Israel D. Rupp

A Collection of Upwards of Thirty Thousand Names

of German, Swiss, Dutch, French and other immigrants in Pennsylvania from 1727

to 1776

Israel D. Rupp

A Collection of Upwards of Thirty Thousand Names
of German, Swiss, Dutch, French and other immigrants in Pennsylvania from 1727 to 1776

ISBN/EAN: 9783337187804

Printed in Europe, USA, Canada, Australia, Japan

Cover: Foto ©Andreas Hilbeck / pixelio.de

More available books at **www.hansebooks.com**

RELATING TO

PENAL AND RFEORMATORY INSTITUTIONS

AND TO

DESTITUTE AND DELINQUENT CHILDREN,

COMPILED FROM THE REVISED STATUTES OF CANADA, 1886,
AND SUBSEQUENT STATUTES, AND FROM THE
REVISEDSTATUTES OF ONTARIO, 1887,
AND SUBSEQUENT STATUTES.

BY THE

SECRETARY OF THE PRISONER'S AID ASSOCIATION OF CANADA.

TORONTO
THE CARSWELL Co. Ltd., LAW PUBLISHERS, Etc.
1895.

PART I.

Provincial Statutes relating to Asylums, Prisons, Gaols, Reformatories, Houses of Refuge, and Aid to Public Charities.

PART II.

Provincial and Dominion Statutes relating to the Protection of Children.

PART III.

PROVINCIAL STATUTES.

1.—The Gibson Act for the Protection of Children.
2.—Houses of Refuge for Females (Bronson.)
3.—Amendment to the Gibson Act for the Protection of Chi

PART IV.

Dominion Statutes relating to Penitentiaries, Reformatories, and for the Protection of Children.

RELATING TO THE

ASYLUMS, PRISONS

AND

PUBLIC CHARITIES,

OF

ONTARIO.

COMPILED FROM THE REVISED STATUTES OF 1887.

TORONTO:
Printed by Warwick & Sons, 26 and 28 Front Street West.
1888.

PRISONS AND PUBLIC CHARITIES.

CHAPTER 238.

An Act respecting the Central Prison.

HER MAJESTY, by and with the advice and consent of the Legislative Assembly of the Province of Ontario, enacts as follows :—

3. The Lieutenant-Governor may appoint for said central prison, a warden, a surgeon, a schoolmaster, an accountant, a matron, and such other officers and servants as may be necessary, to hold office respectively during pleasure; and may also fix and determine the salary of every such officer and servant. R. S. O. 1877, c. 217, s. 3.

4. The Lieutenant-Governor may also appoint a central prison bailiff or central prison bailiffs, who shall be employed for the purpose of conveying prisoners from any gaol or other place in which they may be in custody, to the central prison, or from the central prison to any other place to which they may be lawfully removed, and in the performance of such other duties as may be assigned to him or them by the inspector of prisons and public charities. R. S. O. 1877, c. 217, s. 4.

5. The inspector of prisons and public charities shall, by virtue of his office, be the inspector of the central prison and shall have the same powers in respect thereof as are conferred upon him in respect of the Provincial reformatory by *The Prison and Asylum Inspection Act.* R. S. O. 1877, c. 217, s. 5.

6. The said inspector shall have power, and it shall be his duty, to make rules and regulations for the management, discipline and police of the said central prison, and for fixing and prescribing the duties and conduct of the warden and every other officer or servant employed therein, and for the diet, clothing, maintenance, employment, classification, instruction, discipline, correction, punishment and reward of persons confined therein, and to annul, alter and amend the same from time to time; but no such rule or regulation shall have any effect until approved of by the Lieutenant-Governor in Council. R. S. O. 1877, c. 217, s. 6

7. In order to encourage good behaviour and industry, it shall be lawful for the inspector to make rules so that a correct record of the conduct of every inmate of the prison may be made with a view to permit such criminal to earn a remission of a portion of the term for which he is sentenced to be confined. R. S. O. 1877, c. 217, s. 7.

8. The inspector shall have power summarily to suspend any of the officers or servants of the central prison for misconduct, until the circumstances of the case (of which the Lieutenant-Governor shall be at once notified) have been decided upon by the Lieutenant-Governor, and the inspector may, until such decision has been intimated to him, cause any officers or persons so suspended to be removed beyond the precincts of the prison; and it shall be the duty of the inspector to recommend the removal of any of the above-named officers or servants whom he finds incapable, inefficient or negligent in the execution of his duty, or whose presence in the central prison he deems injurious to the interests thereof; and the pay of every officer or servant so suspended shall cease during the period of such suspension. R. S. O. 1877, c. 217, s. 8.

Power of Inspector over officers of the prison.

9. The inspector may impose a fine, payable in money, upon any officer or servant of the central prison for any act of negligence, carelessness or insubordination by him committed, of reasonable amount, not exceeding one month's pay of the officer or servant, as the inspector may think fit. R. S. O. 1877, c. 217, s. 9.

Power of inspector to impose fines on officers of the prison.

10. The inspector shall have power at all times to enter into the central prison, and have access to every part thereof, and to examine all papers, documents, vouchers, records, books and other things belonging thereto; and to investigate the conduct of any officer or servant employed in or about such central prison, or of any person found within the precincts thereof, and may summon any person before him by order under his hand, and examine such person under oath, touching any matter relating to any breach of the rules of the central prison, or any matter affecting the interests of the institution; and may by the same or like order compel the production of books, papers and writings before him; and any person who neglects or refuses to appear at the time and place specified in the order, having been duly served with a copy thereof, or refuses to give evidence, or to produce the books, papers or writings demanded of him, may be taken into custody by virtue of a warrant under the hand of the inspector, in that behalf, and imprisoned in the common gaol of the locality, as for contempt of Court, for a period not exceeding fourteen days. R. S. O. 1877, c. 217, s. 10. *See* Cap. 250, s. 11.

Inspection of prison by inspector.

11. It shall also be the duty of the inspector to audit the accounts of the warden of the central prison; to inquire into all money transactions when requisite; to demand and obtain a statement of all cash transactions of the prison every month; and to administer to the warden and accountant an oath or affirmation to the effect following, viz:

Audit by inspector.

"I,   , Warden, and I,   , Accountant, of the Central Prison of this Province, make oath (*or* affirm) and say, that the foregoing statement of revenue and expenditure of the said Central Prison for the month of   , 18 , is true and correct."

R. S. O. 1877, c. 217, s. 11.

Prisoners to be transferred from common gaol to central prison. **12.** All persons from time to time confined in any of the common gaols of the Province, under sentence of imprisonment for any offence against any Act of the Legislature of the Province, may by direction of the Provincial Secretary be transferred from such common gaols respectively to the central prison, there to be imprisoned for the unexpired portion of the term of imprisonment to which any such person was originally sentenced or committed to such common gaols respectively; and such persons shall thereupon be imprisoned in the central prison for the residue of the said respective terms, and shall be subject to all the rules and regulations of the central prison. R. S. O. 1877, c. 217, s. 12. *See* R. S. C. c. 183, s. 20.

Imprisonment in central prison on conviction by Justices. **13.** Every person convicted before one or more Justice or Justices of the Peace, or by a Police Magistrate, of any offence cognizable by such Justice or Justices, or Police Magistrate, and for which punishment by imprisonment in the common gaol may be awarded, for any period not less than fourteen days, and committed to a common gaol under such conviction, may be removed and transferred by order of the Provincial Secretary from the common gaol to the central prison, and there imprisoned for the unexpired portion of his sentence in the central prison instead of the common gaol of the county. R. S. O. 1877, c. 217, s. 13.

Convicts may be sentenced to central prison instead of common gaol. **14.** Every Court before which any person is convicted of an offence against any Act of the Legislature of this Province, punishable by imprisonment in the common gaol, may sentence such person to imprisonment in the central prison instead of the common gaol of the county where the offence was committed or was tried. R. S. O. 1877, c. 217, s. 14. *See* R. S. C. c. 183, s. 19.

Operation of ss. 12-14, declared. **15.** The next preceding three sections of this Act shall be held to extend to persons convicted of offences created under the authority of an Act of the Legislature of this Province, as well as to persons convicted of offences directly created by the said Legislature, and to any case where imprisonment is imposed in whole or in part, in default of the payment of a fine or penalty in money, notwithstanding the offender is entitled to be discharged upon payment of such fine or penalty; if the fine or penalty is paid after the removal of the offender to the central prison, the same shall be paid to the proper officer of the said prison, to defray the expense of removal, and otherwise for the use of the said prison; but nothing herein contained shall affect the right of any private person to the said fine, or any part thereof. 44 V. c. 32, s. 1.

Detention of offenders until removal to central prison. **16.** Any sheriff or other person having the custody of an offender convicted of an offence punishable by virtue of a statute of this Province, for which such offender has been sentenced to imprisonment in the central prison, may detain the offender, or cause him or her to be detained, in the common gaol of the county or district in which such offender is sentenced, or other place of confinement in which the said offender may be, until a provincial bailiff or other person lawfully authorized in that behalf requires the delivery of the said offender for the purpose of being conveyed to the central prison. 44 V. c. 32, s. 2.

17. The Lieutenant-Governor may from time to time, by warrant, signed by the Provincial Secretary, or by such other officer as may be authorized by the Lieutenant-Governor in Council in that behalf, direct the removal, from the central prison to the provincial reformatory, or from the central prison back to the common gaol, or from the said reformatory to the central prison, of any person under sentence of imprisonment for an offence against any Act of the Legislature of this Province. R. S. O. 1877, c. 217, s. 15. *See* R. S. C. c. 183, s. 24.

Transfer of prisoners from Central Prison to reformatory or gaol.

18. The warden of the central prison or reformatory, or the keeper of any common gaol having the custody of any convict or offender ordered to be removed, shall, when required so to do, deliver up the convict or offender, together with a copy, attested by the warden, of the sentence and date of conviction of the convict or offender, as given him on reception of the person into his custody, to the constable or other officer or person who produces the warrant. R. S. O. 1877, c. 217, s. 16.

Wardens and gaolers to deliver up prisoners for removal.

19. The sheriff or deputy-sheriff of any county, or any bailiff, constable or other officer or person, by his direction, or by direction of the Court, or other lawful authority, may convey to the central prison any convict sentenced or liable to be imprisoned therein, and deliver him to the warden or keeper thereof, without any further warrant than a copy of the sentence, taken from the minutes of the Court before which the offender was tried, and certified by a Judge or the clerk or acting clerk of such Court. R. S. O. 1877, c. 217, s. 17.

Conveyance of prisoners to central prison.

20. The warden shall receive into the central prison every offender legally certified to him as sentenced to imprisonment therein, and shall there detain him, subject to all the rules, regulations and discipline thereof, until the time to which he has been sentenced is completed, or until he is otherwise discharged in due course of law. R. S. O. 1877, c. 217, s. 18. *See* R. S. C. c. 183, s. 22.

Warden to receive prisoner and detain him.

21. The sheriff or other officer or person employed by competent authority to convey such offender to the central prison, or to or from the provincial reformatory, penitentiary, or common gaol, as by law provided, may secure and convey

Powers of sheriff, etc., in that behalf.

him through any county or district through which he may have to pass; and until such offender has been delivered to the warden of the central prison, reformatory, or penitentiary, or the keeper of the common gaol, the sheriff, or other officer or person, shall have in every part of this Province through which it may be necessary to convey the offender, the same power and authority over and with regard to the offender, and to command the assistance of any person to prevent his escape, and in recapturing him in case of an escape, as the sheriff of the county in which he was convicted would himself have in conveying him from one part to another of that county. R. S. O. 1877, c. 217, s. 19.

Sheriff, etc., to give and take receipt for prisoners. **22.** The sheriff, or other officer or person, shall give a receipt to the warden or gaoler for the convict or offender, and shall thereupon, with all convenient speed, convey and deliver up such convict or offender with the attested copy into the custody of the warden or gaoler of the central prison, reformatory, or common gaol, mentioned in the warrant, who shall give a receipt in writing for every convict or offender so received into his custody, to the sheriff or other officer or person, as his discharge; and the convict or offender shall be kept in custody in the central prison, reformatory or common gaol to which he has been so removed, until the termination of his sentence, or until his pardon, or release, or discharge by law, unless he is in the meantime again removed under competent authority. R. S. O. 1877, c. 217, s. 20.

Powers and duty of warden. **23.** The warden of the central prison shall reside within the prison, and shall be the chief executive officer of the same, under the direction of the inspector, and as such shall have the entire execution, control and management of all its affairs, subject to the rules, regulations and written instructions from time to time duly made by the inspector, and approved by the Lieutenant-Governor in Council, and he shall be held responsible for the faithful and efficient administration of the offices of every department of the institution. R. S. O. 1877, c. 217, s. 21.

To give security. **24.** The warden, the accountant, and every storekeeper and steward of the central prison shall severally execute to Her Majesty a bond, with sufficient sureties, conditioned for the faithful performance of the duties of their respective offices, according to law, in the respective sums following, that is to say:

Amount.
1. The Warden in........................... $8,000
   With two sureties in (each) 4,000
2. The Accountant, Storekeeper and Steward (each) 4,000
   With two sureties (each) in............... 2,000

Bond to be filed. which bond shall be filed in the office of the Provincial Secretary and Registrar. R. S. O. 1877, c. 217, s. 22.

25. The warden and every other officer or servant employed permanently in the central prison shall severally take and subscribe, in a book to be kept for that purpose by the accountant at his office, the oath of allegiance to Her Majesty, and the following oath of office, viz. :

" I *(A. B.)* do promise and swear (*or* affirm), that I will faithfully, diligently and justly serve and perform the office and duties of in the Central Prison of this Province to the best of my ability, and that I will carefully observe and carry out all the regulations of the said Prison : So help me God."

which oath may be administered by the inspector, or in the case of any other of the said officers, by the warden. R. S. O. 1877, c. 217, s. 23.

26. No inspector, warden or other officer or servant em- ployed in such central prison, shall, either in his own name, or in the name of or in connection with any other person, provide, furnish or supply any materials, goods or provisions, for the use of such central prison ; nor shall be concerned, directly or indirectly, in furnishing or supplying the same, or in any con- tract relating thereto, under pain of forfeiting $1,000, with full costs of suit, to any person who sues for the same in any Court of competent jurisdiction in this Province, one-half thereof to belong to Her Majesty for the public services of this Province. R. S. O. 1877, c. 217, s. 24.

27. No warden, officer or servant, except the surgeon, shall be allowed to carry on any trade or calling of profit or emolu- ment in such central prison ; nor shall any such officer buy from or sell to any convict in the said prison anything what- ever ; or take or receive to his own use, or for the use of any other person, any fee, gratuity or emolument from any prisoner or visitor or any other person ; nor employ any convict in working for him. R. S. O. 1877, c. 217, s. 25.

28. No spirituous or fermented liquors shall, on any pretence whatever, be brought into the central prison for the use of any officer or person in the institution, except the warden, or for the use of any convict confined therein (except under the rules of the institution) ; and any person other than an officer of the prison, giving any spirituous or fermented liquors, and any person or officer giving any tobacco, snuff, or cigars to any convict (except under the rules of the institution), or con- veying the same to any such convict, shall forfeit and pay the sum of $40 to the warden, to be by him recovered for the use of the prison, in any Court of competent jurisdiction. R. S. O. 1877, c. 217, s. 27. *For penalty in case of officers giving liquor, see* Cap. 243, s. 1.

29. The female convicts or prisoners shall be kept distinct and secluded from the male convicts, and shall be under the charge of the matron. R. S. O. 1877, c. 217, s. 28.

Hard labour and solitary confinement.

30. The said central prison shall be furnished with all requisite means for enforcing the performance of hard labour by the inmates thereof; and solitary confinement shall form part of the discipline thereof. R. S. O. 1877, c. 217, s. 29.

Cells for solitary confinement.

31. The central prison shall contain not less than fifty penal cells for the separate and solitary confinement of such prisoners as are sentenced to solitary confinement, or for enforcing obedience to the rules and discipline of the said prison. R. S. O. 1877, c. 217, s. 30.

Lieut.-Governor may acquire lands.

32. The Lieutenant-Governor may cause to be procured and provided, adjacent to or surrounding the central prison, a tract of land fit for agricultural or mechanical purposes, not exceeding two hundred acres, and may cause the same to be securely enclosed. R. S. O. 1877, c. 217, s. 31.

Employment of prisoners without the precincts of the prison, under certain regulations.

33.—(1) The Lieutenant-Governor by Order in Council, may from time to time authorize, direct or sanction the employment upon any specific work or duty, without or beyond the walls or limits of such central prison, of any of the prisoners confined or sentenced to be imprisoned therein; and all such prisoners shall, during such last mentioned employment, be subject to all the provisions of this Act, and to all the rules, regulations and discipline of the said central prison, so far as the same may be applicable, and to such other regulations for the purpose of preventing escapes and otherwise as may be approved by the Lieutenant-Governor in that behalf.

Under supervision.

(2) No such prisoner or prisoners shall be so employed without the walls or limits of such central prison, except under the strictest care and supervision of officers appointed to that duty. R. S. O. 1877, c. 217, s. 32. *See* R. S. C. c. 183, s. 23.

Prisoner not to be discharged on a Sunday.

34. Whenever the time of the sentence of any prisoner committed to the central prison for an offence against any Act of the Legislature of Ontario expires on a Sunday, he shall be discharged on the previous Saturday, unless he desires to remain until the following Monday. R. S. O. 1877, c. 217, s. 33. *See* R. S. C. c. 183, s. 45.

Prisoners labouring under certain diseases not to be discharged until cured.

35. No prisoner shall be discharged from the central prison at the termination of his sentence if then labouring under any contagious or infectious disease, or under any acute or dangerous illness, but he shall be permitted to remain in the prison until he recovers from such disease or illness: and any convict or prisoner remaining from such cause in the central prison shall be under the same discipline and control as if his sentence were still unexpired. R. S. O. 1877, c. 217, s. 34.

Escape, etc., punishable according to the rules of the prison.

36. Any escape, prison breach or attempt to escape by any person confined in or sentenced to the central prison shall be punished as may be provided by the rules and regulations of the prison in that behalf. R. S. O. 1877, c. 217, s. 35.

37. The central prison shall be held to include all the land and real estate procured or acquired under section 32 of this Act; and all buildings and machinery erected or used thereon, and all carriages, waggons, sleighs or other vehicles for land carriage, and all boats, scows and other vessels for water carriage, being the property of such central prison, or employed in its service; and the real property of every such prison, and every other property or description of property belonging .thereto, shall be and remain vested in Her Majesty, Her Heirs and Successors; but the warden for the time being shall have the custody and care thereof, under such regulations as may be provided in that behalf; and all such property, real and personal, shall be exempt from taxation for municipal purposes. R. S. O. 1877, c. 217, s. 36.

38. All dealings and transactions on account of the central prison, and all contracts for goods, wares or merchandise, necessary for maintaining and carrying on the said institution, or for the sale of goods prepared or manufactured in such central prison, or for the hire, labour or employment of any of the prisoners, either within or without the limits of the central prison, shall be entered into and carried out in the corporate name of the said inspector on behalf of Her Majesty. R. S. O. 1877, c. 217, s. 37.

39. All books of account, and other books, bills, registers, returns, receipts, bills of parcels and vouchers, and all other papers and documents of every kind relating to the affairs of the said central prison, shall be considered the property of the prison, and shall remain therein; and the warden of the central prison shall preserve therein at least one copy of all official reports made to the Legislature respecting the same, for which purpose, and for the purpose of enabling him to distribute such official reports in exchange for like documents from other similar institutions abroad, he shall be furnished by the Clerk of the Legislative Assembly, on application, with fifty copies of such reports as printed by the Legislative Assembly. R. S. O. 1877, c. 217, s. 38.

[*See as to fees payable to Sheriffs and Gaol Surgeons for services in connection with offenders sentenced or liable to be removed or sentenced to the Central Prison*, Rev. Stat. Cap. 83, ss. 9, 10 *and* Schedule, p. 838].

For the Dominion Acts relating to the Central Prison, see Revised Statutes of Canada, 1886, Cap. 183, Part II.

CHAPTER 239.

An Act Respecting the Andrew Mercer Ontario Reformatory for Females.

———

———

HER MAJESTY, by and with the advice and consent of the Legislative Assembly of the Province of Ontario, enacts as follows :—

1. The word "county," wherever it occurs in this Act, shall include a union of counties for judicial purposes, and every judicial or territorial division or district now existing or which may be hereafter formed out of any portion of the unorganized territory in this Province.   42 V. c. 38, s. 1.

2. The Andrew Mercer Ontario Reformatory for females shall be for the reception, confinement and employment, of such female offenders as are hereinafter mentioned.   42 V. c. 38, s. 2.

3. The Lieutenant-Governor may from time to time appoint for the said reformatory, a female superintendent, an accountant, a surgeon, a school mistress, and such other officers and servants as may be necessary.   42 V. c. 38, s. 3.

4. The Lieutenant-Governor may also appoint an officer or officers, who shall be employed for the purpose of conveying prisoners from any gaol or other place in which they may be in custody, to the reformatory, or from the reformatory to any other place to which they may be lawfully removed, and in the performance of such other duties as may be assigned to such officer or officers by the inspector of prisons and public charities.   42 V. c. 38, s. 4.

5. The inspector of prisons and public charities shall, by *Inspector.* virtue of his office, be the inspector of the reformatory. 42 V. c. 38. s. 5.

6. The said inspector shall have power, and it shall be his *Inspector to make rules, etc.* duty, to make rules and regulations for the management, discipline and police of the reformatory, and for fixing and prescribing the duties and conduct of the superintendent and every other officer or servant employed therein, and for the diet, clothing, maintenance, employment, classification, instruction, dicipline, correction, punishment, and reward of persons confined therein, and to annul, alter, and amend the same from time to time: but no such rule or regulation shall have any effect until and unless it is first approved of by the Lieutenant Governor in Council.   42 V. c. 38, s. 6.

7. In order to encourage good behaviour and industry, it *Encouragement of good behaviour.* shall be lawful for the inspector to make rules so that a correct record of the conduct of every inmate of the prison may be made, with a view to permit each offender to earn a remission of a portion of the term for which she is sentenced to be confined.   42 V. c. 38, s. 7.

8. The inspector shall have power summarily to suspend *Powers of Inspector over officers.* any of the officers or servants of the reformatory for misconduct, until the circumstances of the case (of which the Lieutenant-Governor shall be at once notified) have been decided upon by the Lieutenant-Governor, and the inspector may, until such decision has been intimated to him, cause any officers or persons so suspended to be removed beyond the precincts of the reformatory; and it shall be the duty of the inspector to recommend the removal of any of the above-named officers or servants whom he finds incapable, inefficient, or negligent in the execution of his duty, or whose presence in the reformatory he may deem injurious to the interests thereof; and the pay of every officer or servant so suspended shall cease during the period of such suspension.   42 V. c. 38, s. 8.

9. The inspector may impose a fine, payable in money, upon *Power of Inspector to impose fines.* any officer or servant of the reformatory for any act of negligence, carelessness, or insubordination committed by such officer or servant, of reasonable amount, not exceeding one month's pay of the officer or servant, as the inspector may think fit.   42 V. c. 38, s. 9.

10. The inspector shall have power at all times to enter into *Inspection of Reformatory.* the reformatory, and have access to every part thereof, and to examine all papers, documents, vouchers, records, books, and other things belonging thereto; and to investigate the conduct of any officer or servant employed in or about the reformatory, or of any person found within the precincts thereof, and may summon any person before him by order under his hand,

and examine such person under oath, touching any matter relating to any breach of the rules of the reformatory, or any matter affecting the interests of the institution ; and may, by the same or like order, compel the production of books, papers, and writings before him ; and any person who neglects or refuses to appear at the time and place specified in the order, having been duly served with a copy thereof, or refuses to give evidence, or to produce the books, papers, or writings demanded of him, may be taken into custody by virtue of a warrant under the hand of the inspector, in that behalf, and imprisoned in the common gaol of the locality, as for contempt of Court, for a period not exceeding fourteen days.　42 V. c. 38, s. 10.

Audit by Inspector.

11. It shall also be the duty of the inspector to audit the accounts of the accountant of the reformatory ; to inquire into all money transactions when requisite ; to demand and obtain a statement of all cash transactions of the prison every month ; and to administer to the accountant an oath or affirmation to the effect following, viz. :

Oath of Accountant.

"I　　　　　　　　　　　　　　Accountant of the Andrew Mercer Ontario Reformatory for Females, make oath (or affirm) and say, that the foregoing statement of revenue and expenditure of the said Reformatory for the month of　　　, 18 , is true and correct."

42 V. c. 38, s. 11.

Transfer from Gaol to Reformatory.

12. All females confined from time to time in any of the common gaols of the Province, under sentence of imprisonment for any offence against any Act of the Legislature of the Province, may by direction of the Provincial Secretary be transferred from such common gaols respectively to the said reformatory, to be imprisoned for the unexpired portion of the term of imprisonment to which any such female was originally sentenced or committed to such common gaols respectively ; and such females shall thereupon be imprisoned in the reformatory aforesaid, for the residue of the said respective terms, and shall be subject to all the rules and regulations of the reformatory.　42 V. c. 38, s. 12.

Convict may be sentenced to Reformatory.

13. Every Court before which any female is convicted of an offence against any Act of the Legislature of this Province, punishable by imprisonment in the common gaol, may sentence such female to imprisonment in the said reformatory instead of the common gaol of the county where the offence was committed or was tried ; but this section shall not authorize the imposition of such sentence by any Justice of the Peace, or Police or Stipendiary Magistrate.　42 V. c. 38, s. 13.

Application of ss. 12 and 13.

14. The next preceding two sections shall be held to extend to persons convicted of offences created under the authority of an Act of the Legislature of this Province as well as to persons convicted of offences directly created by the said Legislature and to any case where imprisonment is imposed in whole or in part in default of the payment of a fine or penalty in money, notwithstanding the offender is entitled to be discharged upon payment of such fine or penalty ; if the fine or penalty is paid after the removal of the offender to the reformatory the same shall be paid to the proper officer of the reformatory to defray the expense of removal and otherwise for the use of the said reformatory, but nothing herein contained shall affect the right of any private person to the said fine or any part thereof.   44 V. c. 32, s. 1.

15. The Lieutenant-Governor may from time to time, by warrant signed by the Provincial Secretary, or by such other officer as may be authorized by the Lieutenant-Governor in Council in that behalf, direct the removal from the reformatory back to the common gaol, of any person under sentence of imprisonment for an offence against any Act of the Legislature of this Province.   42 V. c. 38, s. 14. *Transfer from Reformatory to Gaol.*

16. The superintendent of the reformatory, or the keeper of any common gaol, having the custody of any offender ordered to be removed, shall, when required so to do, deliver up to the constable or other officer or person who produces the said warrant, the offender, together with a copy, attested by the superintendent or gaoler, of the sentence and date of conviction of the offender, as given him on reception of the offender into his custody.   42 V. c. 38, s. 15. *Superintendent or Gaoler to deliver up prisoners.*

17. Any officer appointed under section 4, or other officer or person by his direction, or by direction of the Court or other lawful authority, may convey to the reformatory any convict sentenced or liable to be imprisoned therein, and deliver her to the superintendent or keeper thereof, without any further warrant than a copy of the sentence, taken from the minutes of the Court before which the offender was tried, and certified by a Judge or the clerk or acting clerk of the Court.   42 V. c. 38, s. 16. *Copy of sentence sufficient warrant.*

18. The superintendent shall receive into the reformatory every offender legally certified to her as sentenced to imprisonment therein, and shall there detain her, subject to all the rules, regulations, and discipline thereof, until the time to which she has been sentenced shall be completed, or until she is otherwise discharged in due course of law.   42 V. c. 38, s. 17. *Superintendent to receive and detain prisoners.*

19. The officer or other person employed by competent authority to convey such offender to the reformatory or back to a common gaol, as by law provided, may secure and convey her through any county or district through which he may have to pass ; and until the offender shall have been delivered to the superintendent of the reformatory, or the keeper of such common gaol, the said officer or other person shall have *Powers of officer in charge of prisoner.*

20. The said officer or other person, shall give a receipt to the said superintendent or gaoler for the offender, and shall thereupon, with all convenient speed, convey and deliver up the offender with the said attested copy into the custody of the superintendent of the reformatory or gaoler of the gaol mentioned in the warrant, who shall give a receipt in writing for every offender so received into his custody, to such officer or other person, as his discharge ; and the offender shall be kept in custody in the reformatory or gaol to which she has been so removed, until the termination of her sentence, or until her pardon, or release, or discharge by law, unless she is in the meantime again removed under competent authority. 42 V. c. 38, s. 19.

21. The superintendent of the reformatory shall reside within the prison, and shall be the chief executive officer of the same, under the direction of the inspector, and as such shall have the entire execution, control, and management of all its affairs, subject to the rules, regulations, and written instructions from time to time duly made by the inspector, and approved by the Lieutenant-Governor in Council, and she shall be held responsible for the faithful and efficient administration of the offices of every department of the institution. 42 V. c. 38, s. 20.

22. The accountant of the reformatory shall execute to Her Majesty a bond, with sufficient sureties, conditioned for the faithful performance of the duties of the office, according to law, in the sum of $4,000 with two sureties for $2,000 each, which bond shall be filed in the office of the Provincial Secretary and Registrar. 42 V. c. 38, s. 21.

23. The superintendent and every other officer or servant employed permanently in the reformatory, shall severally take and subscribe, in a book to be kept for that purpose, by the accountant at his office, the oath of allegiance to Her Majesty, and the following oath of office, viz :

" I (*A. B.*), do promise and swear (*or affirm*) that I will faithfully, diligently, and justly serve and perform the office and duties of
in the Andrew Mercer Ontario Reformatory for females to the best of my ability, and that I will carefully observe and carry out all the regulations of the said prison, so help me God."

Which oath may be administered by the inspector, or, in case of any other of the said officers, by the superintendent. 42 V. c. 38, s. 22.

24. No inspector, superintendent, or other officer or servant employed in the reformatory, shall either in his own name, or in the name of, or in connection with any other person, provide, furnish, or supply any materials, goods, or provisions for the use of the said reformatory ; nor shall be concerned, directly or indirectly, in furnishing or supplying the same, or in any contract relating thereto, under pain of forfeiting $1000, with full costs of suit, to any person who sues for the same in any Court of competent jurisdiction in this Province, one-half thereof to belong to Her Majesty for the public services of this Province.   42 V. c. 38, s. 23. *Officers not to be interested in any contract.*

25. No superintendent, officer, or servant, except the surgeon, shall be allowed to carry on any trade or calling of profit or emolument in the reformatory ; nor shall any such superintendent, officer, or servant buy from or sell to any convict in the said prison anything whatever ; or take or receive to his own use, or for the use of any other person, any fee, gratuity, or emolument from any prisoner or visitor, or any other person, or employ any convict in working for him.   42 V. c. 38, s. 24. *Officers not to engage in trade, etc., in the Reformatory.*

26. Except under the rules of the institution, no spirituous or fermented liquors shall, on any pretence whatever, be brought into the reformatory for the use of any officer or person in the institution, or for the use of any convict confined therein ; and any person, other than an officer of the reformatory, giving any spirituous or fermented liquors, and any person or officer giving any tobacco, snuff, or cigars, to any convict (except under the rules of the institution), or conveying the same to any such convict, shall forfeit and pay the sum of $40 to the superintendent, to be by her recovered for the use of the reformatory, in any Court of competent jurisdiction.   42 V. c. 38, s. 25. *Liquors, etc., not to be taken into Reformatory.*

27. The reformatory shall be furnished with all requisite means for enforcing the performance of hard labour by the inmates thereof.   42 V. c. 38, s. 26. *Hard labour.*

28. All the land enclosed and used in connection with the reformatory building shall be held to be part of the Andrew Mercer Ontario Reformatory for females.   42 V. c. 38, s. 27. *Reformatory, what to include.*

29. All dealings and transactions on account of the reformatory, and all contracts for goods, wares, or merchandise, necessary for maintaining and carrying on the said institution, or for the sale of goods prepared or manufactured in the reformatory, or for the hire, labour, or employment of any of the prisoners, shall be entered into and carried out in the corporate name of the said inspector on behalf of Her Majesty.   42 V. c. 38, s. 28. *Contracts, etc., how made.*

Prisoners not to be discharged on Sunday.

30. Whenever the time of the sentence of any prisoner committed to the reformatory, for an offence against any Act of the Legislature of Ontario, expires on a Sunday, she shall be discharged on the previous Saturday, unless she desires to remain until the following Monday. 42 V. c. 38, s. 29.

Prisoners not to be discharged if labouring under certain diseases.

31. No prisoner shall be discharged from the reformatory at the termination of her sentence, if then labouring under any contagious or infectious disease, or under any acute or dangerous illness, but she shall be permitted to remain in the prison until she recovers from the disease or illness, and any convict or prisoner remaining from any such cause in the reformatory, shall be under the same discipline and control as if her sentence were still unexpired. 42 V. c. 38, s. 30.

Books of account to remain in Reformatory.

Official reports.

32. All books of account, and other books, bills, registers, returns, receipts, bills of parcels, and vouchers, and all other papers and documents of every kind, relating to the affairs of the reformatory, shall be considered the property of Her Majesty and shall remain in the reformatory, and the superintendent of such reformatory shall preserve therein at least one copy of all official reports made to the Legislature respecting the same, for which purpose, and for the purpose of enabling her to distribute such official reports in exchange for like documents from other similar institutions abroad, she shall be furnished by the Clerk of the Legislative Assembly, on application, with fifty copies of such reports as printed by the said Legislative Assembly. 42 V. c. 38, s. 31.

For the Dominion Acts relating to the Reformatory, see Revised Statutes of Canada, 1886, Chapter 183, Part II.

CHAPTER 240.

to establish an Industrial Refuge for Girls.

———

———

HER MAJESTY, by and with the advice and consent of the Legislative Assembly of the Province of Ontario, enacts as follows:—

1. The Lieutenant-Governor in Council may set apart such portion of the Andrew Mercer Ontario Reformatory for females as he may think fit for the reception of girls under the age of fourteen years. 42 V. c. 39, s. 1. *Portion of the Mercer Reformatory may be set apart for Refuge.*

2. The said portion so set apart shall be called "The Industrial Refuge for girls." 42 V. c. 39, s. 2. *Name of portion set apart*

3. The inspector of prisons and public charities and the superintendent, accountant, surgeon and school mistress of the Andrew Mercer Ontario Reformatory for females, shall be also the inspector, superintendent, accountant, surgeon, and school mistress of the said industrial refuge for girls, and shall perform similar duties in respect to both institutions. 42 V. c. 39, s. 3. *Certain officers of Mercer Reformatory to act as officers of Refuge*

4. The Lieutenant-Governor may appoint for the refuge such other officers and servants as may be required, or he may require any officer or servant of the said reformatory to act for both of the said institutions. 42 V. c. 39, s. 4. *Appointment of other officers.*

5. Whenever a girl under the age of fourteen years is convicted under any Act of the Legislature of Ontario of an offence punishable on summary conviction and is thereupon sentenced and committed to prison in any common gaol, any Judge of the High Court, or the Judge of any County Court (in a case occurring within his county) may examine and enquire into the circumstances of such case and conviction, and may direct the offender to be sent either *What convicts may be sent to Refuge.*

forthwith or the tirpiration of her sentence to the said
fuge, to be the refctained for a period of not less than :
years and not exceeding five years, and such offender shall
liable to be detained pursuant to such direction unless, in
manner hereinafter provided or otherwise lawfully, sooner d
charged: provided no one sent to the refuge under this s
tion shall be discharged under this Act until the period 1
which she is sentenced for her said offence has expired. 42
c. 39, s. 5.

Proviso.

Removal from Reformatory to Refuge.

6. The inspector of prisons may, upon the application c
the superintendent, direct the removal from the reforma
tory to the said refuge of any girl under sixteen who is con
fined in the said reformatory for any offence within the jurisdiction of the Legislature of Ontario. 42 V. c. 39, s. 6.

In certain other cases girls may be sent to Refuge.

7. A County or District Court Judge or Police Magistrate
may by his war ant commit to the refuge any girl apparently
under the age f fourteen years who comes within any of the
following descriptions:

1. Who is found begging or receiving alms or being in any
street or public place for the purpose of begging or receiving
alms;

2. Who is found wandering and not having any home or
settled place of abode or proper guardianship;

3. Who is found destitute and is an orphan, or has a surviving parent who is undergoing penal servitude or imprisonment;

4. Whose parent, step-parent or guardian represents to
the Judge or Police Magistrate that he is unable to control the
girl and that he desires her to be sent to the refuge:
the word guardian as used herein shall include any officer of a
society under whose charge the girl is, or any person standing
in fact in the place of a parent although not lawfully appointed
a guardian;

5. Who by reason of the neglect, drunkenness, or other
vices of her parents or either of them, or of any other persons
in whose charge such girl is, is suffered to be growing up without salutary control and education or in circumstances which
render it probable that such girl will, unless placed under proper control, lead an idle and dissolute life. 42 V. c. 39, s. 7;
50 V. c. 8, Sched.

Mode of proceeding under last section.

8. No formal information shall be requisite to authorize
proceedings being taken under the preceding section, but the
Judge or Police Magistrate before issuing his warrant shall
have such girl brought before him and shall in her presence
take evidence in writing under oath of the facts charged and
shall make reasonable enquiry into the truth thereof. 42 V
c. 39, s. 8.

9. It shall be the duty of the Judge or Police Magistrate to obtain from the witnesses at the hearing, where practicable, the residence of the parents of the girl, or of the persons with whom she resides, and their post office address. 42 V. c. 39, s. 9. Judge to obtain address of parents, etc.

10. The proceedings to be taken and the forms to be followed upon an application for a committal to the refuge shall, unless where otherwise provided by this Act, be, as nearly as may be, in accordance with the proceedings and forms which are authorized in case of prosecutions before a Justice of the Peace for an offence punishable by imprisonment under the laws of Canada upon summary conviction. 42 V. c. 39, s. 10. Proceedings and forms.

11. It shall not be necessary in the said warrant to fix any period for the detention of any girl committed to the refuge, but every girl so committed shall be liable to be there detained for the purpose of learning some proper trade, or being taught some other means of earning her livelihood, or for the formation of industrious habits, for the period of five years, unless the Lieutenant-Governor shall sooner direct her discharge or the inspector shall make an order under section 20. 42 V. c. 39, s. 11. Time of detention in Refuge.

12. The Lieutenant-Governor in his discretion may at any time, and from time to time, order any girl confined in the said refuge, who is reported by the superintendent as incorrigible, to be transferred to the said female reformatory for any period not exceeding two months at any one time. 42 V. c. 39, s. 12. Transfer of prisoners from Refuge to Reformatory.

13. Where the confinement of any girl in the refuge is directed under this Act, the Judge or Police Magistrate may either by his warrant authorize some female to convey the said girl to the refuge, or he may give such directions as he considers advisable for the detention of the girl in some proper place of confinement until a female provincial bailiff, or other person lawfully authorized in that behalf, requires the said girl's delivery for the purpose of being conveyed to the refuge. 44 V. c. 32, s. 3. Judge or Magistrate may give directions as to removal or detention of girls in certain cases.

14. In case the Judge or Police Magistrate directs the girl's detention under the next preceding section, he shall cause the superintendent of the refuge to be forthwith notified of his action in the said matter: in case a female is employed by the said Judge or Police Magistrate to convey the girl to the refuge, she shall be entitled to receive from the county or separate town or city the like fees and charges therefor as a constable would receive for similar services. 44 V. c. 32, s. 4. Notice of detention to be given to superintendent of Refuge. Fees.

Superintendent to report proper cases for discharge.

15. It shall be the duty of the superintendent from time to time to report to the Provincial Secretary, for submission to the Lieutenant-Governor, the cases of such girls as she is of opinion may with propriety be discharged from the refuge. 42 V. c. 39, s. 13.

Applications for discharge of girls committed under section 7.

16. In case an application is made to any Court or Judge for the discharge from the refuge of any girl committed thereto under the provisions of section 7 of this Act, notwithstanding any irregularity in or insufficiency of the warrant or other proceedings, no order shall be made for such discharge in case the Court or Judge shall deem it for the benefit of the girl that she should remain in the refuge and it shall appear by the depositions taken before the committing Judge or Magistrate that she was liable to be committed to the refuge under the provisions of this Act. 42 V. c. 39, s. 14.

Depositions to be delivered to person receiving prisoner.

17. The committing magistrate shall deliver to the constable or other person having the execution of his warrant, the depositions taken by him, or a certified copy thereof, which depositions or copy shall be delivered by the constable or other person to the superintendent or officer receiving the prisoner into the refuge ; such copy shall be *prima facie* proof of the contents of the original depositions and shall be receivable in evidence upon any application for the discharge of any girl committed thereunder. 42 V. c. 39, s. 15.

Expenses of conveying persons to Refuge.

18. The expenses of conveying to the said refuge any girl committed thereto shall be paid by the county, city, or separate town in which such girl is committed. 42 V. c. 39, s. 16.

Superintendent to send notice to parents, etc.

19. The superintendent shall, upon the reception of any girl into the refuge, ascertain from the girl and from the depositions the address of the parents, guardian, or other person with whom such girl has been living, and shall send by mail, registered, a notice that such girl has been committed to the said refuge. 42 V. c. 39, s. 17.

Power to bind girls as apprentices.

20. In case any respectable and trustworthy person is willing to undertake the charge of any girl committed to the refuge, either this Act or any other Act of the Legislature of this Province, whether she be over or under the age of twelve years, as an apprentice to the trade or calling of such person or for the purpose of domestic service, the superintendent may, with the consent of the inspector of prisons, bind the said girl to such person for any term not to extend beyond the girl's attaining the age of eighteen years, and the inspector shall thereupon order that such girl shall be absolutely discharged, or discharged on probation, and she shall be discharged accordingly ; any wages reserved in any such indenture shall be payable to the girl or to some other person for her benefit. 49 V. c. 49, s. 1, *part.*

21.—(1) The Judge of any County or District Court or any Police Magistrate, or the inspector of prisons, may upon satisfactory proof that any girl, who was sentenced under the provisions of this Act or any other Act of the Legislature of this Province, and who has been discharged on probation, has violated the conditions of her discharge, order such girl to be re-committed to the refuge, and thereupon she shall be detained therein under her original sentence, as if she had never been discharged. Re-committ of girls discharged on probation.

(2) The said proof may be by oral evidence, and each of the said officers is hereby authorized to administer an oath to any person requiring to give evidence under this section. 49 V. c. 49, s. 1, *part ;* 50 V. c. 8, Sched.

—————

For Dominion Acts relating to the Refuge, see Revised Statutes of Canada 1886, Chap. 183, Part II.

—————

CHAPTER 241.

An Act respecting the Ontario Reformatory for Boys.

———

———

HER MAJESTY, by and with the advice and consent of the Legislative Assembly of the Province of Ontario, enacts as follows :—

1. The word "county," whenever it occurs in this Act, shall include any union of counties for judicial purposes, and every judicial or territorial district now existing or that may be hereafter formed out of any portion of the unorganized territory in this Province; the word "sentence," unless where the context requires a different meaning, shall include any order made by Interpretation.

lawful authority for the confinement of any boy in the reformatory hereinafter mentioned, and the word " sentenced," shall include the making of such order.   43 V. c. 34, s. 1.

Name of Reformatory.

2. The institution established at Penetanguishene, and known as the reformatory prison, is hereby continued, and shall hereafter be designated the " Ontario Reformatory for Boys."   43 V. c. 34, s. 2.

Property included in Reformatory.

3. The said Ontario reformatory for boys shall be held to include all the lands and buildings now attached and belonging to the reformatory, including the lands acquired from the Ordnance Department, and known as " the redoubts," and whatever land may hereafter be purchased or acquired for the purposes of the reformatory, and whatever buildings may hereafter be erected upon any of the said lands. 43 V. c. 34, s. 3.

Objects of Reformatory.

4. The reformatory shall have for its objects the custody and detention, with a view to their education, industrial training, and moral reclamation, of such boys as shall be lawfully sentenced to confinement therein.   43 V. c. 34, s. 4.

Appointment of certain officers.

5. The Lieutenant-Governor may from time to time appoint for the reformatory a superintendent, a deputy-superintendent, a bursar, a storekeeper and steward, two or more schoolmasters, a surgeon, and such trade-instructors, overseers, and other officers and servants as the efficient management of the said reformatory may require ; and may fix and determine their respective salaries.   43 V. c. 34, s. 5.

Qualification of school masters.

6. No person shall be deemed legally qualified to be a schoolmaster in the reformatory who does not at the time of his appointment, and during his tenancy of the office, hold a first or second-class certificate of qualification as public school teacher in this Province.   43 V. c. 34, s. 6.

Inspector.

7. The inspector of prisons and public charities shall, by virtue of his office, be the inspector of the reformatory. 43 V. c. 34, s. 7.

Notice to be sent to Inspector when any boy is sentenced to Reformatory.

8. Whenever a boy is sentenced to confinement in the said reformatory, the sheriff or other officer having the lawful custody of such boy, shall forthwith notify the inspector of such sentence, and shall at the same time send to the inspector a copy of the sentence of such boy, taken from the minutes of the Court before which such boy was tried, and certified by a Judge, or the clerk, or acting clerk of such Court, or in case the boy is held in custody under the order or warrant of a Judge, Justice of the Peace, or other Magistrate, a copy, certified by such sheriff or other officer, of the said order or warrant, together with a return in accordance with the schedule to this Act, properly filled up.   43 V. c. 34, s. 8.

9. The inspector may thereupon issue his warrant in duplicate under his official seal, to a provincial bailiff requiring the bailiff to take the boy into his custody, and the sheriff or other officer having the lawful custody of such boy, shall when required so to do, upon production of one of the duplicates of the warrant, deliver up the said boy to the bailiff, and in case the sheriff or other officer holds a warrant or order for the confinement of such boy in the reformatory, he shall also deliver the original warrant or order with the boy to the bailiff, in order that he may deliver the same to the superintendent of the reformatory. 43 V. c. 34, s. 9.

Warrant of removal.

10. The bailiff may take into his custody, for the purpose of removal to the said reformatory, any boy sentenced to the reformatory, without any further authority than the said warrant of the inspector, and either the said certified copy of the sentence or the said original warrant or order. 43 V. c. 34, s. 10.

Authority for removal.

11. The bailiff shall give one of the duplicates of the warrant and a receipt for such boy to the sheriff, gaoler, superintendent, or other officer having the custody of such boy, and shall thereupon, with all convenient speed, convey and deliver up such boy, with the certified copy of the sentence, or warrant or order, into the custody of the superintendent of the reformatory, or the warden or keeper of the said place to which such boy may be lawfully removed, and the superintendent, warden, or keeper shall give a receipt in writing for every boy so received into his custody to the bailiff as his discharge ; and such boy shall be kept in custody in the reformatory, or other lawful place to which he has been so removed, until the termination of his sentence, or until his pardon, release, or discharge by law or until he be removed therefrom under competent authority. 43 V. c. 34, s. 11.

Receipt to be given and taken by bailiff.

12. The bailiff may secure and convey such boy through any county through which he may have to pass ; and until such boy shall have been delivered to the superintendent of the reformatory, or to the warden or keeper of any place to which such boy may lawfully be removed from the reformatory, the bailiff shall have, in every part of this Province through which it may be necessary to convey such boy, the same power and authority over and with regard to such boy, and to command the assistance of any person to prevent his escape, and to recapture him in case of his escape, as the sheriff of the county in which he was convicted would himself have in conveying him from one part to another of that county. 43 V. c. 34, s. 12.

Powers of bailiff.

13. The inspector may, whenever it is more convenient so to do, address his warrant for the removal of any boy to or from the reformatory (whose removal is by law required

Warrant may be directed to person not a bailiff.

or authorized) to any fit and proper officer or person other than the bailiff, and such officer and person shall thereupon, as to every such boy and for his removal or to prevent his escape or for his recapture, possess all the rights and authority which a provincial bailiff would have had if such warrant had been addressed to him, and shall perform the like duties. 43 V. c. 34, s. 13.

Contracts how to be made.

14. All dealings and transactions on account of the reformatory, and all contracts for goods, wares, or merchandise necessary for maintaining and carrying on the industrial operations of the said institution, or for the sale of goods prepared or manufactured therein, or for the hire, labour or employment of any boy therein confined, either within or without the limits of the reformatory, shall be entered into and carried out in the corporate name of the inspector on behalf of Her Majesty. 43 V. c. 34, s. 14.

Inspector to make rules, etc.

15. The inspector shall make rules and regulations for the management, interior economy and discipline of the reformatory, and for fixing and prescribing the duties and conduct of the superintendent and every other officer and servant employed therein, and for the clothing, maintenance, education, employment, industrial instruction, classification, discipline, correction, punishment, reward, and general oversight and care of all boys sent to the reformatory, and may repeal and amend the same from time to time; but no such rule or regulation, repeal or amendment shall have any effect unless and until it is first approved of by the Lieutenant-Governor in Council. 43 V. c. 34, s. 15.

Powers of Inspector over officers of Reformatory.

16. The inspector shall have power summarily to suspend any of the officers or servants of the reformatory for misconduct, until the circumstances of the case (of which the Lieutenant-Governor shall be at once notified) have been decided upon by the Lieutenant-Governor in Council, and the inspector may, until such decision shall have been notified to him, cause any officer or servant so suspended to be removed beyond the precincts of the reformatory; and it shall be the duty of the said inspector to recommend the removal of any officer or servant whom he finds incapable, inefficient, or negligent in the execution of his duty, or whose presence in the reformatory he may deem injurious to the interests thereof; and the pay of every officer or servant so suspended shall cease during the period of such suspension. 43 V. c. 34, s. 16.

Inspector may impose fines.

17. The inspector may impose upon any officer or servant of the reformatory, for any act of negligence, carelessness, or insubordination by him committed, a fine of reasonable amount, not exceeding one month's pay of the officer or servant, as the inspector may think fit. 43 V. c. 34, s. 17.

18. The inspector shall have power at all times to enter into the reformatory, and have access to every part thereof, and to examine all papers, documents, vouchers, records, books, and other things belonging thereto ; and to investigate the conduct of any officer or servant employed in or about the reformatory, or of any person found within the precincts thereof, and may summon any person before him by order under his hand, and examine such person under oath touching any matter relating to any breach of the rules of the reformatory, or any matter affecting the interests of the institution, and may by the same or like order compel the production of books papers, and writings before him ; and any person, having been duly served with a copy of such order, who shall neglect or refuse to appear at the time and place specified therein, or shall refuse to give evidence, or to produce the books, papers, or writings demanded of him, may, by virtue of a warrant under the hand of the inspector in that behalf, be taken into custody, and imprisoned in the common gaol as for contempt of Court, for a period not exceeding fourteen days.   43 V. c. 34, s. 18.

19. It shall also be the duty of the inspector to audit the accounts of the bursar of the reformatory, to inquire into all money transactions when requisite, and to demand and obtain a statement of all cash transactions of the reformatory every month.   43 V. c. 34, s. 19.

20. The superintendent of the reformatory shall reside in a house to be provided for him within the grounds of the reformatory, and shall be the chief executive officer of the same, under the direction of the inspector, and as such shall have the entire execution, control, and management of all its affairs, other than those under the control and management of the bursar, subject to the rules and regulations made by the inspector as aforesaid, and he shall be held responsible for the faithful and efficient administration of the offices of every department of the institution.   43 V. c. 34, s. 20.

• 21. The superintendent shall receive into the reformatory every boy legally certified to him as sentenced to confinement therein, and shall there detain him, subject to all the rules, regulations, and discipline thereof, until the time to which he has been sentenced shall be completed, or until he shall be otherwise lawfully discharged.   43 V. c. 34, s. 21.

22. The superintendent shall, upon the reception of any boy into the reformatory, ascertain the address of the parents, guardian, or other person with whom such boy has been living, and shall send by mail, registered, a notice that such boy has been committed to the reformatory.   43 V. c. 34, s. 22.

23. All books of account, bills, registers, returns, receipts, bills of parcels, and vouchers, and all other books, papers, and documents of every kind relating to the affairs of the reformatory, shall be considered the property of Her Majesty and shall. remain in the reformatory; and the superintendent of the reformatory shall preserve therein at least one copy of all official reports made to the Legislature respecting the same, for which purpose, and for the purpose of enabling him to distribute such official reports in exchange for like documents from other similar institutions elsewhere, he shall be furnished by the Clerk of the Legislative Assembly, on application, with fifty copies of such reports as printed by the said Legislative Assembly.   43 V. c. 34, s. 23.

24. Every bursar, and every storekeeper and steward of the reformatory, shall severally execute to Her Majesty a bond, with the security of some guarantee company in good standing in this Province, conditioned for the faithful performance of the duties of their respective offices according to law, in the respective sums following, that is to say: the bursar in $3,000, and the storekeeper and steward in $1,000, which bond shall be filed in the office of the Provincial Secretary and Registrar.   43 V. c. 34, s. 24.

25. Every superintendent, officer, and servant employed permanently in the said reformatory, shall severally take and subscribe in a book to be kept for that purpose by the bursar at his office, the oath of allegiance to Her Majesty, and the following oath of office, viz. :—

" I, (*A. B.*) do promise and swear (*or* affirm) that I will faithfully, diligently, and justly perform the duties of   in the Ontario Reformatory for Boys to the best of my ability, and that I will carefully observe and carry out all the rules and regulations of the said Reformatory, so help me God :"

Which oath may be administered by the inspector, or by a Justice of the Peace, and in the case of any of the said officers or servants other than the superintendent, by the superintendent.   43 V. c. 34, s. 25.

26 No inspector, superintendent, or other officer or servant employed in the reformatory, shall, either in his own name, or in the name of or in connection with any other person, provide, furnish, or supply any materials, goods, or provisions, for the use of the reformatory, or be concerned, directly or indirectly, in furnishing or supplying the same, or in any contract relating thereto, under a penalty of $1,000, with full costs of suit, to any person who sues for the same in any Court of competent jurisdiction in this Province, one-half of the penalty to belong to the person suing for the same, and the other half to Her Majesty for the public services of this Province.   43 V. c. 34, s. 26.

27. Upon complaint and due proof made to the Jud
County or District Court or to any Police Magistrate, b
or guardian of any boy between the ages of ten an
years, that by reason of incorrigible or vicious con
boy is beyond the control of such parent or guardian
a due regard for the material and moral welfare of
manifestly requires that he should be committed to th
tory, the Judge or Police Magistrate may order su
be confined in the reformatory for an undefined per
exceed five years.   43 V. c. 34 s. 27 ; 50 V. c. 8, sche

28. Any Court, Judge, Police or Stipendiary Mag
Justice of the Peace, who, under and by virtue of a
the Legislature of this Province, has, or shall have,
sentence any boy to be confined in the reformatoi
stated period, may sentence such boy to be confil
in for an undefined period ; and such boy shall the
detained in the reformatory until he be reformed
wise fit to be apprenticed or bound out, or be proba
permanently discharged, as hereinafter provided : Prc
such boy shall not be detained for a longer time
maximum term of confinement for which he might
sentenced for the offence of which he was convicted
no boy shall be sentenced under this section who can
prisoned for two years or over.   43 V. c. 34, s. 28.

29. In case a boy is sentenced to confineme:
reformatory, a copy of the sentence of the Court du
as aforesaid, or the warrant or order of the Judge, Ju
Peace, or other Magistrate by whom the boy is sente
be a sufficient authority to the sheriff, constable
officer who may be directed so to do (which directio
verbal) to convey such boy to the common gacl of t
where such sentence is pronounced, and for the gaol
gaol to receive and detain the said boy until the
bailiff or other person entrusted with the warrant
spector shall require the delivery of such boy for :
the reformatory.   43 V. c. 34, s. 29.

30. In case a boy, sentenced under any Act of
lature of Ontario to be confined in the reformatory,
a weak state of health that he cannot safely or co:
be removed to the reformatory, he may be detair
common gaol or other place of confinement in whi
be, until he is sufficiently recovered to be safely an
ently removed to the reformatory ; but any time du
such boy is so detained shall be reckoned in com
time served by such boy in the reformatory.   43 V.

31. In order to encourage good behaviour and
among the boys in the said reformatory, and with
permitting every boy to earn a remission of a port

term for which he was sentenced to the said reformatory, it shall be lawful for the inspector to make rules so that a correct record of the conduct of every boy may be made under the mark system. 43 V. c. 34, s. 31.

Proceedings or remission of sentence.

32. When under the rules in that behalf, a boy shall have obtained the requisite number of good marks, based upon good conduct, proficiency in school and industrious habits, and shall in addition thereto have given satisfactory evidence of being reformed, it shall be the duty of the superintendent to transmit to the inspector a certificate to that effect, and also the separate certificates to a like effect or with such variations as their respective opinions may render necessary, of the minister or other person who has given religious instruction to such boy, of the schoolmaster who has given him secular instruction and of the trade instructors, if any, whom he has been under; whereupon, the inspector, if he considers it requisite, shall make further enquiry into the facts, and having satisfied himself that the boy has earned his discharge shall forthwith transmit the certificates and other papers to the Attorney-General of the Province, with a recommendation that action be taken to have the remaining portion of the sentence of such boy remitted, or to have such boy discharged on probation for a **Proviso.** stated period: Provided that no action shall be taken under this section in respect of any boy who has not been at least one **Proviso.** year in the reformatory: Provided also that the Judge of any County Court or any Police Magistrate may, upon satisfactory proof that any boy who was sentenced under the provisions of an Act of the Legislature of Ontario and who has been discharged on probation, has violated the conditions of his discharge, order such boy to be recommitted to the reformatory, there to be confined for the residue of the term for which he was originally sentenced. 43 V. c. 34, s. 32.

Superintendent may apprentice boys in certain cases.

33. In case any respectable and trustworthy person is willing to undertake the charge of any boy committed to the reformatory, when such boy is over the age of twelve years, as an apprentice to the trade or calling of such person, or for the purpose of domestic service, and such boy is confined in the reformatory by virtue of a sentence pronounced under the authority of any statute of this Province, the superintendent may, with the consent and in the name of the inspector, bind the said boy to such person for any term not to extend beyond a period of five years from the commencement of his imprisonment, without his consent, and the inspector shall thereupon order that such boy shall be discharged from the **Proviso** said reformatory, and he shall be discharged accordingly: Provided that any wages reserved in any indenture of apprenticeship made under this section shall be payable to the said boy or to some other person for his benefit. 48 V. c. 34, s. 33.

34. Whenever the time of any boy's sentence in the reformatory, under any law within the legislative jurisdiction of this Province, shall expire on a Sunday, he shall be discharged on the previous Saturday, unless he desires to remain until the Monday following. 43 V. c. 34, s. 34.

Boys not to be discharged on Sunday.

35. No boy shall be discharged from the reformatory at the termination of his sentence, if then labouring under any contagious or infectious disease, or under any acute or dangerous illness, but he shall be permitted to remain in the reformatory until he recovers from such disease or illness: Provided that any boy remaining in the reformatory from any such cause shall be under the same discipline and control as if his sentence were still unexpired. 43 V. c. 34, s. 35.

Boys not to be discharged if labouring under certain diseases.
Proviso.

SCHEDULE.

(Section 8.)

ONTARIO REFORMATORY FOR BOYS.

RETURN MADE UNDER R. S. O., CAP. 241, SEC. 8, OF BOY IN GAOL LIABLE TO TRANSFER TO THE REFORMATORY.

(☞ A separate return to be made with each boy).

1. Name in full.
2. Age.
3. From what court sentenced.
4. Date of sentence.
5. Period and nature of sentence.
6. Place of residence.
7. Place of birth.
8. Name and post-office address of parents, guardian or other person with whom boy has been living.
9. Trade, occupation or calling of boy, if any.
10. Temperate or intemperate.
11. If married, state the fact.
12. Religious denomination.
13. Degree of education.
14. Offence.
15. Fine, if any.
16. Gaoler's opinion as to physical and mental condition of boy, and his fitness to perform ordinary work.

(Signature of Sheriff.)

(Date of return.)

, 43 V. c. 34, Sched. A.

For Dominion Acts relating to the Reformatory, see R. S. C., Chapter 183, Part II. See also R. S. C., Chapter 182, sec. 49 and 50.

CHAPTER 242.

An Act respecting the removal of persons from County Gaols to Provincial Institutions.

HER MAJESTY, by and with the advice and consent of the Legislative Assembly of the Province of Ontario, enacts as follows :—

Appointment of bailiffs.

1. The Lieutenant-Governor may appoint a bailiff or bailiffs' male or female, who shall be designated and known as provincial bailiffs, and who shall be employed for the purpose of conveying any person from time to time confined in any of the common gaols of the Province or other place of custody, and liable to be thence lawfully removed to any asylum or other institution for the insane in this Province, or to the Reformatory for Boys, or to the Andrew Mercer Ontario Reformatory for Females, or to the Industrial Refuge for Girls, and also in the performance of such other duties as may be assigned to him, her, or them by the Inspector of Prisons and Public Charities. 43 V. c. 35, s. 1.

Warrant for removal.

2. Any bailiff so appointed may convey any person from the gaol or other place of custody to such one of the provincial institutions in the preceding section mentioned in which such person is lawfully directed to be confined, without any further authority than the warrant of the inspector of prisons and public charities under his official seal and in duplicate, and such person shall be received into such provincial institution and there detained subject to the rules, regulations and discipline thereof until legally entitled to be discharged therefrom. 43 V. c. 35, s. 2.

Powers of bailiffs.

3. The bailiff, in the conveyance of such person as aforesaid to any of the provincial institutions hereinbefore mentioned, may secure and convey him through any county or district through which such bailiff may have to pass, and until such person has been delivered to and placed in such provincial institution, such bailiff shall have, in every part of this Province, the same power and authority over and with regard to such person, and to command the assistance of any person to prevent his escape, and in recapturing him in case of an escape, as the sheriff of the county in which he was convicted or confined would himself have in conveying him from one part to another of that county. 43 V. c. 35, s. 3.

Bailiffs to give and take receipts for persons in their charge.

4. The bailiff shall give one of the duplicates of the warrant and a receipt to the sheriff or gaoler for every person so liable to be removed from the gaol or other place of custody, and shall thereupon with all convenient speed convey and deliver up such person with the other duplicate of the warrant to the superintendent or other official head of such provincial institution, who shall give his receipt in writing for every such person so received by him to such bailiff, as evidence of his discharge of duty, and every such person shall be kept in such provincial institution until legally discharged, or removed under competent authority.   43 V. c. 35, s. 4.

5. The county or other municipality, in which the gaol or other place of custody is located and from which such person may be removed by such bailiff as aforesaid, shall be liable to pay to the Treasurer of the Province, on demand, the expenses incurred in the removal and conveyance, as aforesaid, of each person, together with sixty per centum added thereto toward the salary or other remuneration of such bailiff: Provided always that when gaols are maintained jointly by cities and counties, or in case of towns separated from counties, the county shall be held to be the municipality in which the gaol is located, and the cities or towns shall pay their just proportion of such salaries and expenses, and if not mutually agreed upon, the same shall be determined by arbitration as provided by *The Municipal Act.*   43 V. c. 35, s. 5. *Payment by municipalities. Proviso. Rev. Stat. c.*

CHAPTER 243.

An Act respecting the use of Spirituous Liquors in Gaols and Prisons.

HER MAJESTY, by and with the advice and consent of the Legislative Assembly of the Province of Ontario, enacts as follows :—

1. No license shall be granted for retailing spirituous liquors within any gaol or prison ; and if any gaoler, keeper or officer of any gaol or prison, sells, lends, uses or gives away, or knowingly permits or suffers any spirituous liquors or strong waters to be sold, used, lent or given away in such gaol or prison, or to be brought into the same, other than such spirituous liquors or strong waters as may be prescribed by or given by the prescription and direction of a legally qualified medical practitioner, such gaoler, keeper or other officer shall, for every such offence, forfeit the sum of $80, one moiety thereof to Her Majesty, for the public uses of the Province, and the other moiety, with full costs of suit, to the person who sues for the same in any of Her Majesty's Courts of Record in Ontario; and in case any gaoler or other officer, having been so convicted, *No license to be granted for retailing spirituous liquors within gaols. Penalty*

offends again in like manner, and is thereof a second time convicted, such second offence shall be a forfeiture of his office R. S. O. 1877, c. 219, s. 1.

Penalty on persons supplying spirits to a prisoner in gaol.

2. If any person gives, conveys or supplies to any prisoner confined in any common gaol or house of correction, any rum, brandy, whiskey, or other spirituous liquors, contrary to the rules and regulations from time to time established by law, such offender, being duly convicted thereof before two Justices of the Peace, shall be fined a sum not exceeding $20.   R. S. O. 1877, c. 219, s. 2.

CHAPTER 244.

An Act to provide for employing Prisoners without the walls of Common Gaols.

HER MAJESTY by and with the advice and consent of the Legislative Assembly of the Province of Ontario, enacts as follows:—

Lieutenant-Governor may authorize employment of prisoners outside gaol.

1. The Lieutenant-Governor in Council may, from time to time, direct or authorize the employment upon any work or duty, the nature of which is specified in the Order in Council, beyond the limits of any common gaol, of any prisoner who is sentenced to be imprisoned with hard labour in such gaol under the authority of any Statute of Ontario, or for the breach of the by-laws of any municipal corporation in this Province. 48 V. c. 52, s. 1.

Discipline of gaol to be observed during employment.

2. Every such prisoner shall, during such employment, be subject to all the rules, regulations and discipline of the gaol so far as applicable, and to any regulations made by the Lieutenant-Governor in Council under section 8 of chapter 138 of the Revised Statutes of Canada or any Act thereby consolidated, for preventing escapes and preserving discipline. 41 V. c. 24, s. 2.

Supervision.

3. No such prisoner shall be so employed, save under the strictest care and supervision of officers appointed to that duty. 41 V. c. 24, s. 3.

Place of work to be deemed part of gaol.

4. Every street, highway or public thoroughfare of any kind along or across which prisoners may pass in going to or returning from their work, and every place where they may be employed under this Act, shall, while so used, be considered as a portion of the gaol for the purposes of this Act so far as the legislative authority of this Province extends in this behalf. 41 V. c. 24, s. 4.

5. An account shall be kept of the amount earned by the Application of earnings of prisoners. labour of prisoners imprisoned in any common gaol, and such amount shall be divided between the Province and the county in proportion to the amount contributed by them respectively towards the care and maintenance of the said prisoners; the division shall be made by such officer, or other person or persons, and at such times as the Lieutenant-Governor in Council shall direct.   41 V. c. 24, s. 5.

6. In the case of a county in which a city or separated town Application of earnings between county and city or towns. is situate, the share of such earnings which the said city or town shall be entitled to receive from the county shall, in case the councils are unable to agree with respect thereto, be determind annually by arbitration, according to the provisions of *The Municipal Act.*   41 V. c. 24, s. 6. Rev. Stat. c. 184.

See also R. S. C. 1886, Chap. 183, Sec. 8-12.

CHAPTER 245.

An Act Respecting Lunatic Asylums and the Custody of Insane Persons.

HER MAJESTY, by and with the advice and consent of the Legislative Assembly of the Province of Ontario, enacts as follows :—

Interpreta-
tion —

1. Where the words following occur in this Act, or in the schedules thereto, they shall be construed in the manner hereinafter mentioned unless a contrary intention appears ;

"Inspector."
Rev. Stat. c.
250.

1. " Inspector " shall mean the inspector of prisons and public charities, appointed under *The Prison and Asylum Inspection Act.*

" Lunatic."

2. " Lunatic " shall mean any insane person, whether found so by inquisition or not.

" Father."

" Mother."

3 " Father " shall include any husband of the lunatic's mother, and " mother " shall include any wife of the lunatic's father ; provided, in either case, that the birth of such lunatic was legitimate. R. S. O. 1877, c. 220, s. 1.

Certain Asy-
lums vested in
the Crown.

2. The asylums for the insane at Toronto, London, Kingston, Hamilton and Orillia, and any other public asylum established or acquired under any grant from the Legislature of this Province, for the custody and treatment of insane persons, and all the property and effects, real and personal belonging thereto, shall be vested in the Crown. R. S. O. 1877, c. 220, ss. 2, 4.

Designation
of asylums.

3. Such asylums shall be called " The Asylum for the Insane, Toronto," or " The Asylum for the Insane, London," or elsewhere, according to the fact. R. S. O. 1877, c. 220, s. 3.

OFFICERS.

Medical super-
intendent,
appointment
and duties of.

4. The Lieutenant-Governor may from time to time appoint in each asylum a medical superintendent, who shall—

1. Direct and control the medical and moral treatment of the patients ;

2. Hire and discharge from time to time the attendants and servants ;

3. Watch over the internal management, and maintain the discipline and due observance of the by-laws of the institution ;

4. Report the condition thereof to the inspector of prisons and public charities at each visit ;

5. Annually report to the inspector upon the affairs of the institution, with such suggestions as may in his opinion tend to the improvement of the asylum. R. S. O. 1877, c. 220, s. 5.

The Bursar,
appointment
and duties of.

5. The financial business and affairs of each of the said asylums shall be conducted by an officer to be appointed from time to time by the Lieutenant-Governor, to be called " The Bursar," who shall—

1. Report the state of the income and expenditure of the asylum to the inspector quarterly, and to the medical superintendent monthly ;

2. Perform such other duties as may be assigned to him under any rules or regulations in force respecting such asylum, and in accordance with the direction of the inspector. R. S. O. 1877, c. 220, s. 6.

6. The salaries of the medical superintendent and bursar, shall be such amounts as may be appropriated by the Legislature therefor. R. S. O. 1877, c. 220, s. 7 ; 41 V. c. 2, s. 39. Sched. B.

Salary of Superintendent and Bursar.

ADMISSIONS.

7. No person shall be admitted into any of the said asylums as a lunatic (except upon an order of the Lieutenant-Governor) without the certificates (Form A) of two medical practitioners, each attested by the signatures of two subscribing witnesses, and bearing date within three months of the time of such admission. R. S. O. 1877, c. 220, s. 8 ; 45 V. c. 32, s. 3.

No admission without order of Lieutenant-Governor or certificates of two doctors.

8. Every such certificate shall state that the medical practitioner signing the same personally examined the patient separately from any other medical practitioner, and after due inquiry into all necessary facts relating to the case of the patient, found him to be insane ; and the medical practitioner so certifying shall also, in the certificate, specify the facts upon which he has formed his opinion that the person to whom the certificate relates is insane, and he shall therein distinguish the facts observed by himself from facts communicated to him by others. R. S. O. 1877, c. 220, s. 9.

Contents of certificates.

9. The certificate shall be a sufficient authority to any person to convey the lunatic to any of the said asylums, and to the authorities thereof to detain him therein, or to the authorities of any other asylum to which the lunatic may have been or may be removed by the order of the inspector of prisons and public charities to detain him in such asylum as long as he continues to be insane. R. S. O. 1877, c. 220, s. 10.

Effect of certificates as authority to detain.

10. Where any obligation or agreement has been or may be entered into with the bursar of an asylum, or with Her Majesty, to secure the payment of the charges for the maintenance of any patient in an asylum, or to secure the payment of part thereof, such obligation and agreement shall be and continue in force and binding, and the parties thereto shall be and continue liable for the maintenance or partial maintenance of the patient, so long as he is maintained in a provincial asylum, notwithstanding his removal to an asylum different from that named in the obligation or agreement : but where the obligation or agreement is for a limited period of time, nothing herein contained shall be construed to extend the liability beyond the period limited. R. S. O. 1877, c. 220, s. 11.

Agreements for maintenance of patients to continue in force notwithstanding a removal to a different asylum.

xamination
destitute
sane
ersons.

11.—(1) In any municipality within the Province of Ontario, where an insane person is in destitute circumstances, and is a fit subject for asylum treatment, application may be made to the head of the municipality for an examination to be made and certificates given, in accordance with sections 7, 8 and 9, of this Act, and the head of the municipality, if satisfied that the insane person is in destitute circumstances, shall, immediately after receiving the application, notify two medical practitioners to make the required examination.   45 V. c. 32, s. 1.

ayment of
xpenses of
xamination,
c.

(2) The council of the municipality shall pay the medical practitioners for the examination and certificate a sum not exceeding $5 each, and twenty cents for each mile necessarily travelled, and shall also pay the necessary expenses incurred in conveying such insane person or persons to one of the provincial lunatic asylums; said sum to be reimbursed to the municipality by the county, where the municipality is a part of the county.   45 V. c. 32, s. 2.

COMMITTAL OF DANGEROUS LUNATICS.

ustice may
ssue warrant
o apprehend
erson be-
eved to be in-
ane and
angerous to
e at large.

12. Where an information is laid before any of Her Majesty's Justices of the Peace for any territorial division that any person, being within the limits of the jurisdiction of such Justice, is, or is suspected and believed by the person laying the information to be insane and dangerous to be at large, and has exhibited a purpose of committing some crime for which, if committed, such person would be liable to be indicted, such Justice may issue his warrant to apprehend such person and to cause him to be brought before such Justice or any other Justice for the same territorial division.   R. S. O. 1877, c. 220, s. 12.

Warrant to
apprehend,
orm of.

13. Every such warrant (Form B) shall be under the hand and seal of the Justice issuing the same, and may be directed to all or any of the constables or other peace officers of the territorial division within which the Justice issuing the same has jurisdiction, and shall name or otherwise describe the person against whom the information has been laid; and shall state that information has been laid on oath that such person is insane and dangerous to be at large; and the warrant shall order the person or persons to whom it is directed to apprehend the person against whom the information has been laid and to bring him before the Justice issuing the warrant, or before some other Justice of the Peace for the territorial division, in order that inquiry may be made respecting the sanity of such person, and that he may be further dealt with according to law. R. S. O. 1877, c. 220, s. 13.

Proceedings
on apprehen-
ion.

14. Where the person alleged to be insane has been apprehended under the warrant, he shall be brought before the same Justice of the Peace, or some other Justice for the same territorial division, and the Justice may thereupon by his warrant (Form C) commit the said alleged insane person to the common gaol or other prison, or if the Justice thinks fit, to the custody of the constable or other person who apprehended him, or to such other safe custody as the Justice deems fit; and he shall in such case order the person apprehended to be brought up at a certain time or place before the Justice of which order the informant shall have due notice; or the Justice may, if he considers fitting, proceed forthwith to hear the matter as in the next section directed; but no committal under this section shall be for a longer period than three days. R. S. O. 1877, c. 220, s. 14. <small>Warrant of committal.</small>

15. Upon the day so appointed the said Justice shall proceed to hear such evidence under oath as may be adduced with reference to the alleged insanity of the prisoner, and shall then or previously direct inquiry to be made as to the friends and relatives of the prisoner in order that the evidence of some person or persons who is or are acquainted with the family and previous habits of the prisoner may be had before the committal of the prisoner to custody as an insane person is directed. R. S. O. 1877, c. 220, s. 15. <small>Hearing of evidence; inquiry among friends, etc.</small>

16. The Justice may from time to time adjourn the inquiry, and again commit for safe custody until proper inquiry is made as herein directed. R. S. O. 1877, c. 220, s. 16. <small>Adjournment of inquiry.</small>

17. If after reasonable inquiry has been made by the Justice he is satisfied that the prisoner is insane and dangerous to be at large, the Justice shall commit (Form D) the prisoner to the common gaol of the territorial division, there to remain until the pleasure of the Lieutenant-Governor is known, or until the prisoner is discharged by law. R. S. O. 1877, c. 220, s. 17. <small>Committal on finding of insanity.</small>

18. In case it appears to the Justice that the prisoner is not insane, or is not dangerous to be at large, then the Justice shall forthwith discharge such person. R. S. O. 1877, c. 220, s. 18. <small>Discharge as not insane.</small>

19. If the Justice is satisfied that the person so apprehended as aforesaid is insane and dangerous to be at large it shall also be the duty of the Justice to make inquiry whether the prisoner is possessed of any and of what property, and where the same is situated, and also as to the number of persons (if any) who are dependent for support upon the prisoner, so that it may be ascertained whether the prisoner should be sustained as an insane pauper or not. R. S. O. 1877, c. 220, s. 19. <small>Inquiry as to property and dependents.</small>

20. It shall also be the duty of the Justice upon the examination of the witnesses in respect to such alleged insanity, and the danger of permitting the person apprehended to be at <small>Justice to inquire as to matters in schedule 2.</small>

large, to elicit as far as such Justice may be able, all information in respect to the matters set out in Schedule No. 2 to this Act. R. S. O. 1877, c. 220, s. 20.

21. If, in the opinion of the Justice, it will be much less expensive to make the inquiries directed in the preceding two sections in the county town, or in case he finds that the persons whom it is necessary to examine in order to obtain the information desired live at a considerable distance, the Justice may, in lieu of making said inquiries, certify such fact or facts, and the Justice shall in such case be excused from making such inquiries.   R. S. O. 1877, c. 220, s. 21.

22. The Justice shall forthwith send, certified, to the keeper of the gaol to which the insane person is committed, the depositions taken before him, and also the certificate (if any) given under the preceding section, and the keeper of the gaol shall forthwith deliver the same to the sheriff.   R. S. O. 1877, c. 220, s. 22.

23. The Judge of the County Court of the county, or the Deputy or Junior Judge, or if there is no Deputy or Junior Judge, and the said Judge of the County Court is absent from the county, or unable to act, then such other Justice of the Peace as may be requested by the County Court Judge to act in his stead in this behalf, shall as soon as conveniently may be, cause to be made such of the inquiries directed to be made by sections 19 and 20 of this Act as have not been previously fully made ; and the County Crown Attorney shall cause to be summoned the witnesses required therefor ; but should the Judge or other Justice find that such inquries will be expensive, or that sufficient information has been obtained for the purposes of this Act by other means, then the Judge or Justice need not make the inquiries by this section directed. R. S. O. 1877, c. 220, s. 23.

24. A Judge or Justice of the Peace acting in respect of any inquiry herein directed to be made, shall have the like authority for compelling the attendance of witnesses as a Justice would have under any Act in force respecting summary convictions, and may give directions to any constable or peace officer ; and every constable and peace officer is hereby required to obey the same in like manner ; and all the provisions of the said Acts as to procedure under the same shall, as nearly as may be, apply to proceedings under this Act, unless where different provisions are herein made.   R. S. O. 1877, c. 220, s. 24.

25. Every person committed as an insane and dangerous person under this Act shall remain in confinement in the gaol mentioned in the warrant until he is thence removed to some asylum or other place of safe keeping by direction of the Lieutenant-Governor, or until an order for his discharge is made by the Lieutenant-Governor, or until he is discharged under the provisions of section 30.   R. S. O. 1877, c. 220, s. 25.

INSANE CONVICTS.

26. The Lieutenant-Governor upon such evidence of the in- sanity of any person imprisoned for an offence under the authority of any of the statutes of this Province, or imprisoned for safe custody, charged with such an offence as the Lieutenant-Governor considers sufficient, may order the removal of such insane person to an asylum for the insane; and such person shall remain there, or in such other asylum, or other place of safe keeping, as the Lieutenant-Governor may from time to time order, until his complete or partial recovery, or until other circumstances justifying his discharge from such asylum or place are certified to the satisfaction of the Lieutenant-Governor, who may then order such person back to imprisonment if then liable thereto, or otherwise to be discharged.   R. S. O. 1877, c. 220, s. 26.

Removal of prisoners from gaols to asylums.

27. The Judge, Deputy or Junior Judge of the County Court of the county in the common gaol of which any person imprisoned for an offence is confined, and which person is, in the opinion of the gaol surgeon, insane, may, and if required by any regulations, approved by the Lieutenant-Governor in Council, made respecting the admission of patients into asylums for insane persons, shall, as soon as conveniently may be, cause to be made in respect of such prisoner inquiries similar to those directed to be made by sections 19 and 20 of this Act; and in case there is no Deputy or Junior Judge for any such County Court, and the Judge is absent from the county or is unable to act, then the said inquiries may be made by such Justice of the Peace as may be requested by the said County Court Judge to act in his stead in this behalf.   R. S. O. 1877, c. 220, s. 27.

Inquiries as to property, etc., of a person in gaol.

28. The provisions of sections 23 and 24 of this Act shall apply to inquiries made under the preceding section.   R. S. O. 1877, c. 220, s. 28.

Sections 23 and 24 to apply to examinations under s. 27.

29. Where the Judge of the County Court, or the Junior or Deputy Judge, or the Justices acting for such Judge, and the medical practitioners, upon making a personal examination of a person committed to gaol as insane, do not agree in opinion as to whether the person so committed is or is not insane, they, or any of them, may again examine such person and may grant a new certificate, if upon such further examination they change their opinion as to the mental condition of such person.   46 V. c. 30, s. 5.

Where examiners do not agree as to the mental state of a person committed as insane a second examination may be made.

DISCHARGE.

30. If the Judge of the County Court of the county, or the Deputy or Junior Judge, or if there is no such Deputy or Junior Judge, and the said County Court Judge is absent from the county or unable to act, then if such other two Justices of the Peace as may be authorized by the said Judge to act in his stead in this behalf certify (Form E) that he or they has or have personally examined a prisoner committed under the sections of this Act from 12 to 26 inclusive, and that he or they is or are satisfied that such prisoner is not insane, or that such prisoner, though insane, is not dangerous to be at large, and is not, in the opinion of such Judge or Justices, a proper person to be confined in an asylum for the insane, and if two medical practitioners (of whom the gaol surgeon shall be one), each separately from the other, personally examine the prisoner, and certify in like manner (Form F), then, in either of such cases the prisoner shall be forthwith discharged by the keeper of the gaol in which the prisoner is confined. R. S. O. 1877, c. 220, s. 29.

31. Where the insanity of any person committed under the warrant of any Justice or Justices of the Peace to a gaol as insane, has been duly certified under section 33 of this Act, and the gaol surgeon afterwards certifies that such person has recovered and may be safely discharged, the sheriff shall direct the keeper of the gaol to discharge such person from custody under the said warrant, and such person shall be discharged accordingly. 46 V. c. 30, s. 6.

32. Persons confined by virtue of this Act may be discharged by the Lieutenant-Governor or by the medical superintendent, under such regulations as may by the Lieutenant-Governor in Council be made in that behalf. R. S. O. 1877, c. 220. s. 35.

REMOVAL TO AN ASYLUM.

33.—(1) In case the said medical practitioners duly certify (Form G) that they have personally examined such prisoner as aforesaid, and that he is insane, and a proper person to be confined in an asylum for the insane, and in case the said examining Judge or Justices duly certify (Form H) that they have personally examined such prisoner as aforesaid, and that from such examination and from the evidence adduced before him or them, he or they is or are of opinion that the prisoner is insane and a proper person to be confined in an asylum for the insane, the Lieutenant-Governor, upon receipt of such certificates, may, through the Provincial Secretary, direct that the prisoner shall be removed to such asylum for the insane, or other place of safe custody, as may by the Lieutenant-Governor be deemed fit.

(2) Each medical practitioner signing a certificate under this section shall specify therein the facts upon which he has formed his opinion.   R. S. O. 1877, c. 220, s. 30.

34. An order for the removal of any insane person, impris- *Order for removal.* oned or confined under any warrant or order of a Justice of the Peace, may be made by the Lieutenant-Governor, notwithstanding any irregularity or insufficiency in the warrant or order under which such person is imprisoned or confined. R. S. O. 1877, c. 220, s. 31.

35. Every person so removed, as mentioned in section 33, *Custody of person committed to asylum, etc., till discharged.* or already removed, or in custody by authority of the Lieutenant-Governor, in any asylum for the insane, shall remain subject to the custody of the officers and other persons in charge of such asylum or other proper place to which such prisoner has been removed, or in which he is in custody by virtue of any like order, until the discharge of such prisoner is directed by the Lieutenant-Governor.   R. S. O. 1877, c. 220, s. 32.

36. Upon its appearing to the Lieutenant-Governor that any *Lt.-Governor may in certain cases return an insane non-resident of Ontario to the country from whence he came.* insane person confined as aforesaid in any gaol, or in any asylum for the insane, has come or been brought to this Province from some other Province or country, within thirty days prior to his committal to such gaol or asylum, or any other gaol or asylum, it shall be lawful for the Lieutenant-Governor, by his warrant, to authorize the removal of such insane person back to the Province or country from whence he has come or been brought, as aforesaid.   R. S. O. 1877, c. 220, s. 33.

37. The expenses of the inquiries directed by this Act to be *Expenses of inquiries, and conveyance to asylum, how to be borne.* made, and of conveying any insane person from any gaol to an asylum for the insane, shall be paid by the county, city or separate town in which the insane person has been apprehended; but if the insane person had not prior to his being apprehended resided in such county, city or separate town for the period of one year, but had resided for that period in some other county, city or separate town in this Province, then such expenses may be recovered back by the county, city or separate town in which the insane person was apprehended from the county, city or separate town in which the insane person had last resided for the period of a year; or if the insane person, although he had resided for the period of one year in the county, city or separate town in which he was apprehended, had since such residence been resident for the period of one year in some other county, city or separate town in this Province, then in like manner such expenses may be recovered by the county, city or separate town in which the insane person was apprehended from the county, city, or separate town in which the insane person last resided for the period of one year.   R. S. O. 1877, c. 220, s. 34.

ESCAPE AND RECOMMITTAL.

38. In case an inmate of an asylum for the insane escapes therefrom, it shall be lawful for any of the officers or servants of the asylum, or for any other person or persons, at the request of such officers or servants, or any of them, within forty-eight hours after such escape where no warrant has been issued, and within one month after such escape where a warrant (Form I,) has been issued by the medical superintendent in that behalf, to retake such escaped person, and to return him to the asylum from whence he escaped, and he shall remain in custody therein under the authority by virtue of which he was detained prior to the escape.   R. S. O. 1877, c. 220, s. 36.

39. In case the medical superintendent of any asylum considers it conducive to the recovery of any of the persons confined in the asylum that such person should be committed for a time to the custody of his friends, the medical superintendent may allow such person to return on trial to his friends, upon receiving a written undertaking by one or more of the friends of such person, that he or they will keep an oversight over such person.   R. S. O. 1877, c. 220, s. 37.

40. Nothing in the preceding section contained shall be construed to authorize the temporary discharge of any person who has been imprisoned for an offence, and the period of whose sentence has not expired.   R. S. O. 1877, c. 120, s. 38.

41. In case, within six months from such temporary discharge on trial, the insane person again becomes dangerous to be at large, it shall be lawful for the medical superintendent by whom the insane person was so discharged, by his warrant (Form K) directed to any person or persons, or to any constable or peace officer, or to all constables or peace officers, to authorize and direct that such insane person be apprehended and brought back to the asylum from which he was temporarily discharged, and such warrant shall be an authority to any one acting thereunder to apprehend the person named therein and to bring him back to the said asylum.   R. S. O. 1877, c. 220, s. 39.

MAINTENANCE OF LUNATICS.

42. Where a lunatic sent to any asylum is under the age of twenty-one years, and has a father or mother able to pay for his maintenance, or a guardian or committee, it shall be the duty of the bursar and medical superintendent to send a copy of the certificate mentioned in sections 7 to 9, or of the order of the Lieutenant-Governor (as the case may be), attested under their hands, to the father or mother, guardian or committee (as the case may be) of the lunatic, to which copy the said medical superintendent and bursar shall subscribe a certificate of the admission of the lunatic, and of the amount which will become due for him, each quarter, to the asylum, by the regulations of the asylum made in that behalf. R. S. O. 1877, c. 220, s. 40.

43. It shall be lawful for the bursar, conjointly with the medical superintendent, on the 1st day of each of the months of January, April, July and October, and during the time the lunatic remains in the asylum, to demand from the father or mother, guardian or committee (as the case may be) of the lunatic, such sum as may be due for the lunatic to the asylum, which sum shall be forthwith paid on such demand. R. S. O. 1877, c. 220, s. 41. *Liability for maintenance of lunatic.*

44. On the first of the said quarter days after the admission of the lunatic, the demand shall be for a sum proportionate to the broken period elapsed since the admission of the lunatic, and on the discharge of the lunatic a like demand shall be made for the sum due for the broken period since the then last quarter day. R. S. O. 1877, c. 220, s. 42. *Proportion for broken periods of a quarter.*

45. In case of refusal or neglect to pay the same, the said bursar may apply to the County Judge of the county in which the father or mother, guardian or committee, resides, upon affidavit, and if the Judge, on the return of a rule which he shall make upon the proper party, to shew cause, is satisfied that the father or mother of the lunatic is able to pay for his maintenance as aforesaid, or that the guardian or committee is able to pay for the same out of property in his possession belonging to the lunatic, the bursar shall be entitled to an order for the payment of the amount then due and the costs, and a writ of execution may issue thereon in like manner as upon a judgment of the said Court for such amount. R. S. O. 1877, c. 220, s. 43. *Order for payment for maintenance.*

46. The Judge, after hearing the parties and their witnesses under oath, either orally or in writing by affidavit, may make the order herein referred to, or if he thinks fit, may direct an issue to be made up and tried before a jury previous to making such order. R. S. O. 1877, c. 220, s. 44. *Judge may make an order for maintenance or direct an issue.*

47. Any person who is confined in any asylum for the insane, and who has at the time that he is placed in confinement, or who subsequently thereto, comes into the possession of property, shall be liable for his maintenance while in such asylum; and any person whose wife is confined in any asylum for the insane shall be liable for her maintenance while confined therein; and the inspector of prisons and public charities may, by his name of office, recover the amounts owing in respect of such maintenance; but it shall not be the duty of the inspector to enforce payment in accordance with such liability, unless upon inquiry, regard being had to the claims *Maintenance, liability for.* *Maintenance of married woman, liability of husband.*

of persons having a moral or legal right to maintenance out of the estate of such insane person, the inspector considers that the claim for maintenance ought to be collected.   R. S. O. 1877, c. 220, s. 45.

When property of a lunatic may be taken possession of to pay for maintenance.

48. If a lunatic, upon or at any time after his admission into any asylum, possesses or becomes possessed of or entitled to any real or personal property whereby the expenses of his maintenance in the asylum or any part thereof can be paid, and has no guardian or committee lawfully appointed to take the care or management of the same for the benefit of the lunatic, then if any sum due for the maintenance of the lunatic in the asylum is not paid on demand, or there is no one of whom it can be demanded, and such property, in the opinion of the inspector of prisons and public charities, is more than sufficient or is not required to maintain the family (if any) of the lunatic, the inspector may take possession of such property, or so much thereof as he thinks necessary to pay or to secure the payment of the sum due or to become due for the support and maintenance of the lunatic in the asylum, and he shall have full power over and be competent to manage and appropriate, take or recover possession of, lease, mortgage, sell and convey all or any part of such property in the name of the lunatic, or as his committee under this Act, as fully and effectually to all intents and purposes as the lunatic could or might if of full age and of sound and disposing mind ; and notwithstanding the lunatic may have ceased to be an inmate of the asylum, or may have recovered or died, the inspector may complete any lease, mortgage, sale or conveyance in respect of which proceedings have been commenced while the lunatic was confined in the asylum ; but no such lease, mortgage, sale or conveyance, shall take place without the concurrence of the Attorney-General of Ontario.   R. S. O. 1877, c. 220, s. 46.

Inspector may exercise powers conferred by s. 48, where he deems expedient.

49. The inspector may exercise the powers by the next preceding section conferred upon him if he thinks it expedient so to do, notwithstanding the property of the insane person is not more than sufficient to maintain the family of the lunatic and notwithstanding by reason thereof it is not the intention of the Government to require payment for the maintenance of the lunatic.   43 V. c. 36, s. 3.

Payment by Inspector to family of insane person may be authorized.

50. Where any moneys or other property belonging to the estate of an insane person has been received by the inspector of prisons and public charities, as the statutory committee of such insane person, and the Lieutenant-Governor in Council does not think it fitting on account of the necessities of the family of such insane person to require from the estate of such insane person payment of the amount payable for maintenance, or which, except for the abatement made by such order, would afterwards become payable, the Lieutenant Governor in Council may by order authorize the inspector to pay

over to any member or members of the family of such insane person, or other person or persons dependent upon him, such amount or amounts as it may not be considered proper to claim in respect of his maintenance, and the inspector, as such committee, in respect of every amount so paid, shall be as fully discharged as if he had paid the same for the maintenance of the said insane person in the asylum in which he is or has been confined.　43 V. c. 36, s. 4.

51. Any gift, grant, alienation, conveyance or transfer of any real or personal property made by any person, after having been insane, shall be held to be fraudulent and void, as against the inspector of prisons and public charities, unless the same is made for full and valuable consideration actually paid, or sufficiently secured to such person, or unless the purchaser had no notice of the insanity.　R. S. O. 1877, c. 220, s. 47. *Conveyances by insane persons void as against Inspector, unless for value or without notice.*

52. If the inspector considers it necessary, in order to secure the payment of the maintenance of the lunatic, or for the interest of the estate of the said lunatic so to do, he may exercise his powers in section 48 given, or any of them, although no sum is overdue for such maintenance.　R. S. O. 1877, c. 220, s. 48. *Inspector may deal with property, though nothing due for maintenance.*

53.—(1) The inspector of prisons and public charities shall *ex officio*, and by his name of office, be the committee of every lunatic who has no other committee, and who is detained in any public asylum referred to in sections 2 and 3 of this Act, and whether the lunatic is detained under an order from the Lieutenant-Governor or otherwise. *Lunatics of whom the Inspector is the committee.*

(2) The High Court may at any time appoint a committee of any such lunatic if such Court considers it expedient so to do, and upon such committee being appointed the inspector shall, while such other committee exercises such office, cease to be the committee of the lunatic, but the inspector upon delivering up the lunatic's estate shall retain so much thereof as may be required to pay any sums then due for maintenance.　R. S. O. 1877, c. 220, s. 49. *High Court may appoint another committee.*

54. Notwithstanding another committee may have been appointed by the High Court, every act of the inspector of prisons and public charities, as the committee of a lunatic or other insane person, shall be valid and binding upon the estate of such lunatic or other insane person, if done previously to a copy of the order appointing another committee, together with a notice of the persons who have been approved by the Court, as the sureties of such committee, being served upon the inspector.　R. S. O. 1877, c. 220, s. 50. *When acts of the Inspector valid as against the committee appointed by the Court.*

55. In case any action or other proceeding is brought against a person confined as insane in a public asylum for the insane, it shall not be sufficient in order to bind the estate *Proceedings against persons confined in public asylums.*

of such insane person, or to make the proceedings otherwise valid, to serve any process, bill, paper or other document upon the inspector of prisons and public charities, although the inspector is named therein as committee, but the same proceedings shall and may be taken for the appointment of some person or persons to protect the interest of the insane person aforesaid in the action or other proceeding as would be requisite or might be taken if the said inspector was not the committee of the lunatic under this Act.   43 V. c. 36, s. 1.

56. Nothing contained in this Act shall be construed to make it the duty of the inspector to institute proceedings on behalf of an insane person confined in any public asylum, or to intervene in respect of his estate, but the inspector may institute such proceedings and otherwise intervene in respect of the estate of an insane person confined as aforesaid, who has no other committee of his estate, wherever the inspector considers it expedient in the interest of the estate of the insane person, or necessary in order to secure in the manner least burdensome to the estate of the insane person, moneys due or to become due for his maintenance in an asylum.   43 V. c. 36, s. 2.

57. In case at the time of the death of an insane person the inspector of prisons and public charities is the committee of such insane person, the said inspector shall, until probate of the will or letters of administration of the estate of the insane person is granted to some other person or persons, and the grant notified to the inspector in writing, continue to have, and may, if he considers it requisite so to do, exercise by his name of office aforesaid the same powers in respect of the real and personal estate of the deceased as an executor and devisee would have in respect of the estate of his testator, in case the same were bequeathed and devised to him in trust for the payment of debts and the distribution of the residue. R. S. O. 1877, c. 220, s. 51.

58. The inspector shall be liable to render an account as to the manner in which he has managed the property and effects of the lunatic, in the same way and subject to the same responsibilities as any trustee, guardian or committee duly appointed for a similar purpose may be called upon to account, but he shall only be liable for wilful misconduct. R. S. O. 1877, c. 220, s. 53.

59. In all cases mentioned in the preceding eleven sections if doubt or opposition arises as to the right of property, it shall be lawful for the inspector or the person claiming the property to apply to the County Judge of the county in which the property is, to cause an inquisition to be held before such County Judge, and to try and determine, either by himself, or by a jury when required by either party but not otherwise, the right of property, which such Judge shall accordingly do. R. S. O. 1877, c. 220, s. 54.

60. The costs, charges and expenses which the inspector may incur in respect of the estate of an insane person shall be the first charge upon any moneys coming into the hands of the inspector and belonging to such estate. 43 V. c. 36, s. 5.

Costs of Inspector a first charge on estate.

61. The High Court shall, upon any application, made therefor by the inspector, direct to be paid to the inspector from time to time, out of any funds or moneys in Court belonging to the lunatic, the amount payable in respect to charges for maintenance of the lunatic. R. S. O. 1877, c. 220, s. 55.

Moneys in Court may be paid to Inspector for maintenance.

62. In case the insanity of any lunatic confined in any of the asylums is of such a nature, and he is possessed of such property, real or personal, as would in the opinion of the medical superintendent justify the supply to the lunatic of greater comfort and attention than are supplied under the ordinary regulations of the asylum, it shall be lawful for the inspector to make any specific regulation in respect thereto as he may deem fitting. R. S. O. 1877, c. 220, s. 56.

Inspector may make special order as to comfort of lunatic.

PROVISIONS RESPECTING THE PROPERTY OF INSANE PERSONS IN GAOLS.

63. The inspector of prisons and public charities shall, *ex officio*, and by his name of office, be the committee of the estate of every person, certified in the manner required by section 33 to be insane, who is detained in any gaol or other prison which is under the authority of the Government of this Province, if such person has no other committee lawfully appointed, whether such person has been committed to gaol under this Act, or has been committed for safe custody, or in default of sureties to keep the peace, or is imprisoned upon conviction for any offence, or otherwise howsoever. 48 V. c. 51, s. 1.

When inspector to be committee of person certified as insane under s. 33.

64.—(1) The inspector shall have the same authority and power to take or recover possession of, lease, mortgage, sell and convey any property of any insane person of whom he is committee under the preceding section as he has with respect to the property of lunatics of whom he is committee under the other provisions of this Act, and he may, notwithstanding such insane person may have been discharged from gaol, or may have recovered or died, complete any lease, mortgage, sale or conveyance in respect of which proceedings have been commenced while such insane person was confined in gaol.

Authority of inspector over property.

(2) No such lease, mortgage, sale or conveyance shall take place without the concurrence of the Attorney-General of Ontario.   48 V. c. 51, s. 2.

Application of ss. 54, to 61.   **65.** Sections 54 to 61, inclusive, shall apply to the inspector in his dealings with any such estate referred to in the next preceding two sections and as committee thereof.   48 V. c. 51, s. 3.

SCHEDULE No. 1.

FORM A.

(*Section 7.*)

CERTIFICATE OF MEDICAL PRACTITIONER IN ORDINARY CASES.

I, the undersigned C. D. (*here set forth the qualification or degree of the person certifying : for example, Licentiate of the Medical Board; M.D. of the University of Toronto, etc.*), a legally qualified medical practitioner, residing and practising at   , in the County of   , hereby certify that I, on the   day of   , A. D. 18   , at   , in the County of   , separately from any other medical practitioner, personally examined A. B., of (*insert residence and profession or occupation, if any*), and after making due inquiry into all facts in connection with the case of the said A. B., necessary to be inquired into in order to enable me to form a satisfactory opinion, I certify that the said A. B. is insane, and is a proper person to be confined in an asylum for the insane [*if the insane person is an idiot* ADD and that the said A. B. is an idiot,] and that I have formed this opinion upon the following grounds, namely :

1. Facts indicating insanity observed by myself (*here state the facts*).

2. Other facts (*if any*) indicating insanity, communicated to me by others (*here state the information, and from whom received*).

Signed this   day of   , A. D. 18   , at   , in the County of

Signed in presence of }
      F. G.   }
      H. K.   }

R. S. O. 1877, c. 220, Sched. No. 1, Form A.

FORM B.

(*Section 13.*)

WARRANT FOR APPREHENSION OF DANGEROUS LUNATIC.

Province of Ontario. }
      County of   }

To all or any of the Constables or other Peace Officers in the said County of

Whereas information upon oath has this day been laid before the undersigned, one (*or as the case may be*) of Her Majesty's Justices of the Peace in and for the said County of   , that *A. B.* is insane, and dangerous to be at large :

These are therefore to command you, in Her Majesty's name, forthwith to apprehend the said *A. B.* and bring him before me (*or us*), or some one or more of Her Majesty's Justices of the Peace in and for the said County, in order that inquiry may be made respecting the sanity of the said *A. B.*, and that he may be further dealt with according to law.

Given under my (*or our*) hand and seal this   day of   , in the year of our Lord   , at   , in the County of

[L. S.]

R. S. O. 1877, c. 220, Sched. No. 1, Form B.

FORM C.

(Section 14.)

WARRANT OF COMMITTAL FOR SAFE CUSTODY PENDING INQUIRY.

Province of Ontario, ⎱
County of   ⎰

To all or any of the Constables or Peace Officers in the County of   ,
and to the keeper of the Common Gaol (or Lock-up House) at   .

Whereas on the   day of   last past, information upon oath was laid before me (*or us*)   , ono (*or as the case may be*) of Her Majesty's Justices of the Peace in and for the said County of   , that *A. B.* is insane, and dangerous to be at large ; and whereas the hearing of the same is adjourned to the   day of   , at   o'clock in the (*fore*) noon, at   , and it is necessary that the said *A. B.* should in the meantime be kept in safe custody :

These are therefore to command you or any of you, the said Constables or Peace Officers, in Her Majesty's name, forthwith to convey the said *A. B.* to the Common Gaol (*or* Lock-up House) at   , and there deliver him to the custody of the keeper thereof, together with this precept : And I hereby require you the said keeper to receive the said *A. B.* into your custody in the said Common Gaol (*or* Lock-up House), and there safely keep him until the   day of   (instant), when you are hereby required to convey and have him the said *A. B.* at the time and place to which the said hearing is so adjourned as aforesaid, before such Justice or Justices of the Peace for the said County as may then be there to make further inquiry respecting his sanity, and to be further dealt with according to law.

Given under my (*or* our) hand and seal this   day of   in the year of our Lord,   , at   , in the County aforesaid.

[L. S.]

R. S. O. 1877, c. 220, Sched. No. 1, Form C.

FORM D.

(*Section* 17).

FINAL WARRANT OF COMMITTAL.

Province of Ontario, }
County of

To all or any of the Constables or other Peace Officers in the County of
    , and to the keeper of the Common Gaol of the County of
    , at   , in the county aforesaid.

Whereas information was laid before me (*or us*), one (*or as the case may
be*) of Her Majesty's Justices of the Peace for the said County of   ,
on the oath of   , that *A. B.* was insane and dangerous to
be at large : and whereas inquiry has been made by me (*or us*) respecting
the sanity of the said *A. B.* : and whereas I (*or we*) have found and adjudged
the said *A. B.* to be insane and dangerous to be at large :

These are therefore to command you, the said Constables or other Peace
Officers, or any of you, to take the said *A. B,* and him safely convey to the
Common Gaol at   aforesaid, and there deliver him to the
keeper thereof, together with this precept ; and I do hereby command
you, the keeper of the said Common Gaol, to receive the said *A. B.* into
your custody in the said Common Gaol, and there safely keep him until
the pleasure of the Lieutenant-Governor be known, or until he be discharged
by law.

Given under my or our hand and seal this   day of
in the year of our Lord 18 , at   , in the county aforesaid.
    [L. S].

R. S. O. 1877, c. 220, Sched. No. 1, Form D.

FORM E.

(*Section* 30.)

CERTIFICATE OF JUDGE OR JUSTICE WHEN PRISONER IS NOT FIT FOR AN ASYLUM.

Province of Ontario, }
County of

I, the undersigned *C. D.*, Judge of the County Court of the County of
    (*or, we E. F.* and *G. H.*, Esquires, two of Her Majesty's
Justices of the Peace for the County of   , who have been requested by *C. D.*, Esquire, Judge of the County Court of the said County,
to act in his stead in this matter) do hereby certify that I (*or we*) have
on this   day of   A.D. 18 , personally examined *A. B.*,
an inmate of the Gaol of the said County of   , and I (*or we*)
do hereby further certify that I am (*or we are*) satisfied that the said *A.
B.* is not insane (*or that the said A. B.*, though insane is not dangerous to
be at large) ; and is not in my (*or our*) opinion a fit person to be confined
in an Asylum for the Insane.

Signed this   day of   , A. D. 18 , at   , in the
County of

R. S. O. 1877, c. 220, Sched. No. 1, Form E.

FORM F.

(Section 30.)

CERTIFICATE OF MEDICAL PRACTITIONER WHERE PRISONER IS NOT FIT FOR AN ASYLUM.

I, the undersigned *C. D.* (*here set forth the qualification or degree of the person certifying: for example, Licentiate of the Medical Board; M. D. of the University of Toronto, etc.*), a legally qualified medical practitioner, residing and practising at   , in the County of   , do hereby certify that I, on the   day of   , A.D. 18 , at   , in the County of   , separately from any other medical practitioner, personally examined *A. B.*, an inmate of the Common Gaol of the County of   , and I further certify that I am satisfied that the said *A. B.* is not insane (*or that the said A. B., though insane, is not dangerous to be at large*), and is not in my opinion a fit person to be confined in an Asylum for the Insane.

Signed this   day of   , A.D. 18 , at in the County of   .

R. S. O. 1877, c. 220, Sched. No. 1, Form F.

FORM G.

(Section 33.)

CERTIFICATE OF MEDICAL PRACTITIONER WHERE PRISONER IS INSANE.

I, the undersigned *C.D.* (*here set forth the qualification or degree of the person certifying: for example, Licentiate of the Medical Board; M. D. of the University of Toronto, etc.*), a legally qualified medical practitioner, residing and practising at   , in the County of   , do hereby certify that I, on the   day of   , A.D. 18 , at   , in the County of   , separately from any other medical practitioner, personally examined *A.B.*, an inmate of the Common Gaol of the County of   , and I further certify that the said *A. B.* is insane, and is a proper person to be confined in an Asylum for the Insane ; and that I have formed this opinion upon the following grounds, namely : (*here state the facts upon which the certificate is based.*)

Signed this   day of   , A.D. 18 , at   , in the County of   .

R. S. O. 1877, c. 220, Sched. No. 1, Form G.

FORM H.

(Section 33.)

CERTIFICATE OF JUDGE OR JUSTICE WHEN PRISONER IS INSANE.

Province of Ontario, ⎫
County of   ⎰

I, the undersigned *C. D.*, Judge of the County Court of the County of   (*or we E. F. and G. H.*, Esquires, two of Her Majesty's Justices of the Peace for the County of   , who have been requested by *C. D.*, Esquire, Judge of the County Court of the said County, to act in his stead in this matter), do hereby certify that I (*or* we) have on this   day of   , A.D. 18   , personally examined *A.B.*, an inmate of the Gaol for the said County of   , and I (*or* we) do hereby further certify that from such personal examination, and from the evidence adduced thereon, I (*or* we) am (*or* are) of opinion that the said *A. B.* is insane, and that the said *A. B.* is a proper person to be confined in an Asylum for the Insane.

Signed this   day of   , A.D. 18   , at   , in the County of   .

R. S. O. 1877, c. 220, Sched. No. 1, Form H.

FORM I.

(*Section* 38.)

WARRANT TO RETAKE ESCAPED PATIENT.

Asylum for the Insane at
To   , and all or any of the Constables or Peace Officers in the County of

Whereas on the   day of   last past, being within one month from this date, *A. B.*, an insane person confined in the Asylum for the Insane at   , of which I (*name*) am Medical Superintendent, did escape from the said Asylum :

These are therefore to command you or any of you the said Constables or Peace Officers, in Her Majesty's name, to retake the said *A. B.*, and safely convey him to this Asylum and deliver him into my charge.

Given under my hand and seal this   day of   in the year of our Lord   , at   in the County aforesaid.

[L. S.]

R. S. O. 1877, c. 220, Sched. No. 1, Form I.

FORM K.

(*Section* 41).

WARRANT TO RETAKE PROBATIONARY PATIENTS.

Asylum for the Insane at   ,
To   , and all or any of the Constables or Peace Officers in the County of

Whereas on the   day of   last past, being within six months of this date, *A. B.*, an insane person confined in the Asylum for the Insane at   , was allowed by me, *C. D.*, the Medical Superintendent of the said Asylum, to return on trial to the care of his friends ; and whereas it appears to me from information received by me, that the said *A. B.* has again become dangerous :

These are therefore to command you or any of you the said Constables or Peace Officers, in Her Majesty's name, to retake the said *A. B.*, and safely convey him to this Asylum and deliver him into my charge.

Given under my hand and seal this   day of   , in the year of our Lord   , at   , in the County aforesaid.

[L. S.]

R. S. O. 1877, c. 220, Sched. No. 1, Form K.

SCHEDULE No. 2.

INFORMATION TO BE ELICITED UPON INQUIRY.

(Sections 19 and 20.)

1. The names in full and age of prisoner.
2. Occupation, religion and country.
3. Whether married or single ; and if single, whether ever married.
4. How many children, if any.
5. Address of parents or nearest relatives ; and in case of such relatives how connected.
6. How long prisoner has been insane.
7. Duration of the present attack, and whether the first.
8. How the insanity first shewed itself, and the supposed causes.
9. Whether any delusions, and if so, what they are.
10. Whether the prisoner is suicidal or dangerous to others.
11. Whether any offence has ever been committed by the prisoner, and whether the prisoner has been convicted of the same, with all particulars.
12. Whether the prisoner is subject to epilepsy or paralysis. •
13. Whether any of the other members of the prisoner's family have suffered in a similar way, and whether the prisoner has ever been in an asylum, and if so when and where.
14. What have been the habits of the prisoner as to temperance, industry and general conduct, and in what manner they have changed—whether the change has been recent, gradual or sudden.
15. Whether the prisoner has been subject to any bodily ailments, and if so, their nature.
16. Degree of education of prisoner, and any other information that will in the opinion of the Justice or Justices aid the Medical Superintendent in the treatment of the case.
17. Whether the prisoner is idiotic, imbecile or incurable.
18. Whether the friends of the prisoner, or any of them, if such there be, are able to contribute to the maintenance of the prisoner while in an asylum, and which, if any, of such friends, and how much they, or any of them, can contribute.
19. The information required by section 19 of this Act.

R. S. O. 1877, c. 220, Sched. No. 2.

See Revised Statutes of Canada, 1886, Chapter 182, Sections 70, 71, 72, 73, 74, as regards the removal of insane convicts from the Penitentiary whose sentences have expired.

CHAPTER 246.

An Act respecting Private Lunatic Asylums.

HER MAJESTY, by and with the advice and consent of the Legislative Assembly of the Province of Ontario, enacts as follows:—

Interpretation. **1.** Where the words following occur in this Act or in the schedules thereto they shall be construed in the manner hereinafter mentioned unless a contrary intention appears :

"Inspector." **Rev. Stat. c. 250.** 1. " Inspector " shall mean the inspector appointed under *The Prison and Asylum Inspection Act.*

"Private Asylum." 2. " Private Asylum " shall mean a house licensed under the provisions of this Act, and " house " and " licensed house " shall include a private asylum ; 46 V. c. 28, s. 1.

"County." 3. " County " shall mean a county or union of counties, or a city or town having a separate Commission of the Peace ;

"Lunatic." 4. " Lunatic " shall mean every insane person, and every person being an idiot or lunatic or of unsound mind ;

"Patient." 5. " Patient " shall mean every person received or detained as a lunatic, or taken care or charge of as a lunatic ;

"Proprietor." 6. " Proprietor " shall mean every person to whom any license is granted under the provisions of this Act, and every person keeping, owning or having any interest or exercising any duties or powers of a proprietor in any licensed house ;

7. "Clerk of the Peace" shall mean every clerk of the "Clerk of the Peace and person acting as such, and every deputy duly Peace." appointed ;

8. "Justice" shall mean a Justice of the Peace ;   "Justice."

9. "Medical Attendant" shall mean every physician who "Medical Attendant." keeps any licensed house, or in his medical capacity attends any licensed house ;

10. "Physician" shall mean every person of the male sex "Physician." authorized to practise medicine, surgery or midwifery in this Province ;   •

11. "Licensed house" shall mean a house licensed under "Licensed House." the provisions of this Act.   R. S. O. 1877, c. 221, s. 1.

LICENSE, HOW OBTAINED, ETC.

2. When the proprietor of a private asylum desires to obtain Proprietors of asylum desiring license to notify Inspector. a license for such private asylum under the provisions of this Act, he shall give notice thereof to the inspector.   46 V. c. 28, s. 2.

3. The notice shall contain the true Christian name and Contents of notice. surname, place of abode, and occupation of the person to whom the license is desired to be granted, and a true and full description of his estate or interest in such house ; and in case the person to whom the license is desired to be granted, does not propose to reside himself in the licensed house, the notice shall contain the true Christian name and surname, place of abode and occupation of the superintendent who is to reside therein.   R. S. O. 1877, c. 221, s. 19.

4. The notice shall be accompanied by a plan of the house, Plan of the house, etc. drawn upon a scale of not less than one-eighth of an inch to a foot, with a description of—

1. The situation thereof ;   Its situation.

2. The length, breadth and height of, and a reference by a Size of room. figure or letter, to every room and apartment therein ;

3. A statement of the quantity of land, not covered by any Extent of grounds. building, annexed to such house, and appropriated to the exclusive use, exercise and recreation of the patients proposed to be received therein ; and

4. Also a statement of the number of patients proposed to be Number of patients provided for. received into such house, and whether the license so applied for is for the reception of male or female patients, or of both, and if for the reception of both, of the number of each sex proposed to be received in such house, and of the means by which the one sex may be kept distinct and apart from the other.   R. S. O. 1877, c. 221, s. 20.

Time notice to be sent to Inspector.

5.—(1) The notice, with the plan and statement required by the next preceding section shall be sent to the inspector at least two weeks before the private asylum is ready for the reception of patients.

Inspector to report to Lieutenant-Governor.

(2) The inspector shall thereupon visit the proposed private asylum and minutely inspect the same, and report thereon to the Lieutenant-Governor in Council. 46 V. c. 28, s. 3.

License to proprietors.

6. If the inspector reports that the buildings and premises referred to in the said notice are ready and fit for occupation as a private asylum for the insane, the Lieutenant-Governor in Council may issue a license to the proprietors to keep and maintain the same for the purposes of a private asylum ; and such license shall continue in force until revoked by the Lieutenant-Governor in Council. 46 V. c. 28, s. 4.

Securities by licensee.

7. No such license shall be granted unless the person to whom the license is granted enters into a bond to Her Majesty in the sum of $400, with two sufficient sureties, each in the sum of $200, or one sufficient surety in the sum of $400, under the usual conditions for the good behaviour of such person during the time for which the license continues in force. R. S. O. 1877, c. 221, s. 23 ; 46 V. c. 28, s. 4.

BOARD OF VISITORS.

Board of Visitors.

8.—(1) Every private asylum or house licensed under the provisions of this Act shall be under the supervision and inspection of a board of visitors, composed of the Judge (or in the case of his absence or disqualification the Junior or Deputy Judge) of the County Court of the county wherein the private asylum is located, the warden of the county for the time being, the clerk of the Peace for the county, together with a local physician, who shall be appointed by the Lieutenant-Governor in Council, and shall hold office for three years unless sooner removed by the Lieutenant-Governor.

Chairman.

(2) The Judge shall be the chairman of the board, and the clerk of the peace shall be its secretary.

Allowance to secretary.

(3) The secretary shall be paid out of the license fees, or by the proprietors of the asylum, such allowance for his services as the Lieutenant-Governor in Council may direct. 46 V. c. 28, s. 5.

Visitors not to have a pecuniary interest in any asylum.

9.—(1) No member of the board of visitors shall be pecuniarily interested in any private asylum, either directly or indirectly and any visitor who, after his appointment, becomes interested in any private asylum, either by profits as proprietor, or by the sale of merchandise to such an asylum, or in any other way, shall thereupon become disqualified from acting, and shall not thereafter act in such capacity.

(2) In case a Judge or clerk of the peace is or becomes Appointmen so disqualified, the Lieutenant-Governor may appoint some one in case of dis qualification to act in his stead; and in case a warden is or becomes so official visito disqualified, the county council may appoint some one to act in his stead. 46 V. c. 28, s. 6.

(3) If an assistant-secretary to any board after his appoint- Assistant-secretary be-ment becomes so interested he shall be disqualified from coming inter-acting, and shall cease to act in such capacity. R. S. O. 1877, ested to be di qualified. c. 221, s. 16.

10.—(1). The visitors shall, before acting, take an oath to Oath of visi-the following effect: tors.

" I *A.B.* do swear that I will discreetly, impartially and faithfully execute all the trusts and powers committed to me by virtue of the Act entitled *An Act respecting Private Lunatic Asylums,* and that I will keep secret all such matters as come to my knowledge in the execution of my office, except when required to divulge the same by legal authority, or so far as I feel myself called upon to do so for the better execution of the duty imposed upon me by the said Act."

(2) The oath may be administered by any Justice of the By whom ad Peace to the clerk of the peace, who may then administer the ministered. same to the other members of the board. 46 V. c. 28, s. 8.

11. The secretary shall summon the board of visitors to Meeting of meet for the purpose of executing the duties of this Act. Visitors to b called. R. S. O. 1877, c. 221, s. 8; 46 V. c. 28, s. 5.

12. Every such appointment, summons and meeting shall be Visitors' made and held as privately as may be, and in such manner meetings to private. that no proprietor, superintendent or person interested in or employed about or connected with any house to be visited, has notice of such intended visitation. R. S. O. 1877, c. 221, s. 9.

13.—(1) If the secretary at any time, desires to employ an Assistant assistant in the execution of the duties of his office, he shall Clerk. certify such desire, and the name of the proposed assistant to one of the other members of the board of visitors, being a Justice of the Peace, and if such member approves thereof, he shall administer the following oath to such assistant:

"I, *A. B.,* do solemnly swear that I will faithfully keep secret all such Oath of. matters and things as come to my knowledge in consequence of my em-ployment as assistant to the Secretary of the Board of Visitors, appointed for the County of by virtue of *The Act respecting Private Lunatic Asylums,* unless required to divulge the same by legal authority : So help me God."

(2) The secretary may thereafter, at his own cost, employ At whose co such assistant. R. S. O. 1877, c. 221, s. 13.

14. No physician being a member of the board of visitors Restrictions shall sign any certificate for the admission of any patient into upon physi-sicians being any licensed house or hospital, or shall professionally attend visitors.

upon any patient in any licensed house or hospital unless he is directed to visit such patient by the person upon whose order such patient has been received into such licensed house or hospital, or by the Provincial Secretary, or one of the Judges of the High Court or by a committee appointed by one of the said Judges. R. S. O. 1877, c. 221, s. 15.

enalty on
ysicians.

15. If a physician, being a member of the board of visitors, signs a certificate for the admission of a patient into any licensed house or hospital, or professionally attends a patient in such house or hospital (except as aforesaid), such physician shall for each offence forfeit the sum of $200. R. S. O. 1877, c. 221, s. 17.

Removal of Superintendent.

emoval of
perinten-
nt.

16. Any person to whom a license is granted may remove the superintendent named in the notice, and may at any time appoint another superintendent, upon giving to the board of visitors a notice containing the true Christian name and surname, place of abode and occupation of the new superintendent. R. S. O. 1877, c. 221, s. 24.

Fees for Licenses.

es thereon.

17. For every license there shall be paid to the clerk of the peace, for every patient proposed to be received into such house, the sum of $2 ; and if the total amount of such sums of $2 does not amount to $60, then so much more as together therewith will make up the sum of $60, and no such license shall be delivered until the sum payable for the same has been paid. R. S. O. 1877, c. 221, s. 30.

pplication
fees.

18. All moneys to be received for licenses granted under this Act shall be applied towards the payment of the allowance to the secretary for his services and the discharge of the costs, charges and expenses incurred by or under the authority of the board of visitors, in the execution of or by virtue of this Act. R. S. O. 1877, c. 221, s. 32.

erk of the
ace to keep
counts of
oneys re-
ived or ex-
nded.

19. The clerk of the peace shall keep an account of all moneys received and paid by him under or by virtue of or in the execution of this Act, and such accounts shall be made up to the last day of December in each year inclusively, and shall be signed by two at least of the members of the board of visitors. R. S. O. 1877, c. 221, s. 33.

ADDITIONS AND ALTERATIONS TO LICENSED PREMISES.

e license for
ch house.

20. No one license shall include or extend to more than one house ; but if there is any place or building detached from a house to be licensed, but not separated therefrom by ground belonging to any other person, and if such place or building is specified, delineated and described in the notice, plan and statement hereinbefore required to be given, in the same manner in all particulars as if the same had formed part of such house, then such detached place or building may, if the Lieutenant-Governor in Council thinks fit, be included in the license for the house, and if so included, shall be considered part of such house for the purposes of this Act. R. S. O. 1877, c. 221, s. 25.

21. No addition or alteration shall be made to, in or about any licensed house, or the appurtenances, unless previous notice in writing of such proposed addition or alteration, accompanied with a plan thereof, to be drawn upon the scale aforesaid, and accompanied by such description as aforesaid, has been given to the inspector, by the person to whom the license has been granted, nor unless the approval of the Lieutenant-Governor in Council has been previously obtained. R. S. O. 1877, c. 221, s. 26. *Alterations i asylums.*

TRANSFERS AND REMOVALS.

22. If a person to whom a license has been granted under this Act, by sickness, or other sufficient reason, becomes incapable of keeping the licensed house, or dies before the expiration of the license, the Lieutenant-Governor in Council may authorize the transfer of the license, with all the privileges and obligations annexed thereto for the term then unexpired, to the person who at the time of such incapacity or death was the superintendent of such house, or had the care of the patients therein, or to such other person as the Lieutenant-Governor in Council may approve, and in the meantime the license shall remain in force, and have the same effect as if granted to the superintendent of the house. R. S. O. 1877, c. 221, s. 34; 46 V. c. 28, s. 9. *When license assignable.*

23. In case a license has been granted to two or more persons, and one or more of such persons die, leaving the other or others surviving, the license shall remain in force and have the same effect as if granted to the survivor or survivors. R. S. O. 1877, c. 221, s. 35. *Survivorshi*

24.—(1) If a licensed house is pulled down or occupied under the provisions of any statute, or is by any *vis major*, or by fire, tempest or other accident, rendered unfit for the accommodation of lunatics or if the person keeping such house desires to transfer the patients to another house, the Lieutenant-Governor in Council, may grant to the person whose house has been so pulled down, occupied or rendered unfit as aforesaid, or who desires to transfer his patients as aforesaid, license to *Removal to other premises.*

keep such other house for the reception of lunatics, for such time as the Lieutenant-Governor in Council thinks fit ; but the same notice of such intended change of house, and the same plans and statements and descriptions of and as to such intended new house, shall be given as are required when application is first made for license for any house, and shall be accompanied by a statement in writing of the cause of such change of house. R. S. O. 1877, c. 221, s. 36, *part ;* 46 V. c. 28, s. 4.

(2) A fee of $4 shall be payable by the licensee to the clerk of the peace upon the issue of the license. R. S. O. 1877, c. 221, s. 36, *part.*

Notice of in-
tended re-
moval.

25. Except in cases in which the change of house is occasioned by fire or tempest, seven clear days' previous notice of the intended removal, shall be sent by the person to whom the license for keeping the original house was granted to the person who signed the order for the reception of each patient, or the person by whom the last payment on account of each patient had been made. R. S. O. 1877, c. 221, s. 36, *part.*

REVOCATION OF LICENSES.

Revocation of
license.

26. In case a majority of the Justices of any county, in General Sessions assembled, resolve to recommend to the Lieutenant-Governor the revocation of any license granted under this Act, such Justices shall cause to be given to the person licensed, or to the resident superintendent of the licensed house, or to be left at the licensed house, seven clear days' previous notice in writing of the intended recommendation. R. S. O. 1877, c. 221, s. 37.

When the
Lieutenant-
Governor may
revoke.

27. Upon the receipt of such recommendation the Lieutenant-Governor in Council may revoke such license ; and in the case of a revocation, the same shall take effect at a period to be named in the Order in Council not exceeding two months from the time a copy or notice thereof has been published in the *Ontario Gazette.* R. S. O. 1877, c. 221, s. 38.

How revoca-
tion notified
and promul-
gated.

28. A copy or notice of the Order in Council shall be transmitted to the person licensed or to the resident superintendent of, or be left at the licensed house, after which the same shall be published in the *Ontario Gazette.* R. S. O. 1877, c. 221, s. 39. *As to revocation on report of Inspector of Prisons and Public Charities, see* Cap. 250, s. 18.

ADMISSION OF PATIENTS.

Orders for
admission of
patient.

29. No person, whether being or represented to be a lunatic, or only a boarder or lodger, in respect of whom any money is received or agreed to be received for board, lodging or any other accommodation, shall be received into or detained in any licensed house without an order under the hand of some person according to the form, and stating the particulars mentioned in Schedule A, nor without the medical certificates, according to the Form of Schedule B, of two physicians not being partners Medical Certi- or brothers, or father and son, and each of whom separately ficates. from the other had personally examined the person to whom it relates not more than fifteen clear days previous to the reception of such person into such house, and each of whom signed .and dated the certificate on the day on which such person was so examined.   R. S. O. 1877, c. 221, s. 40 ; 48 V. c. 53, s. 4.

30. Every physician who signs such certificate shall Facts to be specify therein that he has personally examined the person to certified. whom the certificate relates, and that from such examination, and from the evidence adduced before him, he is of opinion that such person is a lunatic (or an insane person, or an idiot, or a person of unsound mind) and a proper person to be confined in an asylum, and shall also specify in the certificate the fact or facts and the evidence adduced before him which led to such opinion, and he shall therein distinguish the facts observed by himself from facts communicated to him by others.   49 V. c. 50, s. 1.

31. A medical superintendent of a private asylum may Admission of admit to and detain therein any patient from any Province patients from of the Dominion of Canada, who is certified to be insane by vinces. two physicians duly authorized to practise as such in the Province where such patient has his domicile, provided such certificates of insanity are made in accordance with the requirements of section 29 and Schedule B therein mentioned, but any patient so admitted and detained in a private asylum from any other Province must, within fifteen days of such admission, be examined by one duly qualified physician of the Province of Ontario.   48 V. c. 53, s. 3.

32. No person shall receive to board and lodge in any house Lunatics not not licensed under this Act, or take the charge or care of any to be received insane person without having first obtained the medical certi- sed houses ficates required by this Act for the admission of an insane per- without medi- son into a licensed house.   R. S. O. 1877, c. 221, s. 42. calcertificates.

33. Every person who receives to board or lodge in a Notice thereof house not licensed under this Act, or takes the care or charge to be sent to of an insane person, shall within three months next after re- of the Visitors. ceiving such insane person into his house, or under his care, transmit to the secretary of the board of visitors of the county a copy of such medical certificates, sealed and endorsed *Private Return*, and every such person shall also (if the insane person continues in his house or under his care) on the 1st day of January, of every year, or within seven clear days thereafter, transmit to such secretary a certificate, signed by two physicians describing the then actual state of mind of such insane person, and endorsed *Private Return*, and all such private returns shall be preserved by the said secretary and shall be open to the inspection of the members of the board of visitors only. R. S. O. 1877, c. 221, s. 43.

When certificate of one physician sufficient.

34. Any person may, under special circumstances, be received into such house, upon such order with the certificate of one physician alone, provided the order states the special circumstances which prevented the person from being examined by two physicians; but in every such case another certificate shall be signed by some other physician, not connected with any house licensed as aforesaid, and who has specially examined such person within three days after his reception into such house. R. S. O. 1877, c. 221, s. 44.

When physician not allowed to certify.

35. No physician who, or whose father, brother, son or partner, is wholly or partly the proprietor of or a regular professional attendant in a licensed house, shall sign any certificate for the reception of a patient into such house; and no physician who, or whose father, brother, son or partner, signs the order hereinbefore required for the reception of a patient, shall sign any certificate for the reception of the same patient. R.S.O. 1877, c. 221, s. 45.

Penalty on physician giving false certificate maliciously.

36. Any physician who with express malice, or corruptly, signs any false certificate of insanity for the purpose of aiding to procure the confinement of any sane person in a private asylum shall, upon judgment being given against him in the High Court in an action for damages on account of such malicious or corrupt act, *ipso facto* be incapacitated from practising as a physician in Ontario for the period of five years thereafter, unless the Court shall see fit to remove such incapacity or shorten the limit thereof. The name of such physician shall, upon production of a certified copy of the judgment to the registrar of the College of Physicians and Surgeons of Ontario, be removed from the register, and shall not be restored thereto during such incapacity. 48 V. c. 53, s. 7.

Admission of person requiring treatment.

37. The medical superintendent of a private asylum may upon the written application of the person desiring admission, receive and detain therein as a patient, any person who though not insane, is desirous of submitting himself for the treatment of epilepsy, hysteria, chorea-amentia, or any nervine or physical ailment, provided that one physician certifies in writing that such patient is afflicted with epilepsy, hysteria, chorea-amentia, or some other nervine or physical ailment, and that there is a danger such ailment will develop into mental derangement unless it is properly treated, but no patient thus voluntarily admitted shall be detained more than three days after he has given notice in writing to the medical superintendent of his or her intention or desire to leave such asylum.   48 V. c. 53, s. 5.

38. When a patient is received into a private asylum upon his own application, the medical superintendent shall give immediate notice of such reception to the secretary of the board of visitors, stating all the particulars of the case ; and one or more members of the board or the secretary thereof shall forthwith visit such patient in order to verify the fact of such patient's having been admitted voluntarily : and all the facts in connection with such case shall be forthwith recorded in the visitors' book by the person making the inquiry.   48 V. c. 53, s. 6.   ·

Notice of admission to be given to Board of Visitors.

39. Every proprietor or superintendent who receives a patient into a licensed house, shall, within two days after the reception of such patient, make an entry with respect to such patient in a book to be kept for that purpose, to be called " The Book of Admissions," according to the form and containing the particulars required in Schedule C, so far as he can ascertain the same, except as to the form of the mental disorder, and except also as to the discharge or death of the patient, which shall be made when the same happens ; and every person who so receives such patient and does not, within two days thereafter, make such entry (except as aforesaid), shall forfeit a sum not exceeding $10.   R. S. O. 1877, c. 221, s. 46.

Books to be kept, and entries made therein.

40. The form of the mental disorder of every patient received into any licensed house, shall, within seven days after the reception, be entered in the said " Book of Admissions " by the medical attendant of the house ; and every medical attendant who omits to make any such entry within the time aforesaid, shall, for every such omission, forfeit a sum not exceeding $10.   R. S. O. 1877, c. 221, s. 47.

The form of mental disorder to be entered.

Under penalty.

41. The proprietor or resident superintendent of every licensed house shall, after two clear days, and before the expiration of seven clear days from the day on which any patient has been received into the house, transmit to the secretary of the board of visitors within whose jurisdiction the house is situate, a copy of the order and medical certificates or certificate on which the patient has been received, and also a notice and statement according to the form of Schedule D. R. S. O. 1877, c. 221, s. 48.

Copy of order to be sent by proprietor to Secretary of Visitors.

42. When a patient has escaped from a licensed house, the proprietor or superintendent of the house shall, within two clear days next after the escape, transmit a written notice

In cases of escape, what steps to be taken.

5

thereof to the secretary of the board of visitors within whose jurisdiction the house is situate; and the notice shall state the Christian name and surname of the patient who so escaped, and his or her then state of mind, and also the circumstances connected with the escape; and if the patient is brought back to such house, the proprietor or resident superintendent shall within two clear days after the patient has been brought back, transmit a written notice thereof to the secretary; and the notice shall state when the patient was so brought back, and the circumstances connected therewith, and whether with or without a fresh order and certificates or certificate, and every proprietor or resident superintendent omitting to transmit such notice whether of escape or of return, shall for every such omission forfeit a sum of $40. R. S. O. 1877, c. 221, s. 49.

Under penalty.

REMOVAL, DISCHARGE, DEATH, ETC.

Removal, discharge, etc., to be entered.

43. When a patient is removed or discharged from a licensed house, or dies therein, the proprietor or superintendent of the house shall, within two clear days next after such removal, discharge or death, make an entry thereof in a book to be kept for that purpose, according to the form and stating the particulars in Schedule E to this Act, and shall also within the same two days transmit a written notice thereof, and also of the cause of the death, removal or discharge of the patient, if known to the secretary of the board of visitors in whose jurisdiction the house is situate, according to the form, and containing the particulars in Schedule F to this Act. R. S. O. 1877, c. 221, s. 50.

And notice given.

Certificate required in case of death.

44. In case of the death of a patient in a licensed house, a statement of the cause of the death of the patient, with the name of any person present at the death, shall be forthwith drawn up and signed by the medical attendant of the house, and a copy thereof, duly certified by the proprietor or superintendent of such house, shall, within forty-eight hours after the death of the patient, be by such proprietor or superintendent transmitted to the nearest coroner, and also to the secretary of the board of visitors in whose jurisdiction the house is situate, and also to the person who signed the order for the patient's confinement, or if such person is dead or absent from the Province, then to the person who made the last payment on account of the patient, and every medical attendant, proprietor or superintendent who neglects or omits to draw up, sign, certify, or transmit such statement as aforesaid, shall, for every such neglect or omission, forfeit and pay a sum of not exceeding $200. R. S. O. 1877, c. 221, s. 51.

Under penalty.

Penalty for illegal confinement.

45. In case any person released from confinement in any licensed house considers himself to have been unjustly confined, the secretary of the board of visitors within whose jurisdiction the house is situate shall at his request, furnish to him, or to his solicitor, without fee or reward, a copy of the certificates and order upon which he has been confined; and the Lieutenant-Governor may cause to be prosecuted on the part of the Crown, any person who has been concerned in the unlawful taking of any of Her Majesty's subjects as an insane patient, and likewise any person who has been concerned in the neglect or ill-treatment of any patient or persons so confined.   R. S. O. 1877, c. 221, s. 52.

MEDICAL ATTENDANCE.

46. In every house licensed for one hundred patients or more, *Every house to have a resident or* there shall be a resident physician as the superintendent or medical attendant thereof; and every house licensed for less *attendant physician.* than one hundred, and more than fifty patients (in case such house is not kept by, or has not a resident physician), shall be visited daily by a physician, and every house licensed for less than fifty patients (in case such house is not kept by, or has not a resident physician) shall·be visited twice in every week by a physician; but the board of visitors of any house may direct that such house shall be visited by a physician at any other time or times, not being oftener than once in every day. R. S. O. 1877, c. 221, s. 53.

47. Where a house is licensed to receive less than eleven *When a physician to visit,* lunatics, any two members of the board of visitors of such house, *if less than* if they respectively think fit, may, by writing under their *eleven* hands, permit the house to be visited by a physician at such *lunatics.* intervals more distant than twice every week, as such visitors appoint, but not at a greater interval than once in every two weeks.   R. S O. 1877, c. 221, s. 54.

48. Every physician, in case there is only one, keeping or *Entries to be* residing in or visiting any licensed house, and in case there are *made in "The Medical Visit-* two or more physicians keeping or residing in or visiting any *ation Book."* licensed house, then one at least of such physicians, shall once in every week (or, in the case of any house at which visits at more distant intervals than once a week are permitted then shall on every visit), enter and sign in a book to be kept at such house for that purpose, to be called "The Medical Visitation Book," a report shewing:

1. The date thereof;

2. The number, sex, and state of health of all the patients then in the house;

3. The Christian name and surname of every patient who has been under restraint, or in seclusion, or under medical treatment, since the date of the last preceding report;

4. The condition of the house, and every death, injury and act of violence which has happened to or affected any patient since the then last preceding report, according to the form in

Schedule H, and every such physician who omits to enter or sign such report, shall for every such omission forfeit and pay the sum of $80.   R. S. O. 1877, c. 221, s. 55.

A book to be kept called "The Case Book."

Entries.

49. There shall be kept in every licensed house a book to be called "The Case Book," in which the physician keeping or residing in or visiting such house shall from time to time make entries of the mental state and bodily condition of each patient, together with a correct description of the medicine and other remedies prescribed for the treatment of his disorder, and the board of visitors within whose jurisdiction any licensed house is situate may, whenever they see fit, by an order in writing, require the physician keeping or residing in or visiting such house, to transmit to them a correct copy of the entries or entry in the case book kept under the provisions of this

Penalty.

Act relative to the case of any lunatic who is or has been confined in such house, and every physician who neglects to keep the said case book, or to enter therein the particulars of each patient's case, or to transmit a copy of any entry therein pursuant to any such order, shall for every such neglect forfeit a sum not exceeding $40.   R. S. O. 1877, c. 221, s. 56.

INSPECTION BY BOARD OF VISITORS.

Visitors to visit licensed houses.

50. Every licensed house within the jurisdiction of any board of visitors shall be visited by two at least of the members of the board (one of whom shall be a physician), four times at the least in every year.   R. S. O. 1877, c. 221, s. 57.

Duties of, in making visits.

51. The visitors, when visiting any such house, shall inspect every part of the house, and every house, out-house, place and building communicating therewith, or detached therefrom but not separated by ground belonging to any other person, and every part of the ground and appurtenances held, used or occupied therewith, and shall see every patient then confined therein, and shall enquire whether any patient is under restraint, and why, and shall inspect the order and certificates or certificate for the reception of every patient who has been received into the house since the last visit of the visitors, and shall enter in the visitors' book a minute :

1. Of the then condition of the house, and of the patients therein ;

2. The number of patients under restraint, with the reasons thereof as stated :

3. Such irregularity (if any) as exists in such order or certificate ;

4. Whether the previous suggestions (if any) of the visitors, have or have not been attended to ; and

5. Any observations which they deem proper as to any of the matters aforesaid, or otherwise.   R. S. O. 1877, s. 221, s. 58.

52. The proprietor or superintendent of every licensed house shall shew to the visitors so visiting the same, every part thereof and every person detained therein as a lunatic. R. S. O. 1877, c. 221, s. 59. *Duties of proprietor or superintendent towards the Visitors.*

53. The visitors upon their several visitations to a licensed house shall inquire: *Inquiries to be made by the Visitors.*

1. Where divine service is performed therein, to what number of the patients, and the effect thereof;

2. What occupations or amusements are provided for the patients, and the result thereof;

3. Whether there has been adopted any system of non-coercion, and if so, the result thereof;

4. As to the classification of patients;

5. And such other inquiries as to such visitors seem expedient. R. S. O. 1877, c. 221, s. 60.

54. Upon every visit of the visitors to a licensed house, there shall be laid before them by the proprietor or superintendent of the house: *What information to be laid before the Visitors.*

1. A list of all the patients then in the house (distinguishing males from females, and specifying such as are deemed curable);

2. The several books by this Act required to be kept by the proprietor or superintendent, and by the medical attendant of a licensed house;

3. All orders and certificates relating to patients admitted since the visitation of the visitors;

4. The license then in force for such house;

5. All such other orders, certificates, documents and papers relating to any of the patients at any time received into such house, as the visitors from time to time require to be produced to them; and the visitors shall sign the said books as having been so produced. R. S. O. 1877, c. 221, s. 61.

55. There shall be hung up in some conspicuous part of every licensed house a copy of the plan sent to the inspector on applying for the license for such house; and there shall be kept in every such house a Queen's Printer's copy of this Act, bound in a book, to be called "The Visitors' Book," and the said visitors shall at the time of their visitations enter in such book the result of the inspections and inquiries hereinbefore directed or authorized to be made by them, with such observations (if any) as they think proper; and there shall also be kept in every such house a book, to be called "The Patients' Book," and the said visitors shall, at the times of their visitations, enter therein such observations as they think fit respecting the state of mind or body of any patient in such house. R. S. O. 1877, c. 221, s. 62. *Information to be hung up in every licensed house.* *"The Visitors' Book."* *"The Patients' Book."*

Copies of
Visitors'
entries to be
sent to the
Secretary.

56.—(1) The proprietor or resident superintendent of every licensed house shall, within three days after every visit by the said visitors, transmit to the secretary of the visitors a true and perfect copy of the entries made by them in "The Visitors' Book," "The Patients' Book" and "The Medical Visitation Book" respectively, distinguishing the entries in the several books. R. S. O. 1877, c. 221, s. 63.

Report to be
made to
Inspector.

(2) The proprietor or resident superintendent of every licensed house shall, within five days after the admission of any lunatic, or of an insane or idiotic patient, or of a person of unsound mind, to such licensed house, report to the inspector of prisons and public charities for Ontario, the fact of such admission, together with copies of the certificates and papers upon which the patient was admitted, and shall at any and all times furnish to the inspector such other reports and information relative to any such patient or patients as may be required by him.   49 V. c. 50, s. 2.

Penalty on
proprietor
omitting.

57. Every proprietor or superintendent who omits to transmit to the secretary of the board of visitors a true and perfect copy of every such entry, shall, for every omission, forfeit a sum not exceeding $40.   R. S. O. 1877, c. 221, s. 65.

Nocturnal
visits.

58. Any two members of the board of visitors may visit and inspect a licensed house within their jurisdiction at such hour of the night as they think fit.   R. S. O. 1877, c. 221, s. 66.

DISCHARGE OF PATIENTS.

Order for dis-
charge.

59. In case the person who signed the order on which a patient has been received into a licensed house, by writing, under his hand, directs the patient to be removed or discharged, such patient shall forthwith be removed or discharged accordingly.   R. S. O. 1877, c. 221, s. 67.

If person who
signed the
order for ad-
mission be-
comes incapa-
ble, what to
be done.

60. If the person who signed the order upon which a patient has been received into a licensed house is incapable by reason of insanity or absence from the Province, or otherwise, of giving an order for the discharge or removal of the patient, or if such person is dead, then, the husband or wife of the patient, or if there is no such husband or wife, the father of the patient, and if there is no father, the mother of the patient, or if there is no mother, then any one of the nearest of kin for the time being of the patient, or the person who made the last payment on account of the patient, may, by writing under his or her hand, give such direction for the discharge or removal of the patient, and thereupon the patient shall be forthwith discharged or removed accordingly.   R. S. O. 1877, c. 221, s. 68.

61. No patient shall be discharged or removed from a licensed house under any of the powers hereinbefore contained, if the physician by whom the same is kept, or who is the regular medical attendant thereof, by writing under his hand, certifies that in his opinion the patient is dangerous and unfit to be at large, together with the grounds on which such opinion is founded, unless the board of visitors of the house after such certificate has been produced to them, give their consent, in writing, to the discharge or removal of the patient. R. S. O. 1877, c. 221, s. 69.

What to be done if the physician in charge objects.

62. Nothing herein contained shall prevent any patient from being transferred from one licensed house to another licensed house, or to an asylum for the insane, but in such case every patient shall, for the purpose of such removal, be placed under the control of an attendant belonging to the licensed house to or from which he is about to be removed, and shall remain under such control until the removal has been duly effected. R. S. O. 1877, c. 221, s. 70.

Transfer from one house to another or to an asylum for the insane.

63. Any two or more members of the board of visitors of any licensed house, of whom one shall be a physician, may make special visits to any patient detained in such house, on such days and at such hours as they think fit; and if after two distinct and separate visits made by the same visitors it appears to them that the patient is detained without sufficient cause, they may order his discharge and the patient shall be discharged accordingly. R. S. O. 1877, c. 221, s. 71.

Special visits by Visitors and when they may order discharge of patients.

64. Every order by the visitors for the discharge of a patient from a licensed house shall be signed by them, and they shall not order the discharge of a patient from such house without having previously examined the medical attendant of the house, if he tenders himself for that purpose, as to his opinion respecting the fitness of the patient to be discharged. R. S. O. 1877, c. 221, s. 72.

To sign the orders, etc.

And examine medical attendant if required.

65. If the visitors, after examining the medical attendant, discharge a patient, and the medical attendant furnishes them with a statement in writing, containing his reasons against the discharge of the patient, they shall forthwith transmit such statement to the secretary of the board of visitors, to be kept and registered in a book for that purpose. R. S. O. 1877, c. 221, s. 73.

If physician in charge objects, what to be done.

66. Not less than seven days shall intervene between the first and second of such special visits, and the board of visitors shall, seven days previously to the second of such special visits, give notice thereof, either by post, or by an entry in "The Patients' Book," to the proprietor or superintendent of the licensed house in which the patient intended to be visited is detained, and the proprietor or superintendent shall, forth-

Time to intervene between special visits, etc.

with, if possible, transmit by post a copy of the notice to the person by whose authority the patient has been received into such house, or by whom the last payment on account of such patient was made, and also to the secretary of the board of visitors.   R. S. O. 1877, c. 221, s. 74.

What lunatics the visitors cannot discharge.

67. None of the powers of discharge hereinbefore contained, shall extend to a lunatic confined under an order or authority of the Lieutenant-Governor, or under the order of any Court of criminal jurisdiction.   R. S. O. 1877, c. 221, s. 75.

ORDER FOR INFORMATION.

Information to be given to persons who apply respecting individuals detained as lunatics.

68. If a person applies to a member of the board of visitors to be informed whether any particular person is confined in a licensed house within the jurisdiction of the board, the member, if he thinks it reasonable to permit the inquiry to be made, shall sign an order to the secretary of the board of visitors, and the secretary shall, on receipt of such order, and on payment to him of a sum not exceeding twenty cents for his trouble, make search amongst the returns made to him in pursuance of this Act, whether the person inquired after is, or, within the then last twelve months, has been confined in any licensed house within the jurisdiction of the board; and if it appears that such person is or has been so confined, the secretary shall deliver to the person applying a statement in writing, specifying :

1. The situation of the house in which the person so inquired after appears to be or to have been confined ;

2. The name of the proprietor or resident superintendent thereof ;

3. The date of the admission of such person into such licensed house : and

4. (In case of his having been removed or discharged) the date of his removal or discharge therefrom.   R. S. O. 1877, c. 221, s. 76.

ORDERS FOR ADMISSION.

Admission of relatives, order for.

69. Any member of the board of visitors of a licensed house may, at any time, give an order in writing under his hand for the admission to any patient confined in such house, of any relation or friend of such patient or of any medical or other person whom any relation or friend of the patient desires to be admitted to him.   R. S. O. 1877, c. 221, s. 77.

Extent of such order.

70. The order of admission may be either for a single admission, or for an admission for any limited number of times or for admission generally at all reasonable times, and either with or without restriction as to the admission or admissions being in the presence of a keeper or not, or otherwise.   R. S. O. 1877, c. 221, s. 78.

71. If the proprietor or superintendent of such house refuses admission to, or prevents or obstructs the admission to any patient, of any relation, friend or other person who produces such order of admission, he shall for every such refusal, prevention or obstruction, forfeit a.sum not exceeding $80. R. S. O. 1877, c. 221, s. 79.

Penalty for refusing admission.

MISCELLANEOUS PROVISIONS.

72. In case the medical superintendent of a private asylum considers it conducive to the recovery of any of the persons confined in the asylum that such person should be entrusted for a time to the care of his friends, the medical superintendent may allow such person to return on trial to his friends, upon receiving a written undertaking by one or more of the friends of such person, that he or they will keep an oversight over such person.　48 V. c. 53, s. 1.

Medical Superintendent may give patient into custody of his friends.

73. In case, within six months from such probational leave, the patient again becomes dangerous or unfit to be at large, it shall be lawful for the medical superintendent by whom the patient was so enlarged, with the consent of the inspector of prisons and public charities, or one of the visitors, to be endorsed on the warrant, by his warrant directed to any person or persons, or to any constable or peace officer, or to all constables or peace officers, to authorize and direct that such patient be apprehended and brought back to the asylum from which he was probationally enlarged, and the warrant so endorsed shall be an authority to, any one acting thereunder to apprehend the person named therein and to bring him back to the said asylum.　48 V. c. 53, s. 2.

Recommittal to asylum.

74. The proprietor or superintendent of a licensed house, with the consent in writing of any two of the visitors of the house, may send or take, under proper control, any patient to any specified place for any definite time for the benefit of his health; but before such consent is given by any visitors, the approval in writing of the person who signed the order for the reception of the patient, or by whom the last payment on account of the patient has been made, shall be produced to such visitors, unless they, on cause shewn, dispense with the same.　R. S. O. 1877, c. 221, s. 80.

On what authority patients may be taken on excursions for benefit of health.

75. In every case in which a patient under any of the powers or provisions of this Act, is removed temporarily from the licensed house into which the order for his reception has been given, or is transferred from such house into any new house, and also in every case in which any patient has escaped from any such house and has been retaken within fourteen days next after such escape, the certificate or certificates relating to and the original order for the reception of the patient shall respectively remain in force, in the same manner as the same

What temporary circumstances not to affect original certificates and order.

would have done if the patient had not been so removed or transferred, or had not so escaped and been retaken. R. S. O. 1877, c. 221, s. 81.

76. Every proprietor or superintendent of a licensed house who receives a proper order in pursuance of this Act, accompanied with the required medical certificates or certificate for the reception or taking care of any person as a lunatic, and the assistants and servants of such proprietor or superintendent, may take charge of, receive and detain such patient until he dies or is removed or discharged by due authority ; and in case of the escape of the patient, may retake him at any time within fourteen days after his escape, and again detain him as aforesaid. R. S. O. 1877, c. 221, s. 82.

Persons licensed authorized to receive and detain patients, etc.

77. The board of visitors of any licensed house, or any two members of the board may, from time to time, by summons under their hands and seals (according to the form in Schedule G, or as near thereto as the case permits), require any person to appear before them to testify, on oath, the truth touching any matters respecting which such visitors are by this Act authorized to inquire (which oath they are hereby empowered to administer) ; and every person who does not appear before such visitors pursuant to such summons, or does not assign some reasonable excuse for not appearing, or appears and refuses to be sworn or examined, shall, on being convicted thereof before one of Her Majesty's Justices for the county, forfeit a sum not exceeding $200 for every such neglect or refusal. R. S. O. 1877, c. 221, s. 83.

Visitors may compel the attendance of witnesses.

Penalty for non-attendance, etc.

78. Any visitors who summon a person to appear and give evidence as aforesaid, may direct the secretary of the board to pay to such person all reasonable expenses of his appearance and attendance, in pursuance of the summons ; the same to be considered as expenses incurred by the board of visitors in the execution of this Act, and to be taken into account and paid accordingly. R. S. O. 1877, c. 221, s. 84.

Expenses of witnesses.

PROSECUTIONS AND PENALTIES.

79. Every complaint or information of or for any offence against this Act, where any pecuniary penalty is imposed may be made before one Justice. R. S. O. 1877, c. 221, s. 85.

One Justice may receive complaints.

80. When any person is charged upon oath, before a Justice, for any offence against this Act, the Justice may summon the person charged to appear at a time and place to be named in the summons, and if he does not appear then upon proof of due service of the summons (either personally or by leaving the same at his last or usual place of abode), any two Justices

Procedure on non-appear-

may either proceed to hear and determine the case, or may issue their warrant for apprehending such person and bringing him before any two Justices., R. S. O. 1877, c. 221, s. 86.

81. Any two Justices upon the appearing of such person pursuant to the summons, or upon such person being apprehended under a warrant, or upon the non-appearance of such person, shall hear the matter of every such complaint or information, and make such determination thereon as the Justices think proper. R. S. O. 1877, c. 221, s. 87.

Adjudication by Justices.

82. Upon conviction of any person, the Justices may, if they think fit, reduce the amount of the penalty by this Act imposed for the offence, to any sum not less than one-fourth of the amount thereof, and shall issue a warrant under their hands and seals for levying such penalty, or reduced penalty, and all costs and charges of the summons, warrant and hearing, and all incidental costs and charges, by distress and sale of the goods and chattels of the person convicted. R. S. O. 1877, c. 221, s. 88.

Penalties ma be reduced, and how levied.

83. Such two Justices may order any person so convicted to be detained and kept in the custody of any constable or other peace officer until return can be conveniently made to such warrant of distress, unless the offender gives security by way of recognizance or otherwise to the satisfaction of the Justices, for his appearance before them on such day as they appoint for the return of the warrant of distress ; such day not being more than seven days from the time of taking such security. R. S. O. 1877, c. 221, s. 89.

Detention of defendant.

84. If, upon the return of the warrant of distress, it appears that no sufficient distress can be had whereupon to levy the penalty or reduced penalty, and the costs and charges, and if the same are not forthwith paid, or in case it appears to the satisfaction of the Justices, either by the confession of the offender or otherwise, that the offender has not sufficient goods and chattels whereupon the penalty or reduced penalty, costs and charges can be levied, the Justices shall, by warrant under their hands and seals, commit the offender to the common gaol or house of correction of the county, as the case may be, for any term not exceeding three months, unless the penalty or reduced penalty, costs and charges, are sooner paid, R. S. O. 1877, c. 221, s. 90.

If no sufficie distress.

85. All penalties and reduced penalties, when recovered shall be paid to the clerk of the peace for the county in which the offence was committed, to be by him applied and accounted for as hereinbefore directed with respect to moneys received for licenses ; and the overplus (if any) arising from such distress and sale, after payment of the penalty or reduced penalty, and all costs and charges as aforesaid, shall be paid upon demand, to the owner of the goods and chattels so distrained. R. S. O. 1877, c. 221, s. 91.

How penalti to be dispos of.

86. The Justices before whom any person is convicted of any offence against this Act for which a pecuniary penalty is imposed, may cause the conviction to be drawn up in the following form, or in any other form to the same effect, as the case may require ; and no conviction under this Act shall be void through want of form :

" Be it remembered, that on the   day of
in the year of our Lord   at   , in the
County of   , A. B. was convicted before us,
of Her Majesty's Justices of the Peace for the said county, for that he
the said   ·   ·   did   and we the
said   adjudge the said
for his said offence to pay the sum of   .

R. S. O. 1877, c. 221, s. 92.

87. Any person who thinks himself aggrieved by the order or determination of any Justices under this Act, may, within four months after such order made or given, appeal to the Justices at General Sessions ; the person appealing having first given at least fourteen clear days' notice in writing of the appeal and the nature and matter thereof, to the person appealed against, and forthwith after such notice entering into a recognizance before some Justice, with two sufficient sureties, conditioned to try such appeal and to abide the order and award of the said Court thereupon.   R. S. O. 1877, c. 221, s. 93.

88. The Justices at General Sessions, upon the proof of such notice and recognizance having been given and entered into, shall, in a summary way, hear and determine the appeal, or if they think proper, may adjourn the hearing thereof until the next General Sessions, and if they see cause, may mitigate any penalty to not less than one-fourth of the amount imposed by this Act, and may order any money to be returned which has been levied in pursuance of the order or determination appealed against, and may also award such further satisfaction to the party injured, or such costs to either of the parties, as they judge reasonable and proper ; and all such determinations of the said Justices at General Sessions shall be final and conclusive upon all parties to all intents and purposes whatsoever. R. S. O. 1877, c. 221, s. 94.

89. If an action is brought against any person for anything done in pursuance of this Act, the same shall be commenced within twelve months next after the release of the party bringing the action, and shall be laid or brought in the county where the cause of action arose, and not elsewhere. R. S. O. 1877, c. 221, s. 95.

90. The defendant in every such action may, at his election, plead specially or may plead not guilty by statute, and give this Act and the special matter in evidence at any trial to be had thereupon, and that the same was done in pursuance and by the authority of this Act; and if the same appears to have been so done, or if it appears that the action has been brought in any other county than where the cause of action arose, or was not commenced within the time hereinbefore limited for bringing the same, then the Judge or jury (as the case may be) shall find a verdict for the defendant; and upon a verdict being so found, or if the plaintiff is non-suited or discontinues his action after the defendant has appeared, or if upon demurrer judgment is given against the plaintiff, then the defendant shall recover double costs, and have such remedy for recovering the same as any defendant has in other cases by law.   R. S. O. 1877, c. 221, s. 96.

91. In every writ, action and other proceeding preferred or brought against any proprietor or superintendent, or against the assistant or servant of any proprietor or superintendent, for taking, confining, detaining or retaking any person as a lunatic, the party complained of may plead in defence the order and certificates or certificate hereinbefore mentioned, and such order and certificates or certificate shall, as respects such party, be a justification for taking, confining, detaining or retaking the lunatic or alleged lunatic.   R. S. O. 1877, c. 221, s. 97. *Defence in case of prosecution.*

92. The secretary of any board of visitors may, on the order of the board, prosecute any person for any offence against the provisions of this Act committed within the jurisdiction of such board, and may sue for and recover any penalty to which any person within the jurisdiction of the board is made liable by this Act.   R. S. O. 1877, c. 221, s. 98. *When Secretary of Board of Visitors to prosecute.*

93. All penalties sued for and recovered by such secretary shall be paid to him, and shall be by him applied and accounted for the same as hereinbefore enacted with respect to moneys received for licenses.   R. S. O. 1877, c. 221, s. 99. *How penalties recovered by him to be disposed of.*

94. No one shall prosecute any person for any offence against the provisions of this Act, or sue for any penalty to which any person is made liable by this Act, except by order of the board of visitors having jurisdiction in the place where the cause of prosecution has arisen or the penalty has been incurred, or with the consent of Her Majesty's Attorney-General for Ontario.   R. S. O. 1877, c. 221, s. 100. *Order of Visitors necessary to authorize suits for penalties or prosecutions for offences. Except, etc.*

95. In case any person is proceeded against for omitting to transmit or send any copy, list, notice, statement or other document hereinbefore required to be transmitted by such person, and such person proves by the testimony of one person upon oath, that the copy, list, notice, statement or other document in respect of which the proceeding has been taken, was put into the proper post-office in due time or (in case of documents required to be transmitted to a clerk of the peace), left at the *What to be sufficient proof of compliance with certain regulations in case of prosecution.*

office of such clerk of the peace, and was properly addressed, such proof shall be a bar to all further proceedings in respect of such omission.   R. S. O. 1877, c. 221, s. 101.

Costs under orders, etc., of Visitors provided for.

96. The costs, charges and expenses incurred by or under the order of any board of visitors, shall be paid by the clerk of the peace for the county, and be included by him in the account of receipts and payments hereinbefore directed to be kept by him.   R. S. O. 1877, c. 221, s. 102.

ADMISSION OF INEBRIATES.

Inebriates may be admitted.

97. If the license so directs, admission to a private asylum shall be awarded to inebriates who are *bona fide* residents of the Province, upon the voluntary application in writing of the person desiring to be admitted : provided it is certified to the satisfaction of the superintendant that the person so applying is an inebriate, and further, that he is a reasonably hopeful subject for treatment with a view to the cure of his inebriety. 36 V. c. 33, s. 13.

Time of detention in hospital.

Terms of admission.

98. Such inebriate may be detained in the asylum for a period of one year, and no longer ; and it shall be a condition of his admission to the asylum that he shall remain therein such length of time, not exceeding one year, as, in the opinion of the superintendent, is required to effect a permanent cure of his inebriety ; and before admission is awarded he shall sign a pledge agreeing and consenting to such specified condition, and to faithfully conform himself to all the rules and regulations of the asylum while an inmate of the same.   36 V. c. 33, s. 14.

Authority of superintendent to discharge patients.

99. The superintendent, with the consent and authority of the inspector, shall have full authority to discharge at any time from the asylum any person who has been awarded admission to it by his own voluntary application for the following causes, viz :—

1. That such person is cured ;

2. That such person is incurable and incapable of being benefited by the treatment and discipline of the said asylum ;

3. That such person, who, being able to pay for maintenance and support therein, or that any other person who has become security for maintenance and support, has failed to pay therefor ;

4. Such person who has been guilty of vicious conduct prejudicial to the good order and discipline of the asylum.   36 V. c. 33, s. 15.

Commitment of habitual drunkards.

100. On petition under oath, presented to the Judge of the County Court of the county in which the alleged habitual drunkard resides, by any relations, whether by blood or affinity, or, in default of such relations, by any friend of the alleged habitual drunkard, setting forth that the alleged habitual drunkard, being a *bona fide* resident of the Province, is so given over to drunkenness as to render him unable to control himself, and is incapable of managing his affairs, or that by reason of such drunkenness he either squanders or mismanages his property, or places his family in danger or distress, or transacts his business prejudicially to the interest of his family or his creditors, or that he uses intoxicating liquors to such an extent as to render him dangerous to himself or others, or incurs the danger of ruining his health and shortening his life thereby, and praying that a hearing and examination of the matters and allegations set forth in the said petition may be had, the Judge shall cause and direct that a copy of the petition shall forthwith be served upon the alleged habitual drunkard, and with such copy there shall be served an appointment signed by the Judge, appointing a time and place for the hearing of the matters and allegations contained in the petition, and such service shall be at least eight clear days before the time fixed for the hearing.   36 V. c. 33, s. 18.

101. The Judge shall attend at the time and place named in the appointment, and then and there proceed to enquire into the matters and allegations set forth in the petition: provided always that he may in his discretion adjourn the said enquiry from time to time.   36 V. c. 33, s. 19. *Hearing the petition.*

102. The Judge shall have power to summon such relations, or such other persons as are acquainted with the alleged habitual drunkard, before him, by order under his hand, and examine such persons under oath touching the truth or falsity of the mattters and allegations set forth in the petition respecting the alleged habitual drunkard; and any person who shall neglect or refuse to appear before the Judge at the time and place named in the order, having been duly served with a copy thereof, or shall refuse to give evidence before the Judge, may be taken into custody by virtue of a warrant under the hand of the Judge, and imprisoned in the common gaol of the county in which the enquiry is held, as for contempt of Court, for a period not exceeding fourteen days.   36 V. c. 33, s. 20. *Summoning of witnesses.*

103. In proceeding to the examination of the matters and charges contained in the petition, it shall not be necessary that the person charged with such habitual drunkenness be interrogated before the Judge, nevertheless the Judge shall have power so to do, but it shall be sufficient that he be satisfied with the evidence given before him by the relations or such other persons as are acquainted with the alleged habitual drunkard.   36 V. c. 33, s. 21. *Examination of the habitual drunkard discretionary.*

104. The alleged habitual drunkard may produce before the Judge witnesses to contradict the matters and allegations of the petition, and the witnesses in support of the same, and each party may retain counsel to conduct the proceedings before the Judge and to examine the witnesses.   36 V. c. 33, s. 22. *Habitual drunkard may produce and examine witnesses.*

If judge find party petitioned against to be an habitual drunkard, to report to Provincial Secretary.

105. If the Judge, upon such examination, finds the person petitioned against to be an habitual drunkard, and so given over to drunkenness as to render him unable to control himself and incapable of managing his affairs; or for the like reasons squanders or mismanages his property; or places his family in danger or distress; or transacts his business prejudicially to the interest of his family or his creditors; or that he uses intoxicating liquors to such an extent as to render him dangerous to himself or others; or incurs the danger of ruining his health or shortening his life, the Judge shall forthwith report the fact to the Provincial Secretary, and with the report shall transmit the evidence taken.   36 V. c. 33, s. 23.

Provincial Secretary may direct removal to hospital.

106. Upon the receipt of the report and evidence, the Provincial Secretary may, by order directed to the sheriff of the county where the habitual drunkard resides, direct the said sheriff to forthwith remove the habitual drunkard to the asylum, to be placed under treatment and detained therein for a period not exceeding one year; nevertheless, the Provincial Secretary may, upon the report of the superintendent, at any time, order the discharge of the person so committed for any of the causes specified in sub-sections 1, 2 and 4 of section 99 of this Act.   36 V. c. 33, s. 24.

Provision in case any party detained escape.

107. In case an inmate of the asylum, whether admitted or committed as hereinbefore provided, shall escape therefrom, it shall be lawful for any of the officers or servants of the asylum, or for any other person or persons, at the request of the superintendent within forty-eight hours after such escape, or within one month thereafter, when a warrant has been issued by the superintendent in that behalf, to retake such escaped person, and to return him to the asylum where he shall remain under the authority by virtue of which he was detained prior to such escape.   36 V. c. 33, s. 25.

Application of provisions as to voluntary admission.

108. The provisions respecting the voluntary admission of inebriates shall extend to any person, whether male or female, who is a habitual consumer of stimulating or narcotic drugs to such excess as to cause mental or physical derangement or disease.   46 V. c. 28, s. 11.

Rev. Stat. c. 250, ss. 10, 11, to apply to Private Asylums. Application of Act.

109. Sections 10 and 11 of *The Prison and Asylum Inspection Act* shall hereafter apply to private as well as to public asylums for the insane.   48 V. c. 53, s. 8.

Rev. Stat. c. 245.

110. Nothing in this Act contained shall extend to the asylum for the insane at Toronto, or to the asylums referred to in sections 2 and 3 of *The Act respecting Lunatic Asylums and the Custody of Insane Persons.*   R. S. O. 1877, c. 221, s. 103.

SCHEDULE A.

(Section 29.)

ORDER FOR THE RECEPTION OF A PATIENT.

I, the undersigned, hereby request you to receive *A. B.*, a lunatic (*or*, an insane person, *or*, an idiot, *or*, a person of unsound mind) as a patient into your house.

(Signed*)*   *Name.*

Occupation (if any), place of abode, degree of relationship, (if any), or other circumstances of connection with the patient.

1. Name of Patient, with Christian name at length.
2. Sex and age.
3. Married, single, or widowed.
4. Condition of life and previous occupation (if any).
5. Previous place of abode.
6. Religious persuasion, so far as known.
7. Duration of existing attack.
8. Whether first attack.
9. Age (if known) on first attack.
10. Whether subject to epilepsy.
11. Whether suicidal or dangerous to others.
12. Previous place of confinement (if any).
13. Whether found lunatic by Commission, and date of Commission.
14. Special circumstances (if any) preventing the patient being examined, before admission, separately by two physicians.
15. Special circumstances (if any) preventing the insertion of any of the above particulars.

Dated this   day of   , 18
                    (Signed,)   *Name.*

To
          Proprietor (*or*, Superintendent) of
(describing house by situation and name, if any.)

R. S. O. 1877, c. 221, Sched B.

SCHEDULE B.

(Section 29.)

FORM OF MEDICAL CERTIFICATE.

I,   being a physician duly authorized to practise as such, hereby certify that I have this day, separately from any other medical practitioner, visited and personally examined *A. B.*, the person named in the accompanying statement and order, and that the said *A. B.* is a lunatic, (*or* an insane person, *or* an idiot, *or* a person of unsound mind,) and a proper person to be confined, and that I have formed this opinion from the following fact (*or* facts,) viz. :

               (Signed,)   *Name.*
                              Place of abode.

Dated this   day of   , 18
               R. S. O. 1877, c. 221, Sched. C.

SCHEDULE C.

(Section 59.)

REGISTRY OF ADMISSIONS – REGISTER OF PATIENTS.

Date of last previous Admission (if any).	No. in order of Admission.	Date of Admission.	Christian and Surname at length.	Sex.		Age.	Condition as to Marriage.			Condition of life and previous occupation (if any).	Previous place of abode.	By whose authority sent.	Dates of Medical Certificates, and by whom signed.	Bodily condition.	Name of Disorder (if any).	Form of mental Disorder.	Supposed cause of Insanity.	Epileptics.	Congenital Idiots.	Duration of existing attacks.			Number of previous attacks.	Age on first attack.	Date of Discharge, or Death or Removal.	Discharged.				Removed.	Died.	Observations.
				M.	F.		Married.	Single.	Widowed.											Years.	Months.	Weeks.				Recovered.	Relieved.	Not Improved.				

R. S. O. 1877, c. 221, Sched. D.

SCHEDULE D.

(Section 41.)

NOTICE OF ADMISSION.

I hereby give you notice, that *A. B.* was received into this house as a patient, on the   day of   , and I hereby transmit a copy of the Order and Medical Certificates (*or* Certificate) on which he was received.

Subjoined is a statement with respect to the mental and bodily condition of the above named patient.

(Signed),   *Name.*

Superintendent (*or* Proprietor) of

Dated this   day of   , 18 .

———

STATEMENT.

I have this day seen and personally examined *A. B.*, the patient named in the above notice, and hereby certify that, with respect to mental state, he (*or* she),   , and that, with respect to bodily health and condition, he (*or* she)

(Signed),   *Name.*

Medical Proprietor (*or* Superintendent, or Attendant of

Dated this   day of   , 18 .

R. S. O. 1877, c. 221, Sched. E.

SCHEDULE E

(Section 45.)

REGISTER OF DISCHARGES AND DEATHS.

Date of Death or Discharge.	Date of last Admission.	No. in Register of Patients.	Name and Surname at length.	Sex.		Discharged.								Died.		Removed.		Assigned cause of Death.	Age at Death.		Observations.
				M.	F.	Recovered.		Relieved.		Not Improved.									M.	F.	
						M.	F.	M.	F.	M.	F.			M.	F.	M.	F.				

R. S. O. 1877, c. 221. Sched. F.

SCHEDULE F.

(Section 43.)

FORM OF NOTICE OF DISCHARGE OR DEATH.

I hereby give you notice that   a patient received
into this house on the   day of   was discharged
therefrom, recovered (*or* relieved, *or* not improved) *or* was removed
therefrom) by the authority of   (*or* died therein) on the
day of

        (Signed)   *Name.*

                                   Superintendent (*or* Proprietor)
                                   of house, at

Dated this   day of   , 18 .

In case of death, add—and I further certify that *A. B.* was present
at the death of the said   , and that the apparent cause
of the death of the said   (ascertained by *post
mortem* examination, *if so*) was

                   R. S. O. 1877, c. 221, Sched. G.

SCHEDULE G.

(Section 77.)

FORM OF SUMMONS.

We, whose names are hereunto set and seals affixed, being two of
the visitors appointed under or by virtue of chapter 246 of The Revised
Statutes of Ontario, respecting Private Lunatic Asylums, do hereby
summon and require you personally to appear before us at
in   on
the   day of   , at the hour of
in the   noon of the same day, and then and there to be
examined, and to testify the truth touching certain matters relating to the
execution of the said Act.

Given under our hands and seals, this   day of
in the year of our Lord, 18 .

                   R. S. O. 1877, c. 221, Sched. H.

SCHEDULE H.

(Section 48, sub-section 4.)

FORM OF MEDICAL JOURNAL, AND WEEKLY REPORT.

Date of Report.	Number of Patients.		Names of Patients under restraint (and by what means), or in seclusion.		Names of Patients under Medical Treatment.		Report on state of health of Patients, and condition of House.	Deaths, injuries, and violences to Patients.
	Males.	Females.	Males.	Females.	Males.	Females.		

CHAPTER 54.

An Act respecting Lunatics.

HER MAJESTY, by and with the advice and consent of the Legislative Assembly of the Province of Ontario, enacts as follows:—

1. The word "lunatic" in this Act shall include an idiot or other person of unsound mind. R. S. O. 1877, c. 40, s. 57. *Interpretation "lunatic."*

2. In the case of lunatics and their property and estates the jurisdiction of the High Court shall include that which in England is conferred upon the Lord Chancellor by a Commission from the Crown, under the Sign Manual. R. S. O. 1877, c. 40, s. 58. *Jurisdiction over lunatics and their estates.*

INQUISITION BY COMMISSION.

3.—(1) Where a Commission has been issued and an inquisition thereupon returned into Court, by which a person is found lunatic, in case any one entitled to traverse the inquisition desires to do so, he may, within three months from the day of the return and filing of the inquisition, present a petition for that purpose to the Court, and the Court shall hear and determine the petition subject to the following provisions: *Traverse of inquisition of lunacy.*

(2) In every order giving effect to the petition, the Court shall limit a time not exceeding six months from the date of the order, within which the person desiring to traverse, and all other proper parties, shall proceed to the trial of the traverse; but the Court may under the special circumstances of any case, verified by affidavit, and upon a petition being presented for that purpose, allow the traverse to be had or tried after the time limited; and in such special case the Court may make such orders as seem just. *Time to be limited.*

(3) The trial may be ordered to take place in any Court of Record in Ontario, with the aid of a jury, according to the circumstances of the case and the situation of the parties. R. S. O. 1877, c. 40, s. 59 (1-3). *May be tried in any Court of Record.*

What security the traverser shall give. (4) The Court may order that the person to traverse, if he is not the party who has been found lunatic, shall, within one month after the date of the order, file, with such officer as the Court may appoint, a bond, with one or more sureties, in favour of the Accountant, or other officer appointed by the Court, and conditioned for all proper parties proceeding to the trial of the traverse within the time limited. The bond before the filing thereof shall be approved of and certified to be sufficient by the Judge of the County Court of the County in which the parties reside, or by one of the Masters of the Supreme Court of Judicature. R. S. O. 1877, c. 40, s. 59 (4); 50 V. c. 8, Sched.

When the traverser barred. (5) Every person who does not present his petition, or who neglects to give the security, or who does not proceed to the trial of the traverse within the times respectively limited therefor, and the heirs, executors and administrators of every such person, and all others claiming through him, shall be absolutely barred of the right of traverse. R. S. O. 1877, c. 40, s. 59 (5).

New trials may be granted. **4.** The Court if dissatisfied with the verdict returned upon a traverse, may order a new trial, or new trials, as in other cases. R. S. O. 1877, c. 40, s. 60.

INQUIRY WITHOUT COMMISSION.

Inquiry as to lunacy. **5.** Instead of issuing a Commission of Lunacy the High Court may, with or without the aid of a jury (which the Court or a Judge thereof may cause to be empanelled as in other cases) hear evidence and inquire into and determine upon the alleged lunacy, or may send the inquiry to any Court of **Alleged lunatic may require a jury.** Record; but the alleged lunatic shall have a right in such cases to demand that the inquiry be submitted to a jury. R. S. O. 1877, c. 40, s. 61.

No traverse allowed but new trial may be granted by Court. **6.** Where such inquiry is had, no traverse shall be allowed, but the Court, if dissatisfied with the finding of a jury, may, at the instance of any party who would be entitled to traverse an inquisition under commission of lunacy, direct a new trial or new trials from time to time upon application therefor made to the Court within three months from the time the verdict is rendered, or such further time as the Court, under special circumstances, permits, and subject to such directions and upon such conditions as to the Court seem proper, and the Court may order such new trial to be had before the same Court in which the verdict was rendered or before any other Court. R. S. O. 1877, c. 40, s. 62.

Alleged lunatic may be examined openly or privately as Judge directs. **7.** On every such inquiry the alleged lunatic, if he is within the jurisdiction of the Court, shall be produced, and shall be examined at such times and in such manner either in open Court or privately before the jury retire to consult about their verdict as the presiding Judge may direct, unless the Court ordering the inquiry has, beforehand, by order, dispensed with the examination. R. S. O. 1877, c. 40, s. 63.

8. The High Court or a Judge thereof may, on sufficient evidence, declare a person a lunatic without the delay or expense of issuing a commission to inquire into the alleged lunacy, except in cases of reasonable doubt; and any person who might traverse an inquisition to the same effect may move against the order containing the declaration, or may appeal therefrom, as the case requires; and the right so to move or appeal shall, as to time, be subject to the same rules as the right to traverse. R. S. O. 1877, c. 40, s. 65.

Declaration of lunacy without commission.

Proceedings in lieu of traverse when no commission issued.

SCOPE OF INQUIRY.

9. Every inquiry, under a Commission of Lunacy, or before any Court of Record, shall be confined to the question, whether or not the person who is the subject of inquiry is, at the time of the inquiry, of unsound mind and incapable of managing himself or his affairs, and the verdict rendered by a jury shall, in every case, be returned to the Court, certified by the Judge before whom the inquiry has been had, and shall be final as to the question on the inquiry, unless the same is set aside. R. S. O. 1877, c. 40, s. 64.

Question to be tried.

PROTECTION OF PROPERTY.

10. In order to afford due protection to the property of lunatics, the following provisions shall in every case be observed:

Property of Lunatics.

1. The committee of the estate shall, within six months after being appointed, file in the office of the Master to whom the matter is referred, or of such officer as may be appointed for that purpose, a true inventory of the whole real and personal estate of the lunatic, stating the income and profits thereof, and setting forth the debts, credits and effects of the lunatic, so far as the same have come to the knowledge of the committee;

The committee to file an inventory of present property.

2. If any property belonging to the estate is discovered after the filing of an inventory, the committee shall file a true account of the same from time to time, as the same is discovered;

Also, of after discovered property.

3. Every inventory shall be verified by the oath of the committee; and

To be verified on oath.

4. The committee of the estate shall give two or more responsible persons as sureties, in double the amount of the personal estate, and of the annual rents and profits of the real estate, for duly accounting for the same once in every year, or oftener if required by the Court, and for filing the inventory aforesaid; and the security shall be taken by bond in the name

Security to be given by the committee.

of the Accountant or other officer appointed by the Court for that purpose, and the same shall be filed in the office of the Accountant or other officer so appointed.   R. S. O. 1877, c. 40, s. 66.

When estate not sufficient to pay debts.

11. Where the personal estate of a lunatic is not sufficient for the discharge of his debts, the following steps may be taken :

Committee to apply for leave to mortgage or sell, &c.

1. The committee of his estate shall petition for authority to mortgage, lease or sell so much of the real estate as may be necessary for the payment of the debts ;

What the petition is to contain.

2. The petition shall set forth the particulars and amount of the estate, real and personal, of the lunatic, the application made of any personal estate, and an account of the debts and demands against the estate ;

Truth of petition to be inquired into.

3. The Court shall, by one of the Masters of the Supreme Court of Judicature, or otherwise, inquire into the truth of the representations made in the petition, and hear all parties interested in the real estate ;

If personal estate insufficient, real estate may be disposed of.

4. If it appears to the Court that the personal estate is not sufficient for the payment of debts, and that the same has been applied to that purpose as far as the circumstances of the case render proper, the Court may order the real estate or a sufficient portion of it to be mortgaged, leased or sold either by the committee or otherwise ;

Debts to be paid out of the proceeds.

5. The Court shall direct the committee to discharge the debts out of the money so raised, and the Court may order the committee to execute conveyances of the estate, and to give security for the due application of the money, and to do such other acts as may be necessary in such manner as the Court may direct ; and

Ratably and without preference.

6. In the application of moneys so raised, the debts shall be paid in equal proportion without giving preference to those secured by sealed instruments.   R. S. O. 1877, c. 40, s. 67.

If effects not sufficient to maintain the lunatic, his real estate may be applied.

12. Where the personal estate, and the rents, profits and income of the real estate of the lunatic are insufficient for his maintenance or that of his family, or for the education of his children, an application may be made by the committee, or by a member of the family of the lunatic, that the committee be authorized or directed to mortgage or sell the whole or part of the real estate as may be necessary ; upon which the like reference and proceedings shall be had, and a like order made, as for the payment of debts.   R. S. O. 1877, c. 40, s. 68.

Surplus sums how to be applied or disposed of.

13. In case of a mortgage, lease or sale being made, the lunatic and his heirs, next of kin, devisees, legatees, executors, administrators and assigns shall have the like interest in the surplus which remains of the money raised as he or they would have in the estate, if no mortgage, lease or sale had been made; and the money shall be of the same nature and character as the estate mortgaged, leased or sold; and the Court may make such orders as are necessary for the due application of the surplus. R. S. O. 1877, c. 40, s. 69.

14. Where a lunatic is seised or possessed of real estate, by way of mortgage, or as a trustee for others in any manner, the committee may apply to the Court for authority to convey such real estate to the person entitled thereto, in such manner as the Court may direct; and thereupon the like proceedings shall be had as in the case of an application to sell the real estate; and the Court, upon hearing all the parties interested, may order a conveyance to be made; and on the application of any person entitled to a conveyance, the committee may be compelled by the Court, after hearing all parties interested, to execute the conveyance. R. S. O. 1877, c. 40, s. 70. *Where a lunatic is trustee or mortgagee his committee may act, and how far.*

15. Every conveyance, mortgage, lease and assurance made by the committee under direction of the Court, pursuant to any of the provisions of this Act, shall be as valid as if executed by the lunatic when of sound mind. R. S. O. 1877, c. 40, s. 71. *Instruments executed by the committee to be valid.*

16. The Court may compel the specific performance of any contract made by a lunatic while capable of contracting, and may direct the committee to execute all necessary conveyances for the purpose; and the purchase money, or so much thereof as remains unpaid, shall be paid to the committee or otherwise as the Court directs. R. S. O. 1877, c. 40, s. 72. *Specific performance of contracts made by lunatic.*

APPEAL.

17. An order made by a Judge in a matter of lunacy shall be subject to appeal to a Divisional Court and to the Court of Appeal within the same times and under the same conditions as in other cases in the High Court. R. S. O. 1877, c. 40, s. 73. *Appeal.*

COSTS.

18. The Court may order the costs, charges and expenses of and incidental to a petition for a commission of lunacy or to any inquiry, inquisition, issue, traverse, order, direction, conveyance or other proceeding in lunacy, to be paid by the party or parties presenting the petition or prosecuting the same or such inquiry or other proceeding in lunacy, or by the party or parties opposing the same, or out of the estate of the lunatic, or alleged lunatic, or partly in one way and partly in another. R. S. O. 1877, c. 40, s. 74. *By whom the Court may order costs to be paid.*

EXTRACTS FROM VARIOUS ACTS RELATING TO LUNATICS, IDIOTS AND PERSONS OF UNSOUND MIND.

CHAPTER 44, SECTION 21, SUB-SEC. 2.

Equitable jurisdiction.

21. The High Court shall also, subject as in this Act mentioned, have the like jurisdiction and powers as by the laws of England were on the 4th day of March, 1837, possessed by the Court of Chancery in England, in respect of the matters hereinafter enumerated, that is to say :

(2) In all matters relating to trusts, executors and administrators, co-partnership and account, mortgages, awards, dower, infants, idiots, lunatics and their estates.

SECTION 32, SUB-SEC. 1, 3, 4, 5.

Jurisdiction of Court of Chancery in respect to leases, settled estates, estates of infants, and special cases.

32.—(1) The High Court shall have the same jurisdiction as the Court of Chancery in England had on the 18th day of March, 1865, in regard to leases and sales of settled estates, and in regard to enabling infants, with the approbation of the Court, to make binding settlements of their real and personal estate on marriage ; and in regard to questions submitted for the opinion of the Court in the form of special cases on the part of such persons, as may by themselves, their committees or guardians, or otherwise, concur therein. R. S. O. 1877, c. 40, s. 85 ; 44 V. c. 5, s. 9.

(3) Infants and persons of unsound mind (not so found), required to be served with notice of any application to the High Court, may be served by delivering to the official guardian *ad litem* a copy of the petition or other proceeding required to be served ; and from the time of such service, the said official guardian shall be the guardian *ad litem* of the infant or person of unsound mind, unless and until the Court or Judge, otherwise orders ; and the said official guardian, or any other guardian appointed by the Court for the infant or person of unsound mind, shall take all such proceedings as he may think necessary for the protection of the interests of the infant or person of unsound mind in the proceeding in which he is so appointed guardian.

(4) In case there be more than one infant or person of unsound mind (not so found) for whom service is made on the official guardian *ad litem*, one copy only of the petition or other proceeding, need be so served, but the name of each person on whose behalf the official guardian is served, is to be stated on the copy served.

(5) Money realized from the sale or leasing of any settled estate or any interest therein, shall be paid, applied or invested as the Court or a Judge shall direct. 49 V. c. 16, s. 8.

SECTION 34, SUB-SEC. 3.

34. The High Court shall also have jurisdiction— Jurisdiction.

3. In respect of lunatics and infants and their property and Lunatics and estates, as provided by *The Act respecting Lunatics* and *The Infants.* *Act respecting Infants.* R. S. O. 1877, c. 40, ss. 58, 75.

CHAPTER 61, SECTION 11.

11. In an action or proceeding by or against a person found In actions by or by inquisition to be of unsound mind, or being an inmate of a against luna-lunatic asylum, an opposite or interested party shall not obtain dence of oppo-a verdict, judgment or decision therein, on his own evidence, site party to be unless such evidence is corroborated by some other material corroborated. evidence. R. S. O. 1877, c. 62, s. 11.

CHAPTER 111, SECTION 40.

40. The time during which any person otherwise capable of Time during resisting any claim to any of the matters mentioned in sec-which a party tions 34 to 39 inclusive of this Act, is an infant, idiot, *non* not to be com-*compos mentis*, or tenant for life, or during which any action puted against has been pending and has been diligently prosecuted until Imp. Act 2-3 abated by the death of any party or parties thereto, shall be W. iv, c. 71, excluded in the computation of the period in said sections s. 7. mentioned, except only in cases where the right or claim is thereby declared to be absolute and indefeasible. R. S. O. 1877, c. 108, s. 40.

CHAPTER 114, SECTION 45.

45. Where the witnesses to any instrument are dead or are Witnesses in-out of this Province, or have become insane, idiotic, imbecile, sane, absent, or of unsound mind or understanding, and whether so found etc. by inquisition or not, or where any instrument, not by law requiring an attesting or subscribing witness thereto, has been executed without any attesting or subscribing witness thereto, or in case it is proved to the satisfaction of the Judge in this section mentioned that the place of abode or residence of such first above mentioned witnesses is unknown, any person who is or claims to be interested in the registration of the instrument, may make proof before the Judge of any County Court in Ontario, of the execution of the instrument, and upon a certificate (according to the form of Schedule F to this Act), endorsed on the instrument and signed by the Judge, that the Judge is satisfied by the proof adduced of the due execution of the instrument, the Registrar shall register the instrument and certificate. R. S. O. 1877, c, 111, s. 47.

CHAPTER 132, SECTION 21, SUB-SEC. 1.

In what cases a married woman may obtain an order of protection for the earnings of her minor children.

21.—(1) Any married woman having a decree for alimony against her husband, or any married woman who lives apart from her husband, having been obliged to leave him from cruelty or other cause which by law justifies her leaving him and renders him liable for her support, or any married woman whose husband is a lunatic with or without lucid intervals, or any married woman whose husband is undergoing sentence of imprisonment in the Provincial Penitentiary or in any gaol for a criminal offence, or any married woman whose husband from habitual drunkenness, profligacy, or other cause, neglects or refuses to provide for her support and that of his family, or any married woman whose husband has never been in this Province, or any married woman who is deserted or abandoned by her husband, may obtain an order of protection, entitling her, notwithstanding her coverture, to have and to enjoy all the earnings of her minor children, and any acquisitions therefrom, free from the debts and obligations of her husband and from his control or dispositions, and without his consent, in as full and ample a manner as if she continued sole and unmarried.

Purport and effect of such order.

CHAPTER 133—SECTIONS 10, 11, 12 AND 13.

Dower on conveyance where wife is a lunatic confined in an asylum.

10.—(1) Where an owner of land whose wife is a lunatic, or of unsound mind, and confined as such in a Lunatic Asylum, is desirous of selling or mortgaging the land free from dower, he may apply in that behalf to the Judge of the County Court of the County in which he resides or to a Judge of the High Court, and if the Judge approves, he may, by an order to be made by him in a summary way, upon such evidence as to the Judge seems meet, and either *ex parte* or upon such notice as he may deem requisite, dispense with the concurrence of the wife for the purpose of barring her dower, and also he shall ascertain and state in the order the value of such dower, and order such amount to remain a charge upon the property, or to be secured otherwise for the wife's benefit or to be paid and applied for her benefit as he deems best, and thereupon a conveyance or mortgage by the husband, expressed to be free from his wife's dower, shall, subject to the terms and conditions mentioned in the order, be sufficient to bar her right thereto, as if she were of sound mind, and had duly executed a deed jointly with her husband for that purpose.

Dower to be ascertained and to be charge on land or secured for wife's benefit.

Fee.

(2) On every such application the Judge shall be entitled to his own use to a fee of $5, and no other fee or charge of

any kind shall be payable in respect thereof, either to the Clerk, or otherwise. R. S. O. 1877, c. 126, s. 8 (1, 2) ; 44 V. c 14, s. 3.

(3) This section shall apply to any case in which an agreement for sale has been made and a conveyance has been executed by the husband, and any part of the purchase money has been retained by the purchaser on account of dower, and to any case in which an indemnity has been given against the dower of the wife. R. S. O. 1877, c. 126, s. 9 *part;* 43 V. c. 14, s. 4.

Similar appli cation to as- certain dowe1 in certain other cases.

11. In case the Gaol Surgeon of any County or District in which a married woman resides, and another medical practitioner to be named by the Judge, shall each certify (Form A) that he has personally examined such married woman and that he is of opinion that she is insane, and the Judge of the County Court of the County in which such married woman resides, or a Judge of the High Court, also certifies (Form B) that he has personally examined such married woman, and that from such examination and from the evidence adduced before him, if such Judge thinks it expedient to hear evidence, he is of opinion that such married woman is insane, the said Judge may make the like order as by the preceding section of this Act is authorized in the case of a married woman of unsound mind who is confined in an Asylum for the Insane. The examination and certificates required by this section must all be made and granted within a period of one month, or such certificates shall not be acted upon by the said Judge, and the application shall not be entertained unless it is made within one month of the day upon which the last of such examinations took place. 44 V. c. 14, s. 2.

Judge's orde1 as to dower where wife i1 lunatic but not confined in an asylum

12. In case a Judge makes an order under any of the preceding three sections of this Act with reference to any parcel of land, he may afterwards make orders in respect of other sales or mortgages, either on the like evidence as is required for the first application or on any other evidence which may satisfy him of the continued insanity of the married woman. 44 V. c. 14, s. 4.

Subsequent orders by Judge as to other sales o mortgages.

13. Sections 9. 10, 11 and 12 of this Act shall apply to any case where any person owns or has the right to sell or mortgage (whether as trustee or otherwise) land which is subject to dower, whether such dower is inchoate or complete and whether the person applying is or is not the husband of the doweress. 46 V. c. 12, s. 1.

Application ss. 9, 10, 11 a1 12.

FORM A.

(Section 11.)

CERTIFICATE OF MEDICAL PRACTITIONER.

I, the undersigned   *(here set forth the qualification or degree of the person certifying: for example, " Licentiate of the Medical Board," " M. D. of the University of Toronto," etc.)*   a legally qualified Medical Practitioner, residing and practising at   in the County of   do hereby certify that I, on the   day of   A. D. 18   , at in the County of   separately from any other Medical Practitioner, personally examined *A. B.*, of the Township of in the County of   wife of *C. D.*, of the Township of in the County of   and I further certify that the said   is insane, and that I have formed this opinion upon the following grounds, namely : *(here state the facts upon which the Certificate is based).*

Signed this   day of A. D. 18   , at   in the County of

44 V. c. 14, *Form* A.

FORM B.

(Section 11.)

CERTIFICATE OF JUDGE.

Province of Ontario, }   I, the undersigned *E. F.*, County of   }

Judge of the County Court of the County of do hereby certify, that I on the   day of A. D. 18   , personally examined *A. B.*, of the   of in the County of   wife of *C. D.*, of the   of   in the County of   and I do hereby further certify that from such personal examination (and from the evidence of *G. H.* and *J. K.* adduced before me, *if evidence has been taken by the judge*) I am of the opinion that the said   is insane.

Signed this   day of   A. D. 18   , at in the County of

44 V. c. 14, *Form* B.

CHAPTER 149, SECTION 1.

Certain bodies may be delivered for study of anatomy.

1. In all localities coming under the provisions of this Act the body of any person found dead, publicly exposed, or sent to a public morgue, or who immediately before death had been supported in and by any public institution, shall be delivered to persons qualified as hereinafter mentioned, unless such body be within forty-eight hours after death claimed by relations or *bona fide* friends, or being a lunatic, dies in any Provincial Asylum for the insane ; provided, nevertheless, that the authorities in whose care any body may be, shall not deliver the same to any person other than a known relative unless such person shall pay to the said authorities the sum of $5 to defray

the funeral expenses of the body so claimed, the said sum to Proviso.
be paid over to the undertaker by the said authorities when
satisfied that the body has been properly interred.   48 V.
c. 31, s. 2

CHAPTER 157, SECTIONS 74 AND 45.

74.—(1) Where a company incorporated under any special Appointment of companies
Act or under this Act is authorized to execute the office of to act as trustee, etc.
executor, administrator, trustee, receiver, assignee, guardian of
a minor, or committee of a lunatic, then in case the Lieutenant-
Governor in Council shall approve of such company being
accepted by the High Court as a Trusts Company for the purposes of such Court, the said Court, or any Judge thereof, and
every other Court or Judge having authority to appoint such
an officer, may, with the consent of the company, appoint such
company to exercise any of the said offices in respect of any
estate, or person, under the authority of such Court or Judge,
or may grant to such company probate of any will in which
such company is named an executor; but no company which
has issued, or has authority to issue, debentures shall be
approved as aforesaid.

(2) Notwithstanding any rule of practice. or any provision
of any Act requiring security, it shall not be necessary for the
said company to give any security for the due performance of
its duty as such executor, administrator, trustee, receiver,
assignee, guardian or committee, unless otherwise ordered.

(3) The Lieutenant-Governor in Council may revoke the
approval given under this section, and no Court, or Judge,
after notice of such revocation, shall appoint any such company
to be an administrator, trustee, receiver, assignee, guardian or
committee, unless such company gives the like security for
the due performance of its duty as would be required from a
private person.   45 V. c. 17, s. 2 (1-3).

75. The liability of the company to persons interested in Liability of
an estate held by the said company as executor, administra- company acting as trustee.
tor, trustee, receiver, assignee, guardian or committee as afore-
said, shall be the same as if the estate had been held by any
private person in such capacities respectively, and its powers
shall be the same.   45 V. c. 17, s. 2 (4).

CHAPTER 184, SECTION 520.

520. The County Council of each County shall, from time County coun-
to time, make provision for the whole or partial support either cil to make provision for
in the County gaol or some other place within the County, of the destitute
such insane destitute persons as cannot properly be admitted insane.
to the provincial asylums, and shall determine the sum to be
paid for such support, and also the parties to whom such sums
shall be paid by the County Treasurer.   46 V. c. 18, s. 520.

CHAPTER 247.

An Act respecting Institutions for the Education and Instruction of the Deaf and Dumb and the Blind.

HER MAJESTY, by and with the advice and consent of the Legislative Assembly of the Province of Ontario, enacts as follows :—

The Institution at Belleville to be for the public use of the Province, etc.

Name.

1. The institution founded and established at Belleville, for the education and instruction of the deaf and dumb, with all the lands, buildings, real estate and appurtenances thereunto attached, and whatever lands or real estate may hereafter be purchased or acquired for the same, and whatever buildings may hereafter be erected thereupon, shall be for the public use of the Province, and shall be known and designated as " The Ontario Institution for the Education and Instruction of the Deaf and Dumb." R. S. O. 1877, c. 222, s. 1.

The Institution at Brantford to be for the public use of the Province, etc.

Name.

2. The institution founded and established at Brantford, for the education and instruction of the blind, with all the lands, buildings, real estate and appurtenances thereunto attached, and whatever lands or real estate may hereafter be purchased or acquired for the same, and whatever buildings may hereafter be erected thereupon, shall be for the public use of the Province, and shall be known and designated as " The Ontario Institution for the Education and Instruction of the Blind." R. S. O. 1877, c. 222, s. 2.

Objects of the institutions.

3. Such institutions respectively shall be for the purpose of educating and imparting instruction in some manual art to such deaf and dumb persons and to such blind persons as are born of parents, or are wards of a person *bona fide* resident of and domiciled in the Province of Ontario. R. S. O. 1877, c. 222, s. 3.

Appointment of officers.

Salaries.

4. The Lieutenant-Governor may appoint to the said institutions respectively, to hold office during pleasure, a principal who shall be the chief executive officer of the same, a bursar, a physician, a matron, and such other officers, instructors and servants as he deems necessary ; and may also fix and determine the salary of every such officer and servant. R. S. O. 1877, c. 222, s. 4.

Inspector and his powers.

5. The inspector of prisons and public charities shall be the inspector of the said institutions, and shall have and perform the same powers and duties in respect to the said.

institutions as are conferred on him in respect of asylums for the insane by *The Prison and Asylum Inspection Act.* R. S. O. 1877, c. 222, s. 5.

Rev. Stat. c. 250.

6.—(1) The inspector shall have power, and it shall be his duty, to make such rules and by-laws as he deems expedient for the government, discipline and management of the said institutions; for prescribing and regulating the duties of the principals, bursars, physicians, matrons, and every other officer, instructor and servant employed in or about such institutions; for the education and instruction of the pupils admitted to the same; and, subject to the provisions hereinbefore contained, for fixing the terms and conditions upon which pupils shall be admitted to, and remain in, the said institutions respectively, and the period they shall be allowed to remain therein, and their discharge therefrom.

Inspector to make rules for management, etc.

(2) No such rules or by-laws shall have any effect until and unless they are first approved by the Lieutenant-Governor in Council.   R. S. O. 1877, c. 222, s. 6.

7. No person shall be admitted to either of such institutions except for the purposes of education and instruction, nor if over the age of twenty-one years, except upon the assent in writing of the inspector of prisons and public charities, and upon his report to the Provincial Secretary of the particulars and special circumstances which in the opinion of the inspector justify such admission; and the maintenance and support of any person admitted shall be in the discretion of the inspector, who, on exercise thereof in favour of such person, shall report every six months to the Provincial Secretary the particulars and special circumstances which justify such maintenance and support; and the Provincial Secretary in either case may annul the right of admission or of continuance in such institutions, and annul or vary the terms of continuance, support or maintenance.   R. S. O. 1877, c. 222, s. 7.

Admittance.

Maintenance.

Annulling admission.

CHAPTER 248.

An Act to regulate Public Aid to Charitable Institutions.

HER MAJESTY, by and with the advice and consent of Legislative Assembly of the Province of Ontario, enacts as follows :—

Short title. **1.** This Act may be cited as " *The Charity Aid Act.*" R. S. O. 1877, c. 223, s. 1.

Aid to be given to certain charitable institutions. **2.** Aid from the public funds or moneys of this Province shall be given to charitable institutions hitherto receiving public aid, and named in schedules A, B and C, upon the terms and under the provisions of this Act. R. S. O. 1877, c. 223, s. 2.

Amount of aid. **3.** In case of public moneys being appropriated for the purposes of this Act by the Legislative Assembly, every institution named in said Schedules complying with the requirements of this Act, and of all Orders made hereunder by the Lieutenant-Governor in Council, shall receive in each year aid from such moneys to the extent and amount following, that is to say :

1. Every institution named in Schedule A shall so have and receive 20 cents for each day's actual treatment and stay of every patient admitted to, or being within such institution during the calendar year next preceding the year for which such aid is given ;

2. Every institution named in Schedule B shall so have and receive 5 cents for each day's actual lodgment and maintenance therein of any indigent person during the calendar year next preceding that for which such aid is given ;

3. Every institution named in Schedule C shall so have and receive 1½ cents for each day's actual lodgment and

maintenance therein of any orphan or neglected and abandoned child, during the calendar year next preceding that for which such aid is given. R. S. O. 1877, c. 223, s. 3.

4.—(1) In every year, every such institution shall also *Further aid.* be entitled to have and receive from such public funds further aid to the extent and amount following, that is to say:

1. Every institution named in Schedule A, 10 cents;

2. Every institution named in Schedule B, 2 cents; and

3. Every institution named in Schedule C, one-half cent,

for every such day's actual stay and treatment, or lodgment and maintenance of any patient or person therein, as aforesaid;

(2) But the aggregate amount of such further aid, at the *Proviso—* rate aforesaid, shall not, in any one year, exceed one-fourth of *Limit of amount of aid.* the entire moneys received by such institution in said preceding year from all sources other than the Province, towards the ordinary yearly maintenance thereof, and in every such case, where said further aid in the aggregate would exceed said one-fourth of the last-mentioned moneys, there shall be substituted and given in lieu thereof, from the public moneys so appropriated, a sum equal to the said one-fourth of the last mentioned moneys. R. S. O. 1877, c. 223, s. 4.

5. In calculating the amount of aid so to be given under *How amount* this Act to any institution as aforesaid, the day of departure *to be calculated.* of any patient or person from such institution shall not be counted or reckoned. R. S. O. 1877, c. 223, s. 5.

6. No warrant shall issue for the payment of any sum of *No money to* money granted by the Legislature to any hospital to which *be paid to any Hospital ad-* small-pox patients are admitted unless a certificate has been *mitting small-* filed with the Clerk of the Executive Council signed by a *pox patients unless it has* medical officer of such hospital, to the effect that there is in *a special ward.* such hospital a distinct and separate ward set apart for the exclusive accommodation of patients afflicted with small-pox. R. S. O. 1877, c. 223, s. 6.

7. The Treasurer of the Province, with the authority of the *Treasurer of* Lieutenant-Governor in Council, may, from any moneys appro- *Province to pay over* priated for that purpose by the Legislative Assembly, advance *amounts.* and pay, by such periodical payments in every year as the Lieutenant-Governor in Council deems fit, to any institution entitled to receive aid under this Act, all sums to which such institution may be so entitled; but if in any year the aggregate aid payable under this Act exceeds the amount of the moneys so appropriated, then every such institution shall in such year receive by way of aid, as aforesaid, such sum only as will *Proviso in case* bear the same proportion to the amount of aid, which, but for *aid is in excess* this section it would receive, as the amount of moneys so *of sum* appropriated, bears to such aggregate aid as aforesaid. R. S. O. *granted.* 1877, c. 223, s. 7.

Case of a residue of appropriation.

8. If there is a residue of the moneys so appropriated, because of the same being more than sufficient to pay the sums payable to the said institution as aforesaid, then every of the institutions named in the schedules, which may not be entitled to receive under the foregoing provisions the sum set opposite to its name in the schedules, that being the sum heretofore granted thereto, shall receive out of the residue such an amount by way of supplementary aid as will make the total aid under this Act received by the institution equal to the sum so set opposite its name, if the residue is sufficient for that purpose, or if insufficient, then such proportion thereof as the residue will permit of.   R. S. O. 1877, c. 223, s. 8.

Returns.

9. The Lieutenant-Governor in Council shall from time to time, by Order in Council, fix and direct the particulars to be contained in, and the form, manner and time of making such return or returns as to the Lieutenant-Governor in Council may, for the due carrying out of the provisions of this Act, seem proper with regard to such institution, and, by like Order in Council shall fix and direct the form and manner of oath (if any) required for the verification of any such return, and the person by whom such oath shall be made; and any such oath may be taken before and administered by a Justice of the Peace or commissioner for taking affidavits.   R. S. O. 1877, c. 223, s. 9.

Penalty in case of false return.

10. Any person who knowingly and wilfully makes, or is a party to, or procuring to be made, directly or indirectly, any false return, either under this Act or any Order in Council, shall thereby incur a penalty of $1,000, which penalty may be recovered, with costs, by civil action or proceeding, at the suit of the Crown only, in any form allowed by law, and before any Court of the Province having jurisdiction to the amount of such penalty in cases of simple contract.   R. S. O. 1877, c. 223, s. 10.

Inspector.

11. The inspector of prisons and public charities shall, by virtue of his office, be the inspector of every institution receiving aid under this Act.   R. S. O. 1877, c. 223, s. 11.

Duties of Inspector.

12. The inspector shall, from time to time, visit and inspect every such institution, and make all proper inquiries as to the maintenance, management and affairs thereof; and by examination of the registers and such other means as he may deem necessary, particularly satisfy himself as to the correctness of any returns made under this Act, or under any Order in Council in that behalf, as aforesaid; upon all which matters he shall make report to the Lieutenant-Governor in Council. R. S. O. 1877, c. 223, s. 12.

13.—(1) The Lieutenant-Governor in Council may, by Order in Council, direct that any institution(naming it)similar to those named in either of said schedules, shall be thereafter taken as named in such one of the schedules as in that behalf is specially designated in such Order ; and thereupon and thereafter said last mentioned institution shall receive aid under this Act after the manner and to the same extent as the other institutions now named in said last mentioned schedule.

(2) No Order in Council shall be made except upon report of the inspector of prisons and public charities to and for the information of the Lieutenant-Governor in Council, shewing that the institution named in the Order has all the usual and proper requirements for one of its nature and objects and that, for reasons therein stated, the same ought to be aided under this Act.

(3) Every Order in Council shall, as soon as conveniently may be after the making thereof, be laid before the Legislative Assembly for its ratification or rejection, and no Order shall be operative unless and until the same has been ratified by a resolution of the Legislative Assembly. R. S. O. 1877, c. 223, s. 13.

14. The Lieutenant-Governor in Council may, by Order in Council, direct that any institution receiving aid under this Act shall not, after the date of the Order, receive any aid ; and thereupon, and whilst the Order remains unrevoked, such last mentioned institution shall not be entitled to or receive any further aid from the public moneys of the Province; but upon report of the inspector, disclosing good and sufficient grounds in that behalf, it shall always be competent for the Lieutenant-Governor in Council to revoke such last mentioned Order by a subsequent Order in Council, and thereafter such institution shall again receive aid under this Act, and shall be subject to all its provisions, as if the Order in Council firstly in this section mentioned had not been made ; and if at any time, upon report of the inspector, it is found that any institution of the character named in Schedule A is insufficient, or without the necessary and proper accommodation or requirements for one of its nature and objects, the Lieutenant-Governor in Council shall thereupon make such Order as is firstly in this section mentioned. R. S. O. 1877, c. 223, s. 14.

15. No by-laws or regulations adopted by the directors or managers, or other body or persons having the control or management of any institution named in Schedules A and B, for the government and management of such institution, or for prescribing the method and terms of admission thereto, or defining and regulating the duties and powers of the officers and servants thereof, and the salaries (if any) of such officers and servants, shall have force or effect unless and until the

same have been approved of by the Lieutenant-Governor in
Council, upon the report of the inspector of prisons and public
charities.   R. S. O. 1877, c. 223, s. 15.

SCHEDULE A.

(Sections 2, 3, 4, 8 and 13.)

Toronto General Hospital	$11,200 00
The City Hospital, Hamilton	4,800 00
Kingston Hospital, Kingston	4,800 00
Hotel Dieu Hospital, Kingston	1,000 00
County of Carleton General Protestant Hospital, Ottawa	1,200 00
The General Roman Catholic Hospital, Ottawa	1,200 00
The General Hospital, London	2,400 00
The General and Marine Hospital, St. Catharines	1,000 00
The Burnside Lying-in Hospital, Toronto	480 00
The Toronto Eye and Ear Infirmary	1,000 00

R. S. O. 1877, c. 223, Sched. A.

Belleville Hospital, Belleville.
John H. Stafford Hospital, Brantford.
General Hospital, Guelph.
St. Joseph's Hospital, Guelph.
General Hospital, Mattawa.
House of Mercy Lying-in Hospital, Ottawa.
General Hospital, Pembroke.
St. Joseph's Hospital, Port Arthur.

SCHEDULE B.

(Sections 2, 3, 4, 8 and 13.)

The House of Industry, Toronto	$2,900 00
The House of Providence, Toronto	1,000 00
The House of Industry and Refuge for Indigent Sick, Kingston.	2,400 00
The House of Refuge, Hamilton	720 00

R. S. O. 1877, c. 223, Sched. B.

Home for Incurables, Toronto.
Aged Women's Home, Toronto.
Home for Aged Women, Hamilton.
House of Providence, Kingston.
Home for Aged and Friendless, London.
Home for Aged Women, London.
Roman Catholic House of Refuge, London.
St. Patrick's House of Refuge, Ottawa.
St. Charles' Hospice, Ottawa.
House of Providence, Guelph.
Protestant Home (Refuge Branch), St. Catharines.
The Home, St. Thomas.
House of Providence, Dundas.
Home for the Friendless, Chatham.
Widow's Home, Brantford.
Home for the Friendless, Belleville.
Protestant Home, Peterborough.

SCHEDULE C.

(Sections 2, 3, 4, 8 and 13.)

The Orphans' Home and Female Aid Society, Toronto	$640 00
Roman Catholic Orphan Asylum, Toronto.	640 00
The Toronto Magdalen Asylum	480 00
The Girls' Home and Public Nursery, Toronto	320 00
The Boys' Home, Toronto	320 00
The Orphans' Home, Kingston	640 00
The Roman Catholic Orphan Asylum, London	640 00
The St. Mary's Orphan Asylum, Hamilton	640 00
The Hamilton Orphan Asylum	640 00
The St. Patrick's Orphan Asylum, Ottawa	480 00
The Orphans' Home, Ottawa	480 00
The St. Joseph's Orphan Asylum, Ottawa	480 00
The Magdalen Asylum, Ottawa..............................	480 00

R. S. O. 1877, c. 224, Sched. C.

Industrial Refuge, Toronto.
Newsboys' Lodgings, Toronto.
Infants' Home, Toronto.
St. Nicholas' Home, Toronto.
Hospital for Sick Children, Toronto.
Boys' Home, Hamilton.
Girls' Home, Hamilton.
Home of the Friendless and Infants' Home, Hamilton.
House of Providence Orphan Asylum, Kingston.
Hotel Dieu Orphan Asylum, Kingston.
Protestant Orphans' Home, London.
Women's Refuge and Infants' Home, London.
Protestant Home (Orphanage Branch), St. Catharines.
Orphan Asylum, St. Agatha.
The Home (Orphanage Branch), St. Thomas.
Orphans' Home, Fort William.

EXTRACTS FROM CHAPTER 142, RELATING TO APPRENTICING MINORS.

6. A parent, guardian, or other person having the care or charge of a minor, or any charitable society being authorized by the Lieutenant-Governor in Council to exercise the powers conferred by this Act, and having the care or charge of a minor, the minor being a male and not under the age of fourteen years, may, with the consent of the minor, put and bind him as an apprentice by indenture to any respectable and trustworthy master-mechanic, farmer, or other person carrying on a trade or calling, for a term not to extend beyond the minority of the apprentice; or in case of a female not under the age of twelve years, may, with her consent, bind the minor to any respectable and trustworthy person carrying on any trade or calling, or to

Power of parents, charitable societies, etc., to bind minors.

domestic service with any respectable and trustworthy person for any term not to extend beyond the age of eighteen years. R. S. O. 1877, c. 135, s. 6.

Charitable societies may be authorized to exercise powers under this Act.

29. The Lieutenant Governor in Council may authorize any charitable society, incorporated or unincorporated, to exercise for a limited time or otherwise, the powers conferred by this Act, and may revoke or suspend any Order in Council made for that purpose; and after such revocation such Society shall not possess the authority to exercise such powers unless and until again authorized by Order in Council. R. S. O. 1877, c. 135, s. 29.

CHAPTER 249.

An Act for the Protection of Women in Certain Cases.

HER MAJESTY, by and with the advice and consent of the Legislative Assembly of the Province of Ontario, enacts as follows :—

Protection of persons confined in asylums. Rev. Stat. c. 250.

1. No person shall at any time or place within the precincts of any institution to which *The Prison and Asylum Inspection Act* applies, unlawfully and carnally know any female who is capable in law of giving her consent to such carnal knowledge while she is a patient or is confined in such institution. 50 V. c. 45, s. 1.

Penalty.

2. Whosoever violates section 1 of this Act is guilty of an offence, and shall be liable to be imprisoned in any gaol or place of confinement, other than the Penitentiary, for any term less than two years, with or without hard labour. 50 V. c. 45, s. 2.

Accused a competent witness.

3. The person charged shall be a competent witness in his own behalf. 50 V. c. 45, s. 3.

Civil remedy not affected.

4. Nothing in this Act contained nor any conviction obtained in pursuance thereof shall deprive any person of the right to maintain an action for damages against the person so charged. 50 V. c. 45, s. 4.

See R. S. C. 1886, Chap. 157, Sec. 3 (b).

CHAPTER 250.

An Act to provide for the Inspection of Asylums, Hospitals, Prisons and Court Houses.

HER MAJESTY, by and with the advice and consent of the Legislative Assembly of the Province of Ontario, enacts as follows:—

1. This Act may be cited as "*The Prison and Asylum Inspection Act.*" R. S. O. 1877, c. 224, s. 1. Short title.

2. In the construction of this Act the word "county" shall be held to mean county or union of counties. R. S. O. 1877, c. 224, s. 2. Meaning of "County."

3. The rules and regulations in force for the government of all public asylums, hospitals, common gaols, and reformatory and other prisons in this Province, other than the provincial penitentiary, may, from time to time, be amended, altered, changed, rescinded, or suspended, by order of the Lieutenant-Governor in Council. R. S. O. 1877, c. 224. s. 3. Amendment of rules.

4. The Lieutenant-Governor may appoint two fit and proper persons to be each an inspector of the public asylums, hospitals, common gaols and reformatories in this Province, other than the provincial penitentiary. R. S. O. 1877, c. 224, s. 4; 46 V. c. 30, s. 1. Appointmen of Inspector

5. The Lieutenant-Governor may, from time to time, by Order in Council, designate what public and other institutions requiring inspection are to be inspected by each inspector, or by either inspector, or by both inspectors, and may otherwise define the duties of the inspectors, and each of them. 46 V. c. 30, s. 2. Lieutenant-Governor ma define duties of Inspector.

Senior Inspector to be a corporation sole.

6. For the purposes of chapters 238 to 248 of these Revised Statutes, the inspector for the time being whose commission bears the earlier date, shall be a corporation sole, by the name of "The Inspector of Prisons and Public Charities," and by that name he and his successors in office shall have perpetual succession, and may sue and be sued, and may plead and be impleaded in any of Her Majesty's Courts in this Province; and he may hereafter be referred to in any Statute or otherwise as the senior inspector of prisons and public charities. R. S. O. 1877, c. 224, s. 5; 46 V. c. 30, s. 3 (1) *part.*

Rev. Stat. c. 245, ss. 47-49, 51-54, 57-59, to apply to the Senior Inspector.

7.—(1) Sections 47, 48, 49, 51, 52, 53, 54, 57, 58 and 59 of *The Act respecting Lunatic Asylums, and the Custody of Insane Persons,* shall apply to the senior inspector. 46 V. c. 30, s. 3 (1) *part.*

(2) In case of the death, removal or resignation of such senior inspector, all the rights, powers, duties, obligations, moneys or estates under the said sections, or under anything done in pursuance thereof, which shall be vested in him, or shall belong to him, either by his name of office or in his corporate capacity, at the time of his death, removal or resignation, shall thereupon become vested in, and shall belong to, the surviving inspector, as the successor of the senior inspector; or if there is then no other inspector, the same shall immediately upon the first appointment of an inspector, vest in, and belong to, the inspector so appointed.

(3) The Lieutenant-Governor in Council may by order direct that the rights, powers, duties, obligations, moneys or estates vested in or belonging to the senior inspector, shall become vested in and shall belong to the other inspector; and thereupon the rights, powers, duties, obligations, moneys or estates, vested in or belonging to the senior inspector as aforesaid, shall upon and by virtue of such order become vested in and belong to the other inspector as fully as if the senior inspector had died. 46 V. c. 30, s. 3 (2, 3).

Reference in Statutes to Inspector to apply to either Inspector.

8. Except as in the next preceding two sections provided, where the inspector of prisons and public charities is referred to in any Statute, by this or any other name. the reference shall be held to apply to either of such inspectors, or to that one of them to whom, under an order of the Lieutenant-Governor in Council, the duty or power to which the reference relates belongs. 46 V. c. 30, s. 4.

Inspectors' salaries.

9. The salaries of the inspectors shall be such amount as may be appropriated by the Legislature therefor. R. S. O. 1877, c. 224, s. 6; 41 V. c. 2, s. 39, Sched. B.

Inspectors' duties.

10. It shall be the duty of one of the inspectors to visit and inspect every gaol, house of correction, reformatory and prison or place kept or used for the confinement of persons, in any part of this Province, other than the provincial penitentiary, at least twice in each year, and he may examine any person holding any office or receiving any salary or emolument in such place of confinement, as aforesaid, and call for and inspect all books and papers relating to such place of confinement; and may enquire into all matters concerning the said place of confinement; and each inspector shall make a separate and distinct report in writing to the Lieutenant-Governor of the state of every place of confinement visited by him. R. S. O. 1877, c. 224, s. 7. *Report to Lieutenant-Governor.*

11. Where the inspector considers it expedient to institute an enquiry into the management of any of the said institutions, or of any other institution subject to be inspected by him, or into any matter in connection therewith, or into the truth of any return made by the officers of any of the said institutions, and considers it expedient that any of the officers of such institution or any other person should be required to give evidence before him on oath, the inspector shall have the same power to summon such officers or other persons to attend as witnesses, to enforce their attendance, and to compel them to produce documents and to give evidence, as any Court has in civil cases. R. S. O. 1877, c. 224 s. 8. *Power of Inspector in instituting inquiries into institutions subject to his inspection.*

12.—(1) The inspectors shall have power from time to time, subject to the approval of the Lieutenant-Governor in Council, to alter, amend, cancel or rescind any existing rules or regulations for the government of the common gaols of this Province, and to frame and adopt other rules and regulations in that behalf, touching or extending to— *Power to rescind existing regulations, and to frame others.*

(*a*) The maintenance of prisoners in regard to diet, clothing, bedding, and other necessaries ;

(*b*) Their employment ;

(*c*) Medical attendance ;

(*d*) Religious instruction ;

(*e*) The conduct of the prisoners, and the restraint and punishment to which they may be subjected ;

(*f*) Also to the treatment and custody of the prisoners generally, the whole internal economy and management of the gaol, and all such matters connected therewith as may be considered by them expedient, which rules and regulations shall be submitted to the Lieutenant-Governor for his approval and confirmation. *Regulations to be submitted to Lieut.-Governor.*

(2) Nothing herein contained shall be held to prevent the county councils in this Province from making such special regulations as the peculiar circumstances of their respective gaols and localities may, in their opinion, require, such special regu- *Special regulations by County Councils.*

lations not being inconsistent with this Act, or with the general rules and regulations to be made by the inspectors and approved by the Lieutenant-Governor, as aforesaid.   R. S. O. 1877, c. 224, s. 9.

Examination of lunatic asylums.

13. With respect to the asylums for the insane, at Toronto, London, Hamilton, Kingston and Orillia, an inspector shall at least three times a year, thoroughly examine the manner in which the said institutions are conducted, respectively, and examine the reports respectively made to him by the medical superintendents and bursars.   R. S. O. 1877, c. 224, s. 10.

By-laws.

14. The inspectors shall from time to time frame such by-laws as seem to them most conducive to the peace, welfare and good government of the said asylums, which said by-laws shall have effect when the Lieutenant-Governor has signified his assent thereto.   R. S. O. 1877, c. 224, s. 11.

Inspector's annual report.

15. Each inspector shall, with his annual report to the Lieutenant-Governor, transmit the reports made to him by the medical superintendents and bursars, with his observations thereon.   R. S. O. 1877, c. 224, s. 12.

Inspection of hospitals.

16. An inspector shall, at least twice a year, and oftener if ordered by the Lieutenant-Governor, visit, examine and report upon the state and management of every hospital or other benevolent institution supported wholly by grant of public money, or by money levied under the authority of law. R. S. O. 1877, c. 224, s. 13.

Report of the management, etc.

17. An inspector, whenever required by the Lieutenant-Governor so to do, shall visit, examine, and report to him upon the state, management and condition of every hospital or other benevolent institution supported, in part, by grant of public money, and, in case of refusal of admission into the same for the purpose of inspection, shall forthwith report such refusal to the Lieutenant-Governor, with the circumstances attending the same.   R. S. O. 1877, c. 224, s. 14.   *See* cap. 248, s. 11.

Report on private lunatic asylums.

Rev. Stat. c. 246.

Revo license.

18. An inspector, whenever required to do so by the Lieutenant-Governor, and at least once in the year, shall visit, examine and report to him upon the state and management of every private lunatic asylum established under the provisions of *The Act respecting Private Lunatic Asylums*, and upon the condition of its inmates, and the Lieutenant-Governor in Council, after the receipt of any such report of the inspector may, suspend or revoke the license granted under the said Act. R. S. O. 1877, c. 224, s. 15.

Asylum for idiots, deaf, dumb, and blind.

19. Each inspector shall have and perform the same powers and duties with respect to any other lunatic asylum or any asylum for idiots, or for the deaf, dumb or blind, that may have been, or may be, erected at the public expense, as are vested in him by this Act with respect to the asylums for the insane hereinbefore mentioned. R. S. O. 1877, c. 224, s. 16. *See* cap. 247, s. 5.

20. Each inspector shall keep an exact record of his pro- Copy of pro-ceedings, and transmit a copy thereof to the Lieutenant-Gover- ceedings to be sent to Lieut.-nor, under the hand of the said inspector. R. S. O. 1877, c. 224, Governor. s. 17.

21. Each inspector shall make an annual report to the Lieu- General Annual Report. tenant-Governor as soon as may be after the 1st day of October in each year, which report shall contain a full and accurate report on the state, condition and management of the several asylums, hospitals, gaols and other institutions under his inspection, and inspected by him during the preceding year, together with such suggestions for the improvement of the same Suggestions for improvements. as he may deem necessary and expedient, and which report, as far as respects the reformatories under his inspection, shall comprise and embrace the following particulars, viz. :

1. A copy of the warden's report to the inspector ; Particulars.

2. Copies of the chaplain's report to the inspector ;

3. Copy of the physician's annual report ;

4. A return of the names, ages, country, calling and crimes of the offenders received into the reformatory during the year, and the township, county, town and city from which each came ;.

5. A return of the names, ages, callings and crimes of the offenders who died in the reformatory during the year, and the township, county, town and city from which each came ;

6. A similar return of the offenders liberated during the year, by the expiration of the term for which they were sentenced ;

7. A similar return of the offenders who had the Royal pardon extended to them during the year ;

8. A tabular statement shewing the number of prisoners in the reformatory at the date to which the last previous annual report was made up, the number received during the year, the number discharged, the number then in confinement, and the average number in the reformatory during the year, shewing the particulars separately as to the male and female prisoners ;

9. A balance sheet of the affairs of the institution, at the 1st day of October of the year reported upon, shewing the amount of cash received from the public exchequer since the commencement of the institution and the existing assets thereof ;

10. A cash balance for the past year, shewing the sum on hand on the 1st day of October, the cash received through

the year from Government towards the support and expenses of the prison, the amount received for convict labour, and the amounts received on all other accounts during the year; the said balance sheet shall also shew separately the sums paid . for food, bedding, clothing and hospital stores for the offenders, the salaries of the officers, fuel and light, for the erection of new buildings and repairs, for the support of the stable, and for all other items of expenditure, also the cash on hand at the close of the year;

11. A statement of all debts due by the institution, shewing the names of the parties to whom each sum is due, also shew-ing the debts, if any, due to the institution, with the amounts and ground of each debt;

12. An inventory and valuation of all the property, estate and effects of the institution, distinguishing the estimated value of the several descriptions of property;

13. An estimate of the receipts and expenditures for the current year, and of the amount of aid likely to be required from the Provincial Exchequer;

14. A statement shewing in what manner the offenders were employed as at the 1st day of October of the year reported on, and the average number at each trade or occupation during the year. R. S. O. 1877, c. 224, s. 18.

Construction of gaols.
22. Every gaol erected in this Province shall be constructed and built according to a plan to be approved of by the inspec-tor, and sanctioned by the Lieutenant-Governor; and no gaol built after the 4th day of March, 1868, in any county in Ontario, otherwise than according to a plan approved and sanc-tioned as aforesaid, or that does not, after its completion, receive the approval of the inspector, shall be deemed to be in law the gaol of such county. R. S. O. 1877, c. 224, s. 19.

Gaol plans, consideration of.
23. An inspector, before deciding in any case upon the plan of a gaol most proper to be adopted, shall take into considera-tion—

Particulars.
1. The nature and extent of the ground upon which such gaol or court house has been or is to be built;

2. Its relative situation to any streets and buildings, and to any river or other water;

3. Its comparative elevation and capability of being drained .

4. The material of which it has been or is to be composed ;

5. The necessity of guarding against cold and dampness, and of providing properly for ventilation;

6. The proper classification of prisoners, having regard to their age, sex, and cause of their confinement;

7. The best means of ensuring their safe custody without the necessity of resorting to severe treatment;

8. The due accommodation of the keeper of the gaol, so that he may have ready access to the prisoners and conveniently oversee them;

9. The exclusion of any intercourse with persons without the walls of the building;

10. The prevention of nuisances, from whatever cause;

11. The combining provision, as well for the reformation of convicts, as far as may be practicable, as for their employment, in order that the common gaols may really serve for places of correction;

12. The admission of prisoners to air and exercise without the walls of the building; and

13. The enclosure of the yard and premises with a secure wall.   R. S. O. 1877, c. 224, s. 20.

24. In case an inspector at any time finds that the common gaol in any county or city in this Province is out of repair—or is or has become unsafe or unfit for the confinement of prisoners, or is not constructed or maintained in conformity with the provisions of the next preceding section, or that the same does not afford sufficient space or room for the number of prisoners usually confined therein—he shall forthwith report the fact to the Lieutenant-Governor, and shall at the same time furnish a copy of such report to the council of the county or city to which such common gaol belongs, and the council shall thereupon appoint a special committee to confer with the inspector, and to arrange with him as to the repairs, alterations or additions that may be deemed necessary to remedy the defect so reported upon by the inspector, and to report the same to the council, and in case the inspector and the committee do not agree upon the repairs, alterations and additions, the matter shall then be referred to the Lieutenant-Governor in Council to decide between them, which decision shall be reported to the council; and it shall be the duty of the council in either case, by by-law, to order and provide for the making of the repairs, alterations or additions, and for the appropriation of any money that may be required for that purpose, and in default thereof the council may be proceeded against by *mandamus* issued out of the High Court at the instance and prosecution either of the Attorney-General for Ontario or any private prosecutor, to compel the making by the council of such repairs, alterations or additions, and the council and the members and officers thereof shall be subject to all the process of the Courts for contempt of the orders or process thereof. R. S. O. 1877, c. 224, s. 21.

Marginal notes: Gaol repairs. Report to the Lieut.-Governor. Copy furnished to the County Council. By-law for repairs. In default of repairs—proceeding by *mandamus*.

Repairs to be made with due regard to the ability of the Council to meet the expense.

25. The inspector and the special committee of the county or city council shall, in arranging the particulars of the necessary repairs, alterations or additions, as aforesaid, have due regard to the plan of the gaol, and to the ability of the council to meet the expense thereof, and in the case of alterations or additions, shall make the same as few and inexpensive as, in their opinion, the requirements of this Act and of the public service will admit.   R. S. O. 1877, c. 224, s. 22.

Inspection of court houses.

26. The provisions of this Act as to the inspection, construction, and repairing of gaols shall, so far as may be, apply to court houses.   44 V. c. 5, s. 89.

Lt.-Governor may authorize persons to assist the Inspector of Prisons and Public Charities.

27. The Lieutenant-Governor may authorize such person or persons as he thinks fit, to perform, under the supervision of an inspector, or otherwise as the Lieutenant-Governor may direct, any of the duties belonging to the office of the inspector, and in the performance of the duties such person or persons may exercise the like powers and authorities as are possessed by the inspector.   R. S. O. 1877, c. 224, s. 25.

Action for anything done under this Act.

28. All actions and prosecutions against any person or persons for anything done in pursuance of this Act, shall be laid and tried in the county where the fact was committed, and shall be commenced within six months after the fact committed, and not otherwise or afterwards.   R. S. O. 1877, c. 224, s. 26.

EXTRACTS FROM CERTAIN ACTS RELATING TO COMMON GAOLS, LOCK-UPS AND COURT-HOUSES.

CHAPTER 1, SEC. 8, SUB-SEC. 29.

Imprisonment where to be when no special place is mentioned.

27. If in any Act any party is directed to be imprisoned or committed to prison, such imprisonment or committal shall, if no other place is mentioned or provided by law, be in or to the Common Gaol of the locality in which the order for such imprisonment is made, or if there be no Common Gaol there, then in or to that Common Gaol which is nearest to such locality ; and the keeper of any such Common Gaol shall receive such person, and him safely keep and detain in such Common Gaol under his custody until discharged in due course of law, or bailed in cases in which bail may by law be taken.

CHAPTER 24, SEC. 13,

Lands may be set apart for certain public purposes, and

13. The Lieutenant-Governor in Council may set apart and appropriate such of the Crown Lands as he may deem expedient for the sites of Wharves and Piers, Market Places, Gaols,

Court Houses, Public Parks or Gardens, Town Halls, Hospitals, free grants thereof made in trust. Places of Public Worship, Burying Grounds, Schools, and for purposes of Agricultural Exhibitions, and for other like public purposes, and for Model or Industrial Farms; and at any time before the issue of letters patent therefor, may revoke such appropriation as seems expedient; and may make free grants for the purposes aforesaid, and the trust and uses to which they are to be subject shall be expressed in the letters patent; but no such grant shall be for more than ten acres in any one instance, and for any one of the purposes aforesaid, except for Proviso. a Model or Industrial Farm, which shall not exceed one hundred acres. R. S. O. 1877, c. 23, s. 13.

CHAPTER 44, SEC. 150

All Gaols in Ontario shall be prisons of the High Court· Gaols to be prisons of the High Court. R. S. O. 1877, c. 40, s. 18.

CHAPTER 80, SEC. 3.

3. Upon the death of any prisoner, the Warden, Gaoler, Proceedings in case of the death of any prisoner. Keeper or Superintendent of any Penitentiary, Gaol, Prison, House of Correction, Lock-up house, or House of Industry in which the prisoner dies, shall immediately give notice thereof to some Coroner of the County, City or Town in which the death has taken place, and the Coroner shall proceed forthwith to hold an inquest upon the body. R. S. O. 1877, c. 79, s. 3.

CHAPTER 184, SEC. 452, ET SEQ.

452. Every County Council may pass by-laws for erecting, County council may pass by-laws as to county buildings; improving and repairing a Court-House, Gaol, House of Correction, and House of Industry, upon land being the property of the Municipality, and shall preserve and keep the same in repair, and provide the food, fuel and other supplies required for the same. 46 V. c. 18, s. 451.

453. Every County Council may, when a Court-House is And for acquiring land for court-houses in cities. required to be erected within the limits of a city, pass by-laws for entering upon, taking, using, and acquiring such land as may be necessary or convenient for the purposes of such Court-House. 46 V. c. 18, s. 452.

454. The Gaol, Court-House, and House of Correction of Gaols and court-houses in counties and cities, etc. not separated the County in which a Town or City, not separated for all purposes from a County, is situate, shall also be the Gaol, Court-House, and House of Correction of the Town or City, and shall, in the case of such City, continue to be so until the Council of the City otherwise directs; and the Sheriff, Gaoler and Keeper of the Gaol and House of Correction shall receive and safely keep, until duly discharged, all persons committed thereto by any competent authority of the Town or City. 46 V. c. 18, s. 453.

City councils may erect, etc., certain public buildings.

455. The Council of any City may erect, preserve, improve and provide for the proper keeping of a Court-House, Gaol, House of Correction and House of Industry, upon lands being the property of the Municipality, and may pass by-laws for all or any of such purposes. 46 V. c. 18, s. 454.

Lock-up houses may be established by county councils.

456. The Council of every County may establish and maintain a Lock-up House, or Lock-up Houses, within the County, and may establish and provide for the salary or fees to be paid to the Constable to be placed in charge of every such Lock-up House, and may direct the payment of the salary out of the funds of the County. 46 V. c. 18, s. 455.

A constable to be placed in charge.

457. Every Lock-up House shall be placed in the charge of a Constable specially appointed for that purpose by the Magistrates of the County at a General Sessions of the Peace therefor. 46 V. c. 18, s. 456.

Lock-up houses.

458. The Council of every City, Town, Township, and incorporated Village may, by by-law, establish, maintain and regulate Lock-up Houses for the detention and imprisonment of persons sentenced to imprisonment for not more than ten days under any by-law of the Council; and of persons detained for examination on a charge of having committed any offence; and of persons detained for transmission to any Common Gaol or House of Correction, either for trial or in the execution of any sentence; and such Councils shall have all the powers and authorities conferred on County Councils in relation to Lock-up Houses. 46 V. c. 18, s. 457.

Joint lock-up houses.

459. Two or more Municipalities may unite to establish and maintain a Lock-up House. 46 V. c. 18, s. 458.

Land may be acquired for industrial farms, house of industry, refuge, etc.

460—(1) The Council of every County, City or Town separated from a County may acquire an estate in landed property for an Industrial Farm, and may establish a House of Industry and a House of Refuge, and provide by-law for the erection and repair thereof, and for the appointment, payment and duties of Inspectors, Keepers, Matrons and other servants for the superintendence, care and management of such House of Industry or Refuge, and in like manner make rules and regulations (not repugnant to law) for the government of the same.

Proviso as to united or contiguous counties.

(2) Two or more United Counties, or two or more contiguous Counties, or a City and one or more Counties, or a Town and one or more Counties, may agree to have only one House of Industry or Refuge for such united or contiguous

Counties, or City and Counties, or Town and Counties, and maintain and keep up the same in the manner herein provided.

(3) The Council may provide by by-law, for requiring such persons as may be sent to such Industrial Farm or other place to work on the said Farm, or at any work or service for the said Municipality at such times, and for such hours, and at such trade or labour as they may appear to be adapted for respectively, and for buying and selling material therefor, and for applying the earnings, or parts thereof, of such persons for their maintenance or the maintenance of the wife and child or wife and children (if any) of such persons, or for the general maintenance of the farm or other place as aforesaid, or for aiding such persons to reach their friends (if any) or any place to which it may be deemed advisable to send them. 46 V. c. 18, s. 459.

Power to compel persons sent to industrial farms, etc., work thereo

461. The Inspector of a House of Industry or Refuge appointed as aforesaid, shall keep an account of the charges of erecting, keeping, upholding and maintaining the House of Industry or Refuge, and of all materials found and furnished therefor, together with the names of the persons received into the House, as well as those discharged therefrom, and also of the earnings; and such account shall be rendered to the County Council every year, or oftener when required by a by-law of the Council; and a copy thereof shall be presented to the Legislature. 46 V. c. 18, s. 460.

Inspectors t keep and re der accounts of expenses, etc.

462. The Council of every City and Town may respectively pass by-laws:

By-laws ma be passed establishing workhouses and houses correction.

1. For erecting and establishing within the City or Town or on such Industrial Farm, or on any ground held by the Corporation for public exhibitions, a Workhouse or House of Correction, and for regulating the government thereof.

2. For committing and sending, with or without hard labour, to the Workhouse or House of Correction, or to the Industrial Farm, House of Industry, House of Refuge, or House for the Poor, Aged, and Infirm, or Lock-up, or to any work or service for the said Municipality as aforesaid, by the Mayor, Police Magistrate, or Justice of the Peace, while having jurisdiction in the Municipality, such disorderly persons, drunkards, vagrants, indigent persons, and such description of persons as are set forth or referred to in section 369 of chapter 48 of the Acts passed in the 36th year of Her Majesty's reign, and as may by the Council be deemed, and by by-law be declared, expedient; and such Farm, House of Correction, House of Industry, House of Refuge, or House for the Poor, Aged, or Infirm, Lock-up House, or ground held as aforesaid, shall, for the purposes in this sub-section mentioned, be deemed to be within the Municipality and the jurisdiction thereof. 46 V. c. 18, s. 461.

Who liable be committ thereto.

Until houses of correction erected, the common gaols are constituted houses of correction. **463.** Until separate Houses of Correction are erected in the several Counties in Ontario, the Common Gaol in each County respectively shall be a House of Correction ; and every idle and disorderly person, or rogue and vagabond, and incorrigible rogue, and any other person by law subject to be committed to a House of Correction, shall, unless otherwise provided by law, be committed to the said Common Gaols, respectively. 46 V. c. 18, s. 462.

Custody of gaols. **464.**—(1) The Sheriff shall have the care of the County Gaol, gaol offices and yard, and gaoler's apartments, and the appointment of the keepers thereof, whose salaries shall be **Keepers.** fixed by the County Council, subject to the revision or requirement of the Inspector of Prisons and Public Charities.

Appointment and dismissal of gaolers. (2) Every appointment, or dismissal, of a gaoler shall be subject to the approval of the Lieutenant-Governor. 46 V. c. 18, s. 463.

Gaoler to have a yearly salary in place of all fees, perquisites or impositions whatever. **465.** The salary of the gaoler shall be in lieu of all fees, perquisites or impositions of any sort or kind whatever ; and no gaoler or officer belonging to the gaol shall demand or receive any fee, perquisite or other payment from any prisoner confined within the gaol or prison. 46 V. c. 18, s. 464.

County council to have care of court-house, etc. **466.** The County Council shall have the care of the Court House and of all offices and rooms and grounds connected therewith, whether the same forms a separate building or is connected with the Gaol, and shall have the appointment of the keepers thereof, whose duty it shall be to attend to the proper lighting, heating and cleaning thereof; and shall from time to time provide all necessary and proper accommodation, fuel, light and furniture for the Courts of Justice other than the Division Courts, and for the library of the Law Association of the County (such last-mentioned accommodation to be provided in the Court House), and shall provide proper offices, together with fuel, light and furniture for all officers connected with such Courts other than (1) officers of the Maritime Court (not being in the County of York), and (2) official assignees. 46 V. c. 18, s. 465 ; 48 V. c. 39, ss. 11, 13.

City gaols to be regulated by by-laws of city councils. **467.** In any City, not being a separate County for all purposes, but having a gaol or court-house separate from County Gaol or Court-House, the care of such City Gaol or Court-House shall be regulated by the by-laws of the City Council. 46 V. c. 18, s. 467.

Upon separation of union of counties, gaol and court-house regulations to continue. **468.** In case of a separation of a union of Counties, all rules and regulations, and all matters and things in any statute for the regulation of, or relating to Court Houses or Gaols, in force at the time of the separation, shall extend to the Court-House and Gaol of the Junior County. 46 V. c. 18, s. 468.

469. Cities and Towns separated from Counties shall, as parts of their respective Counties for judicial purposes, bear and pay their just share or proportion of all charges and expenses from time to time as the same may be incurred in erecting, building and repairing and maintaining the Court-House and Gaol of their respective Counties, and of the proper lighting, cleansing and heating thereof, and of providing all necessary and proper accommodation, fuel, light, and furniture for the Gaol and Courts of Justice, other than the Division Courts, and for the library of the Law Association of the County, and of providing proper offices, together with fuel, light, and furniture for offices connected with such Courts, where the same are required to be provided by the County Council; and all other charges relating to Criminal Justice, payable by the County in the first instance, except Constables' fees and disbursements, and charges connected with Coroners' inquests, and such other charges as the Counties are entitled to be repaid by the Province; and in case the Council of the City or Town separate as aforesaid, and the Council of the County in which such City or Town is situate for judicial purposes cannot, by agreement from time to time, settle and determine the amount to be so payable by such City or Town respectively, then the same shall be determined by arbitration, according to the provisions of this Act. 46 V. c. 18, s. 469 : 48 V. c. 39, s. 12. *Liability of cities and towns separated from counties for erection and maintenance of court-house, etc. Reference to arbitration cases of disagreement.*

470. The Council shall not be liable to pay for any furniture which they are required to provide under the provisions of sections 471 and 474 of this Act, unless the same has been ordered by the Council or by some person duly authorized by them so to do. 46 V. c. 18, s. 470. *Liability for furniture for use of county officials.*

471. The Corporation of any County and City or Town separated from the County, are hereby dcelared to have respectively insurable interests in the Court House and Gaol of the County and the furniture thereof in the proportion in which they shall for the time being be liable to contribute towards the erection, building, repairing, and maintaining the same, and towards providing necessary accommodation and furniture for the said Gaol and Courts of Justice, and for the officers connected with such Courts, and any such Corporation may insure its said interest accordingly. 46 V. c. 18, s. 471. *Insurable interests of corporations in certain cases*

472. In all cases in which any city is required to contribute to the cost of erecting or building a court house or gaol, not commenced before the fifth day of March, 1880, the council of such city shall not be bound to pay for any part of the expenditure thereafter incurred in respect thereof, unless the same has been concurred in by the council of such city, or in case of dispute has been determined by arbitration, according to the provisions of this Act, and the council of the city shall have a voice in the selection of the site of the court house and gaol ; and in case the council of the county and city *Liability of city to contribute to cost erecting court houses and gaols.*

shall fail to agree upon the selection of such site, the same shall be settled and determined by arbitration, according to the provisions of this Act. 46 V. c. 18, s. 472.

Compensation by city or town for use of court-house, etc.

473. While a City or Town uses the Court House, Gaol or House of Correction of the County, the City or Town shall pay to the County such compensation therefor, and for the care and maintenance of prisoners as may be mutually agreed upon, or settled by arbitration under this Act. 46 V. c. 18, s. 473.

Compensation for mainten- ance of prisoners.

(2) In case of arbitration under the preceding provisions of this section, in determining the compensation to be paid for the care and maintenance of prisoners confined in the gaol, the arbitrators shall, so far as they deem the same just and reasonable, take into consideration the original cost of the site and erection of the gaol buildings, and of repairs and insurance, so far as the same may have been borne or sustained by one or other of the municipalities, and shall also take into consideration the cost of maintaining and supporting the prisoners, as well as the salaries of all officers and servants connected therewith ; but the provisions of this sub-section shall apply only to the determining of the compensation to be paid for the care and maintenance of any such prisoners subsequent to the first day of January, 1886. 49 V. c. 37, s. 10.

For procedure in cases where the gaol of one county is insecure and it is desirable to use that of a neighbouring county, see Revised Statutes of Canada, 1886, Chapter 183, ss. 1-7.

INDEX.

2*

PART II.

LAWS AFFECTING CHILDREN

COMPILED FROM THE

DOMINION AND ONTARIO STATUTES.

BY

J. J. KELSO,

SUPERINTENDENT OF NEGLECTED and DEPENDENT CHILDREN OF ONTARIO.

PRINTED BY AUTHORITY OF THE PROVINCIAL SECRETARY.

TORONTO:
PRINTED BY WARWICK BROS. & RUTTER, 68 AND 70 FRONT ST. W.
1895.

INTRODUCTION.

. This handbook of laws of Ontario and the Dominion of Canada relating to the protection of children is issued under the auspices of the Ontario Government, and is sent out in the hope that it will be found of service in the work of caring for and protecting children. The need of such a compilation has long been felt by those having the welfare of neglected children at heart, and much good work has been hampered by the difficulty of readily ascertaining the various provisions for their protection. I have also known intelligent persons to advocate the adoption of measures that were for years on our statute books but were practically dead letters because buried away and forgotten. What is now wanted is that all engaged in the work of uplifting fallen humanity should familiarize themselves with existing laws and put them to practical test. The keynote of our work is *prevention.*—We believe it is not poverty but vice and drunkenness that send children out to beg and steal and that are responsible for much of the child abuse ending in a ruined life and a heritage of misery. In the suppression of these evils lies our greatest hope of future success. Where milder methods prove of no avail, these laws should certainly be resorted to, and it must be remembered that every prosecution has a powerful educational effect upon the public mind. The wider the publicity given to these laws the better.—The more they are understood the more will they be obeyed, and it would, in my opinion, be a paying investment if a copy of this pamphlet could be placed in the hands of every householder. In the meantime let each of us do what we can to further the interests of this great work. Any service done towards securing for childhood a pure and happy life will be amply repaid in the great economy of God, and in this thought there should be much to stimulate and encourage all true workers.

J. J. KELSO.

PARLIAMENT BUILDINGS,
    TORONTO, January 15, 1895.

ONTARIO'S INSTITUTIONS

FOR THE CARE OF

DEFECTIVE OR DELINQUENT CHILDREN.

CARE OF THE FEEBLE-MINDED.

The Ontario Home for the care and training of the Feeble-Minded is located at Orillia, Ontario, where every provision has been made for the education of this unfortunate class. Defective children should certainly be sent to this Home, as even the worst cases may be greatly improved by early training. The certificate of two practising physicians is necessary for admittance, but parties interested should first communicate with the Superintendent, Dr. Beaton, Orillia, who will supply the requisite papers.

EDUCATION OF THE BLIND.

The Ontario Institution for the Education of the Blind is at Brantford, Ontario, and is well-equipped for its work of training the blind to enjoy life and become self-supporting in spite of their affliction. The best results are obtained when children are sent young, and parents who fail to take advantage of the facilities here offered are almost criminally negligent. The very little ones are trained by Kindergarten methods, and make rapid progress. Parties knowing of blind children or parents themselves, should communicate with the Principal, Mr. A. H. Dymond, Brantford, who will gladly furnish particulars.

DEAF AND DUMB INSTITUTE.

The Ontario Institution for the Deaf and Dumb is situated at Belleville, Ontario, and is under the superintendence of Mr. R. Mathison. It has the reputation of being one of the best conducted institutions on the continent, and the children are well-equipped to take an honorable part in life's work. The following is a description of the work undertaken, published in the school paper : "The object of the Province in founding and maintaining this Institute is to afford educational advantages to all the youth of the Province who are, on account of deafness, either partial or total, unable to receive instruction in the common schools. All deaf mutes between the ages of seven and twenty, not being deficient in intellect, and free from contagious diseases, who are *bona fide* residents of the Province of Ontario, will be admitted as pupils." Any information regarding the work of the school can be obtained by communicating with Mr. R. Mathison, Superintendent, Belleville, Ontario.

REFORMATORY FOR BOYS.

The Ontario Reformatory for Boys is located at Penetanguishene, Ontario, and is intended for the reformation of lads of criminal tendencies between the ages of 13 and 16. Mr. Thos. McCrosson is Superintendent. No boy should be committed who is not dangerous to society as this is not a "home" in the ordinary sense. Too many lads have been committed in the past to these institutions simply as the easiest method of disposal.

ONTARIO REFUGE FOR GIRLS.

The Ontario Refuge for Girls is located in the same building as the Mercer Reformatory, Toronto, but the work is kept entirely separate from the adult branch. This institution is intended for the care and reformation of wayward girls under sixteen, committed by magistrates or judges.

VICTORIA INDUSTRIAL SCHOOL.

The Victoria Industrial School at Mimico, Ontario, seven miles from Toronto, is intended for the industrial training of wayward boys under 14 years of age. Boys are only received on legal commitment. The institution is admirably conducted, and the results of the past five years' work have been very satisfactory. Mr. Thos. Hassard is superintendent and Mr. C. J. Atkinson, secretary, from whom any information can be obtained.

INDUSTRIAL SCHOOL FOR GIRLS.

The Alexandra Industrial School for Girls is located in the Village of East Toronto, three miles from the City of Toronto, and is intended for the industrial training of wayward girls under 14 years of age. Miss Walker is the superintendent of the school, Mrs. W. T. Aikens is the president, and Miss M. Wilkes, 84 Gloucester Street, Toronto, the secretary of the Ladies Board of Management. The procedure for committal is the same as in the case of the Victoria Industrial School for Boys.

CHILDREN'S ACT OF 1893.

The Children's Protection Act of 1893, sometimes referred to as the "Gibson Act," is printed in separate pamphlet form, and may be had on application to the Superintendent of Neglected and Dependent Children of Ontario, Parliament Buildings, Toronto. Under this Act—which will probably absorb and consolidate, later on, all laws for the protection of children—the Children's Aid Societies now being organized throughout the Province operate. Anyone interested in the extension of this movement should write for particulars, which will be freely given.

HOMES FOUND FOR CHILDREN.

It is important to note that Mr. Kelso is prepared to arrange through the agency of the Children's Aid Societies and the Children's Visiting Committees for the placing in foster homes of dependent children. Charitable institutions are particularly invited to test the efficacy of this medium for happily placing and supervising their charges. Good homes are constantly offering and it is a pity that dependent children should be deprived of the many advantages offered ; their absorption into the general community by this satisfactory process is most desirable from every standpoint.

ADOPTED CHILDREN.

Parties who have adopted children and are desirous of remembering them in their wills, should be particular to name them expressly, as otherwise they would not share in the division of an estate. In justice to the children this matter should be attended to in good time.

CORRESPONDENCE WELCOMED.

For the information of the general public it might be stated that the Superintendent of Neglected Children will be glad to receive communications on any of the following, among other subjects :

Giving particulars of the need for child-saving work in Ontario, or reporting work done for the benefit of neglected children.

Asking information as to the formation of a Children's Aid Society in towns where there is no organization.

Reporting cases of continued ill-treatment or gross neglect of children.

Reporting children in need of homes.—Good homes found for dependent children of all ages.

Making application for the care of a child.—Parties willing to give a home to a little boy or girl are asked to write.

Offering assistance in carrying on this work, especially in rural districts, or offering to distribute child-saving literature at conventions or among friends.

Address—J. J. Kelso, Parliament Buildings, Toronto.

MAINTENANCE OF WIVES DESERTED BY HUSBANDS.

CHAPTER 23, ONTARIO STATUTES, 1888.

Sec. 2.—Any married woman deserted by her husband may summon her husband before any stipendiary or police magistrate, or any two of Her Majesty's justices of the peace ; and thereupon such magistrate or justices, if satisfied that the husband, being able wholly or in part to maintain his wife, or his wife and family, has wilfully refused or neglected so to do, and has deserted his wife, may order that the husband shall pay to his wife such weekly sum, not exceeding $5.00, as the magistrate or justices may consider to be in accordance with his means and with any means the wife may have for support and the support of her family.

5.—(1) In case of non-payment of any sum so ordered, together with the costs, for the space of twenty-one days after order has been made, or such time, if any, as the order may provide, and when and so often as the payment so ordered is in arrears, such married woman may procure from the magistrate or justices making the said order, a summons returnable on the tenth day after the service thereof, and such·summons may be served either personally on the husband, or in such other manner as the magistrate or justices may in writing direct, requiring the husband to attend at the time and place mentioned in said summons, to shew cause why a warrant of distress should not issue for the levying by distress of any of the sums ordered to be paid by him under the preceding section, together with the said costs and the costs of and incidental to such summons under this section.

6.—All cases arising under this Act shall be tried in private, at the discretion of the magistrate or justices.

PROTECTION OF MARRIED WOMEN.

CHAPTER 132, R. S. O.

21.—Any married woman whose husband from habitual drunkenness, profligacy or other cause neglects or refuses to provide for her support and that of his family, or any woman who is deserted or abandoned by her husband, may obtain an order of protection, entitling her to have and to enjoy all the earnings of her minor children and any acquisitions therefrom, free from the debts of her husband and without his consent, in as full and ample a manner as if she continued sole and unmarried.

(5) The hearing of an application for an order of protection or for an order discharging the same may be public or private at the discretion of the judge or police magistrate.

POWERS OF MUNICIPAL COUNCILS.

CHAPTER 184, R. S. O.

The aldermen or councillors of any municipality may pass laws as follows:

Giving Intoxicating Liquors to Minors.—Sec. 489, sub-sec. 32.—For preventing the sale or gift of intoxicating drink to a child, apprentice or servant, without the consent of a parent, master or legal protector;

Public Morals.—Sub-sec. 33.—For preventing the posting of indecent placards, writings or pictures, or the writing of indecent words, or the making of indecent pictures or drawings, on walls or fences in the streets or public places;

Sub-sec. 34.—For preventing vice, drunkenness, profane swearing, obscene, blasphemous or grossly insulting language, and other immorality and indecency.

FOR SUPPRESSION OF BABY-FARMS.

CHAPTER 209, R. S. O.

Sec. 1.—It shall not be lawful for any person to retain or receive for hire or reward more than one infant—and in case of twins, more than two infants—under the age of one year, for the purpose of nursing or maintaining such infants apart from their parents for a longer period than twenty-four hours, except in a house which has been registered as herein provided.

Subsequent sections provide for police regulation and inspection.

Penalty. A fine of $20. and costs, or in default of payment, six months imprisonment. Cases may be brought before any magistrate or two justices of the peace.

TRIAL OF YOUNG PERSONS.

CHAPTER 58, CANADA STATUTES, 1894.

The trials of young persons apparently under the age of 16 years shall take place without publicity, and separately and apart from the trials of other accused persons, and at suitable times to be designated and appointed for that purpose.

SELLING LIQUOR TO MINORS.

CHAPTER 194, R. S. O.

Sec. 76.—Any licensed person who allows to be supplied in his licensed premises by purchase or otherwise, any description whatever of liquor to any person apparently under the age of eighteen years, of either sex, not being resident on the premises or a *bona fide* guest or lodger shall, as well as the person who actually gives or supplies the liquor, be liable to pay a penalty of not less than $10 and not exceeding $20 for every such offence.

(2) Any licensed person who allows to be supplied in his licensed premises, by sale or otherwise, any description whatever of liquor to any person under the age of twenty-one years (hereinafter called minor) in respect of whom a notice in writing has been given to any such licensed person, signed by the father, mother, guardian or master of such minor, correctly stating the age of such minor, and forbidding such licensed person to sell or supply such minor with liquor, the said minor not being resident on the premises or *bona fide* guest or lodger shall, as well as the person who actually gives or supplies the liquor be liable to pay a penalty of not less than $10 and not exceeding $20 besides costs for every such offence.

SELLING TOBACCO TO MINORS.
CHAPTER 52, ONTARIO STATUTES, 1892.

Sec. 1.—Any person who either directly or indirectly, sells or gives or furnishes to a minor under 18 years of age, cigarettes, cigars or tobacco in any form, shall on summary conviction thereof before a justice of the peace, be subject to a penalty of not less than $10 or more than $50 with or without costs of prosecution, or to imprisonment, with or without hard labor, for any time not exceeding thirty days.

MINORS IN BILLIARD ROOMS.
CHAPTER 204, R. S. O.

1. The keeper of a licensed pool or bagatelle room, who directly or indirectly keeps the same for hire or gain, admitting a minor under the age of sixteen years thereto, or allowing him to remain therein, without the consent of his parent or guardian, shall be subject to a fine of not exceeding $10 for the first, and not exceeding $20 for each subsequent offence, to be imposed by any justice of the peace, one half of which fine shall go to the informer ; provided always that this Act shall not apply to a minor who is a member of the family of the keeper, or his servant, or who does not go to the billiard, pool or bagatelle therein ; nor shall this Act apply to any case where the keeper, in the opinion of the justice of the peace, had reasonable cause to believe that such consent had been given by the parent or guardian, or that such minor was not under the age of sixteen.

MINORS AND PAWNBROKERS.
CHAPTER 155, R. S. O.

34. No pawnbroker shall :

(1) Purchase, receive or take any goods in pledge, from any person who appears to be under the age of fifteen years, or to be intoxicated with liquor ; nor

(2) Purchase or take in pawn, pledge or exchange, the note or memorandum aforesaid of any other pawnbroker ;

(3) Employ any servant or other person under sixteen years of age to take any pledge.

EDUCATION AND SCHOOL AGE.

" An Act Revising and Consolidating the Public School Acts," of Ontario, provides that

(1) All public schools shall be free schools, and every person between the ages of five and twenty-one years shall have the right to attend some school. Pupils may attend Kindergarten schools from four to seven years.

TRUANCY AND COMPULSORY SCHOOL ATTENDANCE.

CHAPTER 56, ONTARIO STATUTES, 1891.

2. All children between eight and fourteen years of age shall attend school for the full term during which the school of the section or municipality in which they reside is open each year, unless excused for the reasons hereinafter mentioned, and if the parents or guardians having the legal charge of such children shall fail to send them to school regularly for said full term, or if such children shall absent themselves from school without satisfactory excuse, such parents, guardians and children shall be subject to the provisions and penalties of section 9 of this Act.

3. Any person who receives into his house a child of any other person under the age of fourteen years, and who is resident with him or in his care or legal custody, shall be deemed thereby to be subject to the same duty with respect to the instruction of such child during such residence as a parent, and shall be liable to be proceeded against as in the case of a parent, if he should fail to cause such child to be instructed as required by this Act ; but the duty of the parent under this Act shall not thereby be affected or diminished and shall continue in full force.   .   .   .

9. If the parent, guardian or other person having the legal charge or control of any child, shall neglect or refuse to cause such child to attend some school after being notified as herein required (unless such child has been excused from such attendance, as provided by this Act),* the truant officer shall make, or cause to be made, a complaint against such parent, guardian or other person, before any police magistrate or justice of the peace having jurisdiction in the municipality in which the offence occurred, and upon conviction of such refusal or neglect, such parent, guardian or other person, shall be liable to a fine of not less than five dollars, nor more than twenty dollars, or the court may, in its discretion, require persons so convicted to give bonds in the penal sum of one hundred dollars, with one or

* Valid excuses are : sickness, school over two miles away and child under 10 years ; efficient training at home or elsewhere.

more sureties, to be approved of by said court, conditioned that the persons so convicted shall cause the child or children under their legal charge or control, to attend some school within five days thereafter, and to remain at school as required by this Act.　　.　　.　　.

11. The assessors of every municipality shall annually, when making their assessment, enter in a book, to be provided by the clerk of the municipality, in the Form A in the schedule to this Act, the name, age and residence of every child between the age of eight and fourteen years, resident in the municipality, and the name and residence of such child's parent or guardian, and return the said book to the clerk of the municipality, with the assessment roll for the use of the truant officer.

———

CHILDREN EMPLOYED IN FACTORIES.

Chapter 208, R. S. O.

6—(1) No boy under twelve years of age, and no girl under fourteen years of age shall be employed in any factory.

6—(3) It shall not be lawful for a child, young girl or woman to be employed for more than ten hours in one day, nor more than for sixty hours in any one week, unless a different apportionment of the hours of labor per day has been made for the sole purpose of giving a shorter day's work on Saturday.

6—(4) In every factory the employer shall allow every child and every young girl and woman therein employed not less than one hour at noon of each day for meals, but such hour shall not be counted as part of the time herein limited as respects the employment of children, young girls and women.

6—(5) If the inspector so directs in writing, the employer shall not allow any child, young girl or woman to take meals in any room wherein any manufacturing process is then being carried on. And if the inspector so directs in writing, the employer shall, at his own expense, provide a suitable room or place in the factory or in connection therewith, for the purpose of a dining and eating-room for persons employed in the factory.

7. A child shall not be allowed to clean any part of the machinery in a factory while the same is in motion by the aid of steam, water or other mechanical power ;

A young girl or woman shall not be allowed to clean such part of the machinery in a factory as is mill-gearing, while the same is in motion for the purpose of propelling any part of the manufacturing machinery ;

A child or young girl shall not be allowed to work between the fixed and traversing part of any self-acting machine while the machine is in motion by the action of steam, water or other machinery power.

17. The parent of any child or young girl employed in a factory in contravention of this Act, shall be guilty of an offence and shall, on conviction therefor, incur and pay a fine of not more than $50 and costs of prosecution, and in default of immediate payment of such fine and costs, shall be imprisoned in the common gaol of the county wherein the offence was committed for a period not exceeding three months

CHILDREN SENT BEGGING.

CHAPTER 45, ONTARIO STATUTES, 1893.

·4. Any person who causes or procures any child, being a boy under the age of fourteen years, or being a girl under the age of sixteen years, to be in any street for the purpose of begging or receiving alms, or of inducing the giving of alms, whether under the pretence of singing, playing, or performing for profit, offering anything for sale or otherwise, shall, on conviction thereof by a court of summary jurisdiction, be liable, at the discretion of the court, to a fine not exceeding one hundred dollars, or in default of payment of the said fine, or in addition thereto, to imprisonment, with or without hard labor, for any term not exceeding three months.—(Gibson Act).

CHILDREN IN PUBLIC PERFORMANCES.

CHAPTER 45, ONTARIO STATUTES, 1893.

4—(c) Any person who causes or procures any child under the age of ten years, to be at any time in any street or in any premises licensed for the sale of intoxicating liquor, or in premises licensed according to law for public entertainments, or in any circus or other place of public amusement, to which the public are admitted by payment, for the purpose of singing, playing, or performing for profit, or offering anything for sale, shall, on conviction thereof, be liable to a fine not exceeding $100, and to a term of imprisonment not exceeding three months.—(Gibson Act).

THE CURFEW LAW.

CHAPTER 45, ONTARIO STATUTES, 1893.

31. Municipal councils in cities, towns, and incorporated villages shall have power to pass by-laws for the regulation of the time after which children shall not be in the streets at nightfall without proper guardianship, and the age or apparent age, of boys and girls respectively, under which they shall be required to be in their homes at the hour appointed, and such municipal council shall in such case cause a bell or bells to be rung at or near the time appointed as a warning, to be cal'ed the "curfew bell," after which

the children so required to be in their homes or off the streets shall not be upon the public streets except under proper control or guardianship or for some unavoidable cause.

Any child so found after the time appointed shall be liable to be warned by any constable or peace officer to go home, and if after such warning the child shall be found loitering on the streets such child may be taken by such constable to its home.

Any parent or guardian may be summoned for permitting his child to habitually break said by law after having been warned in writing, and may be fined for the first offence $1, without costs, and for the second offence $2, and for a third, or any subsequent offence, $5.—(Gibson Act).

MINORS EMPLOYED IN SHOPS.

Chapter 23, R. S. O.

3 (3) A young person shall not be employed in or about a shop for a longer period than seventy-four hours, including meal times, in any one week ; nor shall a young person be so employed during any Saturday for more than fourteen hours, including meal times, nor during any other day for more than twelve hours, including meal times, unless a different apportionment of the hours of labor per day has been made for the sole purpose of giving a shorter day's work on some other day of the week ; and there shall be allowed as meal times to every young person so employed, not less than one hour for the noonday meal on each day, and to every young person so employed on any day to any hour later than seven of the clock in the afternoon, not less than forty-five minutes for another or evening meal, between five and eight of the clock in the afternoon.

SEATS FOR GIRLS EMPLOYED IN SHOPS.

Chapter 33, R. S. O.

(7) The occupier of any shop in which are employed females shall at all times provide and keep therein, a sufficient and suitable seat or chair for the use of every such female, and shall permit her to use such seat or chair when not necessarily engaged in the work or duty for which she is employed in such shop ; and any person offending against any of the provisions of this sub-section shall, upon conviction thereof, be liable to a fine not exceeding $20, with costs of the prosecution, and in default of immediate payment of such fine and costs, to be imprisoned in the common gaol of the county within which the offence was committed, for a period not exceeding one month.

BOYS EMPLOYED IN MINES.

CHAPTER 10, ONT. STATS., 1891.

4. No boy under the age of fifteen years shall be employed in or allowed to be for the purposes of employment in any mine below ground ; and no girl or woman shall be employed at mining work or allowed to be for the purposes of employment at mining work in or about any mine.

5. A boy or male young person of the age of fifteen and under the age of seventeen years shall not be employed in or allowed to be for the purpose of employment in any mine to which this part applies below ground for more than forty-eight hours in any one week, or more than eight hours in any one day.

REGULATIONS WHERE WOMEN ARE EMPLOYED.

CHAPTER 54, ONT. STATS., 1892.

2. This Act applies to every place of business whether for the sale or manufacture of goods, or for any other kind of business, in which women or girls are employed, and to all rooms and buildings used in connection with or for the purposes of the business.

3. Every building or apartment or place to which this Act applies shall be kept properly ventilated so as not to be injurious to the persons employed therein, and shall have in connection therewith, or within convenient distance and with convenient access thereto, a sufficient number and description of privies, earth or water-closets and urinals for the employees of the business ; such closets and urinals shall at all times be kept clean and well ventilated ; and separate sets thereof shall be provided for the use of male and female employees, and shall have respectively separate approaches.

ACT RESPECTING APPRENTICES AND MINORS.

CHAPTER 142, R. S. O.

2. Any parent, guardian or any other person having the care or charge of a minor, or any charitable society authorized by the Lieutenant-Governor to exercise the powers conferred by this Act, and having the care or charge of a minor, may, with the minor's consent, if the minor is a male not under the age of fourteen years, or is a female not under the age of twelve years, and without such consent if he or she is under such age, constitute by indenture to be the guardian of the child, any respectable, trustworthy person who is willing to assume, and by indenture does assume, the duty of a parent towards the child. The guardian shall thereupon possess the same authority over the child as he or she would have were the ward his or her own child, and shall be bound to perform the duties of a parent toward such ward.

4. No minor who has been abandoned by his or her parent or guardian, or who is dependent upon charity for support shall not be removed from any public or private charitable institution, or from the custody or control of any private person who is charitably taking care of the minor, by the father or mother or guardian of the minor against the will of the head of such public or private charitable institution, or such private person without an order for such removal, from a judge of the high court or from the judge of the county court of the county, or mayor or police magistrate of the city or town where the minor is, and the judge or other person hereby empowered to make an order for removal, may refuse to grant an order for the removal of the minor unless he is satisfied that the removal will tend to the advantage and benefit of the minor.

6. A parent, guardian, or other person having the care or charge of a minor, or any charitable society being authorized by the Lieutenant-Governor in council to exercise the power conferred by this Act, and having the care or charge of a minor, being a male and not under the age of fourteen years, may, with the consent of the minor, put and bind him as an apprentice by indenture, to any respectable and trustworthy master-mechanic, farmer or other person carrying on a trade or calling, for a term not to extend beyond the minority of the apprentice ; or in case of a female, not under the age of twelve years, may with her consent, bind the minor to any respectable and trustworthy person carrying on any trade or calling, or to domestic service with any respectable and trustworthy person for any term not to extend beyond the age of eighteen years.

29. The Lieutenant-Governor in Council may authorize any charitable society incorporated or unincorporated to exercise for a limited time or otherwise, the powers conferred by this Act, and may revoke or suspend any Order in Council made for that purpose, and after such revocation, such society shall not possess the authority to exercise such powers unless and until again authorized by Order in Council.

FOR THE PROTECTION AND REFORMATION OF NEGLECTED CHILDREN.

CHAPTER 40, ONTARIO STATUTES, 1888.

Her Majesty, by and with the advice and consent of the Legislative Assembly of the province of Ontario, enacts as follows :—

1. In this Act, the word "judge" means a judge of the high court of justice, or a judge of a county court, or a retired judge of the high court or a county or district court, or a stipendiary magistrate, or a police magistrate, or a justice of the peace specially appointed as commissioner for the trial of juvenile offenders.

A judge or retired judge of the high court shall have jurisdiction under this Act in any part of the province. Any other judge, stipendiary magistrate, police magistrate, or justice of the peace specially appointed as aforesaid, shall have jurisdiction in the county or other locality for which he holds his office. A retired judge shall have jurisdiction in the province, county, or district for which he was judge at the time of his retirement.

2. On proof that a child under fourteen years of age, by reason of the neglect, crime, drunkenness, or other vices of its parent, or from orphanage, or any other cause, is growing up in circumstances exposing such child to a bad or dissolute life, or on proof that any child under fourteen years of age, being an orphan, has been found begging in any street, highway, or public place, a judge may order such child to be committed to any industrial school or Refuge for boys or girls, or other institutions, subject to the inspection of the inspector of prisons and asylums, or to any suitable charitable society authorized under *The Act respecting Apprentices and Minors*, and willing to receive such child, to be there kept, cared for and educated, for a period not extending beyond the period at which such child shall attain the age of eighteen years.

3. Any child apparently under the age of sixteen years found frequenting, or being in the company of reputed thieves or prostitutes, or frequenting or being in a reputed house of prostitution or assignation, or living in such a house either with or without the parent or guardian of the child, may be brought before the judge, and may be by him committed to any such institution as mentioned in the preceding section.

4. When any such child is so brought before a judge a summons shall be issued to the father of the child if living and resident within the place where the child was found ; and if not, then to the mother, if she is living and so resident ; and if there is no such father or mother, then to the lawful guardian if there be one so resident ; and if not, then to the person with whom, according to the statement of the child, he or she resides ; and if there is no such person, the judge may appoint some suitable person to act in behalf of the child, requiring him or her to appear at a time and place stated in the summons, and to show cause, if any there be, why the child should not be committed to a refuge, industrial school or other charitable society aforesaid. And if the judge is of opinion that the child should be sent to any such institution as aforesaid, he may order the child to be committed accordingly.

5. No Protestant child shall be committed under this Act to a Roman Catholic institution, and no Roman Catholic shall be committed to a Protestant institution. The certificate of one of the inspectors of prisons and asylums shall be sufficient as to the character of an institution for the purpose of this section.

6. The municipality within which the child is resident at the time of the committal shall be liable for the maintenance of the child to an extent not exceeding $2 per week. The judge's certificate as to the residence of the child shall be sufficient *prima facie* evidence thereof.

2 N.C.

7. The Lieutenant-Governor may, upon request of any municipal council, appoint a commissioner or commissioners each with powers of a police magistrate to hear and determine complaints against juvenile offenders, apparently under the age of sixteen years.

8. Persons under the age of twenty-one years who are charged with offences against the laws of this province, or who are brought before a judge under this Act, shall, as far as practicable, be tried and their cases disposed of, separately and apart from other offenders and at suitable times to be designated and appointed for this purpose.

INDUSTRIAL SCHOOLS.

CHAPTER 234, R. S. O.

1. This Act may be cited as "The Industrial Schools Act," 47 V. c. 46, s. 1.

2—(1) A school in which industrial training is provided, and in which children are lodged, clothed, and fed, as well as taught, shall exclusively be deemed an industrial school within the meaning of this Act. 47, V., c. 46, s 2.

(2) "Philanthropic society," in this Act, shall mean such philanthropic society incorporated as herein mentioned, and approved by the Lieutenant-Governor in Council for the purposes of this Act. 47 V. c. 46, s. 30.

3. In case the public school board of trustees for any city or town, or the separate school trustees therein, establish an industrial school, and provide the necessary building or buildings, either by purchase, lease or otherwise, and provide the other requisites for such schools, and cause notice therefor to be given to the city inspector of public schools, or in case of a Roman Catholic industrial school then to one of the inspectors of separate schools, the said inspector shall make an examination of the school buildings so provided, and of their fitness for the reception of children and shall enquire as to the other requisites provided, and shall enquire also into the means adopted for carrying on the school, and shall report the said particulars to the Minister of Education ; and if the Minister is satisfied with the report of the inspector, he may, in writing under his hand, certify that the school is a fit and proper one for the reception of children to be sent there, and the school shall thereupon be deemed a certified industrial school for the purposes of this Act. 47 V. c. 46, s. 3.

4. The notice of the grant of the certificate shall forthwith be given to the board by the police magistrate, and the judge of the County Court, and shall likewise be inserted by the board in the Ontario Gazette, and a copy of the Gazette containing the notice shall be conclusive evidence of the grant which may also be proved by the certificate itself, or by an instrument purporting to be a copy of the certificate, and attested as such by the Minister of Education for the time being, or his deputy. 47 V. c. 46, s. 4.

5—(1) Any board of school trustees may delegate the powers, rights and privileges conferred upon such board by this Act, respecting the establishment, control and management of an industrial school to any philanthropic society or societies incorporated under the Act respecting benevolent, provident and other societies, or under any other Act in force in this province, and the society or societies to which such powers are delegated, shall have and may exercise all the powers so delegated, and this Act shall thereafter apply to the philanthropic society or societies as fully as to the said boards ; provided, nevertheless, that the chairman and secretary of the board of public school trustees in the city or town, shall be members of the board of management of the society when acting under powers delegated by the board of public school trustees, and the chairman and secretary of the separate shool board shall be members of the board of management when the society is acting under powers delegated by the separate school board.

(2) The by-laws of such society shall be subject to the approval of the Lieutenant-Governor. 47 V. c. 46, s. 5.

6. The respective school boards shall provide the teachers necessary for the industrial school, and the general superintendent of the school shall, when practicable, be selected from the teachers so appointed. 47 V. c. 46, s. 6.

7. Any person may at a special sitting bring before the police magistrate or before the judge of the county court, and except in cities where there is a police magistrate, before any justice of the peace, any child apparently under the age of fourteen years, who comes within any of the following descriptions, namely :

(1) Who is found begging or receiving alms, or being in any street or public place for the purpose of begging or receiving alms ;

(2) Who is found wandering, and not having any home or settled place of abode or proper guardianship, or not having any lawful occupation or business, or visable means of subsistence ;

(3) Who is found destitute, either being an orphan or having a surviving parent who is undergoing penal servitude or imprisonment ;

(4) Whose parent, step-parent or guardian, represents to the judge or magistrate that he is unable to control the child, and that he desires the child to be sent to an industrial school, under this Act ;

(5) Who, by reason of neglect, drunkenness, or other vices of the parents, is suffered to be growing up without salutary parental control and education, or in circumstances exposing him to lead an idle and dissolute life ;

(6) Who has been found guilty of petty crime, and who, in the opinion of the judge or magistrate before whom he has been convicted, should be sent to an industrial school instead of to a gaol or reformatory. 47 V. c. 46. s. 7.

8. No formal information shall be requisite to authorize proceedings being taken under the next preceding section, but the judge or magistrate, before issuing his order shall have such child brought before him, and shall,

in its presence, take evidence in writing under oath of the facts charged, and shall make responsible enquiry into the truth thereof. 47 V. c. 46, s. 8.

9. If the judge or magistrate is satisfied on enquiry that it is expedient to deal with the child under this Act, he may order him to be sent to a certified industrial school ; which order shall be in writing, and shall specify the name of the school, and the time for which the child is to be detained in the school, being such time as to the judge or magistrate seems proper for the teaching and training of the child, but not in any case extending beyond the time when the child will attain the age of sixteen years. 47 V. c. 46, s. 9.

10. The said school corporations or philanthropic societies may admit into the industrial schools established by them, all children apparently under the age of fourteen years who are committed to the said school by the judge or magistrate ; and the said corporations or societies, respectively, shall have power to place the said children at such employment, and cause them to be instructed in such branches of useful knowledge as are suitable to their years and capacities. 47 V. c. 46, s. 10.

11. In case an industrial school is established by the Roman Catholic separate school trustees in any city the judge or magistrate shall endeavor to ascertain the religious persuasion to which every child to be sent by him to an industrial school belongs, and shall, as far as practicable, send Roman Catholic children to the Roman Catholic industrial school and other children to the other industrial school ; and if a parent or guardian, or in case there is no parent or guardian, then if the nearest adult relation of a child in a Roman Catholic separate school claims that the child should be sent to the industrial school under the said board of trustees, or claims that a child in an industrial school established by the latter should be sent to the Roman Catholic separate school, the Minister of Education, on being satisfied of the justness of such claim, shall order a transfer of the child accordingly, provided that the managers of the school to which the transfer is to be made are willing to receive the child. 47 V. c. 46, s. 11.

12. A minister of the religious persuasion to which a child appears to belong may visit the child at the school on such days and at such times as may be from time to time fixed by regulations of the education department in that behalf, for the purpose of instruction in religion. 47 V. c. 46, s. 12.

13. The school corporation, or philanthropic society, may permit a child sent to their industrial school under this Act to live at the dwelling of any trustworthy and respectable person ; provided, that a report is made forthwith to the Minister of Education, in such manner as he thinks fit to require, of every instance in which this discretion is exercised. 47 V. c. 146, s. 13.

14. Any permission for that purpose may be revoked at any time by the school corporation or philanthropic society ; and thereupon the child

to whom the permission relates shall he required to return to the school. 47 V. c. 46, s. 14.

15. The time during which the child is absent from the school under permission shall, except where the permission is withdrawn on account of the child's misconduct, be deemed to be part of the time of his detention in the school, and at the expiration of the time allowed by the permission, he shall be taken back to the school. 47 V. c. 46, s. 15.

16. A child escaping from the person with whom he is placed, or refusing to return to the school on the revocation of his permission or at the expiration of the time allowed thereby, shall be deemed to have escaped from the school. 47 V. c. 46, s. 16.

17. The Minister of Education may at any time order any child to be discharged from a certified industrial school, either absolutely or on such conditions as he thinks fit, and the child shall be discharged accordingly. 47 V. c. 46, s. 17.

18. In case an application is made to any court or judge for the discharge from the industrial school of any child committed thereto under the provisions of section 7 of this Act, notwithstanding any irregularity in or insufficiency of the order or other proceedings, no order shall be made for such discharge in case the court or judge shall deem it for the benefit of the child that it should remain in the industrial school, and it shall appear by the depositions taken before the committing judge or magistrate that the child was liable to be committed to the industrial school under the provisions of this Act. 47 V. c. 46, s. 18.

19. The committing judge or magistrate shall deliver to the constable or other person having the execution of his order, the deposition taken by him, or a certified copy thereof, which depositions or copy shall be delivered by the constable or other person to the superintendent or officer receiving the child into the said industrial school ; such copy shall be *prima facie* proof of the contents of the original depositions and shall be receivable in evidence upon any application for the discharge of the child committed thereunder. 47 V. c. 46, s. 19.

20. The school corporation or philanthropic society may at any time during the period of detention of a child in a school, exercise all the powers conferred by section 2 and 6 of the Act respecting apprentices and minors, upon the charitable societies therein mentioned. 47 V. c. 46, s. 20.

21. The school corporation or philanthropic society may from time to time make rules for the management and discipline of the certified industrial school established by the board or society, such rules not being inconsistent with the provisions of this Act ; but the rules shall not be enforced until they have been approved by the education department ; and rules so approved shall not be altered without the like approval ; a printed copy of

the rules purporting to be rules of a school so approved and signed by the Minister of Education shall be evidence of the rules of the school. 47 V. c. 46, s. 21.

22. On the complaint of the school corporation or philanthropic society, or of any agent of the school corporation or philanthropic society at any time during the detention of a child in a certified industrial school, the judge of the division court of the division in which the parent, step-parent or guardian resides, shall in the form or to the effect of the schedule to this Act issued and served according to the ordinary practice of the court, examine into his ability to maintain the child, and the judge may, if he thinks fit, make an order on such parent, step-parent or guardian for the payment to the school corporation or philanthropic society of such weekly sum, not exceeding $1.50* per week, as to the judge seems reasonable, during the whole or any part of the time during which the child is liable to be detained in the school, and the said order shall for all purposes be a judgment of the division court. 47 V. c. 46, s. 22 ; 50 V. c. 7, s. 26.

23. The judge making such order, or any other judge holding the division court, may from time to time vary any such order as circumstances require, on the application either of the person on whom the order is made, or of the school corporation or philanthropic society or its agent, on fourteen days' notice of the application being first given to the other party. 47 V. c. 46, s. 23.

Sec. 24.—The officers of the court shall be entitled to charge fees upon proceedings had under the next preceeding two sections, according to the lowest division court scale, and in every case all costs shall be in the discretion of the judge. 47 V. c 46, s. 24.

Sec. 25.—(1) In case a child sent by judge or magistrate to an industrial school has not resided in the city or town in which said school is situated, or to which it is attached for a period of one year, but has resided for that period in some other county, city or separated town, the school corporation or philanthropic society may recover from the corporation of such county, city or separated town the expense of maintaining the child.

(2) If the child although he or she had resided for a period of one year, in the city in which the industrial school is situated, or to which it is attached, had, since such residence, been resident for a period of one year in some other municipality, the school corporation or philanthropic society, may, in like manner, recover the expense of maintenance from the county, city or separated town in which the child last resided for a period of one year.

(3) When the child resided for one year last preceeding its admission to said school in the city or town in which the industrial school is situated or to which it is attached, such city or town shall pay a sum of not less than $1.50

---

*Since increased to $2.

per week* towards the expenses of maintaining in the school each child whose maintenance is not otherwise fully provided for ; and such city or town shall have the power to recover the amount so paid from the parents if able to pay it. 47 V. c. 46, s. 25 ; 50 V. c. 7, s. 26.

Sec. 26.—If a child sent to a certified industrial school, and while liable to be detained there, escapes from the school, or neglects to attend thereat, he may at any time before the expiration of his period of detention, be apprehended without warrant, and may be brought back to the same school ; there to be detained during the period equal to so much of his period of detention as remained unexpired at the time of his escape. 47 V. c. 46, s. 26.

Sec. 27.—In case any money is granted or provided by the Legislature for the support of industrial schools, it shall be the duty of the Minister of Education, and he is hereby empowered, to apportion the money on or before the 1st day of May, to the several industrial schools in the Province, according to the average number of pupils at such school from time to time during the proceeding year as compared with the whole average number at the industrial schools established under this Act. 47 V. c. 46, s. 27.

Sec. 28 —Industrial schools established under this Act shall be under the same inspection, and subject to the same laws in all respects as other schools, except so far as may be inconsistent with this Act. 47 V. c. 46, s. 28.

Sec. 29.—Whenever it is satisfactorily proved that the parents of any child committed under the provisions of this Act have reformed and are leading orderly and industrious lives, and are in a condition to exercise salutary parental control over their children, and to provide them with proper education and employment, or whenever said parents being dead, any person offers to make suitable provision for the care, nurture and education of such child as will conduce to the public welfare, and will give satisfactory security for the performance of the same, then the board of school trustees or philanthropic society may discharge said child to the parents or to the party making provision for the care of the child as aforesaid. 47 V. c. 46, s. 29.

———

NOTE.—Girls under 14 may be committed to the Industrial School for Girls at East Toronto under the same procedure in all respects as boys. Both schools are under the same management.

———

* An amendment made in 1888 (chapt. 39) increases the payment to $2 per week.

SCHEDULE.

(*Section 22.*)

[L. S.]

SUMMONS FOR MAINTENANCE IN INDUSTRIAL SCHOOL.

In the

Division Court of the County of

BETWEEN the Public School Board of

Plaintiffs.

and

C. D.

Defendant.

You the above named defendant are hereby summoned to appear at the next sitting of the court to holden at   in the County of   on   the   day of   A. D. 188   , at the hour of ten o'clock in the forenoon, to answer the allegation of the plaintiff, that you the said   are liable for the expense of maintaing one *E. D.*, a boy detained in the Industrial School, under the charge of the above named plaintiffs, in the City of

And, further, you are hereby required to take notice that the plaintiffs claim that you are able to pay the sum of $ per week towards the said expenses, and if you do not appear at the said time and place, such order will be made in your absence as may seem just.

Dated this   day of   A. D. 189   .

By the Court,

X, Y.,

Clerk.

NOTE.—I have not heard of even one case where the above has been acted upon. In my opinion the plaintiff should be the municipal corporation.—Ed.

For other Acts affecting Industrial Schools see the following :

Escapes from an Industrial School or a reformatory— Dominion Act, 53 Vic., chap. 37.

Incorrigible boys may be transferred to the Reformatory—Chapter 76, Ontario Statutes, 1890.

Judicial order deciding the municipality liable for maintenance—Chapter 76, sec. 5, Ontario Statutes, 1890.

Temporary provision for boys under 13 committed to reformatory—Chapter 75, Ontario Statutes, 1890.

School Boards may assist Industrial Schools—Chapter 59, Ontario Statutes, 1891.

Authorizing Government to aid Industrial Schools—Chapter 50, Statutes of 1893.

PLACING OUT CHILDREN.

CHAPTER 59, ONTARIO STATUTES, 1891.

4. The board of management of any Industrial School, in addition to the powers they now possess, may arrange for the maintenance and education of any child committed to their care in any satisfactory home outside of such school, provided that the control of the board over such child shall not thereby be abated or diminished, nor the liability of any municipality for the maintenance of such child thereby increased, and in all cases when the cost of maintenance at such house is less than the statutory liability of any municipality such municipality shall be chargeable only with the amount paid by said board of management.

ONTARIO REFUGE FOR GIRLS.

CHAPTER 240, R. S. O.

7. A county or district county judge or police magistrate may by his warrant commit to the Ontario Refuge for Girls any girl apparently under the age of ~~fourteen~~ years who comes within any of the following descriptions :—

1. Who is found begging or receiving alms or being in any street or public place for the purpose of begging or receiving alms.

2. Who is found wandering about and not having any home or settled place of abode or proper guardianship.

3. Who is found destitute and is an orphan, or who has a surviving parent who is undergoing penal servitude or imprisonment.

4. Whose parent, step-parent, or guardian represents to the judge or police magistrate that he is unable to control the girl, and that he desires her to be sent to the Refuge. The word guardian as used herein shall include any officer of a society under whose charge the girl is or any person standing in fact in the place of a parent, although not lawfully appointed a guardian.

5. Who by reason of the neglect, drunkenness, or other vices of her parents or either of them, or any other persons in whose charge such girl is, is suffered to be growing up without salutary control and education or in circumstances which render it probable that such girl will, unless placed under proper control, lead an idle and desolute life.

Girls Under Sixteen.—It is very important to note here that under Chapter 40, Ontario Statutes, 1888, Section 3, any girl apparently under the age of 16 years, being in the company of reputed thieves or prostitutes or frequenting houses of prostitution or assignation or living in such a house with or without the parent or guardian may be committed to the Refuge for Girls.

Sec. 20.—In case any responsible and trustworthy person is willing to undertake the charge of any girl committed to the Refuge, either under this Act or any other Act of the Legislature of this Province, whether she be over or under the age of twelve years, as an apprentice to the trade or calling of such person or for the purpose of domestic service, the superintendent may, with the consent of the Inspector of Prisons, bind the said girl to such person for any term not to extend beyond the girl's attaining the age of eighteen years, and the inspector shall thereupon order that such girl shall be absolutely discharged or discharged on probation, and she shall be discharged accordingly ; any wages reserved in any such indenture shall be payable to the girl or to some other person for her benefit.

For the entire Act see Chapter 240, R. S. O. For Dominion Acts relating to the Refuge see Revised Statutes of Canada, 1886, Chapter 183, Part II.

ONTARIO REFORMATORY FOR BOYS.

CHAPTER 241, R. S. O.

2. The Reformatory shall have for its objects the custody and detention, with a view to their education, industrial training, and moral reclamation, of such boys (between the ages of 13 and 16) as shall be lawfully sentenced to confinement therein.

BOYS UNDER THIRTEEN.—Sec. 1. No boy shall be received for confinement in the Ontario Reformatory for Boys who appears to the superintendent of the Reformatory to be under the age of thirteen years. Chapter 26, Ontario Statutes, 1890.

THIRTEEN TO SIXTEEN.

CHAPTER 76, ONTARIO STATUTES, 1890.

Sec. 6. Section 27 of the Act respecting the Ontario Reformatory for Boys is amended by striking out the words ten and thirteen, and inserting in lieu thereof the words "thirteen and sixteen." [The ages governing committal to this institution]

For further particulars as to Ontario Reformatory for Boys, appointment of officials, etc., see the Act, Chapter 241, R. S. O. For Dominion Acts, see R. S. C., Chapter 182, sec. 49-50.

PARENT AND CHILD. *

CHAPTER 137, R.S.O.

1. The High Court or Surrogate Court may, upon the application of the mother of an infant, make such order as the court or judge sees fit regarding the custody of the infant and the right of access thereto of either parent,

---

* This Act applies to children in general, and does not come within the scope of child-saving work. Only such clauses as seem of general interest are given here.—ED.

having regard to the welfare of the infant and to the conduct of the parents, and to the wishes as well of the mother as of the father, and may afterwards alter, vary, or discharge the order on the application of either parent, and in every case may make such order respecting the costs of the mother and the liability of the father for the same as the court or judge may think fit.

The court or judge may also make an order for the maintenance of the infant by payment by the father thereof or by the payment out of any estate to which the infant is in·itled of such sum or sums of money from time to time as acccording to the pecuniary circumstances of the father or the value of the estate the court or judge thinks just and reasonable.

10. The Surrogate Court for the county within which an infant resides may appoint the father of the infant to be guardian or may, with the consent of the father, appoint some other suitable person or persons, but if the infant is of the age of fourteen years or over neither of such appointments shall be made without the consent of the infant, or if the infant have no father living or any legal guardian authorized by law to take the care of his person and the charge of his estate the said court may appoint a guardian or guardians of the infant.

11. Upon the written application of the infant, or the friend or friends of the infant, residing within the jurisdiction of the Surrogate Court to which application is made, and after proof of twenty days public notice of the application, the judge of the court may appoint some suitable and discreet person or persons to be guardian or guardians of the infant.

13. On the death of the father of an infant the mother, if surviving, shall be the guardian of the infant, either alone, when no guardian has been appointed by the father, or jointly with any guardian appointed by the father.

Where no guardian has been appointed by the father the High Court or Surrogate Court may appoint a guardian or guardians to act jointly with the mother.

14. The mother of an infant may, by deed or will, provisionally nominate some fit person or persons to act as guardian or guardians of the infant after her death, jointly with the father of the infant, and the court or a judge after her death, if it be shown to the satisfaction of the court or a judge that the father is for any reason unfitted to be the sole guardian of his children, may confirm the appointment of such guardian or guardians, who shall thereupon be empowered to act as aforesaid.

18. The guardian of any infant shall have authority to act for and on behalf of the said ward, may appear in any court and prosecute or defend any action in his or her name, and shall have the charge and management of his or her estate, and the care of his or her person and education. The guardian may also, with the consent of the ward and the approbation of two justices of the peace, place or bind him or her an apprentice to any lawful trade, profession, or employment.

DOMINION CRIMINAL CODE.

INDECENT ACTS.

Sec 177.—Every one is guilty of an offence and liable, on summary conviction before two Justices of the Peace, to a fine of fifty dollars or to six month's imprisonment with or without hard labour, or to both fine and imprisonment, who wilfully—

(a) In the presence of one or more persons does any indecent act in any place to which the public have or are permitted to have access ; or

(b) Does any indecent act in any place intending thereby to insult or offend any person.

INCEST.

Sec. 176.—Every parent and child, every brother and sister, and every grandparent and grandchild who cohabit or have sexual intercour e with each other, shall each of them if aware of this consanguinity, be deemed to have committed incest and be guilty of an indictable offence and liable to fourteen years imprisonment, and the male person shall also be liable to be whipped.

PUBLISHING OBSCENE MATTER.

Sec. 179.—Every one is guilty of an indictable offence and liable to two years' imprisonment who knowingly, without lawful justification or excuse—

(a) Publicly sells, or exposes for public sale or to public view, any obscene book or other printed or written matter, or any picture, photograph, model or other object, tending to corrupt morals ; or

(b) Publicly exhibits any disgusting object or any indecent show.

SEDUCTION.

Sec. 181.—Every one is guilty of an indictable offence and liable to two years' imprisonment who seduces or has illicit connection with any girl of previously chaste character, of or above the age of fourteen years.

SEDUCTION OF WARD OR SERVANT.

Sec. 183.—Every one is guilty of an indictable offence and liable to two years' imprisonment, who, being a guardian, seduces or has illicit connection with his ward, and every one who seduces or has illicit connection with any woman or girl of previously chaste character and under the age of twenty-one years who is in his employment in a factory, mill or workshop, or who being in common employment with him in such factory, mill or workshop, is, in respect of her employment or work in such factory, mill or workshop, under or in any way subject to his control or direction.   53 V., c. 37, s. 4.

PARENT OR GUARDIAN PROCURING DEFILEMENT.

Sec. 186.—Every one, who, being the parent or guardian of any girl or woman.

(*a*) Procures such girl or woman to have carnal connection with any man other than the procurer ; or

(*b*) Orders, is party to, permits or knowingly receives the avails of the defilement, seduction or prostitution of such girl or woman, is guilty of an indictable offence. and liable to fourteen years' imprisonment if such girl or woman is under the age of fourteen years, and if such girl or woman is of or above the age of fourteen years to five years imprisonment.

HOUSEHOLDERS PERMITTING DEFILEMENT OF GIRLS ON THEIR PREMISES.

Sec. 187.—Every one who, being the owner and occupier of any premises, or having, or acting or assisting in, the management or control thereof, induces or knowingly suffers any girl of such age as is in this section mentioned to resort to or be in or upon such premises for the purpose of being unlawfully and carnally known by any man, whether such carnal knowledge is intended to be with any particular man, or generally, is guilty of an indictable offence and—

(*a*) Is liable to ten years' imprisonment if such girl is under the age of fourteen years ; and

(*b*) Is liable to two years' imprisonment if such girl is of or above the age of fourteen and under the age of sixteen years.

VAGRANCY.

Sec. 207.—Every one is a loose, idle or disorderly person or vagrant, and liable to a fine not exceeding $50 or to six months imprisonment who—

Not having any visible means of maintaining himself lives without employment.

Being able to work and therefor, or by other means, to maintain himself, and willfully refuses or neglects to do so.

Loiters in any street, road, highway or public place, and obstructs passengers by standing across the foot path, or by using insulting language, or in any other way.

Causes a disturbance in or near any street, road or highway or public place, by screaming, swearing or singing or by being drunk, or by impeding or incommoding peaceable passengers.

Being a common prostitute or night walker, wanders in the public streets or highways, lanes or places of public meeting or gathering of people and does not give a satisfactory account of herself.

Having no peaceable profession or calling to maintain himself by, for the most part supports himself by gaming or crime, or by the avails of prostitution.

DUTY TO PROVIDE NECESSARIES OF LIFE.

Sec. 209 —Every one who has charge of any other person unable, by reason either of detention, age, sickness, insanity or any other cause to withdraw himself from such charge, and unable to provide himself with the necessaries of life, is, whether such charge is undertaken by him under any contract, or is imposed upon him by law, or by reason of his unlawful act, under a legal duty to supply that person with the necessaries of life, and is criminally responsible for omitting, without lawful excuse, to perform such duty if the death of such person is caused, or if his life is endangered or his health has been or is likely to be permanently injured, by such omission.

NON-SUPPORT OF CHILDREN.

Sec. 210.—Every one who as parent, guardian or head of a family is under a legal duty to provide necessaries for any child under the age of sixteen years, is criminally responsible for omitting, without lawful excuse, to do so while such child remains a member of his or her household, whether such child is helpless or not, if the death of such child is caused, or if his life is endangered or his health is or is likely to be permanently injured by such omission.

(2) Every one who is under a legal duty to provide necessaries for his wife, is criminally responsible for omitting, without lawful excuse, so to do, if the death of his wife is caused, or if her life is endangered, or her health is or is likely to be permanently injured by such omission.

DUTY TOWARDS SERVANTS OR APPRENTICES.

Sec. 211.—Every one who, as master or mistress, has contracted to provide necessary food, clothing or lodging for any servant or apprentice under the age of sixteen years, is under a legal duty to provide the same, and is criminally responsible for omitting, without lawful excuse, to perform such duty if the death of such servant or apprentice is caused or if his life is endangered, or his health has been or is likely to be permanently injured, by such omission.

PENALTY.

Sec. 215.—Every one is guilty of an indictable offence and liable to three years' imprisonment who, being bound to perform any duty specified in sections two hundred and nine, two hundred and ten and two hundred and eleven without lawful excuse neglects or refuses to do so ; unless the offence amounts to culpable homicide.

NEGLECTING CHILDREN ¡UNDER TWO YEARS OLD.

Sec. 216.—Every one is guilty of an indictable offence and liable to three years' imprisonment who unlawfully abandons or exposes any child under the age of two years, whereby its life is endangered, or its health is permanently injured.

(2) The words "abandon" and "expose" include a wilful omission to take charge of the child on the part of the person legally bound to do so, and any mode of dealing with it calculated to leave it exposed to risk without protection.

CAUSING BODILY HARM TO APPRENTICES OR SERVANTS.

Sec. 217.—Every one is guilty of an indictable offence and liable to three years' imprisonment who, being legally liable as master or mistress to provide for, any apprentice or servant, unlawfully does, or causes to be done, any bodily harm to any such apprentice or servant so that the life of such apprentice or servant is endangered or the health of such apprentice or servant has been, or is likely to be, permanently injured.

CONCEALING DEAD BODY OF CHILD.

Sec. 240.—Every one is guilty of an indictable offence, and liable to two years' imprisonment, who disposes of the dead body of any child in any manner, with intent to conceal the fact that its mother was delivered of it, whether the child died before, or during, or after birth.

DEFILING CHILDREN UNDER FOURTEEN.

Sec. 269.—Every one is guilty of an indictable offence and liable to imprisonment for life, and to be whipped, who carnally knows any girl under the age of fourteen years, not being his wife, whether he believes her to be of that age or not.

CONSENT OF CHILD NO DEFENCE.

Sec. 261.—It is no defence to a charge of indictment for any indecent assault on a young person under the age of fourteen years to prove that he or she consented to the act of indecency.

ATTEMPTED ASSAULTS.

Sec. 270.—Every one who attempts to have unlawfully carnal knowledge of any girl under the age of fourteen years is guilty of an indictable offence and liable to two years' imprisonment, and to be whipped.

KILLING UNBORN CHILDREN.

Sec. 271.—Every one is guilty of an indictable offence, and liable to imprisonment for life, who causes the death of any child which has not become a human being, in such a manner that he would have been guilty of murder if such child had been born.

'2.) No one is guilty of any offence, who, by means which he, in good faith, considers necessary for the preservation of the life of the mother of the child, causes the death of any such child before or during its birth.

ABDUCTION.   .

Sec. 283.—Every one is guilty of an indictable offence, and liable to five years' imprisonment who unlawfully takes or causes to be taken, any unmarried girl, being under the age of sixteen years, out of the possession and against the will of her father or mother or of any other person having the lawful care or charge of her.

(2.) It is immaterial whether the girl is taken with her own consent or at her own suggestion or not.

(3.) It is immaterial whether or not the offender believed the girl to be of or above the age of sixteen.

STEALING CHILDREN UNDER FOURTEEN.

Sec. 284.—Every one is guilty of an indictable offence and liable to seven years' imprisonment, who with intent to deprive any parent or guardian, or other person having the lawful charge, of any child, or with intent to steal any article about or on the person of such child, unlawfully—

(a) takes or entices away or detains any such child ; or

(b) receives or harbors any such child knowing it to have been dealt with as aforesaid.

(2.) Nothing in this section shall extend to any one who gets possession of any child, claiming in good faith a right to the possession of the child.—

SELLING PISTOLS TO MINORS.

Sec. 106.—Every one is guilty of an offence and liable on summary conviction to a penalty not exceeding $50 who sells or gives any pistol or air-gun or any ammunition therefor, to a minor under the age of sixteen years, unless he establishes to the satisfaction of the justice before whom he is charged, that he used reasonable diligence in endeavoring to ascertain the age of the minor before making such sale or gift, and that he had good reason to believe that such minor was not under the age of 16.

(2.) Every one is guilty of an offence and liable on summary conviction to a penalty not exceeding $25 who sells any pistol or air-gun without keeping a record of such sale, the date thereof, the name of the purchaser and of the makers' name or other mark by which such arm may be identified.

CHAPTER 28, STATUTES OF CANADA, 1894.

AN ACT RESPECTING THE ARREST, TRIAL AND IMPRISONMENT OF YOUTHFUL OFFENDERS.

[Assented to 23rd July, 1894.]

WHEREAS it is desirable to make provision for the separation of youthful offenders from contact with older offenders and habitual criminals during their arrest and trial, and to make better provisions than now exists for their commitment to places where they may be reformed and trained to useful lives, instead of their being imprisoned ; Therefore Her Majesty, by and with the advice and consent of the Senate and the House of Commons of Canada, enacts as follows :

1. Section 550 of "The Criminal Code, 1892," is hereby repealed and the following section substituted therefor :

" 550. The trials of young persons apparently under the age of sixteen years, shall take place without publicity, and separately and apart from the trials of other accused persons, and at suitable times to be designated and appointed for that purpose."

2. Young persons apparently under the age of sixteen years who are :

(a) Arrested upon any warrant ; or

(b) Committed to custody at any stage of a preliminary enquiry into a charge for an indictable offence ; or

3 N.C.

(*c*) Committed to custody at any stage of a trial, either for an indictable offence or for an offence punishable on summary conviction ; or

(*d*) Committed to custody after such trial, but before imprisonment under sentence, shall be kept in custody separate from older persons charged with criminal offences, and separate from all persons undergoing sentences of imprisonment, and shall not be confined in the lockups or police stations with older persons charged with criminal offences, or with ordinary criminals.

3. If any child, appearing to the court or justice before whom the child is tried to be under the age of fourteen years, is convicted in the Province of Ontario of any offence against the law of Canada, whether indictable or punishable on summary conviction, such court or justice, instead of sentencing the child to any imprisonment provided by law in such case, may order that the child shall be committed to the charge of any home for destitute and neglected children, or to the charge of any Children's Aid Society duly organized and approved by the Lieutenant-Governor of Ontario in Council, or to any certified Industrial School.

4. Whenever in the Province of Ontario an information or complaint is laid or made against any boy under the age of twelve years, or girl under the age of thirteen years, for the commission of any offence against the law of Canada, whether indictable or punishable on summary conviction, the court or justice seized thereof shall give notice thereof in writing to the executive officer of the Children's Aid Society, if there be one in the county and shall allow him opportunity to investigate the charges made, and may also notify the parents of the child, or either of them, or other person apparently interested in the welfare of the child.

(2) The court or justice may advise, and counsel with the said officer and with the parents or such other person, and may consider any report made by the said officer upon the charges.

(3) If, after such consultation and advice, and upon the consideration of any report so made, and after hearing the matter of information or complaint, the court or justice is of opinion that the public interest and the welfare of the child will be best served thereby, then, instead of committing the child for trial, or sentencing the child, as the case may be, the court or justice may, by order :

(*a*) Authorize the said officer to take the child and, under the provisions of the law of Ontario, bind the child out to some suitable person until the child has attained the age of twenty-one years, or any less age ; or place the child out in some approved foster home ;

(*b*) Impose a fine not exceeding $10 ; or

(*c*) Suspend sentence for a definite period or for an indefinite period ; or

(*d*) If the child has been found guilty of the offence charged, or is shown to be wilfully wayward and unmanageable, commit the child to a certified

Industrial School, or to the Provincial Reformatory for boys, or to the Refuge for girls, as the case may be, and in such cases the report of the said officer shall be attached to the warrant of commitment.

5. Whenever an order has been made under either of the two sections next preceding, the child may thereafter be dealt with under the law of the Province of Ontario, in the same manner in all respects as if such order had been lawfully made in respect of a proceeding instituted under authority of a statute of the Province of Ontario.

6. No Protestant child dealt with under this Act, shall be committed to the care of any Roman Catholic Children's Aid Society, or to be placed in any Roman Catholic family as its foster home ; nor shall any Roman Catholic child dealt with under this Act, be committed to the care of any Protestant Children's Aid Society, or be placed in any Protestant family as its foster home. But this section shall not apply to the care of children in a temporary home or shelter, established under the Act of Ontario, 56 Victoria, chapter 45, intituled "An Act for the Prevention of Cruelty to, and the better Protection of Children," in a municipality in which there is but one Children's Aid Society.

INDEX.

PART III.

PROVINCIAL STATUTES.

An Act for the Prevention of Cruelty to, and better
Protection of Children.

HER MAJESTY, by and with the advice and consent of
the Legislative Assembly of the Province of Ontario,
enacts as follows : —

1. In this Act the expression "court of summary jurisdiction" means and includes any police or stipendiary magistrate
or two justices of the peace acting together.

The expression " street " includes any highway or public
place, whether a thoroughfare or not.

"Children's Aid Society" shall mean any duly incorporated
and organized society having among its objects the protection
of children from cruelty and the care and control of neglected
and dependent children, such society having been approved by
the Lieutenant-Governor in Council for the purposes of this
Act.

The expression "place of safety" includes any industrial
school or house of industry for boys or girls, or any shelter or
temporary home established by any children's aid society or
society for the protection of children, approved of by the
Lieutenant-Governor for the purposes of this Act, or any
other institution subject to the inspection of the inspector of
prisons and asylums, or any suitable charitable society authorized to exercise the powers conferred by *The Act respecting
Apprentices and Minors,* but not a gaol prison or police cell.

The expression " parent," when used in relation to a child
includes guardian and every person who is by law liable to
maintain the child.

The word "constable," in the fifth section of this Act
shall include the agent or officer of any children's aid society
or any other society for the protection of children from cruelty
approved as aforesaid, such agent or officer having been duly
commissioned by the mayor of any city or town, or other chief
officer of any municipality, to act as a police officer within the
limits of such city or town or other municipality, whether with
or without salary, payable by such city, town or other muni-

"Superinten-dent."

The word "superintendent" means the provincial officer appointed under the provisions of this Act.

"Minister."

The word "minister" means the Provincial Secretary or such other member of the Executive Council as may from time to time, by order of the Lieutenant-Governor, have control over the administration of the provisions of this Act.

Penalty for neglecting or ill-treating children.

2. Any person over sixteen years of age who, having the care, custody, control, or charge of a child, being a boy under the age of fourteen years, or being a girl under the age of sixteen years, wilfully ill-treats, neglects, abandons, or exposes such child, or causes or procures such child to be ill-treated neglected, abandoned, or exposed, in a manner likely to cause such child unnecessary suffering, or serious injury to its health, shall be guilty of an offence under this Act, and, on conviction thereof by a court of summary jurisdiction, shall be liable, at the discretion of the court, to a fine not exceeding one hundred dollars, or alternatively, or in default of payment of such fine, or in addition thereto, to imprisonment, with or without hard labour, for any term not exceeding three months.

Increased penalty on proof of interest in death of child.

3. If upon the trial of any person under the preceding section it be proved that such person was interested in any sum of money accruable or payable in the event of the death of the child, and had knowledge that such sum of money was accruing or becoming payable, the court may, in its discretion, increase the amount of the said fine so that the fine shall not exceed two hundred and fifty dollars, or increase the imprisonment, with or without hard labour, to any term not exceeding nine months.

4.—(1) Any person who—

Causing children to beg in streets

(a) Causes or procures any child, being a boy under the age of fourteen years, or being a girl under the age of sixteen years, to be in any street for the purpose of begging or receiving alms, or of inducing the giving of alms, whether under the pretence of singing, playing, performing, offering anything for sale, or otherwise; or

or to sing, etc., in streets or taverns between 10 p.m. and 6 a.m.,

(b) Causes or procures any child, being a boy under the age of fourteen years, or being a girl under the age of sixteen years, to be in any street, or in any premises licensed for the sale of any intoxicating liquor, for the purpose of singing, playing, or performing for profit, or offering anything for sale, between ten p.m. and six a.m.; or

or to sing or perform in public places

(c) Causes or procures any child under the age of ten years to be at any time in any street, or in any premises licensed for the sale of intoxicating liquor, or in premises licensed according to law for public entertainments, or in any circus or other place of public amusement to which the public are admitted by payment, for the purpose of singing, playing, or performing for profit, or offering anything for sale;

shall, on conviction thereof by a court of summary juris- Penalty. diction, be liable, at the discretion of the court, to a fine not exceeding one hundred dollars, or alternatively, or in default of payment of the said fine, or in addition thereto, to imprisonment, with or without hard labour, for any term not exceeding three months.

(2) Provided also, that in the case of any entertain- License for employmen of child ove seven years age in circuses, et in certain cases. ment, or series of entertainments, to take place in premises used for public entertainments, or in any circus or other place of public amusement as aforesaid, where it is satisfactorily shown that proper provision has been made to secure the health and kind treatment of any children proposed to be employed thereat, it shall be lawful for the police magistrate or the head of the municipality, anything in this Act notwithstanding, to grant a license for such time, and during such hours of the day, and subject to such restrictions and conditions as he may think fit for any child exceeding seven years of age of whose fitness to take part in such entertainment or series of entertainments without injury the said police magistrate or municipal officer aforesaid is satisfied; and such license may at any time be varied, added to, or rescinded by the same authority upon sufficient cause being shewn; and such license shall be sufficient protection to all persons acting under or in accordance with the same.

(3) The municipal council shall assign to some officer of the Municipal officers to e to compliai with conditions of license. municipality, or other person, the duty of seeing whether the restrictions and conditions of any license under this section are duly complied with, and such officer or person shall have the same power to enter, inspect, and examine any place of public entertainment at which the employment of a child is for the time being licensed under this section, as an inspector has to enter, inspect, and examine a factory or workshop under *The Ontario Factories Act*. This duty shall be dis- Rev. Stat. 208. charged by the chief constable of the municipality until some other officer or person is appointed by the municipal council as aforesaid.

(4) So much of clause (c) of sub-section 1 of this section as Time from which subsection (c) shall be in force. makes it an offence to cause or procure a child to be in premises for public entertainment, or in any circus or other place of public amusement, for the purpose of singing,

playing, or performing for profit, shall not come into operation until the first day of October, 1893.

Powers of constable as to arresting without warrant or removing child.

5.—(1) Any constable may take into custody without warrant any person who, within view of such constable, commits an offence under section 2 of this Act, where the name and residence of such person are unknown to and cannot be ascertained by such constable; and any constable may take to a place of safety any child in respect of whom an offence under section 2 or clause (*a*) of sub-section 1 of section 4 of this Act has been committed, and the child may there be detained until it can be brought before a court of summary jurisdiction, and such court may cause the child to be dealt with as circumstances may admit and require until the charge made against any person in respect of the said offence has been determined by the committal for trial, or conviction, or discharge of such person.

Release of person arrested without warrant on bail being given.

(2) Where a constable arrests any person without warrant in pursuance of this section the officer or constable in charge of the station to which such person is conveyed shall, unless in his belief the release of such person on bail would tend to defeat the ends of justice, or to cause injury or danger to the child against whom the offence is alleged to have been committed, release the person arrested on his entering into such a recognizance, with or without sureties, as may in his judgment be required to secure the attendance of such person upon the hearing of the charge.

Disposal of child by order of court.

6.—(1) Where a person having the custody or control of a child, being a boy under the age of fourteen, or a girl under the age of sixteen years, has been

(*a*) Convicted of committing in respect of such child an offence under section 2 of this Act.

(*b*) Committed for trial for any such offence; or

(*c*) Bound over to keep the peace towards such child,

any person may bring such child before a judge, and the judge, if satisfied on inquiry that it is expedient so to deal with the child, may order that the child be taken out of the custody of such person and committed to the charge of a relative of the child, or some other fit person named by the judge, such relation or other person being willing to undertake such charge until it attains the age of fourteen years, or in the case of a girl sixteen years, or in either case for any shorter period, or to the charge of any duly authorized children's aid society, and may of his own motion, or on the application of any person, from time to time renew, vary, and revoke any

71

such order; provided that no order shall be made under this section unless a parent of the child is under committal for trial for having been, or has been proved to have been, party or prvy to the offence, or has been bound over to keep the peace towards such child.

(2) Any person or society to whom a child is so committed shall, whilst the order is in force, have the like control over the child as if such person or society were its parent, and shall be responsible for its maintenance, and the child shall continue under the control of such person or society, notwithstanding that it is claimed by its parent ; and any judge having power so to commit a child shall have power to make the like orders on the parent of the child to contribute to its maintenance during such period as aforesaid as if the child were detained under *The Industrial Schools Act*, and as he might make under section 20 of the said Act, and such orders may be made on the complaint or application of the person or society to whom the child is for the time being committed, and the sums contributed by the parent shall be paid to such person or society as the judge may name, and be applied for the maintenance of the child. In determining on the person or society to whom the child shall be so committed, the judge shall endeavour to ascertain the religious persuasion to which the child belongs, and shall, if possible, select a person or society of the same religious persuasion, and such religious persuasion shall be specified in the order; and in any case where the child has been placed pursuant to any such order with a person or society not of the same religious persuasion as that to which the child belongs, the judge shall, on the application of any person in that behalf, and on its appearing that a fit person or society of the same religious persuasion is willing to undertake the charge, make an order to secure his being placed with a person or society of the same religious persuasion.

Provided that if the order to commit the child to the charge of some relation or other person be made in respect of any person having been committed for trial for an offence, as specified in sub-section (1) (*b*) of this section, the judge shall not be empowered to order the parent of the child to contribute to its maintenance prior to the trial of such person ; and if he be acquitted of such charge, or if such charge be dismissed for want of prosecution, then any order that may have been made under this section shall forthwith be void, except with regard to anything which may have been lawfully done under it.

(3) The Lieutenant-Governor in Council or the Minister may at any time discharge a child from the custody of any person to whom it is committed in pursuance of this section, either absolutely, or on such conditions as may be approved of, and may from time to time make, alter, or revoke rules in relation to children so committed to any person and to the duties of such persons with respect to such children. (See Imperial Act, 52 and 53 Vic., Cap. 44, sec. 5.)

Power of search.

7.—(1) If it appears to any police magistrate, or to any two justices of the peace, on information made before him or them on oath by any person who, in the opinion of the magistrate or justices, is *bona fide* acting in the interest of any child, that there is reasonable cause to suspect that such child, being a boy under the age of fourteen years, or a girl under the age of sixteen years, has been or is being ill treated or neglected in any place within the jurisdiction of such magistrate or justices in a manner likely to cause the child unnecessary suffering, or to be injurious to its health, such magistrate or justices may issue a warrant authorizing any person named therein to search for such child, and if it is found to have been or to be ill-treated or neglected in manner aforesaid, to take it to and detain it in a place of safety until it can be brought before a judge, and the judge before whom the child is brought may cause it to be dealt with in the manner provided by section 6 ;

Proviso.

Provided always, that the powers hereinbefore conferred on any two justices may be exercised by any one justice, if upon the information the case appears to him to be one of urgency.

Issuing warrant for arrest in addition to said warrant.

(2) The magistrate or justices or justice issuing such warrant may by the same warrant cause any person accused of any offence in respect of the child to be apprehended and brought before a judge and proceedings to be taken for punishing such person according to law.

Power to enter and remove child.

(3) Any person authorized by warrant under this section to search for any child, and to take it to and detain it in a place of safety, may enter (if need be by force) any house, building, or other place specified in the warrant, and may remove the child therefrom.

Warrants, who may execute.

(4) Where there is no superior officer of police the warrant may be addressed to and executed by any policeman or constable approved of for that purpose by the head of the municipality or by any such society as mentioned in the first section of this Act.

Not necessary to specify child.

(5) It shall not be necessary in any information or warrant for the purpose of this section to specify any particular child

Evidence of children.

8. Where, in any proceeding against any person for an offence under this Act, the child in respect of whom the offence is charged to have been committed, or any other child of tender years who is tendered as a witness, does not in the opinion of the judge understand the nature of an oath, the evidence of such child may be received, though not given upon oath, if, in the opinion of the judge, such child is possessed of sufficient intelligence to justify the reception of the evidence and understands the duty of speaking the truth.

71

(2) A person shall not be liable to be convicted of an offence, Corrobora
unless the testimony admitted by virtue of this section and tion.
given on behalf of the prosecution, is corroborated by some
other material evidence implicating the accused ; and

(3) Any child whose evidence is received as aforesaid, and Punishme
who shall wilfully give false evidence, shall be liable to be of childrei
tried for such offence, and on conviction thereof may ments.
be adjudged such punishment as is provided for by sec-
tion three of *The Juvenile Offenders Act*, (R.S.C. c. 177) in the R.S.C., c.
case of juvenile offenders.

9. The Lieutenant-Governor in Council may appoint an Appointm
officer who shall be known as the Superintendent of Neglected superintei
and Dependent Children, and whose salary shall be paid out ent.
of such moneys as may be from time to time set apart for the
purpose by the Legislative Assembly of the Province ; and it
shall be the duty of such officer :

(a) To encourage and assist in the organization and estab- To assist i
lishment in various parts of the Province of chil- establishir
dren's aid societies for the protection of children societies.
from cruelty, and for the due care of neglected and
dependent children in temporary homes or shelters
and the placing of such children in properly selected
foster homes ;

(b) To visit and inspect industrial schools and tem- Inspectio
porary homes or shelters as often as occasion may industrial
require, and not less often than may be directed ers, etc.
by Order in Council or departmental regulation in
that behalf ;

(c) When specially directed, to visit any home or place Special in
where any child is boarded out or placed pursuant spections.
to the provisions of this Act ;

(d) To advise children's visiting committees and to in- Advising
struct them as to the manner in which their duties mittees.
are to be performed :

(e) To see that a record of all committals is kept by the Records (
various children's aid societies and of all children committa
placed out in foster homes under this Act, and of
all particulars connected with each case ;

(f) To inspect houses registered for the reception of chil- Inspectic
dren under the *Act for the Protection of infant* registere
Children, and to instruct local children's aid socie- under Ri
ties and visiting committees as to the proper
supervision of such houses ;

(g) To prepare and submit an annual report on the various Annual
matters dealt with by him under the provisions of report.
this Act.

(h) To perform such other duties as may be prescribed by Other du
the Lieutenant-Governor in Council.

10.—(1) For the better protection of neglected children between the ages of three and fourteen years there shall be provided in every city or town having a population of over 10,000 one or more places of refuge for such children only, to be known as temporary homes or shelters. Such homes shall be distant not less than one-half mile from any penal or pauper institution, and no pauper or convict shall be permitted to live or labour therein, and they shall not be used as a permanent provision or residence for any child but for its temporary protection for so long a time only as shall be absolutely necessary for the placing of the child in a well selected foster home. Children demented, idiotic or suffering from incurable or contagious diseases shall not be taken into these temporary homes.

(2) Orphan asylums or other children's homes now in operation in any municipality may, with the consent of the trustees or governing bodies thereof, be used as temporary homes or shelters under this section; and when desirable for economical reasons, not being inconsistent with the welfare of the children to be provided for, such temporary homes or shelters may be established in desirable private families; but in no instance shall such home or shelter be under the same care or management as a poor house or any penal institution.

(3) When in any municipality a Children's Aid Society has been duly organized and has been approved by the Lieutenant-Governor in Council, such Children's Aid Society shall have the supervision and management of any such children in the temporary home or shelter provided by or at the expense of such municipality. This does not apply to any orphan asylum or other children's home mentioned in sub-section 2 of this section without the consent of the trustees or governing bodies thereof.

11.—(1) For each electoral district within the Province of Ontario there shall be appointed a committee consisting of six persons, not less than three of whom shall be women, who shall be known as the "Children's Visiting Committee" for such electoral district. The said committee shall co-operate with the Children's Aid Societies and shall serve without compensation. They shall have the right at all times to visit any temporary home or shelter in the electoral district, and to suggest from time to time such provisions, changes or additions as they may think desirable. They shall also assist, under the direction and advice of the superintendent, in the careful selection of foster homes for the children in the temporary homes or shelters and in the visitation of children when placed in selected families, and such visitation shall be made for each child at least once in every three months; and the said committee shall have power to remove any child from the family in which it may be placed to a temporary home or to another family at their discretion, subject to any rules or regulations in that behalf, to be approved by the Lieutenant-Governor in Council. The said committee shall also have the right at any time to visit and inspect any house registered under the *Act* for the Protection of Infant Children, and to exercise the powers given by section 9 of said Act. Rev. Stat. c. 209.

(2) The said children's visiting committee for each electoral district shall be appointed by the county judge, the sheriff and the warden of the county of which such electoral division forms a part, and in the case of a city forming a separate electoral division, by the county judge, the sheriff and the mayor of such city and such committee shall hold office for a period of three years. The member of the Legislative Assembly for each electoral district shall be one of the said visiting committee for such electoral district. Who to appoint.

(3) The said committee shall, in the selection of homes, endeavour to secure homes where children may be received to be cared for without remuneration, and shall aim at promoting and encouraging a philanthropic sentiment on behalf of neglected, abandoned and destitute children, and adopt such methods as they may think best for securing voluntary subscriptions of money to be devoted to the effective carrying out of the objects of this Act. Selection of homes by committees.

(4) The said committee shall from time to time report to the superintendent the homes which they select and recommend for the care of children, with full particulars in each case ; and shall also annually report to the superintendent as to their visitations and as to each child placed out in their district and as to all other matters coming within their sphere of duty as such committee. They shall also from time to time report to children's aid societies with reference to children placed out by such societies respectively, to the end that such societies may at all times have accurate knowledge regarding the care, oversight, education and general welfare of such children. Reports to be made by committee.

12.—(1) Towards the necessary expenses of supporting children in temporary homes or in foster homes where such children are not cared for without compensation, until they reach the age of twelve years for girls and fourteen years for boys there shall be paid by the municipality to which they belong not less than one dollar weekly per child. The placing of children with the lowest bidder is hereby prohibited. Expenses of supporting children in homes. Municipalities to contribute.

(2) For the purposes of this section any child shall be deemed to belong to the municipality in which such child has last resided for the period of one year; but in the absence of evidence to the contrary, residence for one year in the municipality in which such child was taken into custody, shall be presumed. When child deemed to belong to a municipality,

(3) A municipality having made any payment under this section for the maintenance of a child in respect of whom some Recovery from municipality liable.

other municipality is liable to make such payment, shall be entitled to recover the amount so paid from such other municipality.

Recovery from parents. (4) Every municipality incurring expenditure hereunder may recover the amount of such expenditure from the parent of the child in respect of whom such expenditure may be made.

Order of committal may direct weekly payment. (5) The order of committal of any child under this Act may direct payment by the parent to the municipality of the said sum of one dollar per week and of such further sum to the Children's Aid Society assuming the control of the child as the judge may deem reasonable and may consider the parent able to pay.

maintenance.

Rev. Stat. c. 234. (6) At any time after committal of a child the municipality or the Children's Aid Society may apply to the Judge of the Division Court of the division in which the parent resides, according to the form in the manner and with the force and effect provided by section 22 of *The Industrial Schools Act* for such order for payment of maintenance or of additional maintenance as the circumstances may justify, and any parent may also make application to the Judge of the Division Court in like manner for an order reducing the amount payable under any order, or revoking such order, or varying or suspending in whole or in part the operation of the same.

When officers of children's aid societies act as constables and apprehend children.

Rev. Stat. c. 234. 13. Officers of any children's aid society duly approved by the inspector or superintendent may be authorized by boards of police commissioners in cities and towns having such boards and by the mayors and reeves of other municipalities to act as constables for the purpose of enforcing the provisions of this or *The Industrial Schools' Act*, and such officers may apprehend without warrant and bring before the judge as neglected any child apparently under the age of fourteen years who comes within any of the following descriptions, namely :

(1) Who is found begging or receiving alms or thieving in any street, thoroughfare, tavern or place of public resort, or sleeping at night in the open air ;

(2) Who is found wandering about at late hours and not having any home or settled place of abode, or proper guardianship ;

(3) Who is found associating or dwelling with a thief, drunkard or vagrant, or who by reason of the neglect or drunkenness or other vices of the parents is suffered to be growing up without salutary parental control and education, or in circumstances exposing such child to an idle and dissolute life ;

(4) Who is found in any house of ill-fame, or in company of a reputed prostitute ;

(5) Who is found destitute, being an orphan or having a surviving parent who is undergoing imprisonment for crime.

14.—(1) Any child apprehended under the next preceding section of this Act shall be brought before the judge for examination, and it shall thereupon be the duty of the judge to investigate the facts of the case and ascertain whether such child is dependent and neglected, its age, and the name and residence of parents, and the said judge shall have power to compel the attendance of witnesses, and may, in his discretion, request the attendance of the Crown attorney for such examition, and if requested it shall be the duty of the Crown attorney to attend accordingly. The parents or person having the actual custody of such child shall be duly notified of such examination, and any friend may appear in behalf of any child, and in his discretion the judge may request the duly authorized representative of the local children's aid society to appear in behalf of any child; and if on such examination the judge shall find that any child is dependent or neglected within the meaning of the next preceding section or so as to be in a state of habitual vagrancy or mendicancy, or ill-treated so as to be in peril of life, health or morality by continued personal injury or by grave misconduct or habitual intemperance of the parents or guardian, he shall enter such finding by a proper order in that behalf, and may order delivery of such child to the children's aid society, and the children's aid society may send such child to their temporary home or shelter to be kept until placed in an approved foster home pursuant to the provisions of this Act. The judge shall deliver to the children's aid society procuring such examination a certified copy of the order made in the case, which shall contain, besides the said finding, a statement of the facts so far as ascertained as to the age of such child, name, nationality and residence, and occupation of parents or either of them, and whether either of them is dead or has abandoned the child, and in the case of the examination of two or more children at the same time only one order need be made.

Powers and duty of judge on apprehension of child.

(2) If, in the opinion of the judge, a child apprehended in pursuance of the provisions of this section has been leading an immoral or depraved life, or is not a fit subject to be dealt with under the next preceding sub-section, the judge may order such child to be committed to any industrial school or refuge for boys or girls or other institution subject to the inspection of the Inspector of Prisons and Asylums or to any suitable charitable society authorized to exercise the powers conferred by the *Act respecting Apprentices and Minors,* and willing to receive such child to be there kept, cared for and educated for a period not extending beyond the period at which such child shall attain the age of eighteen years, or for any period not exceeding two years, and thereafter to be delivered to the children's aid society for the purpose of being placed in an approved foster home until such child arrives at the age of eighteen years.

Committal of children on proof of vicious or immoral conduct.

Rev. Stat. c. 142.

Duties of children's aid societies as guardians.

15.—(1) The children's aid society to the care of which any child may be committed under the provisions of this Act, shall, subject to the provisions of sections 17 and 18 of this Act, be the legal guardian of such child, and it shall be the duty of such society to use special diligence in providing suitable homes for such children as may in the said manner be committed to their care ; and such society is hereby authorized to place such children in such families on a written contract during minority, or until 18 years of age, in the discretion of such society, providing for their education in the public schools (or in the case of Roman Catholic children in the separate schools) where they may reside, for teaching them some useful occupation, for kind and proper treatment as members of the family where placed, and for payment on the termination of such contract to the said society for the use of the child of any sum of money that may be provided for in said instrument. All such contracts shall contain a clause reserving the right to withdraw the child from any person having the custody of such child when in the opinion of the society placing out such child the welfare of the child requires it.

Powers as to guardianship.

Rev. Stat. c. 142.

(2) The children's aid society to which any child shall be committed may at any time during the period of their control or guardianship of such child exercise all the powers conferred by sections 2 and 6 of the *Act respecting Apprentices and Minors* upon the charitable societies therein mentioned.

Medical examination of child before committal.

16. Whenever on the examination provided for by section 14 the judge shall determine that the child is dependent and neglected within the meaning of this Act, he shall cause it to be examined by a respectable practising physician and shall in no case order the delivery of the child to the society unless the physician making such examination shall certify in writing filed in court that the child examined by him is, in his opinion, of sound mind and has no chronic or contagious disease, and in his opinion has not been exposed to any contagious disease within fifteen days previous to such examination before the judge ; and a copy of such certificate shall be attached to the other papers required by this Act to accompany such child to any shelter or temporary home.

Term of guardianship.

17.—(1) Where a child is maintained by any children's aid society, or in any foster home, having been placed out by proper authority in that behalf, and such child was deserted by its parents, the children's aid society may at any time resolve that such child shall be under the control of such society until it reaches the age of twenty-one years or such earlier age as may be thought sufficient, and thereupon until the child reaches that age all the powers and rights of such parent in respect of that child shall, subject as in this Act mentioned, vest in the the said society ;

Provided that such society may rescind such resolution if they think that it will be for the benefit of the child that it should be rescinded, or may permit such child to be either permanently or temporarily under the control of such parent, or of any other relative or of any friend.

(2) A judge, if satisfied on complaint made by a parent of the child, that the child has not been maintained by the society, or was not deserted by such parent, or that it is for the benefit of the child that it should be either permanently or temporarily under the control of such parent, or that the resolution of the society should be determined, may make an order accordingly, and any such order shall be complied with by the society, and if the order determines the resolution, the resolution shall be thereby determined as from the date of the order, and the society shall cease to have the rights and powers of the parent as respects such child.

(3) For the purposes of this Act a child shall be deemed to be maintained by a children's aid society if it is wholly or partly maintained by them, either in any shelter or temporary home or other institution conducted by such society, or is boarded out under the provisions of this or any other Act in that behalf.

(4) Where a parent is imprisoned on a criminal charge, or in respect of an offence committed against a child, this section shall apply as if such child had been deserted by that parent.

(5) Nothing in this section shall relieve any person from any liability to contribute to the maintenance of a child, but the fact of such contribution being made shall not deprive any society of any of the powers and rights conferred on them by this section.

18.—(1) Where the parent of a child applies to any court having jurisdiction in that behalf, for a writ or order for the production of the child, and the court is of opinion that the parent has abandoned or deserted the child, or that he has otherwise so conducted himself that the court should refuse to enforce his right to the custody of the child, the court may, in its discretion, decline to issue the writ or make the order.

(2) If at the time of the application for a writ or order for the production of the child, the child is being brought up by

another person, or is boarded out by a children's aid society duly authorized in that behalf, the court may, in its discretion, if it orders the child to be given up to the parent, further order that the parent shall pay to such person or such society the whole of the costs properly incurred in bringing up the child, or such portion thereof as shall seem to the court to be just and reasonable, having regard to all the circumstances of the case.

(3) When a parent has—

(a) Abandoned or deserted his child ; or

(b) Allowed his child to be brought up by another person at that person's expense, or by any children's aid society, for such time and under such circumstances as to satisfy the court that the parent was unmindful of his parental duties ;

the court shall not make an order for the delivery of the child to the parent unless the parent has satisfied the court that having regard to the welfare of the child he is a fit person to have the custody of the child.

(4) Upon any application by the parent for the production or custody of a child, if the court is of opinion that the parent ought not to have the custody of the child, and that the child is being brought up in a different religion from that in which the parent has a legal right to require that the child should be brought up, the court shall have power to make such order as it may think fit to secure that the child be brought up in the religion in which the parent has a legal right to require that the child should be brought up. Nothing in this section contained shall interfere with or affect the power of the court to consult the wishes of the child in considering what order ought to be made, or diminish the right which any child now possesses to the exercise of its own free choice.

19. Every society or person to whose care any child may be committed under the provisions of this Act, and every person entrusted with the care of any such child by any such person or institution shall from time to time permit such child to be visited, and any place where such child may be or reside to be inspected by the superintendent or any of the members of the local children's visiting committee, or any person authorized by or under regulations approved by Order of the Lieutenant-Governor in Council for the time being in force in that behalf.

20. Notwithstanding anything in this Act contained, no Protestant child shall be committed to the care of any Roman Catholic children's aid society, nor shall any Roman Catholic child be committed to a Protestant children's

aid society, and in like manner no Protestant child shall be placed out in any Roman Catholic family as its foster home, nor shall any Roman Catholic child be placed out in any Protestant family as its foster home. This section does not apply to the care of children in a temporary home or shelter, as in this Act provided, in a municipality in which there is but one Children's Aid Society.

21. Subject to such regulations as may be hereafter provided and approved of as aforesaid, all ministers of religion or any person being duly authorized by the recognized head of any religious denomination, shall have admission to every temporary home or shelter and access to such of the children placed or detained therein as may belong to their respective denominations, and may give instruction to them on the days and at the times allotted by such regulations for the religious education of such children of their respective denominations Right of] ministers o religion to visit 'childr in homes and shelter

22. All members of the Parliament of Canada and of the Legislative Assembly of Ontario, all heads of municipal councils, and all judges and justices of the peace shall be entitled to visit every temporary home or shelter, and shall have admission to the same accordingly. Visitors, v may be.

23. Every person entitled to visit any such temporary home or shelter as aforesaid, and every minister of religion may inscribe in a book (to be for that purpose provided and kept in such temporary home or shelter by the superintendent or matron thereof) any remarks or observations which he may think fit to make touching or concerning such temporary home or shelter, and the superintendent, matron, teachers, officers or servants, or the children placed or detained therein, or any of them, and such book shall be produced to the inspector or superintendent whenever he visits such temporary home or shelter. Powers of visitors.

24. Whenever a complaint is made or pending against any boy under the age of 12 years or girl under the age of 13 years for the commission of any offence against the laws of this Province, before any court or magistrate having competent jurisdiction thereof, it shall be the duty of such court or magistrate at once and before any proceedings are had in the case to give notice in writing to the executive officer of the children's aid society, if there be one in the county, who shall have opportunity allowed him to investigate the charge or charges, and upon receiving such notice the officer may proceed to enquire into and make full examination as to the parentage and surroundings of the child and of all the facts and circumstances of the case and report the same to the court or magistrate, who may advise and counsel with the Trial of ch ren for offe ces against Provincial laws.

said officer of the said society ; and if upon consultation after full investigation and proof of the offence charged it shall appear to the court that the public interest and the interest of the child will be best subserved thereby, an order may be made for the return of such child to his or her parents, guardian or friends, or the court may authorize the said officer to take such child and bind him or her out to some suitable person until he or she shall have attained the age of 21 years, or for any less time, or impose a fine, or suspend sentence for a definite or indefinite period, or if the child be found guilty of the offence charged, or be wilfully wayward and unmanageable, the court may cause him or her to be sent to an industrial school or to the provincial reformatory for boys or to the refuge for girls, as the case may be, and in such cases the report of the officers of the society shall be attached to the warrant of commitment.

25. Where a person is charged with an offence under this Act in respect of a child who is alleged to be under any specified age, and the child appears to the judge to be under that age, such child shall for the purposes of this Act be deemed to be under that age, unless the contrary is proved.

26. Nothing in this Act contained shall be construed to take away or affect the right of any parent, teacher or other person having the lawful control or charge of a child to administer punishment to such child as if this Act had not been passed.

27. Where an offence against this Act is also punishable under any other Act, or at common law, it may be prosecuted and punished either under this Act, or under the other Act, or at common law, so that no person be punished twice for the same offence.

28. Any court or magistrate in lieu of committing to prison any child under the age of 14 years convicted before him of any offence against the laws of this Province may hand over such child to the charge of any home for destitute and neglected children or industrial school or children's aid society and the managers of such home or school or society may permit its adoption by a suitable person, and may apprentice it to any suitable trade, calling or service, and the transfer shall be as valid as if the managers were parents of such child. The parents of such child shall have no right to remove or interfere with the said child so adopted or apprenticed except by the express permission in writing of the Minister.

29. No child under 16 years of age held for trial or under sentence in any gaol or other place of confinement shall be placed or allowed to remain in the same cell or room in company with adult prisoners. It shall be the duty of the officer in charge of such place of confinement to secure, as far as the construction of such place will admit, the exclusion of such children from the society of such adult prisoners during their confinement.

30.—(1) In cities and towns with a population of more than ten thousand, children under the age of 16 years who are charged with offences against the laws of this Province, or who are brought before a judge for examination under any of the provisions of this Act shall not before trial or examination be confined in the lock-ups or police cells used for ordinary criminals or persons charged with crime, nor, save as hereinafter mentioned, shall such children be tried or have their cases disposed of in the police court rooms ordinarily used as such. It shall be the duty of such municipalities to make separate provision for the custody and detention of such children prior to their trial or examination, whether by arrangement with some member of the police force or other person who may be willing to undertake the responsibility of such temporary custody or detention, on such terms as may be agreed upon, or by providing suitable premises entirely distinct and separated from the ordinary lock-ups or police cells; and it shall be the duty of the judge to try all such children or examine into their cases and dispose thereof, where practicable, in premises other than the ordinary police court premises, or, where this is not practicable, in the private office of the judge, if he have one, or in some other room in the municipal buildings, or, if this be not practicable, then in the ordinary police court room, but only in such last mentioned case when an interval of two hours shall have elapsed after the other trials or examinations for the day have been disposed of. *[margin: Custody of children pending trial.]* *[margin: Place of trial.]*

(2) Where any children's aid society possesses premises affording the necessary facilities and accommodation, children, apparently under the age of twelve years, may, after apprehension under the provisions of this Act, be temporarily taken charge of by such society until their cases are disposed of; and the judge may hold the examination into the case of such children in the premises of the said society. *[margin: Confinement of children and trial on premises of children's aid society.]*

(3) The judge may, if he thinks fit, hold the preliminary examination or the trial of any case against any parent for alleged cruelty to a child in the house where the parent resides, but only at the request of such parent. *[margin: Preliminary examination into charge of, cruelty may be held in house.]*

(4) The judge shall exclude from the room or place where any child under 16 years of age, or any parent charged with cruelty to his child is being tried or examined, all persons other than the counsel and witnesses in the case, officers of the law or of any children's aid society and the immediate friends or relatives of the child or parent. *[margin: Private trial of children.]*

By-laws to prevent children being on the streets after nightfall.

31.—(1) Municipal councils in cities, towns, and incorporated villages shall have power to pass by-laws for the regulation of the time after which children shall not be in the streets at nightfall without proper guardianship and the age or apparent age, of boys and girls respectively, under which they shall be required to be in their homes at the hour appointed, and such municipal council shall in such case cause a bell or bells to be rung at or near the time appointed as a warning, to be called the " curfew bell," after which the children so required to be in their homes or off the streets shall not be upon the public streets except under proper control or guardianship or for some unavoidable cause.

Children after warning may be taken home.

(2) Any child so found after the time appointed shall be liable to be warned by any constable or peace officer to go home, and if after such warning the child shall be found loitering on the streets such child may be taken by such constable to its home.

Summoning parents, etc., permitting children to break the law

(3) Any parent or guardian may be summoned for permitting his child to habitually break said by-law after having been warned in writing, and may be fined for the first offence $1, without costs, and for the second offence $2, and for a third, or any subsequent offence, $5.

71

BILL.

An Act for the Prevention of Cruelty to, and better Protection of, Children.

First Reading, 10th April, 1893.
Second   "   25th   "   1893
Third   "   19th May,   1893.

CHAPTER 56.

An Act respecting Houses of Refuge for Females.

[Assented to 27th May, 1893.]

HER MAJESTY, by and with the advice and consent of the Legislative Assembly of the Province of Ontario, enacts as follows :—

1. "House of Refuge" in this Act shall mean any institution for the care of young or adult females, named in schedule B. of The Charity Aid Act, or other similar institution, which is subject to the inspection of the inspector of prisons and asylums. "Superintendent," shall mean the matron, superior, or other person in charge of such institution.

2. All females sentenced to, or confined from time to time in any of the common gaols of the Province under sentence of imprisonment by a police magistrate of any city, for any offence against any Act of the Legislature of the Province, or against any by-law of any municipality in the Province, may be committed to any house of refuge situate in the county or union of counties, city or town in which such females respectively were convicted, or may be transferred, by order of such police magistrate, from such common gaol to such house of refuge, to be there respectively imprisoned for the whole of the unexpired portions of the terms of imprisonment to which such females were originally sentenced or committed respectively to such common gaols; and such females shall thereupon be imprisoned in such houses of refuge aforesaid for the whole or the residue of their respective terms of imprisonment, and shall be subject to all the rules and regulations of such houses of refuge respectively; provided that no Protestant female shall be committed or transferred under this Act to a Roman Catholic institution; and no Roman Catholic shall be committed or transferred to a Protestant institution.

3. The next preceding section shall be held to extend to persons convicted of offences created under the authority of any Act of the Legislature of this Province, as well as to persons convicted of offences under any by-laws of any of the municipalities of said Province, or of any other offence directly or indirectly created by the said Legislature, and to any case where imprisonment is imposed in whole or in part in default of the payment of a fine or penalty in money, notwithstanding the offender is entitled to be discharged upon payment of such fine or penalty, and if the fine or penalty is paid after the committal or removal of the offender to any such house of refuge, and whilst such offender is confined therein,

the same shall be paid to the superintendent of the house of refuge to defray the expense of removal and otherwise, for the use of the said house of refuge, but nothing herein contained shall affect the right of any private person to any part thereof.

4. The Police Magistrate may from time to time direct the removal of any such offender from any house of refuge to the common gaol, to which such offender had been originally sentenced, or from which she had been before removed, or to any other place of imprisonment to which the offender may be removed according to law.

5. Any officer to whom the magistrate's warrant in that behalf is directed may convey to the house of refuge for females named in his warrant in that behalf, any offender liable to be imprisoned therein, and deliver her to the superintendent without any further warrant than a copy of the sentence or warrant of commitment against such offender from the proper court in that behalf, certified under the hand of the gaoler to whom the same is directed.

6. The superintendent or other head of the house of refuge, or the keeper of any common gaol having the custody of any offender ordered to be removed from a house of refuge to a common gaol or other place of imprisonment, or from the common gaol to a house of refuge, shall, when required so to do, deliver up to the constable or other officer or person who produces the said warrant, the offender named therein, together with a copy certified by him or her, of the warrant of commitment of the offender, or of the copy thereof as given him or her on the reception of the offender into his or her custody.

7. The officer or other person employed to convey such offender to the house of refuge or back to a common gaol or any other place of imprisonment as by law provided, may secure and convey her through any county or district through which he may have to pass; and until the offender shall have been delivered to the superintendent, superior or other head of the house of refuge or the keeper of such common gaol or other place of imprisonment, the said officer or other person shall have in every part of this Province through which it may be necessary to convey the offender, the same power and authority over and with regard to the offender, and to command the assistance of any person to prevent her escape, and in recapturing her in case of an escape, as the sheriff of the county in which she was convicted would himself have in conveying her from one part to

8. The said officer or other person shall give a receipt to the said superintendent or gaoler for the offender, and shall thereupon, with all convenient speed, convey and deliver up the offender with the said certified copy of the warrant into the custody of the superior of the house of refuge or keeper of the gaol or other place of imprisonment mentioned in the warrant, who shall give a receipt in writing for every offender so received into his or her custody, to such officer or other person as his or her discharge; and the offender shall be kept in custody in the house of refuge or gaol or other place of imprisonment to which she may have been so removed, until the termination of her sentence or until her pardon or release or discharge by law, unless she is in the meantime again removed under competent authority.

9. Any offender who escapes from any such house of refuge before her sentence therein has expired, may be again arrested without any warrant by any sheriff, sheriff's bailiff or constable of the county, city, town or village in which she may be found and conveyed to the house of refuge for females from which she escaped, or to the county gaol of the county from which she was first removed, and she shall there be confined in such house of refuge or gaol for the balance of the period of her sentence which remained unexpired at the time of her escape.

10. Whenever the time of the sentence of any prisoner removed to a house of refuge expires on a Sunday she shall be discharged on the previous Saturday unless she desires to remain until the following Monday.

11. No prisoner shall be discharged from any house of refuge for females at the termination of her sentence, if then labouring under any contagious or infectious disease or under any acute or dangerous illness, but she shall be permitted to remain in the house of refuge until she recovers from the disease or illness, and any prisoner remaining from any such cause in the house of refuge shall be under the same discipline or control as if her sentence were still unexpired.

12. No prisoner shall be committed to any house of refuge without the consent of the superintendent, superior, or other head thereof in that behalf.

13. The said houses of refuge shall be and shall be deemed to be houses of industry or correction, almshouses and workhouses for the purposes of the Revised Act of the Parliament of Canada, intituled An Act respecting Offences against Public Morals and Public Convenience.

No. 87.] **BILL.** [1895.

An Act for the further protection of Children.

HER MAJESTY, by and with the advice and consent of the Legislative Assembly of the Province of Ontario, enacts as follows :—

1. Notwithstanding provisions to the contrary in any Act contained, and notwithstanding the provisions of any by-laws, rules or regulations for the government or control of any duly incorporated orphanage, children's home, infants' home or industrial school, it shall be lawful for the trustees or governing body of such orphanage or children's home, or infants' home or industrial school to take advantage of the provisions of section 15 of the *Act for the Prevention of Cruelty to and Better Protection of Children* by transferring, from time to time, children under their care to the Superintendent or to the children's aid society in the locality of such orphanage or home, to be placed out by the Superintendent or by such children's aid society in pursuance of the provisions of the said Act, and in such case it shall be the duty of the visiting committee to visit any child so placed out, as by the said Act provided, and in all respects such child shall be treated as having been placed out and shall continue subject to the provisions of the said Act.

2. Section 1 of the said Act is amended by inserting at the end of the thirty-seventh line of the said section the words " or two justices of the peace acting together."

3. Subsection (3) of section 6 of the said Act is hereby amended by striking out the words " in pursuance of this section," in the third line of the said subsection, and inserting in lieu thereof the words " under this Act," and by striking out all the words of the said subsection after the words " relation to " in the sixth line thereof and inserting in lieu thereof the words " the procedure of societies operating under the provisions of this Act."

societies in municipalities where no such society exists, with power from time to time to appoint, subject to the approval of the Minister, any person or committee to act for him as occasion may require."

5. Sub-section (1) of section 10 of the said Act is amended by striking out the words " between the ages of three and fourteen years " in the first and second lines thereof, and substituting the words " entirely distinct and separate " for the words " distant not less than one-half mile," in the fifth and sixth lines thereof.

6. Sub-section 1 of section 11 of the said Act, is amended by striking out the words " not less than three," in the third line thereof, and substituting therefor the words " or more, not less than half."

7. Section 13 of the said Act is amended by inserting after the word " years " in the ninth line thereof the words " if a boy, or sixteen years if a girl."

8. Section 14 of the said Act is amended by adding after the word " examination " in the third line the words " within one week after such apprehension."

9. Section 16 of the said Act is repealed and the following substituted therefor :
16. Every society or institution receiving the care or control of a child under the provisions of this Act shall make enquiry into the condition of health of the child so received, and if it be found to be suffering from any disease or bodily infirmity, due provision shall be made for the temporary care or disposal of such child with a view to guarding against its continued ill-health or the spread of any infectious or contagious malady.

10. Sub-section 2 of section 17 of the said Act is amended by inserting the words " or the superintendent, with the Minister's approval " after the word " judge " in the first line thereof.

11. The following is added to section 15 of the said Act as sub-section (3) thereof :
(3) No child between the ages of 2 and 16 years shall be received or boarded in any house or institution established for the reception and care of paupers or other dependent adults. This subsection shall take effect from and after the first day of July, 1895.

12. Section 1 of the *Act respecting the Industrial Refuge for Girls*, is amended by striking out the last two words in the said section and substituting therefor the words

13. It shall be unlawful for any person to induce any child Taking to leave the building or premises of any duly incorporated children of boys' or girls' home or orphans' home or asylum or children's of custody charitable or infants' home inspected by the Inspector of Prisons and institution Charities, and in respect of which aid is paid out of the funds of the Province under the provisions of *The Charity Aid Act,* Rev. Stat. 248. or to attempt to induce such child to leave or quit any service or apprenticeship or any place in which or where the said child has been or may be lawfully placed for the purpose of being nursed, supported, educated or adopted, or to induce, or attempt to induce any child to break any articles of apprenticeship or agreement which have been or may be lawfully entered into by or with the authority of the trustees or directors or governing body of any such home or asylum respecting any such child, or to detain or harbor any such child after demand made by or on behalf of any officer of any of such institutions for delivery up of such child ; and any person who shall violate the provisions of this section shall be liable, upon summary conviction before a justice of the peace, to a fine not exceeding Penalty. $20 and costs, and, in default of payment thereof, to imprisonment not exceeding thirty days.

(2) *No* parent or guardian or other person, who by instrument in writing has heretofore surrendered or may hereafter Parents surrenderi custody of surrender the custody of a child to any of the charitable children to institutions mentioned in the next preceding sub-section hereof charitable institution shall thereafter, contrary to the terms of such instrument, be entitled to the custody of or any control or authority over or any right to interfere with any such child.

(3) Provided, however that any parent or guardian claiming that a child is improperly and unjustly detained by any of Proviso. the charitable institutions in this section referred to or any other person believing that in the case of any child in any of the said institutions a real grievance or just cause of complaint exists, may make complaint to the judge or superintendent, and the judge or, with the minister's approval, the superintendent may make such order as to the disposition of the child as, having regard to the welfare of the child, may under all the circumstances of the case appear to be just and reasonable.

14. The words "the said Act" wherever they occur in this Act mean *The Act for the prevention of cruelty to and better protection of Children,* chapter 45, of the Acts passed in the 56th year of Her Majesty's reign, and this Act will be read with and form a part of the said Act.

BILL.

An Act for the further protection of Children.

First Reading, 1st March, 1895.
Second Reading, 21st March, 1895.
Third Reading, 11th April, 1895.

Mr. GIBSON,
(Hamilton).

TORONTO:
PRINTED BY L. K. CAMERON,
Printer to the Queen's Most Excellent Majesty.

PART IV.

DOMINION STATUTES RELATING TO PENITENTIARIES, REFORMATORIES, SENTENCES, PARDONS, AND THE PROTECTION OF CHILDREN.

CANADA STATUTES.

CHAPTER 177.

An Act respecting Juvenile Offenders.

A. D. 1886.

HER Majesty, by and with the advice and consent of the Senate and House of Commons of Canada, enacts as follows :—

1. This Act may be cited as "*The Juvenile Offenders' Act.*" Short title.

2. In this Act, unless the context otherwise requires,— Interpretation.

(*a.*) The expression "two or more justices," or "the justices" includes,— "Two or more justices" or "the justices."

(1.) In the Provinces of Ontario and Manitoba any judge of the county court being a justice of the peace, police magistrate or stipendiary magistrate, or any two justices of the peace, acting within their respective jurisdictions; In Ontario and Manitoba.

(2.) In the Province of Quebec any two or more justices of the peace, the sheriff of any district, except Montreal and Quebec, the deputy sheriff of Gaspé and any recorder, judge of the Sessions of the Peace, police magistrate, district magistrate or stipendiary magistrate acting within the limits of their respective jurisdictions; In Quebec.

(3.) In the Provinces of Nova Scotia, New Brunswick, Prince Edward Island, and British Columbia, and in the District of Keewatin, any functionary or tribunal invested by the proper legislative authority with power to do acts usually required to be done by two or more justices of the peace; In N.S., N.B., P.E.I., and B.C.

(4.) In the North-West Territories, any judge of the Supreme Court of the said Territories, any two justices of the peace sitting together, and any functionary or tribunal having the powers of two justices of the peace: In the N.-W.T.

(*b.*) The expression "the common gaol or other place of confinement" includes any reformatory prison provided for the reception of juvenile offenders in the Province in which the conviction referred to takes place, and to which, by the law of that Province, the offender may be sent. 32-33 V., c. 33, s. 1 ;—37 V., c. 39, s. 3, *part ;*—39 V., c. 21, sch., *part ;*—40 V., c. 4, sch., *part ;*—47 V., c. 42, s. 2, *part ;*—49 V., c. 25, s. 30. "Common gaol or other place of confinement."

offence which is simple larceny, or punishable as simp[le] larceny, and whose age, at the period of the commission [or] attempted commission of such offence, does not, in the opin[ion] of the justice before whom he is brought or appears, ex[ceed] the age of sixteen years, shall, upon conviction thereo[f] in open court, upon his own confession or upon proof, befor[e] any two or more justices, be committed to the common gao[l] or other place of confinement within the jurisdiction of suc[h] justices, there to be imprisoned, with or without hard labo[ur] for any term not exceeding three months, or, in the discre[tion] tion of such justices, shall forfeit and pay such sum, not ex[ceeding] ceeding twenty dollars, as such justices adjudge. 32-33 V[ict.], c. 33, s. 2.

Compelling person accused to attend.

4. Whenever any person, whose age is alleged not to ex[ceed] ceed sixteen years, is charged with any offence mentioned i[n] the next preceding section, on the oath of a credible witnes[s] before any justice of the peace, such justice may issue hi[s] summons or warrant, to summon or to apprehend the perso[n] so charged, to appear before any two justices of the peac[e] at a time and place to be named in such summons or war[rant] rant. 32-33 V., c. 33, s. 7.

Power to remand or take bail.

5. Any justice of the peace, if he thinks fit, may reman[d] for further examination or for trial, or suffer to go at larg[e] upon his finding sufficient sureties, any such person charge[d] before him with any such offence as aforesaid. 32-33 V[ict.], c. 33, s. 8.

Condition of recognizance.

6. Every such surety shall be bound by recognizance t[o] be conditioned for the appearance of such person before th[e] same or some other justice or justices of the peace for furthe[r] examination, or for trial before two or more justices of th[e] peace as aforesaid, or for trial by indictment at the prope[r] court of criminal jurisdiction, as the case may be. 32-33 V[ict.], c. 33, s. 9.

Enlarging or discharging recognizance.

7. Every such recognizance may be enlarged, from tim[e] to time, by any such justice or justices to such further tim[e] as he or they appoint; and every such recognizance not s[o] enlarged shall be discharged without fee or reward, whe[n] the person has appeared according to the condition thereo[f]. 32-33 V., c. 33, s. 10.

Defendant to be asked if he consents to be tried summarily.

8. The justices before whom any person is charged an[d] proceeded against under this Act, before such person is aske[d] whether he has any cause to show why he should not b[e] convicted, shall say to the person so charged, these word[s] or words to the like effect :

"We shall have to hear what you wish to say in answe[r] "to the charge against you ; but if you wish to be tried b[y] "a jury, you must object now to our deciding upon it a[t] "[once.]"

And if such person, or a parent or guardian of such person, then objects, such person shall be dealt with as if this Act had not been passed; but nothing in this Act shall prevent the summary conviction of any such person before one or more justices of the peace, for any offence for which he is liable to be so convicted under any other Act. 32-33 V., c. 33, s. 3.

If he does not consent.

9. If the justices are of opinion, before the person charged has made his defence, that the charge is, from any circumstance, a fit subject for prosecution by indictment, or if the person charged, upon being called upon to answer the charge, objects to the case being summarily disposed of under the provisions of this Act, such justices shall, instead of summarily adjudicating thereupon, deal with the case in all respects as if this Act had not been passed; and, in the latter case, shall state in the warrant of commitment the fact of such election having been made. . 32-33 V., c. 33, s. 5, *part ;*—38 V., c. 47, s. 6, *part.*

Justices may send the case to be tried by a jury.

10. Any justice of the peace may, by summons, require the attendance of any person as a witness upon the hearing of any case before two justices, under the authority of this Act, at a time and place to be named in such summons. 32-33 V., c. 33, s. 11.

Summoning witnesses.

11. Any such justice may require and bind by recognizance every person whom he considers necesssary to be examined, touching the matter of such charge, to attend at the time and place appointed by him and then and there to give evidence upon the hearing of such charge. 32-33 V., c. 33, s. 12.

Binding witnesses to attend.

12. If any person so summoned or required or bound, as aforesaid, neglects or refuses to attend in pursuance of such summons or recognizance, and if proof is given of such person having been duly summoned, as hereinafter mentioned, or bound by recognizance, as aforesaid, either of the justices before whom any such person should have attended, may issue a warrant to compel his appearance as a witness. 32-33 V., c. 33, s. 13.

Compelling attendance in case of refusal or neglect.

13. Every summons issued under the authority of this Act may be served by delivering a copy thereof to the person, or to some inmate at such person's usual place of abode, and every person so required by any writing under the hand or hands of any justice or justices to attend and give evidence as aforesaid, shall be deemed to have been duly summoned. 32-33 V., c. 33, s. 14.

Service of summons.

14. If the justices, upon the hearing of any such case, deem the offence not proved, or that it is not expedient to

Discharge in certain cases.

inflict any punishment, they shall dismiss the person charged —in the latter case on his finding sureties for his future **Certificate of** good behavior, and in the former case without sureties, and **discharge.** then make out and deliver to the person charged a certificate in the form A in the schedule to this Act, or to the like effect under the hands of such justices, stating the fact of such dismissal. 32-33 V., c. 33, s. 4, *part.*

Effect of such **15.** Every person who obtains such certificate of dismis-
certificate or sal, or is so convicted, shall be released from all further or
of conviction. other criminal proceedings for the same cause. 32-33 V., c. 33, s. 6.

Form of con- **16.** The justices before whom any person is summarily
viction. convicted of any offence hereinbefore mentioned, may cause the conviction to be drawn up in the form B in the schedule hereto, or in any other form to the same effect, and the conviction shall be good and effectual to all intents and purposes. 32-33 V., c. 33, s. 15, *part.*

Conviction **17.** No such conviction shall be quashed for want of form,
not void for or be removed by *certiorari* or otherwise into any court of
want of form, record; and no warrant of commitment shall be held void
&c. by reason of any defect therein, if it is therein alleged that the person has been convicted, and there is a good and valid conviction to sustain the same. 32-33 V., c. 33, s. 16.

Conviction to **18.** The justices before whom any person is convicted
be sent to under the provisions of this Act, shall forthwith transmit
clerk of the the conviction and recognizances to the clerk of the peace
peace, &c. or other proper officer, for the district, city, county or union of counties wherein the offence was committed, there to be kept by the proper officer among the records of the court of General or Quarter Sessions of the Peace, or of any other court discharging the functions of a court of General or Quarter Sessions of the Peace. 32-33 V., c. 33, s. 17.

Returns to **19.** Every clerk of the peace, or other proper officer, shall
Minister of transmit to the Minister of Agriculture a quarterly return
Agriculture. of the names, offences and punishments mentioned in the convictions, with such other particulars as are, from time to time, required. 32-33 V., c. 33, s. 18.

No forfeiture; **20.** No conviction under the authority of this Act shall
but restitu- be attended with any forfeiture, except such penalty as is
tion may be imposed by the sentence; but whenever any person is ad-
ordered. judged guilty under the provisions of this Act, the presiding justice may order restitution of the property in respect of which the offence was committed, to the owner thereof or his representatives. 32-33 V., c. 33, s. 19.

Or the pay- **21.** If such property is not then forthcoming, the justices,
ment of the whether they award punishment or not, may inquire into
value in

think proper, order payment of such sum of money to the true owner, by the person convicted, either at one time or by instalments, at such periods as the justices deem reasonable.   32-33 V., c. 33, s. 20.

22. The person ordered to pay such sum may be sued for the same as a debt in any court in which debts of the like amount are, by law, recoverable, with costs of suit, according to the practice of such court.   32-33 V., c. 33, s. 21. *Recovery of such value.*

23. Whenever the justices adjudge any offender to forfeit and pay a pecuniary penalty under the authority of this Act, and such penalty is not forthwith paid, they may, if they deem it expedient, appoint some future day for the payment thereof, and order the offender to be detained in safe custody until the day so appointed, unless such offender gives security, to the satisfaction of the justices, for his appearance on such day ; and the justices may take such security by way of recognizance or otherwise in their discretion.   32-33 V., c. 33, s. 22. *Enforcing payment of penalties.*

24. If at any time so appointed such penalty has not been paid, the same or any other justices of the peace may, by warrant under their hands and seals, commit the offender to the common gaol or other place of confinement within their jurisdiction, there to remain for any time not exceeding three months, reckoned from the day of such adjudication.   32-33 V., c. 33, s. 23. *Committal for non-payment.*

25. The justices before whom any person is prosecuted or tried for any offence cognizable under this Act, may, in their discretion, at the request of the prosecutor or of any other person who appears on recognizance or summons to prosecute or give evidence against such person, order payment to the prosecutor and witnesses for the prosecution, of such sums as to them seem reasonable and sufficient, to reimburse such prosecutor and witnesses for the expenses they have severally incurred in attending before them, and in otherwise carrying on such prosecution, and also to compensate them for their trouble and loss of time therein,—and may order payment to the constables and other peace officers for the apprehension and detention of any person so charged.   32-33 V., c. 33, s. 24. *Costs of prosecution may be awarded.*

26. The justices may, although no conviction takes place, order all or any of the payments aforesaid to be made, when they are of opinion that the persons, or any of them, have acted in good faith.   32-33 V., c. 33, s. 25. *Even without conviction.*

27. Every fine imposed under the authority of this Act shall be paid and applied as follows, that is to say :— *Application of penalties.*

In Ontario. (*a.*) In the Province of Ontario, to the justices who impose the same, or the clerk of the county court, or the clerk of the peace, or other proper officer, as the case may be, to be by him or them paid over to the county treasurer for county purposes;

In Quebec. (*b.*) In any new district in the Province of Quebec, to the sheriff of such district as treasurer of the building and jury fund for such district, to form part of such fund, and in any other district in the Province of Quebec, to the prothonotary of such district, to be applied by him, under the direction of the Lieutenant Governor in Council, towards the keeping in repair of the court house in such district, or to be added by him to the moneys or fees collected by him for the erection of a court house or gaol in such district, so long as such fees are collected to defray the cost of such erection;

In N.S. and N.B. (*c.*) In the Provinces of Nova Scotia and New Brunswick, to the county treasurer, for county purposes; and—

In P.E.I., Man., and B.C. (*d.*) In the Provinces of Prince Edward Island, Manitoba and British Columbia, to the treasurer of the Province. 32-33 V., c. 33, s. 26 ;—40 V., c. 4, s. 8, *part.*

Certificate of expenses. **28.** The amount of expenses of attending before the justices and the compensation for trouble and loss of time therein, and the allowances to the constables and other peace officers for the apprehension and detention of the offender, and the allowances to be paid to the prosecutor, witnesses and constables for attending at the trial or examination of the offender, shall be ascertained by and certified under the hands of such justices; but the amount of the costs, charges and expenses attending any such prosecution, to be allowed and paid as aforesaid, shall not in any one case exceed the sum of eight dollars. 32-33 V., c. 33, s. 27.

By whom such expenses shall be paid. **29.** Every such order of payment to any prosecutor or other person, after the amount thereof has been certified by the proper justices of the peace as aforesaid, shall be forthwith made out and delivered by the said justices or one of them, or by the clerk of the peace or other proper officer, as the case may be, to such prosecutor or other person; upon such clerk or officer being paid his lawful fee for the same, and shall be made upon the officer to whom fines imposed under the authority of this Act are required to be paid over in the district, city, county or union of counties in which the offence was committed, or was supposed to have been committed, who, upon sight of every such order, shall forthwith pay to the person named therein, or to any other person duly authorized to receive the same on his behalf, out of any moneys received by him under this Act, the money in such order mentioned, and shall be allowed the same in his accounts of such moneys. 32-33 V., c. 33, s. 28

As to certain offences in P.E.I., B.C., **30.** This Act shall not apply to any offence committed in the Provinces of Prince Edward Island or British Colum-

bia, or the District of Keewatin, punishable by imprison- *and Kee-*
ment for two years and upwards; and in such Provinces *watin.*
and District it shall not be necessary to transmit any recognizance to the clerk of the peace or other proper officer.
39 V., c. 21, sch., *part ;*—40 V., c. 4, sch., *part ;*—47 V., c. 42,
s. 2, *part.*

31. This Act shall not authorize two or more justices of *No sentence*
the peace to sentence offenders to imprisonment in a reform- *to a reforma-*
atory in the Province of Ontario.   43 V., c. 39, s. 15, *part.* *tory in Ontario.*

SCHEDULE.

FORM A.

To wit: ,} justices of the peace for
the   of   , (*or if a recorder,*
&c., I, a   , of the
of   , *as the case may be*), do hereby certify, that
on the   day of   , in the year   ,
at   , in the said   of   , (M. N.)
was brought before us, the said justices (*or me, the said*
  ), charged with the following offence, that is
to say (*here state briefly the particulars of the charge*), and that
we, the said justices, (*or I, the said* .   ) thereupon
dismissed the said charge.

Given under our hands (*or my hand*) this   day of

J. P. [L. S.]
J. R. [L. S.]
or S. J. [L. S.]   .

FORM B.

To wit: ,} Be it remembered, that on the   day ot
  , in the year
    , at   , in the district of
    (county *or* united counties, &c., *or as the case*
may be), A. O. is convicted before us, J. P. and J. R., justices
of the peace for the said district (*or city*, &c., *or me*, S. J.,
recorder, &c.,   , of the   , of   , *or*
as the case may be) for that, he, the said A. O. did (*specify the*
offence and the time and place when and where the same was
committed, as the case may be, but without setting forth the evi-
dence), and we, the said J. P. and J. R. (*or I, the said* S. J.),
adjudge the said A. O., for his said offence, to be imprisoned
in the   (*or to be imprisoned in the*   ,
and there kept at hard labor), for the space of   ,

forfeit and pay   (*here state the penalty
actually imposed*), and in default of immediate payment of
the said sum, to be imprisoned in the   (*or to
be imprisoned in the   and kept at hard
labor*) for the term of   , unless the said sum
is sooner paid.

Given under our hand and seals (*or* my hand and seal),
the day and year first above mentioned.

J. P. [L. S.]
J. R. [L. S.]
or S. J. [L. S.]

32-33 V., c. 33, s. 4, *part, and* s. 15, *part.*

<hr />

OTTAWA : Printed by Brown Chamberlin, Law Printer to the Queen's Most
Excellent Majesty.

CHAPTER 181.

An Act respecting Punishments, Pardons and the Commutation of Sentences. A. D. 1886.

HER Majesty, by and with the advice and consent of the Senate and House of Commons of Canada, enacts as follows :—

PUNISHMENTS.

1. Whenever a person doing a certain act is declared to be guilty of any offence, and to be liable to punishment therefor, it shall be understood that such person shall only be deemed guilty of such offence and liable to such punishment after being duly convicted of such act. 32-33 V., c. 29 s. 1, *part.*

Punishment after conviction only.

2. Whenever it is provided that the offender shall be liable to different degrees or kinds of punishment, the punishment to be inflicted shall, subject to the limitations contained in the enactment, be in the discretion of the court or tribunal before which the conviction takes place. 32-33 V., c. 29, s. 1, *part.*

Degree of punishment in the discretion of the court.

3. Whenever any offender is punishable under two or more Acts or two or more sections of the same Act, he may be tried and punished under any of such Acts or sections; but no person shall be twice punished for the same offence. 32-33 V., c. 20, ss. 40, *part and* 41, *part, and* c. 21, s. 90, *part;* —36 V., c. 55, s. 33 ;—40 V., c. 35, s. 6.

If offender is punishable under two or more Acts, &c.

CAPITAL PUNISHMENT.

4. Every one who is indicted as principal or accessory for any offence made capital by any statute, shall be liable to the same punishment, whether he is convicted by verdict or on confession. 32-33 V., c. 29, s. 82.

Conviction by verdict or on confession.

5. In all cases of treason, the sentence or judgment to be pronounced against any person convicted and adjudged guilty thereof shall be, that he be hanged by the neck until he is dead. 31 V., c. 69, s. 4.

Sentence on conviction for treason.

into execution, and all other proceedings upon such sentence and in respect thereof may be had and taken in the same manner, and the court before which the conviction takes place shall have the same powers in all respects, as after a conviction for any other felony for which a prisoner may be sentenced to suffer death as a felon.   32-33 V., c. 20, s. 2.

Court to direct execution of sentence of death.   **7.** Whenever any offender has been convicted before any court of criminal jurisdiction, of an offence for which such offender is liable to and receives sentence of death, the court shall order and direct execution to be done on the offender in the manner provided by law.   32-33 V., c. 29, s. 106.

Report to be made by the judge.   **8.** In the case of any prisoner sentenced to the punishment of death, the judge before whom such prisoner has been convicted shall forthwith make a report of the case to the Secretary of State, for the information of the Governor General ; and the day to be appointed for carrying the sentence into execution shall be such as, in the opinion of the judge, will allow sufficient time for the signification of the **Reprieve in certain cases.** Governor's pleasure before such day, and if the judge thinks such prisoner ought to be recommended for the exercise of the Royal mercy, or if, from the non-decision of any point of law reserved in the case, or from any other cause, it becomes necessary to delay the execution, he, or any other judge of the same court, or who might have held or sat in such court, may, from time to time, either in term or in vacation, reprieve such offender for such period or periods beyond the time fixed for the execution of the sentence as are necessary for the consideration of the case by the Crown.   32-33 V., c. 29, s. 107 ;—36 V., c. 3, s. 1.

Treatment of persons condemned to death.   **9.** Every one who is sentenced to suffer death shall, after judgment, be confined in some safe place within the prison, apart from all other prisoners ; and no person except the gaoler and his servants, the medical officer or surgeon of the prison, a chaplain or a minister of religion, shall have access to any such convict, without the permission, in writing, of the court or judge before whom such convict has been tried, or of the sheriff.   32-33 V., c. 29, s. 108.

Judgment to be executed within walls of prison.   **10.** Judgment of death to be executed on any prisoner shall be carried into effect within the walls of the prison in which the offender is confined at the time of execution. 32-33 V., c. 29, s. 109.

Sheriff, &c., to be present.   **11.** The sheriff charged with the execution, and the gaoler and medical officer or surgeon of the prison, and such other officers of the prison and such persons as the sheriff requires, shall be present at the execution.   32-33 V., c. 29, s. 110.

12. Any justice of the peace for the district, county or place to which the prison belongs, and such relatives of the prisoner or other persons as it seems to the sheriff proper to admit within the prison for the purpose, and any minister of religion who desires to attend, may also be present at the execution. 32-33 V., c. 29, s. 111. *Justices of the peace, &c., may be present.*

13. As soon as may be after judgment of death has been executed on the offender, the medical officer or surgeon of the prison shall examine the body of the offender, and shall ascertain the fact of death, and shall sign a certificate thereof, and deliver the same to the sheriff. 32-33 V., c. 29, s. 112. *Surgeon to certify death.*

14. The sheriff and the gaoler of the prison, and such justices and other persons present, if any, as the sheriff requires or allows, shall also sign a declaration to the effect that judgment of death has been executed on the offender. 32-33 V., c. 29, s. 113. *Declaration to be signed by sheriff, &c.*

15. The duties imposed upon the sheriff, gaoler, medical officer or surgeon by the four sections next preceding, may and shall, in his absence, be performed by his lawful deputy or assistant, or other officer or person ordinarily acting for him, or conjointly with him, in the performance of his duties. 32-33 V., c. 29, s. 114. *Deputies may act.*

16. A coroner of the district, county or place to which the prison belongs, wherein judgment of death is executed on any offender, shall, within twenty-four hours after the execution, hold an inquest on the body of the offender; and the jury at the inquest shall inquire into and ascertain the identity of the body, and whether judgment of death was duly executed on the offender; and the inquisition shall be in duplicate, and one of the originals shall be delivered to the sheriff. 32-33 V., c. 29, s. 115. *Coroner's inquest on the body.*

17. No officer of the prison or prisoner confined therein shall, in any case, be a juror on the inquest. 32-33 V., c. 29, s. 116. *Officers and prisoners not to be jurors.*

18. The body of every offender executed shall be buried within the walls of the prison within which judgment of death is executed on him, unless the Lieutenant Governor in Council, being satisfied that there is not, within the walls of any prison, sufficient space for the convenient burial of offenders executed therein, permits some other place to be used for the purpose. 32-33 V., c. 29, s. 117. *Burial of the body.*

19. Every one who knowingly and wilfully signs any false certificate or declaration required with respect to any execution, is guilty of a misdemeanor, and liable to imprisonment for any term less than two years. 32-33 V., c. 29, s. 120. *Penalty for signing false certificate.*

Certificate, &c., to be sent to Secretary of State, and exhibited at entrance to prison.

20. Every certificate and declaration, and a duplicate of the inquest required by this Act, shall, in every case, be sent with all convenient speed by the sheriff to the Secretary of State, or to such other officer as is, from time to time, appointed for the purpose by the Governor in Council; and printed copies of such several instruments shall, as soon as possible, be exhibited, and shall, for twenty-four hours at least, be kept exhibited on or near the principal entrance of the prison within which judgment of death is executed. 32-33 V., c. 29, s. 121.

Saving clause as to legality of execution.

21. The omission to comply with any provision of the preceding sections of this Act shall not make the execution of judgment of death illegal in any case in which such execution would otherwise have been legal. 32-33 V., c. 29, s. 123.

As to other matters.

22. Except in so far as is hereby otherwise provided, judgment of death shall be carried into effect in the same manner as if this Act had not been passed. 32-33 V., c. 29, s. 124.

IMPRISONMENT.

Offence not punishable with death.

23. Every one who is convicted of any offence not punishable with death shall be punished in the manner, if any, prescribed by the statute especially relating to such offence. 32-33 V., c. 29, s. 88, *part.*

Felony when there is no special punishment.

24. Every person convicted of any felony for which no punishment is specially provided, shall be liable to imprisonment for life:

And misdemeanor on indictment.

2. Every one who is convicted on indictment of any misdemeanor for which no punishment is specially provided, shall be liable to five years' imprisonment:

And on summary conviction.

3. Every one who is summarily convicted of any offence for which no punishment is specially provided, shall be liable to a penalty not exceeding twenty dollars, or to imprisonment, with or without hard labor, for a term not exceeding three months, or to both. 32-33 V., c. 29, s. 88, *part.*

Second conviction for felony.

25. Every one who is convicted of felony, not punishable with death, committed after a previous conviction for felony, is liable to imprisonment for life, unless some other punishment is directed by any statute for the particular offence,—in which case the offender shall be liable to the punishment thereby awarded, and not to any other. 32-33 V., c. 29, s. 83.

be sentenced to any shorter term of imprisonment than the minimum term, if any, prescribed for the offence of which he is convicted. 32-33 V., c. 29, ss. 89 *and* 90, *part.*

27. When an offender is convicted of more offences than one, before the same court or person at the same sitting, or when any offender, under sentence or undergoing punishment for one offence, is convicted of any other offence, the court or person passing sentence may, on the last conviction, direct that the sentences passed upon the offender for his several offences shall take effect one after another. 32-33 V., c. 29, s. 92.

Offender convicted of more offences than one, &c.

28. Every one who is sentenced to imprisonment for life, or for a term of years, not less than two, shall be sentenced to imprisonment in the penitentiary for the Province in which the conviction takes place:

Imprisonment in a penitentiary.

2. Every one who is sentenced to imprisonment for a term less than two years shall, if no other place is expressly mentioned, be sentenced to imprisonment in the common gaol of the district, county or place in which the sentence is pronounced, or if there is no common gaol there, then in that common gaol which is nearest to such locality, or in some lawful prison or place of confinement, other than a penitentiary, in which the sentence of imprisonment may be lawfully executed:

In the common gaol.

3. Provided, that any prisoner sentenced for any term by any military, naval or militia court martial, or by any military or naval authority under any Mutiny Act, may be sentenced to imprisonment in a penitentiary:

Prisoners sentenced by court martial.

4. Imprisonment in a penitentiary, in the Central Prison for the Province of Ontario, in the Andrew Mercer Ontario Reformatory for females, and in any reformatory prison for females in the Province of Quebec, shall be with hard labor, whether so directed in the sentence or not:

Hard labor in penitentiary, &c.

5. Imprisonment in a common gaol, or a public prison, other than those last mentioned, shall be with or without hard labor, in the discretion of the court or person passing sentence, if the offender is convicted on indictment, or under " *The Speedy Trials Act*,"—and, if convicted summarily, may be with hard labor, if hard labor is part of the punishment for the offence of which such offender is convicted,—and if such imprisonment is to be with hard labor, the sentence shall so direct:

And in other places of confinement.

6. The term of imprisonment, in pursuance of any sentence, shall, unless otherwise directed in the sentence, commence on and from the day of passing such sentence, but no time during which the convict is out on bail shall be reckoned as part of the term of imprisonment to which he is sentenced:

Commencement of term of imprisonment.

Prisoners sub-

shall be subject to the provisions of the statutes relating to such penitentiary, gaol or prison, and to all rules and regulations lawfully made with respect thereto. 32-33 V., c. 29, ss. 1, *part*, 91, 93, 94, *part*, 96, *part*, *and* 97 ;—34 V., c. 30, s. 3, *part* ;—43 V., c. 39, s. 14, *part* ;—43 V., c. 40, s. 9, *part* ;— 44 V., c. 32, s. 4 ;—46 V., c. 37, s. 4.

REFORMATORIES.

Certain offenders may be sentenced to imprisonment in a reformatory.

29. The court or person before whom any offender whose age at the time of his trial does not, in the opinion of the court, exceed sixteen years, is convicted, whether summarily or otherwise, of any offence punishable by imprisonment, may sentence such offender to imprisonment in any reformatory prison in the Province in which such conviction takes place, subject to the provisions of any Act respecting imprisonment in such reformatory; and such imprisonment shall be substituted, in such case, for the imprisonment in the penitentiary or other place of confinement by which the offender would otherwise be punishable under any Act or

As to term of imprisonment.

law relating thereto: Provided, that in no case shall the sentence be less than two years' or more than five years' confinement in such reformatory prison; and in every case where the term of imprisonment is fixed by law to be more than five years, then such imprisonment shall be in the penitentiary:

Labor in a reformatory.

2. Every person imprisoned in a reformatory shall be liable to perform such labor as is required of such person. 38 V., c. 43 ;—43 V., c. 39, ss. 1, *part*, *and* 14, *part*, *and* c. 40, ss. 1, *part*, *and* 9, *part*.

WHIPPING.

Whipping.

30. Whenever whipping may be awarded for any offence, the court may sentence the offender to be once, twice or thrice whipped, within the limits of the prison, under the supervision of the medical officer of the prison; and the number of strokes and the instrument with which they shall be inflicted shall be specified by the court in the sentence;

Time for its infliction.

and, whenever practicable, every whipping shall take place not less than ten days before the expiration of any term of imprisonment to which the offender is sentenced for the offence:

No female to be whipped.

2. Whipping shall not be inflicted on any female. 32-33 V., c. 20, ss. 20, 21, *parts*, *and* c. 29, s. 95 ;—40 V., c. 26, s. 6.

SURETIES FOR KEEPING THE PEACE, AND FINES.

Sureties may be required in cases of felony.

31. Every one who is convicted of felony may be required to enter into his own recognizances, and to find sureties, both or either, for keeping the peace, in addition to any punishment otherwise authorized:

2. Every one who is convicted of any misdemeanor may, *And in cases* in addition to or in lieu of any punishment otherwise author- *of misde-* ized, be fined, and required to enter into his own recogni- *meanor.* zances, and to find sureties, both or either, for keeping the peace and being of good behavior:

3. No person shall be imprisoned for not finding sureties *Imprisonment* under this section, for any term exceeding one year. 31 V., *in default* c. 72, s. 5, *part;*—32-33 V., c. 18, s. 34, *and* c. 19, s. 58, *and* *limited.* c. 20, s. 77, *and* c. 21, s. 122, *and* c. 22, s. 74.

32. Whenever any person who has been required to enter *Notice to be* into a recognizance with sureties to keep the peace and *given to a* be of good behavior has, on account of his default therein, *person has* remained imprisoned for two weeks, the sheriff, gaoler or *been im-* warden shall give notice, in writing, of the facts to a judge *two weeks* of a superior court, or to a judge of the county court of *in default of* the county or district in which such gaol or prison is situate, *sureties.* or, in the North-West Territories, to a stipendiary magistrate, —and such judge or magistrate may order the discharge of *Discharge* such person, thereupon or at a subsequent time, upon notice *may be* to the complainant or otherwise, or may make such other *ordered.* order, as he sees fit, respecting the number of sureties, the sum in which they are to be bound and the length of time for which such person may be bound. 41 V., c. 19 s. 1

33. Whenever a fine may be awarded or a penalty im- *Amount of* posed for any offence, the amount of such fine or penalty *fine at the dis-* shall, within such limits, if any, as are prescribed in that *court.* behalf, be in the discretion of the court or person passing sentence or convicting, as the case may be. 32-33 V., c. 29, s. 90, *part.*

SOLITARY CONFINEMENT.—PILLORY.

34. The punishment of solitary confinement or of the *No solitary* pillory shall not be awarded by any court. 32-33 V., c. 29, *confinement* s. 81. *or pillory.*

DEODAND.

35. There shall be no forfeiture of any chattels, which *No deodand.* have moved to or caused the death of any human being, in respect of such death. 32-33 V., c. 29, s. 54.

ATTAINDER.

36. Except in cases of treason, or of abetting, procuring *Except for* or counselling the same, no attainder shall extend to the *high treason* disinheriting of any heir, or to the prejudice of the right or *to disinherit* title of any person, other than the right or title of the *the heir.* offender during his natural life only. 32-33 V., c. 29, s. 55.

The heir may enter after death of offender.

37. Every one to whom, after the death of any such offender, the right or interest to or in any lands, tenements or hereditaments, should or would have appertained, if no such attainder had taken place, may, after the death of such offender, enter into the same. 32-33 V., c. 19, s. 56.

PARDONS.

Pardon when the committal is for non-payment of moneys.

38. The Crown may extend the Royal mercy to any person sentenced to imprisonment by virtue of any statute, although such person is imprisoned for non-payment of money to some person other than the Crown. 32-33 V., c. 29, s. 125.

Effect of pardon.

39. Whenever the Crown is pleased to extend the Royal mercy to any offender convicted of a felony punishable with death or otherwise, and grants to such offender either a free or a conditional pardon, by warrant under the Royal Sign Manual, countersigned by one of the principal Secretaries of State, or by warrant under the hand and seal-at-arms of the Governor General, the discharge of such offender out of custody, in case of a free pardon, and the performance of the condition in the case of a conditional pardon, shall have the effect of a pardon of such offender, under the Great Seal, as to the felony for which such pardon has been granted ;

As to subsequent convictions.

but no free pardon, nor any discharge in consequence thereof, nor any conditional pardon, nor the performance of the condition thereof, in any of the cases aforesaid, shall prevent or mitigate the punishment to which the offender might otherwise be lawfully sentenced, on a subsequent conviction for any felony or offence other than that for which the pardon was granted. 32-33 V., c. 29, s. 126.

COMMUTATION OF SENTENCE.

Crown may commute sentence of death.

40. The Crown may commute the sentence of death passed upon any person convicted of a capital crime, to imprisonment in the penitentiary for life, or for any term of years not less than two years, or to imprisonment in any other gaol or place of confinement for any period less than

Form and effect of commutation.

two years, with or without hard labor ; and an instrument under the hand and seal-at-arms of the Governor General, declaring such commutation of sentence, or a letter or other instrument under the hand of the Secretary of State or of the Under Secretary of State, shall be sufficient authority to any judge or justice, having jurisdiction in such case, or to any sheriff or officer to whom such letter or instrument is addressed, to give effect to such commutation, and to do all such things and to make such orders, and to give such directions, as are requisite for the change of custody of such convict, and for his conduct to and delivery at such gaol or place of confinement or penitentiary, and his detention therein, according to the terms on which his sentence has been commuted. 32-33 V., c. 29, s. 127.

UNDERGOING SENTENCE, EQUIVALENT TO A PARDON.

41. When any offender has been convicted of an offence not punishable with death, and has endured the punishment to which such offender was adjudged,—or if such offence is punishable with death and the sentence has been commuted, then if such offender has endured the punishment to which his sentence was commuted, the punishment so endured shall, as to the offence whereof the offender was so convicted, have the like effect and consequences as a pardon under the Great Seal; but nothing herein contained, nor the enduring of such punishment, shall prevent or mitigate any punishment to which the offender might otherwise be lawfully sentenced, on a subsequent conviction for any other offence. 32-33 V., c. 29, s. 128. *Undergoing sentence equivalent to a pardon.* *Proviso.*

42. When any person convicted of any offence has paid the sum adjudged to be paid, together with costs, under such conviction, or has received a remission thereof from the Crown, or has suffered the imprisonment awarded for non-payment thereof, or the imprisonment awarded in the first instance, or has been discharged from his conviction by the justice of the peace in any case in which such justice of the peace may discharge such person, he shall be released from all further or other proceedings for the same cause. 32-33 V., c. 21, s. 120, *and* c. 22, s. 78. *Undergoing punishment, &c., a bar to further proceedings.*

43. Nothing in this Act shall, in any manner, limit or affect Her Majesty's Royal prerogative of mercy 32-33 V., c. 29, s. 129. *Royal prerogative saved.*

GENERAL PROVISIONS.

44. The Governor in Council may, from time to time, make such rules and regulations to be observed on the execution of judgment of death in every prison, as he, from time to time, deems expedient for the purpose, as well of guarding against any abuse in such execution, as also of giving greater solemnity to the same, and of making known without the prison walls the fact that such execution is taking place. 32-33 V., c. 29, s. 118. *Governor in Council to make rules, &c., as to executions.*

45. All such rules and regulations shall be laid upon the tables of both Houses of Parliament within six weeks after the making thereof, or, if Parliament is not then sitting, within fourteen days after the next meeting thereof. 32-33 V., c. 29, s. 119. *Such rules to be laid before Parliament.*

46. The forms set forth in the schedule to this Act, with such variations or additions as circumstances require, shall *Forms in schedule to be used.*

be used for the respective purposes indicated in the said schedule, and according to the directions contained therein. 32-33 V., c. 29, s. 122.

Laws as to army and navy not affected.

47. Nothing in this Act shall alter or affect any laws relating to the government of Her Majesty's land or naval forces.   32-33 V., c. 29, s. 137.

SCHEDULE.

CERTIFICATE OF SURGEON.

I, A. B., surgeon (*or as the case may be*) of the (*describe the prison*), hereby certify that I, this day, examined the body of C. D., on whom judgment of death was this day executed in the said prison ; and that on such examination I found that the said C. D. was dead.

(Signed),   A. B

Dated this   day of   18 .

DECLARATION OF SHERIFF AND OTHERS.

We, the undersigned, hereby declare that judgment of death was this day executed on C. D., in the (*describe the prison*) in our presence.

Dated this   day of   18 .

E. F., Sheriff of——
L. M., Justice of the Peace for——
G. H., Gaoler of——
&c.,   &c.

32-33 V., c. 29, sch. B.

SURETIES.

COMPLAINT BY THE PARTY THREATENED, FOR SURETIES FOR THE PEACE.

Canada.
Province of   ,
   district (*or* county,
   united counties, *or*
   as the case may be),
   of

, at N., in the said district, (county, *or as the case may be*) of   this   day of   , in the year one thousand eight hundred and   , who says that A. B., of the (*township*) of   , in the district (county, *or as the case may be*), of   , did, on the   day of   . (instant *or* last past, *as the case may be*), threaten the said C. D. in the words or to the effect following, that is to say, (*set them out, with the circumstances under which they were used*) : and that from the above and other threats used by the said A. B. towards the said C. D., he, the said C. D., is afraid that the said A. B. will do him some bodily injury, and therefore prays that the said A. B. may be required to find sufficient sureties to keep the peace and be of good behavior towards him, the said C. D. ; and the said C. D. also says that he does not make this complaint against nor require such sureties from the said A. B. from any malice or ill-will, but merely for the preservation of his person from injury.

FORM OF RECOGNIZANCE FOR THE SESSIONS.

Be it remembered that on the   day of   , in the year   , A. B. of   (*laborer*), L. M. of   (*grocer*), and N. O. of   (*butcher*), personally came before (*us*) the undersigned, (*two*) justices of the peace for the district (*or* county, united counties, *or as the case may be*), of   , and severally acknowledged themselves to owe to our Lady the Queen the several sums following, that is to say : the said A. B. the sum of   , and the said L. M. and N. O. the sum of   , each, of good and lawful money of Canada, to be made and levied of their goods and chattels, lands and tenements respectively, to the use of our said Lady the Queen, her heirs and successors, if he, the said A. B., fails in the condition indorsed (*or* hereunder written).

Taken and acknowledged the day and year first above mentioned, at   before us.

J. S.
J. T.

The condition of the within (*or* above) written recognizance is such that if the within bound A. B. (of, &c.), appears at the next court of General Sessions of the Peace, (*or other court discharging the functions of the court of General Sessions, or as the case may be*), to be holden in and for the said district (*or* county, united counties, *or as the case may be*), of   to do and receive what is then and there enjoined him by the court, and in the meantime keeps the peace and is of good behavior towards Her Majesty and her liege people, and specially towards C. D. (of, &c.), for the term of   now next ensuing, then the said recognizance to be void, otherwise to stand in full force and virtue.

FORM OF COMMITMENT IN DEFAULT OF SURETIES.

Canada.
Province of
  district (or county,
  united counties, or
  as the case may be),
  of ,

To all or any of the constables or other peace officers in the district (or county, united counties, or as the case may be), of   , and to the keeper of the common gaol of the said district (or county, united counties, or as the case may be), at   , in the said district (or county, &c.)

Whereas on the   day of   instant, complaint on oath was made before the undersigned (or J. L., Esquire) a justice of the peace in and for the said district (or county, united counties, or as the case may be), of by C. D., of the township of   , in the said district (or county, or as the case may be) (laborer), that A. B., of (&c.), on the   day of   , at the township of   , aforesaid,   did threaten (&c., follow to end of complaint, as in form above, in the past tense, then): And whereas the said A. B. was this day brought and appeared before the said justice (or J. L., Esquire), a justice of the peace in and for the said district (or county, united counties, or as the case may be), of   , to answer unto the said complaint: and having been required by me to enter into his own recognizance in the sum of   , with two sufficient sureties in the sum of   each, as well for his appearance at the next General Sessions of the Peace (or other court discharging the functions of the court of General Sessions, or as the case may be), to be held in and for the said district (or county, united counties, or as the case may be), of   , to do what shall be then and there enjoined him by the court, as also in the meantime to keep the peace and be of good behavior towards Her Majesty and her liege people, and especially towards the said C. D., has refused and neglected, and still refuses and neglects, to find such sureties: These are therefore to command you, and each of you, to take the said A. B., and him safely to convey to the (common gaol) at   aforesaid, and there to deliver him to the keeper thereof, together with this precept; And I do hereby command you, the said keeper of the (common gaol), to receive the said A. B. into your custody in the said (common gaol), there to imprison him until the said next General Sessions of the Peace (*or the next term of sitting of the said court discharging the functions of the court of General Sessions, or as the case may be*), unless he, in the meantime, finds sufficient sureties as well for his appearance at the said sessions (*or court*) as in the meantime to keep the peace as aforesaid.

Given under my hand and seal, this   day of   , in the year   , at   in the district (*or county, or as the case may be*) aforesaid.

32-33 V., c. 31, sch., *part.*   J. S.   [L. S.]

_____

OTTAWA: Printed by BROWN CHAMBERLIN, Law Printer to the Queen's Most Excellent Majesty.

CHAPTER 182.

An Act respecting Penitentiaries.

HER Majesty, by and with the advice and consent of the Senate and House of Commons of Canada, enacts as follows :—

1. This Act may be cited as "*The Penitentiary Act.*" 46 V., c. 37, s. 81. *Short title.*

2. All the penitentiaries in Canada and such other prisons, hospitals, asylums and other public institutions as are, from time to time, designated for that purpose by the Governor in Council, by proclamation in the *Canada Gazette*, and all prisoners and other persons confined therein and inmates thereof, shall be under the control of the Minister of Justice, who shall exercise over them complete administrative power. 46 V., c. 37, s. 1, *part.* *Penitentiaries, prisons, &c., to be under control of Minister of Justice.*

3. The Minister of Justice shall submit to the Governor General an annual report upon all the penitentiaries, prisons and other institutions under his control, to be laid before both Houses of Parliament within the first twenty-one days of each session thereof, showing the state of each penitentiary, prison or other institution, and the amounts received and expended in respect thereof, with such further information as is requisite. 46 V., c. 37, s. 1, *part.* *Annual report thereon by the Minister.*

4. The penitentiary situate near the city of Kingston, in the Province of Ontario, known as the Kingston Penitentiary,—the penitentiary situate at St. Vincent de Paul, in the Province of Quebec, known as the St. Vincent de Paul Penitentiary,—the penitentiary situate at Dorchester, in the Province of New Brunswick, known as the Dorchester Penitentiary,—the penitentiary situate in the county of Lisgar, in the Province of Manitoba, known as the Manitoba Penitentiary, and the penitentiary situate in the district of New Westminster, in the Province of British Columbia, known as the British Columbia Penitentiary, together with all the land appertaining to the same respectively, according to the respective metes and bounds thereof as now known and defined, and all the buildings and property thereon belonging to the same, are, all and each of them, hereby declared to be penitentiaries of Canada. 46 V., c. 37, s. 2. *Penitentiaries enumerated and described.*

Penitentiaries for the several Provinces.

5. The Kingston Penitentiary, for the Province of Ontario, —the St. Vincent de Paul Penitentiary, for the Province of Quebec,—the Dorchester Penitentiary, for the Provinces of Nova Scotia, New Brunswick and Prince Edward Island,— the Manitoba Penitentiary, for the Province of Manitoba, the North-West Territories and the District of Keewatin, and the British Columbia Penitentiary, for the Province of British Columbia, shall each be maintained as a prison for the confinement and reformation of persons lawfully convicted of crime before the courts of criminal jurisdiction of the Province, Territory or District for which it is the penitentiary, and sentenced to confinement for life, or for any term not less than two years.   32–33 V., c. 29, s. 96, *part ;*—46 V., c. 37. s. 3.

Governor in Council may establish penitentiaries, and declare any lands established as such not to be so.

6. The Governor in Council may declare, from time to time, by proclamation, to be published in the *Canada Gazette*, that any tract of land within Canada, of which the boundaries shall be particularly defined in the proclamation, is a penitentiary, and is to be so held within the meaning of this Act, —and by such proclamation may declare for what part of Canada the same shall be a penitentiary ; and the Governor in Council, by any proclamation published as aforesaid, may declare that any tract of land established as a penitentiary by the fourth section of this Act, or by any other law, or by proclamation under this section, from and after a certain day to be named in such proclamation, shall cease to be a penitentiary, or a penitentiary for a part of Canada named in such proclamation,—and such tract of land shall cease to be a penitentiary, or a penitentiary for such part of Canada, accordingly.   46 V., c. 37, s. 5.

What shall be included as part of a penitentiary.

7. Every penitentiary now established, or hereafter established by virtue of this Act, shall be held to include all carriages, wagons, sleighs and other vehicles for land carriage, and all boats, scows and other vessels for water carriage, being property belonging to such penitentiary, or employed by hire or otherwise in its service,—and also every wharf at or near the said penitentiary, which, although not within the limits mentioned in the proclamation establishing the same, is used for the accommodation of such boats, scows or other vessels, when so employed in or about any work or labor connected with such penitentiary.   46 V., c. 37, s. 6.

Streets, roads, &c., when to be part of a penitentiary.

Escapes.

8. Every street, highway or public thoroughfare of any kind, along or across which it is necessary that convicts should pass in going to and returning from their work, shall be considered, while so used, as a portion of the tract of land forming the penitentiary ; and every escape, or attempt at escape, and every rescue, or aid in rescue, which takes place on such street, highway or public thoroughfare, while so used, shall have the same effect as if such escape, or attempt at escape, or such rescue, or aid in rescue, had taken place within the prison walls or penitentiary limits. 46 V., c. 37, s. 7.

9. The inspector of penitentiaries, with the approval of the Minister of Justice, may authorize the warden of any penitentiary to construct rail or tram roads to communicate between any one part of the penitentiary and any other part, and to carry the same across, upon or along any public road or street intervening, in such manner as to cause the least possible inconvenience to passengers or carriages using such road or street: but the warden of such penitentiary shall not break ground upon any public road or street for the purpose of constructing such rail or tram roads, in virtue of such authority from the inspector, until after the lapse of one month after a copy of the writing giving such authority, certified by the warden, together with a plan showing the line which such rail or tram roads are to occupy, has been served upon the officer or person charged with the care or supervision of such public road. 46 V., c. 37, s. 8.

Tram roads may be made.

Notice to municipality.

10. The construction and repairs of buildings and other works in the penitentiaries shall be under the control of the Minister of Public Works. 46 V., c. 37, s. 9.

Construction and repair of buildings.

INSPECTOR.

11. The Governor in Council may appoint some fit and proper person to be inspector of all penitentiaries, and of such other prisons, hospitals, asylums and other public institutions as are, from time to time, designated by the Governor in Council; and the inspector shall hold office during pleasure, and shall be an officer of the Department of Justice, and, as such inspector, shall act as the representative of the Minister of Justice. 46 V., c. 37, s. 10.

Governor in Council may appoint inspector.

12. The inspector, under direction from the Minister of Justice, shall visit, examine and report to him, upon the state and management of all the penitentiaries, and all suggestions which the wardens thereof make for the improvement of such penitentiaries. 46 V., c. 37, s. 11.

Inspector to visit penitentiaries and report.

13. The inspector shall keep an exact record of all minutes of inspection made by him in the inspection books of the said institutions, together with all his proceedings in connection therewith, and, after each visit of inspection, shall transmit a copy thereof, under his hand, to the Minister of Justice. 46 V., c. 37, s. 12.

To keep minutes and transmit copy to Minister.

14. The inspector, by virtue of his office, without any property qualification, shall be a justice of the peace for every district, county, city or town of Canada, but shall· have power to act in matters connected with the criminal law

To be a justice of the peace.

15. The inspector shall, subject to the approval of the Governor in Council, make rules and regulations for the management, discipline and police of the penitentiaries, and for the duties and conduct of the wardens thereof, and of every other officer or class of officers or servants employed therein, and for the diet, clothing, maintenance, employment, instruction, discipline, correction, punishment and reward of convicts imprisoned therein, and may, from time to time, with such approval, annul, alter or amend the same; and the wardens of the penitentiaries, and every other officer and servant employed in or about the same, shall be bound to obey such rules and regulations when so approved. 46 V., c. 37, s. 14, *part.*

To make rules and regulations, &c., subject to approval of the Governor in Council.

16. The inspector shall make an annual report to the Minister of Justice on or before the first day of December in each year, which shall contain a full and accurate statement of the state, condition and management of the penitentiaries under his control and supervision, and inspected during the preceding fiscal year, together with such suggestions for the improvement of the same as he deems necessary and expedient, and accompanied by copies of the annual reports of the officers of the penitentiaries, and by such financial and statistical statements and tables as the books kept by them contain; and such report shall also comprise and embrace the following particulars, that is to say :—

To make an annual report.

What the report shall contain.

(*a*) Such statistical information in respect to each penitentiary as is embraced in the registers of such penitentiaries, together with any facts which have come to his knowledge with respect to the working of the criminal laws and penal system of Canada, or any injustice or hardship which, in his opinion, has arisen therefrom, and such suggestions for the improvement or amendment of the same, and for the prevention of crime or the reformation of criminals, as he deems expedient ;

Statistics, facts and suggestions.

(*b.*) An inventory and valuation of all the movable and immovable property belonging to the penitentiaries, respectively—distinguishing the estimated value of the several descriptions of property ;

Inventory and valuation of property.

(*c.*) A detailed statement showing the money receipts of the penitentiaries, and the sources from which they have been derived ; also, the expenditures, together with a statement of all debts due on account of the penitentiaries, showing the names of the persons to whom each is due, and showing also the debts, if any, due to the penitentiary, with the amount and nature of each debt ;

Receipts, expenditure and statement of debts.

(*d.*) An estimate of the expense of the penitentiaries for the ensuing year—distinguishing the ordinary from the extraordinary :

Estimates for ensuing year.

2. The wardens and other officers shall furnish to the inspector all information necessary for the preparation of

Officers to furnish information.

his report, on or before the first day of October in each year. 46 V., c. 37, s. 15.

17. If the inspector at any time finds that any penitentiary is out of repair, or does not possess the proper and requisite sanitary arrangements, or has become unsafe or unfit for the confinement of prisoners, or that the same does not afford sufficient space or room for the number of prisoners confined therein, or the requisite amount of shop and yard space for the proper industrial employment of the prisoners, he shall forthwith report the same to the Minister of Justice, and at the same time shall furnish a copy of such report for the Minister of Public Works. 46 V., c. 37, s. 16. *Special reports as to improvements and repairs.* *Copy to Minister of Public Works.*

EXAMINATIONS AND INVESTIGATIONS.

18. The inspector may, at all times, enter into and remain within any penitentiary or other public institution placed under his control as aforesaid, and have access to every part of the same, and examine all papers, documents, vouchers, records and books of every kind belonging thereto. 46 V., c. 37, s. 17, *part.* *Entry and examination of papers, &c.*

19. The inspector may investigate the conduct of any officer or servant employed in or about any penitentiary, or other such public institution, as aforesaid, or of any person found within the precincts thereof; and, for that purpose, by subpœna issued by him, may summon before him any person, and examine such person upon oath,—which oath the inspector may administer, and may compel the production of papers and writings before him ; and if any person duly summoned neglects or refuses to appear at the time and place specified in the subpœna legally served upon him, or refuses to give evidence or to produce the papers demanded of him, the inspector may cause the said person, by warrant under his hand, to be taken into custody and to be imprisoned in the common gaol of the locality, as for contempt of court, for a period not exceeding fourteen days. 46 V., c. 37, s. 17, *part* *Inquiries into conduct of officers, &c.* *Summoning witnesses and administering oaths.* *Punishment for refusal to give evidence.*

20. The Minister of Justice, at any time when he deems it necessary, may appoint one or more persons to make a special report on the state and management of any penitentiary, and in such case the person or persons so appointed, in order to enable him or them to make such special report, shall have the powers given to the inspector by the two sections next preceding. 46 V., c. 37, s. 18. *Minister of Justice may cause special reports to be made by others than inspector.*

ACCOUNTANT OF PENITENTIARIES.

21. The Governor in Council may appoint a fit and proper person to be the accountant of penitentiaries, who shall be an officer of the Department of Justice, and shall be charged *Accountant of penitentiaries.*

His duties.

generally with the direction, inspection and audit of the books, accounts, money transactions and financial affairs of the penitentiaries, and shall have such other powers as are assigned to him by the Governor in Council; and he shall perform such other duties as are required of him by the Minister of Justice:

To audit accounts and inquire into money matters.

2. He shall audit the accounts of the penitentiaries and transmit the same, duly certified as to correctness, to the Minister of Justice: he shall also inquire into the money transactions and financial affairs of the penitentiaries, prisons, hospitals, asylums or other public institutions supported wholly or in part by Canada:

Powers.

3. He shall, in the performance of his duties, have all the powers given to the inspector by sections eighteen and nineteen of this Act. 46 V., c. 37, s. 19.

WARDENS AND OTHER OFFICERS.

Appointment of officers for each penitentiary.

22. The Governor in Council may appoint, for any penitentiary, a warden, a deputy warden, a Protestant chaplain, an assistant Protestant chaplain when required, a Roman Catholic chaplain, an assistant Roman Catholic chaplain when required, a surgeon and an accountant, all of whom shall hold their offices during pleasure:

Inspector may suspend any officer.

2. The inspector may summarily suspend any of the above named officers for misconduct, until the circumstances of the case, of which the Minister of Justice shall be at once notified, have been decided upon by the Minister, and the inspector may, until such decision has been so intimated, cause any officer so suspended to be removed beyond the precincts

Removal may be recommended.

of the prison; and the inspector shall recommend the removal of any of the above named officers whom he deems incapable, inefficient or negligent in the execution of his duty, or whose presence in the penitentiary he considers detrimental to the interests thereof. 46 V., c. 37, s. 20, *part.*

Minister of Justice may appoint certain officers.

23. The Minister of Justice may appoint, for any penitentiary, a schoolmaster, a schoolmistress, a storekeeper, a steward, a chief keeper, an engineer, a matron, a deputy matron, and such trade instructors as are, from time to time, required, who shall hold their offices during pleasure:

Warden may suspend any of them.

2. The warden may, for misconduct, summarily suspend any of the officers named in this section until the next visit of the inspector, when the warden shall submit to the inspector a report of the circumstances of the case, to be dealt with as to the inspector seems meet. 46 V., c. 37, s. 21, *part.*

Warden may appoint certain officers, guards, &c., and suspend or dismiss them.

24. The warden may appoint, for any penitentiary, an assistant deputy matron and a clerk, and such and so many keepers and guards and other servants, for the proper protection and care of the institution, as the Minister authorizes, and may suspend any of them for neglect of duty, for such time as he sees fit, or dismiss them, without further charge than that, in his opinion, they are inefficient; and such suspension or dismissal shall be reported forthwith to the inspector.   46 V., c. 37, s. 22.

25. The pay of every officer so suspended by the inspector or by the warden shall cease during the period of his suspension ; but the Minister of Justice may direct payment of the same.   46 V., c. 37, s. 23.

26. The warden may impose upon any officer or servant appointed by him or by the Minister of Justice, for any act of negligence or carelessness committed by him, a fine, payable in money, of such reasonable amount, not exceeding one month's pay, as the warden, under the circumstances of the case, thinks fit ; and, under like circumstances, the Minister of Justice may impose a like fine on the deputy warden and accountant.   46 V., c. 37, s. 24.

27. The warden of a penitentiary shall be the chief executive officer of the same ; and as such shall have the entire executive control and management of all its concerns, subject to the rules and regulations duly established, and the written instructions of the inspector authorized by the Minister of Justice ; and, in all cases not provided for, and where the said inspector cannot readily be consulted, the warden shall act in such manner as he deems most advantageous for the penitentiary ; he shall be responsible for the faithful and efficient administration of the affairs of every department of the penitentiary, shall reside in the penitentiary, and shall receive such allowance of fuel and light as the Governor in Council sees fit to make.   46 V., c. 37, s. 25.

28. In the absence or during the incapacity of the warden the deputy warden shall exercise all the powers and perform all the duties of the warden ; and in the absence or during the incapacity of the deputy warden the chief keeper shall exercise all the powers and perform all the duties of the deputy warden.   46 V., c. 37, s. 20, *part, and* s. 21, *part.*

29. Every warden, accountant, storekeeper, steward, and every such other officer as is, from time to time, designated by the Governor in Council, shall give and enter into a bond or bonds for the faithful performance of the duties of his office according to law, and in such sum, and with such sufficient surety or sureties, as the Governor in Council or the Minister of Justice approves of, and such bonds shall be filed in the office of the Secretary of State of Canada.   46 V., c. 37, s. 27.

30. Every warden, and every other officer and servant employed permanently in a penitentiary, shall severally take and subscribe, in a book to be kept for that purpose by the accountant in his office, the oath of allegiance to Her Majesty, and an oath of office in the form following, that is to say :—

"I (A. B.) do promise and swear that I will faithfully, "diligently and justly serve in the office and perform the "duties of   in the   penitentiary, to the "best of my abilities; and that I will carefully observe and "carry out all the regulations of the prison. So help me God:"

2. The inspector or warden is hereby authorized to administer such oaths. 46 V., c. 37, s. 28.

31. Every inspector, warden, or other officer or servant employed in a penitentiary, who, either in his own name or in the name of, or in connection with, any other person, provides, furnishes or supplies any materials, goods or provisions for the use of any penitentiary, or is concerned directly or indirectly in furnishing or supplying the same, or in any contract relating thereto, shall incur a penalty of five hundred dollars, recoverable, with costs, by any person who sues for the same in any court of competent jurisdiction. 46 V., c. 37, s. 29.

32. No warden, officer or servant, except the surgeon and chaplain, shall carry on any trade or calling of profit or emolument other than his office in the penitentiary; and, except in the case mentioned in section sixty-four, no officer shall buy from or sell to or for any convict anything whatsoever; or take or receive for his own use, or for that of any other person, any fee or gratuity or emolument from any convict or visitor or other person; or, without the consent of the Minister, employ any convict in working for him. 46 V., c. 37, s. 30.

33. The Governor in Council may, from time to time, fix the sums to be annually paid to the warden and the other officers and servants of any penitentiary established under the provisions of this Act, regard being had to the number of convicts confined therein, and the consequent responsibility attaching to their offices respectively, and to the length of service and amount of labor devolving upon them; but such salaries shall not exceed the sums specified in the schedule to this Act. 46 V., c. 37, s. 31.

34. The warden shall be a corporation sole known by the name of "The Warden of the   Penitentiary," (designating the place as named in this Act, or named in the proclamation establishing it as a penitentiary), and by that name he and his successors shall have perpetual succession, and may sue and be sued, and may plead and be pleaded unto, in any of Her Majesty's courts. 46 V., c. 37, s. 32.

35. All dealings and transactions on account of any penitentiary, and all contracts for goods, wares or merchandise necessary for maintaining and carrying on the penitentiary, or for the sale of goods prepared or manufactured in the penitentiary, shall be entered into and carried out in the corporate name of the warden ; and all personal property belonging to the penitentiary shall be held, in the corporate name of the warden, for Her Majesty. 46 V., c. 37, s. 33.

36. The real property of every penitentiary, as well as all the other property thereto belonging, shall be vested in Her Majesty; but the warden and his successors in office shall have the custody and care thereof under the provisions of this Act. 46 V., c. 37, s. 34.

37. Whenever any difference arises, between the warden and any person having dealings with him on account of the penitentiary, such difference may, by order of the inspector, and with the consent of such person, be referred either to one arbitrator, selected by the warden and such person, or to three arbitrators,—one of whom shall be named by the warden, and another by such other person, and a third by the two so named as aforesaid ; and, in the one case, the award of the arbitrator, and, in the other case, of any two of the arbitrators, shall be final. 46 V., c. 37, s. 35.

38. The warden of a penitentiary shall exercise due diligence in enforcing the payment of debts due to the penitentiary, and with as little expense as possible ; and, on the report of the inspector approved by the Governor in Council, he may accept of such security from any debtor on granting time, or such composition in full settlement, as is thought conducive to the interests of the penitentiary. 46 V., c. 37, s. 36.

39. All books of account and other books, bills, registers, returns, receipts, bills of parcels and vouchers, and all other papers and documents of every kind relating to the affairs of the penitentiary, shall be the property of the penitentiary, and shall remain therein; and the warden shall preserve therein at least one set of copies of all official reports made to Parliament respecting the penitentiary,—for which purpose, and for the purpose of enabling him to distribute such official reports in exchange for like documents from other similar institutions abroad, he shall, as soon as they are printed, be furnished by the clerk of the House of Commons with fifty copies of such reports as are printed by order of the House. 46 V., c. 37, s. 37.

40. The warden and accountant shall transmit monthly, to the accountant of penitentiaries, a statement of the receipts and expenditures for the preceding month, verified under oath in the manner following :—

    " I,   warden, and I,   accountant, of the
"   penitentiary, make oath and say, that the fore-
" going statement of receipts and expenditures on account of

" the said penitentiary for the month of   18   , is true
" and correct.

 " Sworn before me at   the   day
" of   A.D., 18 ,
"   Inspector, *or as the case may be.*"

Storekeeper's oath.   " I,   storekeeper of the
" penitentiary, make oath and say that the articles mentioned
" in the foregoing statement, as purchased for the said peni-
" tentiary for the month of   18 , were duly received.
" Sworn before me at   the
" day of   A.D., 18 .
"   Inspector, *or as the case may be.*"

By whom administered.   2. Such oaths may be administered by the inspector or the accountant of penitentiaries, or by any justice of the peace, notary public, or commissioner for taking affidavits. 46 V., c. 37, s. 38.

PRIVILEGED VISITORS.

Who shall have the right of visiting.   **41.** The following persons, other tnan the inspector or persons specially appointed by the Minister of Justice may visit any penitentiary at pleasure, that is to say,—the Governor General of Canada, the Lieutenant Governor of any Province of Canada, any member of the Queen's Privy Council for Canada, any member of the Executive Council of any of the said Provinces, any member of the Parliament of Canada or of any of the local Legislatures, any judge of any court of record in Canada or in any of the said Provinces, and any Queen's Counsel; but no other person shall be permitted to enter within the walls wherein the prisoners are confined, except by the special permission of the warden, and under such regulations as the inspector prescribes. 46 V., c. 37, s. 39.

CONVEYANCE, RECEIPT AND REMOVAL OF CONVICTS.

What shall be sufficient authority for conveying convicts to penitentiary.   **42.** The sheriff or deputy sheriff of any county or district, or any bailiff, constable, or other officer, or other person, by his direction or by the direction of a court, or any officer appointed by the Governor in Council and attached to the staff of a penitentiary for that purpose, may convey to the penitentiary named in the sentence, any convict sentenced or liable to be imprisoned therein, and shall deliver him to the warden thereof, without any further warrant than a copy of the sentence taken from the minutes of the court before which the convict was tried, and certified by a judge or by the clerk or acting clerk of such court. 46 V., c. 37, s. 40.

When brought from any other penitentiary or gaol.   **43.** Whenever a prisoner is ordered, by competent authority, to be conveyed to any penitentiary from any other penitentiary, or from a reformatory prison, or from a common gaol, there shall be delivered to the warden of the penitentiary receiving such prisoner, together with all other necessary documents, a certificate signed by the medical officer of the institution from which such prisoner has been taken, and countersigned by the warden, if the prisoner has been taken from a penitentiary or a reformatory prison, or by the sheriff or his deputy if from a common gaol, declaring that such prisoner is free from any putrid, infectious or cutaneous disease, and that he is fit to be removed. 46 V., c. 37, s. 41.

44. The warden shall receive into the penitentiary every convict legally certified to him as sentenced to imprisonment therein, and shall there detain him, subject to all the rules, regulations and discipline thereof, until the term for which he has been sentenced is completed, or until he is otherwise discharged in due course of law. 46 V., c. 37, s. 42. Duty of warden as to receiving and detaining convicts.

45. The Governor General may, by warrant signed by the Secretary of State of Canada, or by such other officer as is, from time to time, authorized by the Governor in Council, direct the removal of any convict from any one penitentiary to another; and the warden of the penitentiary having the custody of any convict so ordered to be removed, when required so to do, shall deliver up the said convict to the constable or other officer or person who produces the said warrant, together with a copy, attested by the said warden, of the sentence and date of conviction of such convict as given to him on reception of such convict into his custody; and the constable or other officer or person shall give a receipt to the warden for the convict, and shall thereupon, with all convenient dispatch, convey and deliver up such convict, with the said attested copy, into the custody of the warden of the penitentiary mentioned in the warrant, who shall give a receipt in writing for every convict so received into his custody, to such constable or other officer or person, as his discharge; and the convict shall be kept in custody in the penitentiary to which he is so removed, until his removal to another penitentiary, or until the termination of his sentence, or until his pardon or release, or discharge by law. 46 V., c. 37, s. 43 Governor may authorize removal from or to any penitentiary.

Proceedings in such case.

Detention of convict.

46. The sheriff, or other officer or person employed by competent authority to convey any convict to any penitentiary to which such convict is ordered to be taken, either by sentence of a court or by order of the Secretary of State or other officer, as in the next preceding section mentioned, may secure and convey him through any county or district through which he has to pass in any of the Provinces of Canada; and until the convict has been delivered to the warden of such penitentiary, such sheriff, officer or person shall, in all territorial divisions or parts of Canada through which it may be necessary to convey such convict, have the same authority and power over and with regard to such con- Powers of sheriff or officer conveying convicts to a penitentiary.

Assistance in case of escape. vict, and to command the assistance of any person in preventing his escape, or in recapturing him in case of an escape, as the sheriff of the territorial division in which he w s convicted would himself have, in conveying him from one part of that division to another. 46 V., c. 37, s. 44.

Power to convey a convict whose sentence of death has been commuted, and effect of commutation. **47.** If sentence of death has been passed upon any convict by any court in Canada, and the Governor General, on behalf of Her Majesty, has been pleased to commute such sentence to imprisonment for life, or for any term of years, such commutation shall have the same effect as the judgment of a competent court legally sentencing such convict to such imprisonment for life or other term, and the sheriff, or other officer, or other person having such convict in custody, on receipt of a letter from the Secretary of State or such other officer as aforesaid, notifying him of the fact of such commutation, and directing him to convey such convict to a penitentiary therein named, shall forthwith convey such convict thereto, and shall have the same rights and powers, in conveying such convict to such penitentiary, as if the conveyance took place by virtue of the sentence of a competent court. 46 V., c. 37, s. 45.

What shall be sufficient authority to the warden in such case. **48.** A letter signed by the Secretary of State or such other officer as aforesaid, notifying the warden of the fact of the commutation of any sentence of death to imprisonment for life or for a term of years, and of the term of years or life term to which the sentence has been commuted, shall be sufficient authority to the warden to receive such convict into the penitentiary, and to deal with him as if he had been sentenced by a competent court to confinement therein for the period or life term in the said letter mentioned; and it shall not be necessary, for the purpose of commuting such sentence, or of authorizing the conveyance of a prisoner to any penitentiary, or for his reception and detention therein for the term to which such sentence is commuted, that the warden should have in his possession a copy of any pardon. 46 V., c. 37, s. 46.

TRANSFER OF JUVENILE OFFENDERS FROM AND TO REFORMATORY PRISONS.

Juvenile offenders found incorrigible may be removed from reformatory to penitentiary. **49.** If a juvenile offender has been ordered by competent authority to be imprisoned in any reformatory prison, and after being imprisoned therein has become incorrigible, and is so certified by the warden and one of the chaplains, the Lieutenant Governor of the Province in which the reformatory prison is situate, by a warrant under his hand, addressed to the warden of such reformatory prison, setting forth the sentence or order under which the juvenile offender was imprisoned therein, and the fact that he is incorrigible, may direct that such juvenile offender be removed to any penitentiary named in the said warrant ; and the warden, or any other officer of the prison, or any other person authorized by him, shall have the same powers in conveying such juvenile offender to such penitentiary as are hereinbefore given to a sheriff or other person in like cases :

2. The warden of the penitentiary therein named shall receive such juvenile offender and deal with him for the unexpired term of the sentence or order under which he was ordered to be imprisoned in such reformatory prison, as if he had been sentenced to such penitentiary by a competent court : Provided, that together with the said offender, a copy of the said sentence or order, attested by the warden of the reformatory prison, and also an order from the Lieutenant Governor, directing the warden of such penitentiary to receive such juvenile offender, shall be delivered to the warden of the penitentiary. 46 V., c. 37, s. 47. *And dealt with as if sentenced to the penitentiary. Copy of sentence or order to be delivered.*

50. The Governor General may, at any time, in his discretion, by warrant under his hand, cause any convict in a penitentiary, whose sentence is for a term not less than two years, and who appears to the inspector to be under sixteen years of age, and susceptible of reformation, to be transferred, for the remainder of his term of imprisonment, to the reformatory prison, if there is one, of the Province where such convict was sentenced. 46 V., c. 37, s. 48. *Juvenile offenders in penitentiary may be transferred to reformatory prison.*

TREATMENT OF CONVICTS.

51. The following general rules shall be observed in the treatment of convicts in a penitentiary :— *General rules.*

(a.) Every convict shall, during the term of his confinement, be clothed, at the expense of the penitentiary, in suitable prison garments ; *Clothing.*

(b.) He shall be fed on a sufficient quantity of wholesome food ; *Food.*

(c.) He shall be provided with a bed and pillow with sufficient covering, varied according to the season ; and— *Bedding.*

(d.) He shall, except in case of sickness, be kept in a cell by himself at night, and during the day when not employed. 46 V., c. 37, s. 49. · *Solitary confinement.*

52. Convict labor may be of two descriptions,— *Convict labor.*

(a.) Obligatory, that is to say : every convict, except during sickness or other incapacity, shall be kept constantly at hard labor during at least ten hours, exclusive of hours for meals or schools, of every day, except Sunday, Good Friday, Christ- *Obligatory. Holidays.*

of the penitentiary has certified that the prisoner is in a physical condition to bear such punishment, and unless the surgeon is present during its infliction; and not more than sixty lashes shall be inflicted upon any prisoner for any such offence. 46 V., c. 37, s. 61.

Limited to 60 lashes.

59. Every officer, guard or servant of any penitentiary, or other person, who brings in or carries out, or endeavors to bring in or carry out, or knowingly allows to be brought in or carried out, to or from any convict, or carries to any convict while employed outside the prison walls, any money, clothing, provisions, tobacco, spirits, letters, papers or other articles whatsoever, not allowed by the rules of the penitentiary shall, on summary conviction, be liable to a penalty not exceeding one hundred dollars, or to imprisonment with hard labor, for a term not exceeding three months. 46 V., c. 37, s. 59.

Bringing money, spirits, letters, &c., to convicts.

Penalty.

TRESPASSES.

60. Every person who is found trespassing upon any grounds, buildings, yards, offices or other premises whatsoever, belonging or appertaining to any penitentiary, or who enters the same, not being an officer or servant of the penitentiary, or authorized by the warden, shall, on summary conviction for a first offence, be liable to a penalty not exceeding ten dollars, and in default of payment to imprisonment, with or without hard labor, for a term not exceeding one month; and for a subsequent offence to a penalty not exceeding fifty dollars, and in default of payment to imprisonment with or without hard labor, for a term not exceeding three months. 46 V., c. 37, s. 62.

Punishment of persons trespassing on penitentiary grounds.

Subsequent offence.

61. Every person who moors or anchors, or causes to be moored or anchored, any raft, boat, vessel or craft of any kind within three hundred feet of the shore or wharf bounding the lands of any penitentiary towards any lake, arm of the sea, bay or river, without the permission of the warden of such penitentiary, shall, on summary conviction, be liable to a penalty of twenty dollars, and in default of payment of such penalty and costs, to imprisonment with hard labor, for a term not exceeding two months; and the amount of such penalty may be levied upon such raft, boat, vessel or craft, in whomsoever the property thereof may be, as well as on the offender's own goods and chattels. 46 V., c. 37, s. 63.

Penalty if vessels are moored within 300 feet of shore or wharf bounding penitentiary.

LIQUORS

62. No spirituous or fermented liquors shall be brought into the penitentiary for the use of any officer or person therein (except the warden or deputy warden, if the latter is resident therein), or for the use of any convict confined therein, except under the rules of the penitentiary; and any

No spirits allowed in penitentiary except for warden, &c.

person who gives any spirituous or fermented liquor, tobacco, snuff or cigars, to any convict, except under the rules of the penitentiary, or conveys the same to any convict, shall incur a penalty of forty dollars, which shall be recoverable by the warden before any court of competent jurisdiction, and placed to the credit of the Minister of Finance and Receiver General. 46 V., c. 37, s. 64.

Giving liquor or tobacco, &c., to convicts.

Penalty.

DISCHARGE OF CONVICTS.

63. No convict shall be discharged from a penitentiary on the termination of his sentence, or otherwise, if he is laboring under any contagious or infectious disease; or, unless at his own request, during the months of November, December, January, February or March, or if he is laboring under any acute or dangerous disease; but such convict may remain in the penitentiary until he recovers from such disease, or until the first day of April following the termination of his sentence: but a convict remaining from any cause in a penitentiary after the termination of his sentence, shall be under the same discipline and control as if his sentence were still unexpired:

Discharge of convicts at certain times and under certain circumstances.

2. On the first day of April a list shall be made of all the prisoners whose sentences have expired during the five preceding months, and who are still in prison, according to the dates when their sentences expired; and according to such order they shall be discharged, one convict on the said first day of April, and one on every day thereafter, until the whole are discharged:

Order of discharge of convicts in April.

3. Whenever the term of any prisoner's sentence expires on a Sunday, he shall be discharged on the Saturday preceding, unless he desires to remain until the Monday following:

Sentence expiring on Sunday.

4. Every convict under sentence for life, or for a term not less than two years, shall, upon his discharge, either by expiration of sentence, or otherwise, be furnished, at the expense of the penitentiary, with a suit of clothing other than prison clothing, and with such sum of money as is sufficient to pay his travelling expenses to the place at which he received his sentence, and such other sum in addition, not exceeding twenty dollars, as the warden deems proper; and if any sum remains at his credit for earnings for overwork, such sum shall be paid to him at such times, and in such amounts, as the prison rules direct; but if the warden is of opinion that a convict, on being discharged, does not intend *bonâ fide* to return to the place at which he received his sentence, but intends to go to some other place, nearer to the penitentiary, such convict shall be furnished with such less sum of money as is, in the warden's opinion, sufficient to pay his travelling expenses to such nearer place. 46 V., c. 37, s. 65.

Clothing and money to convicts discharged.

Money for over work.

As to convict not returning to place of conviction.

PRISONERS' EFFECTS.

64. Every article found upon the person of a convict at the time of his reception into the penitentiary, which is con-

Articles found on convict on entry

to be kept for him.

sidered worth preservation, shall be taken from him, and a description thereof entered in a book kept for that purpose; and if the convict does not see fit otherwise to dispose of it at the time, it shall be carefully put away until the day of his discharge, when it shall be delivered up to him again in the state in which it then is; but the warden shall not be liable for any deterioration which takes place in such article in the interval:

May be sold if he desires to dispose of them.

2. If, at the time of his reception, the convict desires to dispose of any such article, and it is so disposed of, a memorandum of the fact shall be noted in the said book, and signed by the proper officer who has charge thereof, and also by the convict; and any money received therefor shall be placed to his credit. 46 V., c. 37, s. 66.

CORONERS' INQUESTS.

Coroner to hold inquest in certain cases.

65. If a convict dies in a penitentiary, and the inspector, warden, surgeon or chaplain has reason to believe that the death of such convict arose from any other than ordinary causes, he shall call upon a coroner having jurisdiction to hold an inquest upon the body of such deceased convict; and upon such requisition by one or more of the officers above named, the said coroner shall hold such inquest, and, for that purpose, he and the jury, and all other persons necessarily attending such inquest, shall have admittance to the prison. 46 V., c. 37, s. 67.

Admittance of coroner and jury.

DECEASED CONVICTS.

How the body of convict shall be disposed of.

66. The body of every convict who dies in a penitentiary shall, if claimed by his relatives, be given up to and shall be taken away by them; but if not so claimed, the body may be delivered to an inspector of anatomy, duly appointed under any Act authorizing such appointment, or to the professor of anatomy in any college wherein medical science is taught; or if not so delivered, shall be decently interred at the expense of the penitentiary. 46 V., c. 37, s. 68.

INSANE CONVICTS.

Kingston penitentiary insane ward.

67. The Governor in Council may direct the warden of the Kingston Penitentiary to set apart a portion thereof for the reception, confinement and treatment of insane convicts; and the portion so set apart shall be used for such purposes accordingly, and shall be known as the ward for the insane. 46 V., c. 37, s. 69.

Surgeons to report cases of insanity among convicts.

68. If at any time it appears to a surgeon of a penitentiary that any convict confined therein is insane and ought to be removed to the ward for the insane, he shall report the same in writing to the warden, and on such report the warden shall forthwith remove such convict to the ward for the insane. 46 V., c. 37, s. 70.

69. If, at any time before the termination of the sentence of such convict, it is certified to the warden by the surgeon that such convict has recovered his reason, and is in a fit state to be removed from the ward for the insane, the warden shall remove such convict therefrom.   46 V., c. 37, s. 71. If insane convict becomes sane.

70. If the term of imprisonment of any convict expires while detained as insane in the ward for the insane, he may continue to be detained therein pending the proceedings authorized by this Act; and in such case the surgeon shall forthwith certify to the warden whether the person is sane or insane.   46 V., c. 37, ss. 72 *and* 73. If insane when his term expires.

71. If the surgeon certifies that such person is sane, he shall be forthwith discharged.   46 V., c. 37, s. 74. Discharge, if sane.

72. If the surgeon certifies that the person is insane, the warden shall report the fact to the inspector; and the Secretary of State shall thereupon communicate the fact to the Lieutenant Governor of the Province within which the person was sentenced, so that he may be removed to a place of safe keeping : Report in order to removal of insane convict.

2. The Lieutenant Governor may, thereupon, order the removal of the person to a place of safe keeping within the Province, and he shall, upon such order, be delivered to the person therein designated, for transport to such place, and he shall remain and be detained there or in such other place of safe keeping as the Lieutenant Governor, from time to time, orders, until it appears to the Lieutenant Governor that he is of sound mind, when the Lieutenant Governor may order him to be discharged; but if, at any time after his removal to such place of safe keeping, and before his complete recovery, the Lieutenant Governor thinks fit to order that he shall be given up to any person by him named, he shall be given up accordingly.   46 V., c. 37, ss. 75 *and* 76. Lt. Governor may order removal. Further power of Lieutenant Governor.

73. If the Lieutenant Governor of the Province within which any such person was sentenced has made arrangements with the Lieutenant Governor of the Province of Ontario for the safe keeping of any such person in Ontario, and such arrangements have been communicated to the Secretary of State by the Lieutenant Governors of the Provinces concerned, the Secretary of State shall, in the case of any such person, communicate, under the next preceding section, with the Lieutenant Governor of Ontario, who shall, in such cases, have all the powers thereby given : Provision if arrangements have been made for safe keeping of convict in Ontario.

2. If the Lieutenant Governor does not, within two months after the Secretary of State has communicated, as provided by the next preceding section, cause the person to be removed under the provisions thereof, the Secretary of State may, on the recommendation of the Minister of Justice, direct the convict to be removed for safe keeping to the gaol in which Provision if Lt. Governor does not provide for removal.

he was last confined previous to his transfer to the penitentiary, or to any other gaol in the Province within which he was sentenced; and, after such removal, all the provisions of the next preceding section shall apply to his case.   46 V., c. 37, ss. 77 *and* 78.

Question of sanity, how decided.

74. If any question arises as to the sanity of any convict, the Minister of Justice may order an inquiry and report to be made by one or more medical men, in conjunction with the surgeon, and may, upon such report, direct such action as is necessary to carry out the provisions of this Act.   46 V., c. 37, s 79.

SCHEDULE.

Warden, not exceeding		$3,000
and not less than	$1,000	
Deputy Warden, not exceeding		1,400
and not less than	600	
Chief Keeper, not exceeding		900
and not less than	500	
Chaplain, not exceeding		1,200
and not less than	400	
Assistant Chaplain, not exceeding		500
and not less than	300	
Surgeon, not exceeding		1,800
and not less than	400	
Accountant, not exceeding		1,000
and not less than	500	
Schoolmaster, not exceeding		600
and not less than	250	
Storekeeper, not exceeding		900
and not less than	400	
Steward, not exceeding		700
and not less than	400	

(If the offices of Steward and Storekeeper are combined, the salary may be that of the Storekeeper).

Chief Trade Instructor, not exceeding		1,100
and not less than	700	
Trade Instructor, not exceeding		750
and not less than	500	
Hospital Keeper, not exceeding		750
and not less than	500	
Engineer, not exceeding		900
and not less than	500	
Farmer and Gardener, not exceeding		650
and not less than	500	
Keeper, not exceeding		600
and not less than	400	

Guard, not exceeding.. $600
   and not less than.. $350
Messenger, not exceeding.................................... 600
   and not less than.. 400
Teamster, not exceeding..................................... 400
   and not less than.. 300
Other male servants, not exceeding per day.............. 1
Matron, not exceeding.. 550
   and not less than.. 250
Deputy Matron, not exceeding.............................. 350
   and not less than.. 200
Assistant Deputy Matron, not exceeding................. 250
   and not less than.. 175
Schoolmistress, not exceeding.............................. 250
   and not less than.. 120
46 V., c. 37, schedule A.

OTTAWA: Printed by BROWN CHAMBERLIN, Law Printer to the Queen's Most Excellent Majesty.

CHAPTER 183.

An Act respecting Public and Reformatory Prisons.

A. D. 1886.

HER Majesty, by and with the advice and consent of the Senate and House of Commons of Canada, enacts as follows :—

1. In this Act, unless the context otherwise requires, the expression "Lieutenant Governor" means the Lieutenant Governor in 'Council.

Interpretation. "Lieutenant "Governor."

PART I.

INSECURE PRISONS.

2. The Lieutenant Governor of any Province of Canada may, by proclamation published in the official Gazette of the Province, and in the *Canada Gazette*, declare that the common gaol of any district, county or place in such Province is insecure, and may name the gaol of any adjoining district, county or place as the gaol to which offenders within such first mentioned district, county or place, may, from and after a time stated, be committed or sentenced. 40 V., c. 37, s. 1.

Lt.-Governor may substitute a neighboring gaol for an insecure one.

3. The Lieutenant Governor may, after the issue of such proclamation, from time to time, direct the sheriff to transfer such of the prisoners then confined in such insecure gaol, as the Lieutenant Governor thinks proper, to the gaol so named as aforesaid ; and such order shall be a sufficient authority to the respective sheriffs and officers to deliver and receive, and to the keeper of such last mentioned gaol to detain therein, any such prisoner, according to the exigency of the warrant or sentence under which he was confined in such insecure gaol. 40 V., c. 37, s. 4.

Transfer of prisoners to substituted gaol.

4. During the continuance of such proclamation, any person who would otherwise be committed to or sentenced to imprisonment in the common gaol so declared insecure, shall be committed to or sentenced to imprisonment in the gaol named in the proclamation for the purpose, and the respective sheriffs and officers shall have authority to deliver and receive such person ; and a warrant directed to the gaoler of the insecure gaol shall be a sufficient authority for the gaoler of the gaol so named as aforesaid to detain in such

Effect of such proclamation as to persons who would otherwise be imprisoned in the insecure gaol.

gaol the person named in such warrant, according to the exigency of the warrant, or until he is removed, as is hereinafter provided. 40 V., c. 37, s. 2.

As to place of trial of prisoners in substituted gaol, &c.

Powers of court and judges.

5. Every person so confined in the gaol named in such proclamation, may be tried in the district, county or place in the gaol whereof he is confined, unless the judge, or other person presiding at the court at which it is proposed to try such person, or a judge of a court having jurisdiction to try the offence, otherwise directs ; and the court of general gaol delivery or General Sessions of the Peace, or other court having like powers, held in such district, county or place, and every judge presiding thereat, shall have jurisdiction to make, in reference to any person committed in default of sureties for good behavior, or to keep the peace, the like order as such court or judge might make if the court was being held in the district, county or place in which such person was committed. 40 V., c. 37, s. 3

Proclamation superseding that first issued.

6. The Lieutenant Governor may, at any time, by his proclamation published in the official Gazette of the Province, and in the *Canada Gazette*, declare that any proclamation issued under the second section of this Act, shall, from and after a time stated, cease to have effect; and such proclamation shall cease to have effect accordingly. 40 V., c. 37, s. 5.

Re-transfer of prisoners in consequence.

7. The Lieutenant Governor may, after the issue of such last mentioned proclamation, direct the sheriff to transfer so many of the prisoners then confined in the gaol so named as aforesaid, as the Lieutenant Governor thinks proper, to the gaol of the district, county or place in which, but for the operation of the preceding sections, such prisoners would have been confined ; and such order shall be sufficient authority to the respective sheriffs and officers to deliver and receive, and to the keeper of such last mentioned gaol to detain therein, any such prisoners, according to the exigency of the warrant or sentence under which they were originally confined. 40 V., c. 37, s. 6.

EMPLOYMENT OF PRISONERS.

Lt.-Governor in Council may make regulations.

8. The Lieutenant Governor of any Province may, from time to time, make regulations for the purpose of preventing escapes and preserving discipline in the case of prisoners in any common gaol, employed beyond the limits thereof. 40 V., c. 36, s. 1.

And may then authorize employment of prisoners outside of gaols.

9. After such regulations are made, the Lieutenant Governor may, from time to time, direct or authorize the employment, upon any specific work or duty, beyond the limits of any common gaol, of any prisoner who is sentenced to be imprisoned with hard labor in such gaol, for any offence against any law of Canada. 48-49 V., c. 81, s. 1.

10. Every such prisoner shall, during such employment, be subject to such regulations and to all the rules, regulations and discipline of the gaol, so far as applicable. 40 V., c. 36, s. 3.

Discipline of the gaol to be observed.

11. No such prisoner shall be so employed, except under the strictest care and supervision of officers appointed to that duty. 40 V., c. 36, s. 4.

Supervision.

12. Every street, highway or public thoroughfare of any kind, along or across which prisoners pass in going to or returning from their work, and every place where they are so employed, shall, while so used, be considered as a portion of the gaol; and any escape or attempt at escape, and any rescue or attempt at rescue, made on such street, highway or thoroughfare, shall be held to have been made within or from such gaol. 40 V., c. 36, s. 5.

Place of work, &c., to be deemed part of gaol.

IMPROVEMENT OF PRISON DISCIPLINE.

13. If, in any Province, there is at any time a prison of such a character as to render practicable the application of the three sections next following to such Province, and if the Lieutenant Governor makes rules for keeping a correct record of the daily conduct of every prisoner in such prison, noting his behavior, industry, diligence and faithfulness, and the strictness with which he observes the prison regulations, and if such prison, and the rules so made, are, by the Governor in Council, declared adequate, the Governor in Council may, by proclamation published in the *Canada Gazette*, reciting the premises, and describing the prison, declare such sections in force within such Province from and after a day named in such proclamation. 40 V., c. 39, ss. 1 *and* 5.

On certain conditions the three sections next following may be declared in force in any Province.

14. Any judge sentencing any prisoner to imprisonment in any prison named in the proclamation in the next preceding section mentioned, may sentence such prisoner for a term not more than one sixth longer than the maximum term at present prescribed by law for the offence; and any such sentence may be carried out in such prison, although it is for any term not exceeding two years and four months. 40 V., c. 39, s. 2.

Power to judge sentencing a prisoner in certain cases.

15. Every prisoner sentenced to such prison shall be entitled to earn a remission of a portion of the time for which he is sentenced, not exceeding five days for every month during which he is exemplary in behavior, industry and faithfulness, and does not violate any of the prison rules;

Prisoner may earn a remission of part of sentence.

and if prevented from labor by sickness, not intentionally produced by himself, he shall be entitled to earn, by good conduct, a remission not exceeding two and one half days for every such month. 40 V., c. 39, s. 3.

Forfeiture of remission in certain cases. **16.** Every such prisoner who commits any breach of the laws or of the prison regulations shall, besides any other penalty to which he is liable, be liable to forfeit the whole or any part of any remission which he has so earned. 40 V., c. 39, s. 4.

PART II.

ONTARIO.

Provisions applicable to Ontario. **17.** The provisions of sections eighteen to forty-eight both inclusive, being Part two of this Act apply only to the Province of Ontario. 43 V., c. 39, s. 16, *part, and* c. 40, s. 10, *part.*

Interpretation. **"Court."** **18.** In this part of this Act, the expression "court" includes a police or stipendiary magistrate, but does not include one or more justices of the peace. 43 V., c. 39, s. 2, *and* c. 40, s. 2;—44 V., c. 32, s. 1, *part, and* s. 6, *part.*

The Central Prison for the Province of Ontario.

Imprisonment in the Central Prison. **19.** Every court in the Province of Ontario, before which any person is convicted for an offence against the laws of Canada, punishable by imprisonment in the common gaol, for the term of two months, or for any longer time, may sentence such person to imprisonment in the central prison for the Province of Ontario, instead of the common gaol of the county or judicial district where the offence was committed, or was tried. 44 V., c. 32, s. 6, *part.*

Transfer of prisoners to the Central Prison. **20.** Every person confined in any one of the common gaols of the said Province, under sentence of imprisonment for any offence, may, by direction of the Provincial Secretary, be transferred from such common gaol to such central prison, there to be imprisoned for the unexpired portion of the term of imprisonment to which such person was originally sentenced or committed to such common gaol; and such person shall thereupon be imprisoned in such central prison for the residue of such term, unless in the meantime he is lawfully discharged or removed, and shall be subject to all the rules and regulations of such central prison. 36 V., c. 69, s. 2.

Transfer although imprisonment is **21.** Such person may be removed to the central prison, notwithstanding such imprisonment, or any part thereof, is imposed in default of the payment of a fine or penalty in money, and that such person is entitled to be discharged for non-pay-
ment of fine. upon payment of such fine or penalty :

2. If the fine or penalty is paid after the removal of the If fine is paid
subsequently. offender, the same shall be paid to the proper officer of such prison, to defray the expenses of the removal of the said offender to such prison, and otherwise for the uses of such prison ; but nothing herein contained shall affect the right of any private person to such fine or penalty, or any part thereof. 44 V., c. 32, s. 5.

22. The warden of the central prison shall receive into Warden to re-
ceive and
detain offen-
ders. the said prison every offender legally certified to him as sentenced to imprisonment therein ; and shall detain him, subject to all the rules, regulations and discipline thereof, until the term for which he has been sentenced is completed, or until he is otherwise discharged in due course of law. 36 V., c. 69, s. 3.

23. The Lieutenant Governor may, from time to time, Employment
of prisoners
on works
without the
prison. authorize, direct or sanction the employment upon any specific work or duty, without or beyond the walls or limits of such central prison, of any of the prisoners confined or sentenced to be imprisoned therein ; and all such prisoners shall, during such last mentioned employment, be subject to all the rules, regulations and discipline of such prison, so far as the same are applicable, and to such other regulations, for the purpose of preventing escapes, and otherwise, as are approved by the Lieutenant Governor in that behalf : Provided, that when prisoners are so employed without the walls or limits of such prison, it shall only be done under the strictest care and supervision of officers appointed to that duty. 36 V., c. 69, s. 4.

24. The Lieutenant Governor may, from time to time, by Transfer of
prisoners to
common gaol. warrant signed by the Provincial Secretary, or by such other officer as is authorized by the Lieutenant Governor in that behalf, direct the removal of any offender from the central prison to the Ontario reformatory for boys, or from the central prison to the common gaol of the county in which he was sentenced, or to any other gaol, or from the said reformatory to the said central prison. 48-49 V., c. 79, s. 1.

Ontario Reformatory for Boys.

25. If any boy, who, at the time of his trial, appears to What offen-
ders may be
sentenced to
the Ontario
Reformatory
for boys. the court to be under the age of sixteen years, is convicted of any offence for which a sentence of imprisonment for a period of three months or longer, but less than five years, may be imposed upon an adult convicted of the like offence, and the court before which such boy is convicted is satisfied that a due regard for the material and moral welfare of the boy manifestly requires that he should be committed to the

Ontario reformatory for boys, then such court may sentence the boy to be imprisoned in such reformatory for such term as the court thinks fit, not being greater than the term o imprisonment which could be imposed upon an adult fo the like offence; and may further sentence such boy to b kept in such reformatory for an indefinite time after th expiration of such fixed term: Provided, that the whol period of confinement in such reformatory shall not excee five years from the commencement of his imprisonment 43 V., c. 39, s. 1, *part*.

As to term of imprisonment.

26. If any boy, apparently under the age of sixteen years is convicted of any offence punishable by law on summar conviction, and thereupon is sentenced and committed t prison in any common gaol for a period of fourteen days a the least, any judge of any one of the superior courts, or an judge of a county court, in any case occurring within hi county, may examine and inquire into the circumstances o such case and conviction, and when he considers the materia and moral welfare of the boy requires such sentence, h may, as an additional sentence for such offence, sentenc such boy to be sent either forthwith or at the expiration o his imprisonment in such gaol, to such reformatory, to b there detained for the purpose of his industrial and mora education, for an indefinite period, not exceeding in th whole five years, from the commencement of his imprison ment in the common gaol. 43 V., c. 39, s. 3.

In certain cases offenders summarily convicted may be sentenced be such reformatory.

27. Every boy so sentenced shall be detained in such reformatory until the expiration of the fixed term, if any, o his sentence, unless sooner discharged by lawful authority and thereafter shall, subject to the provisions hereof and t any regulations made, as hereinafter provided, be detained in such reformatory for a period not to exceed five years from the commencement of his imprisonment, for the pur pose of his industrial and moral education. 43 V., c. 39, s. 4

Detention for purposes of reform.

28. A copy of the sentence of the court, duly certified by the proper officer, or the warrant or order of the judge or other magistrate by whom any boy is sentenced to con finement in such reformatory, shall be a sufficient authority to the sheriff, constable or other officer who is directed verbally or otherwise, so to do, to convey such boy to the com mon gaol of the county where such sentence is pronounced and for the gaoler of such gaol to receive and detain such boy, until some person, lawfully authorized, requires the delivery of such boy for removal to the reformatory. 43 V. c. 39, s. 6.

Commitment of boy to gaol until conveyed to reformatory.

detained in the common gaol or other place of confinement
in which he is, until he is sufficiently recovered to be
safely and conveniently removed to the reformatory.   43 V.,
c. 39, s. 7.

30. No boy shall be discharged from such reformatory at
the termination of his term of confinement, if then laboring
under any contagious or infectious disease, or under any
acute or dangerous illness, but he shall be permitted to remain in such reformatory until he recovers from such disease
or illness : Provided, that any boy remaining in such reformatory for any such cause shall be under the same discipline and control as if his term was still unexpired.   43 V.,
c. 39, s. 13.

*As to dis-
charge when
boy is in bad
health.*

Proviso.

The Andrew Mercer (Ontario) Reformatory for Females.

31. Every court in the Province of Ontario, before which
any female is convicted of an offence against the laws of
Canada, punishable by imprisonment in the common gaol
for the term of two months, or for any longer time, may
sentence such female to imprisonment in the Andrew Mercer
(Ontario) reformatory for females, instead of the common gaol
of the county or judicial district where the offence was committed or was tried.   44 V., c. 32, s. 1, *part.*

*When females
may be sen-
tenced to
Andrew Mer-
cer Reforma-
tory.*

32. Any female, from time to time, confined in any common gaol in the said Province, under sentence of imprisonment for any offence against the laws of Canada, may, by
direction of the Provincial Secretary, be transferred from
such common gaol to such reformatory, to be imprisoned
for the unexpired portion of the term of imprisonment to
which such female was originally sentenced or committed
to the common gaol ; and such female shall thereupon be
imprisoned in such reformatory for the residue of the said
term, and shall be subject to all the rules and regulations of
the reformatory.   44 V., c. 32, s. 2.

*Transfer of
prisoners to
such reforma-
tory.*

33. Any female so sentenced to imprisonment may be
removed to such reformatory, notwithstanding such imprisonment, or any part thereof, is imposed in default of
the payment of a fine or penalty in money, and that such
offender is entitled to be discharged upon payment of such
fine or penalty :

2. If the fine or penalty is paid after the removal of the
offender, the same shall be paid to the proper officer of such
reformatory, to defray the expense of the removal of the said
offender to such reformatory, and otherwise for the uses of
such reformatory ; but nothing herein contained shall affect
the right of any private person to such fine or penalty, or

*Transfer
although im-
prisonment is
for non-pay-
ment of a fine.*

*If fine is paid
subsequently.*

Term of imprisonment in certain cases.

34. Whenever any female is convicted under the eighth section of the *"Act respecting Offences against Public Morals and Public Convenience,"* or, under *"The Summary Trials Act,"* she may be sentenced to the said reformatory for any term less than two years ; but if any term exceeding six months is inflicted, no fine shall be imposed in addition. 44 V., c. 32, s. 3.

Conveyance of prisoners.

35. Any officer appointed by the Lieutenant Governor, or other officer or person, by his direction or by direction of the court or other lawful authority, may convey to such reformatory any convict sentenced, or liable to be imprisoned therein, and deliver her to the superintendent or keeper thereof, without any further warrant than a copy of the sentence, taken from the minutes of the court before which the offender was tried, and certified by a judge or the clerk or acting clerk of such court. 42 V., c. 43, s. 7.

Superintendent to receive and detain offenders.

36. The superintendent of the reformatory shall receive into the same every offender legally certified to her as sentenced to imprisonment therein, and shall there detain her, subject to all the rules, regulations and discipline thereof, until the term for which she has been sentenced is completed, or until she is otherwise discharged in due course of law. 42 V., c. 43, s. 8.

Transfer of prisoners to common gaol.

37. The Lieutenant Governor may, from time to time, by warrant signed by the Provincial Secretary, or by such other officer as is authorized by the Lieutenant Governor in that behalf, direct the removal from such reformatory back to the common gaol, or to any other gaol in Ontario, of any person removed to such reformatory under this Act. 42 V., c. 43, s. 9.

Delivery of offender to the proper officer.

38. The superintendent of such reformatory, or the keeper of any common gaol, having the custody of any offender ordered to be removed, shall, when required so to do, deliver up to the constable or other officer or person who produces the said warrant, such offender, together with a copy, attested by the said superintendent or gaoler, of the sentence and date of conviction of such offender, as given on the reception of the offender into the custody of such superintendent or keeper. 42 V., c. 43, s. 10.

The Industrial Refuge for Girls.

On conviction for certain offences girls may be sentenced to Industrial Refuge.

39. If any girl who at the time of her trial appears to the court to be under the age of fourteen years, is convicted of any offence for which a sentence of imprisonment for a term of one month or longer, but less than five years, may be imposed upon an adult convicted of the like offence, and the court before which the girl is convicted is satisfied that a due regard for her material and moral welfare manifestly requires that she should be committed to the Industrial Refuge for Girls of Ontario, such court may sentence such girl to be imprisoned in the Andrew Mercer (Ontario) reformatory for females, for such fixed term as the court thinks fit, not being greater than the term of imprisonment which could be imposed upon an adult for the like offence, and may further sentence the said girl to be kept in such industrial refuge for girls for an indefinite time after the expiration of such fixed term : Provided, that the whole term of confinement in such reformatory and industrial refuge shall not exceed five years from the commencement of her imprisonment.   43 V., c. 40, s. 1, *part.* As to term of imprisonment.

40. If any girl apparently under the age of fourteen years, is convicted of any offence punishable by law on summary conviction, and thereupon is sentenced and committed to prison in any common gaol for a term of fourteen days at the least, any judge of one of the superior courts, or any judge of a county court, in any case occurring within his county, may examine and inquire into the circumstances of such case and conviction, and if he considers the material and moral welfare of the girl requires it, he may, as an additional sentence for such offence, sentence such girl to be sent either forthwith, or at the expiration of her imprisonment in such gaol, to such industrial refuge for girls, to be there detained for the purpose of her industrial and moral education for an indefinite period, not exceeding in the whole five years from the commencement of her imprisonment in the common gaol.   43 V., c. 40, s. 3. In certain cases offenders summarily convicted may be sentenced to such refuge.

41. Every girl so sentenced shall be detained in such reformatory until the expiration of the fixed term of her sentence, unless sooner discharged by lawful authority ; and such girl thereafter shall, and every girl sentenced under the next preceding section shall, subject, in both cases, to the provisions hereof, and to any regulations made as hereinafter provided, be detained in such industrial refuge for girls for a term not to exceed five years from the commencement of her imprisonment, for the purpose of her industrial and moral education.   43 V., c. 40, s. 4. Detention for purposes of reform.

General Provisions.

42. Any sheriff or other person having the custody of any offender sentenced to imprisonment in the said central prison or either of the said reformatories, may detain the offender in the common gaol of the county or district in which such offender is sentenced, or other place of confinement in which such offender is, until some person lawfully authorized in that behalf requires such offender's delivery for the purpose of being conveyed to such prison or either Detention in gaol until demanded by proper authority.

of such reformatories.   38 V., c. 46, s. 1 ;—42 V., c. 43, s. 4;—43 V., c. 39, s. 5.

If offender is certified to be in weak health.
43. If the gaol surgeon, or other medical practitioner acting in that behalf, certifies that any offender sentenced to the central prison or to the Andrew Mercer (Ontario) reformatory for females, is in such a weak state of health that such offender is unable to perform hard labor, such offender may be detained in the common gaol or other place of confinement in which such offender is, until such offender is sufficiently recovered to be employed at hard labor.   38 V., c. 46, s. 2 ;—42 V., c. 43, s. 5.

Computation of time in such cases.
44. The time for which any person, sentenced to imprisonment in the central prison or in the Andrew Mercer (Ontario) reformatory for females, is held in custody under the provisions of the two sectious next preceding, shall be reckoned in computing the time served by such person in such prison or reformatory.   38 V., c. 46, s. 3 ;—42 V., c. 43, s. 6.

If term expires on Sunday.
45. Whenever the time of any offender's sentence in such prison, reformatories or refuge, under any law within the legislative authority of the Parliament of Canada, expires on a Sunday, such offender shall be discharged on the previous Saturday, unless such offender desires to remain until the Monday following.   36 V., c. 69, s. 6 ;—42 V., c. 43, s. 11 ;—43 V., c. 39, s. 12.

Apprenticeship of juvenile offenders.
46. If any respectable and trustworthy person is willing to undertake the charge of any boy committed to the Ontario Reformatory for Boys, when such boy is over the age of twelve years, or of any girl committed to the Industrial Refuge for Girls, as an apprentice to the trade or calling of such person, or for the purpose of domestic service, and such boy or girl is confined to the reformatory or refuge by virtue of a sentence or order pronounced under the authority of any Act of the Parliament of Canada, the superintendent of the reformatory or refuge may, with the consent and in the name of the inspector of prisons and public charities of Ontario, bind the said boy or girl to such person for any term not to extend, without his or her consent, beyond a term of five years, from the **Discharge on probation in such case.** commencement of his or her imprisonment; and the inspector shall thereupon order that such boy or girl shall be discharged from the said reformatory or refuge on probation, to remain so discharged, provided his or her conduct during the residue of the term of five years, from the commencement of his or her imprisonment, continues good, and such **As to wages.** boy or girl shall be discharged accordingly : Provided, that any wages reserved in any indenture of apprenticeship made under this section shall be payable to such boy or girl, or to some other person for his or her benefit:

2. No boy or girl shall be discharged under this section until after the fixed term of his or her sentence has elapsed, unless by the authority of the Governor General. 43 V., c. 39, ss. 8 *and* 9;—43 V., c. 40, ss. 5 *and* 6. _{Sanction of Governor General.}

Sanction of Governor General.

47. The Governor in Council may make such regulations as he considers advisable for the discharge, after the expiration of the fixed term of sentence, of prisoners confined in such reformatory or refuge under any Act of the Parliament of Canada; and such discharge may be either absolute or upon probation, subject to such conditions as are imposed under the authority of the said regulations. 43 V., c. 39, s. 10;—43 V., c. 40, s. 7.

Regulations as to discharge.

48. The judge of any county court or any police magistrate may, upon satisfactory proof that any boy or girl who was sentenced under the provisions of any Act of the Parliament of Canada, and who has been discharged on probation, has violated the conditions of his or her discharge, order such boy or girl to be recommitted to such reformatory or refuge, and thereupon such boy or girl shall be detained therein under his or her original sentence, as if such boy or girl had never been discharged. 43 V., c. 39, s. 11, *and* c. 40, s. 8.

Re-commitment for violation of conditions of discharge.

PART III.

QUEBEC.

Reformatory Schools for Boys.

49. The provisions of sections fifty to sixty, both inclusive, being Part three of this Act, apply only to the Province of Quebec. 32-33 V., c. 34, s. 10, *part.*

Provisions applicable to Quebec.

50. Every person apparently under the age of sixteen years, who is convicted before any court of criminal jurisdiction or before any judge of the Sessions of the Peace, recorder, district or police magistrate, of any offence for which he would be liable to imprisonment, may be sentenced, on such conviction, to be detained in a certified reformatory school for any term not less than two years nor more than five years, or he may be sentenced to be first imprisoned in the common gaol for a term not in any case exceeding three months, and at the expiration of his sentence, to be sent to a certified reformatory school, and to be there detained for a term of not less than two years and not more than five years. 32-33 V., c. 34, s. 2.

Offenders under 16 years may be sent to Reformatory Schools.

51. The Lieutenant Governor may, at any time, in his discretion, order that any offender detained in such reformatory school, under a summary conviction, be discharged.

Power to discharge.

Removal of incorrigibles. **52.** The Lieutenant Governor may, at any time, on the report of one of the inspectors of prisons for the Province of Quebec, order any offender undergoing sentence in any certified reformatory school, on a conviction for felony, to be removed as incorrigible; and in any such case, the offender shall be imprisoned in the penitentiary for the remainder of the term of his sentence. 32-33 V., c. 34, s. 4.

Detention of offenders under 16 years previous to trial. **53.** A person apparently under the age of sixteen years, arrested on a charge of having committed any offence not capital, shall not, while awaiting trial for such offence, be detained in any common gaol, if there is a certified reformatory school within three miles of such gaol, but shall be detained in such reformatory school while awaiting trial; and if there is more than one such school within such distance, the person so charged shall be detained in that one of them which is conducted nearest in accordance with the religious belief to which his parents belong, or in which he has been educated. 32-33 V., c. 34, s. 5.

Punishment of persons breaking the rules of reformatory schools. **54.** Every offender detained in a certified reformatory school, who wilfully neglects or refuses to conform to the rules thereof, shall, on summary conviction before a justice of the peace having jurisdiction in the place or district in which the school is situate, be imprisoned with hard labor, for any term not exceeding three months; and at the expiration of the term of his imprisonment, he shall, by and at the expense of the managers of the school, be brought back to the school from which he was taken, there to be detained during a period equal to so much of his period of detention as remained unexpired at the time of his being sent to the prison. 32-33 V., c. 34, s. 6.

Reformatory Prisons for Females.

When Reformatory Prisons are established certain female convicts may be sentenced to be detained therein. **55.** Whenever the Lieutenant Governor of the Province of Quebec has declared, by proclamation published in the *Official Gazette* of that Province, that suitable arrangements have been made in any district in that Province, for the detention and proper government and discipline of female convicts in any separate building or separate portion of the common gaol in such district, as a reformatory prison for such convicts, and that such separate building or portion of a common gaol shall be a reformatory prison for the purposes hereof,—then if any female person is convicted in the said Province of any felony, not capital, and for which she would, without this Act, otherwise be punishable by imprisonment for any term not less than two years, but not exceeding seven years, such female convict shall be punishable by imprisonment in the female reformatory prison for any term less than seven, but not less than five years, and she may be sentenced to such imprisonment accordingly, although otherwise she would not be liable to imprisonment in the penitentiary for so long a term as that for which she may be so sentenced to imprisonment in the female reformatory prison. 34 V., c. 30, s. 1.

56. If, after such proclamation, any female is convicted of any felony or misdemeanor otherwise punishable by imprisonment, but not for any term so long as two years, or of any offence under the eighth section of the "*Act respecting Offences against Public Morals and Public Convenience*," then, unless it is proved that she has been previously convicted and imprisoned twice or oftener, each of such convictions being for some such felony, misdemeanor or offence, as aforesaid, such convict shall be asked, by the judge, recorder, judge of the Sessions of the Peace, commissioner of police, district, police or stipendiary magistrate, mayor, warden or the two justices of the peace, or other functionary before whom the conviction is had, whether she consents, instead of the imprisonment to which she is otherwise liable, to be sentenced to imprisonment for a term of five years, in the female reformatory prison; and if she refuses to give such consent, sentence shall be passed upon her as if this Act had not been passed, but if she gives such consent, or it is proved that she has been twice convicted as aforesaid, the fact shall be duly recorded or entered on the proceedings in the case, and she shall be sentenced accordingly to imprisonment in the female reformatory prison for a term of five years. 34 V., c. 30, s. 2.

And certain others after two convictions or with their own consent.

57. If, at the time of the passing of any such sentence, there is more than one female reformatory prison in such Province, the imprisonment under such sentence shall be in that one of such reformatory prisons which is in the same district as the place at which the sentence is passed, or if there is no reformatory prison in such district, then in the reformatory prison nearest to such place; but if there is not more than one such reformatory prison in the Province, then such imprisonment shall be in it; and in any case the sheriff of the district in which the sentence is passed, or any person thereunto by him deputed, shall have the like powers for conveying the convict to the reformatory prison in which she is to be imprisoned, as any sheriff has to convey any convict to the penitentiary. 34 V., c. 30, s. 3, *part*.

In what prison such sentence shall be carried out.

Power to convey prisoner to it.

58. Each such female reformatory prison as aforesaid, shall be a house of correction and a public reformatory prison, within the meaning of the sixth sub-section of the ninety-second section of "*The British North America Act, 1867*," and subject to such laws as the Legislature of such Province makes with respect to the establishment, maintenance and management thereof. 34 V., c. 30, s. 4.

Every such prison to be a house of correction, &c.

Convicts in common gaols may be employed outside the same.

59. Every sheriff or gaoler in the Province of Quebec, being thereunto authorized by the Lieutenant Governor, or in such manner as any Act of the Legislature of the Province provides, and under such regulations as the said Legislature makes or authorizes to be made in that behalf, may employ any male convict sentenced to hard labor in such prison, at hard labor outside the walls or precincts of **Powers for preventing escapes, &c.** such prison, and may exercise the same powers of restraint and discipline, and for preventing escape, while such convict is so outside of the walls or precincts, as if he was inside the same, and whether his labor is so employed directly by the Government of the said Province or by any contractor to whom such labor is let or hired out by the said Govern-**Sentence to include such employment.** ment, or by any competent authority; and the sentence of any such male convict, whether pronounced before or after the passing of this Act, shall be understood to include such employment as aforesaid,—and any time during which a convict is so employed, shall be reckoned as part of the term for which he was sentenced to be confined in such prison 34 V., c. 30, s. 5.

Common Gaols.

Gaols to be houses of correction.

60. Every common gaol in such Province shall be a house of correction, reformatory prison and place of detention. 34 V., c. 30, s. 6.

PART IV.

NOVA SCOTIA.

The Halifax Industrial School.

Certain offenders may be sentenced to Halifax Industrial School.

61. Whenever any boy, who is a Protestant and a minor, apparently under the age of sixteen years, is convicted before the police court in the city of Halifax, or before the stipendiary magistrate for the city of Halifax, of any offence for which, by law, he is liable to imprisonment, the police court or stipendiary magistrate may sentence such boy to be detained in the Halifax Industrial School for any term not exceeding five years, and not less than two years, as to the said police court or stipendiary magistrate appears proper. 33 V., c. 32, s. 1.

As to support of such boys.

62. No such sentence shall be pronounced unless, nor until, provision has been made by the city of Halifax, out of its funds, for the support of boys so sentenced, at the rate of not less than forty dollars per annum for each boy. 33 V., c. 32, s. 2.

63. The said industrial school shall, at all times, be open to inspection by the mayor and aldermen of the city of Halifax, and the stipendiary magistrate for the city of Halifax, or any of them. 33 V., c. 32, s. 3.

School to be open to inspection.

64. The committee of the said industrial school shall be bound to teach and instruct each boy so sentenced and detained as aforesaid, in reading and writing, and in arithmetic as far as the rule of three, and also to teach each such boy such one of the trades or occupations which is, from time to time, taught in the said school, as the committee deems most adapted to his capabilities. 33 V., c. 32, s. 4.

Boys to be educated and taught trades.

Halifax Reformatory School for Boys of the Roman Catholic Faith.

65. As soon as a proclamation has been issued by the Lieutenant Governor of Nova Scotia, declaring that a reformatory, orphanage, industrial school or home for boys of the Roman Catholic faith has been established in the county of Halifax, and made ready for the confinement of prisoners, any boy, who is a Roman Catholic and apparently under the age of sixteen years, who is convicted before the police court of the city of Halifax, or before the stipendiary magistrate for such city, of any offence for which by law he is liable to imprisonment, with or without hard labor, may be sentenced by such police court or stipendiary magistrate to be detained in such home, whether situate in such city or elsewhere in such county, for any term not exceeding five years, as to such police court or stipendiary magistrate appears proper. 47 V., c. 45, s. 1.

Certain offenders may be sentenced to Halifax Roman Catholic Reformatory.

66. The governing body or head of such home may, at any time, notify the mayor of the city of Halifax that no prisoners, beyond those already under sentence in such home, will be received therein; and after the receipt of such notice by such mayor, no such sentence shall be pronounced until notice has been received by the mayor from such governing body or head that prisoners will again be received in such home. 47 V., c. 45, s. 2.

Number of such prisoners may be limited by the governing body.

67. Such home shall, at all times, be open to inspection by any officer appointed by the Governor in Council to inspect the same, and, when and so long as any pecuniary aid is received from the city of Halifax, shall be open to inspection by the mayor, aldermen and stipendiary magistrate of such city, or any of them. 47 V., c. 45, s. 3.

Reformatory to be open to inspection.

68. The governing body of such home shall be bound to teach and instruct each boy so sentenced and detained as aforesaid in reading and writing, and in arithmetic to the end of simple proportion, and also to teach each such boy

Boys to be educated and taught trades.

such one of the trades or occupations which are, from time to time, taught in such home, as such governing body deems most adapted to his capabilities. 47 V., c. 45, s. 4.

Removal of
incorrigibles.

69. If any offender detained in such home becomes incorrigible, he may, on a certificate from the officer in charge of such home, be removed to a penitentiary, as provided in "*The Penitentiary Act.*" 47 V., c. 45, s. 5.

Ticket of
leave may be
granted by
Minister of
Justice.

70. If any boy so sentenced and detained in such Home has, in the opinion of the governing body of such Home, so conducted himself during a term of six consecutive months as by his good behaviour, diligence and industry, to warrant his being set at large and no longer detained in the Home, and if the police court or stipendiary magistrate of the city of Halifax concurs with the said governing body in recommending the issue of a license to such boy to be at large, then the Minister of Justice, or such person as he appoints to issue such licenses, may issue a license to such boy to be at large in the Province of Nova Scotia, or in such part thereof as is specified in such license :

And may be
revoked or
altered.

2. Such license may be revoked or altered at pleasure by the Minister of Justice, or by such person as he appoints as aforesaid :

Minister to
make regula-
tions.

3. The Minister of Justice may make such regulations as he sees fit as to the form of such licenses. the conditions of enjoyment and forfeiture thereof, and for ascertaining that such conditions are duly complied with :

Contraven-
tion of con-
ditions of
ticket of
leave how
dealt with.

4. Upon information on oath that the holder of any such license has contravened any of the conditions thereof, the police court or stipendiary magistrate of the city of Halifax may issue a warrant for his arrest, wherever in the Dominion of Canada he may be, and cause him to be brought before such court or magistrate, and upon conviction of such contravention, shall remand him to such Home, there to serve the remainder of his original sentence, with such additional term, not exceeding one year, as to such court or magistrate seems proper. 49 V., c. 54, s. 1.

Jurisdiction
of police
court, &c.,
extended.

71. The jurisdiction of the police court and of the stipendiary magistrate of Halifax, and of the policemen and other officers of such court or magistrate, shall, for the purposes hereof, extend to every boy so convicted and sentenced as aforesaid, although he is in any place in the county of Halifax beyond the limits of the city of Halifax. 47 V., c. 45, s. 7.

PART V.

PRINCE EDWARD ISLAND.

Reformatory Prison.

72. As soon as a proclamation has been issued by the Lieutenant Governor of the Province of Prince Edward Island, declaring that a reformatory for juvenile offenders has been established and made ready for the confinement of prisoners, any person, apparently under the age of sixteen, who is convicted in that Province, before the Supreme Court or stipendiary magistrate, of any offence for which, by law, he is liable to imprisonment, may, by the said court or stipendiary magistrate, be sentenced to be detained in the said reformatory for any term not exceeding five years and not less than two years, as to the said court or magistrate appears proper. 43 V., c. 41, s. 1. *Certain offenders may be sentenced to P. E. I. Reformatory.*

73. Any person, apparently under the age of sixteen years, thereafter arrested on a charge of having committed any offence within the said Province, not capital, shall not, while awaiting trial for such offence, be detained in any common gaol, but shall be detained in such reformatory. 43 V., c. 41, s. 2. *Offenders awaiting trial.*

74. If any offender, detained in such reformatory, wilfully neglects to conform to the rules thereof, he may, upon summary conviction, be imprisoned in the common gaol, with hard labor, for any term not exceeding three months; and at the expiration of his term of imprisonment, he shall be brought back to the reformatory, there to be detained during a term equal to so much of his term of imprisonment as remained unexpired at the time of his being sent to the prison. 43 V., c. 41, s. 3. *Punishment of offenders violating rules.*

Removal of Prisoners to the Gaol of Queen's County.

75. The Supreme Court of Judicature of the Province of Prince Edward Island, or any judge thereof, may, on the application of the Attorney General or other Crown officer of such Province, whenever any prisoner is sentenced to any term of imprisonment, with hard labor, in either of the counties of Prince County or King's County, make an order or give directions for the transfer and removal of such prisoner from the gaol of the county in which the conviction of such prisoner takes place, to the gaol of the county of Queen's County, and such order may be made or directions given at the time of passing sentence. 17 V. (P.E.I.), c. 13, s. 1, *part.* *Removal of prisoners to gaol of Queen's County may be ordered*

76. Whenever such order is made or directions given, the sheriff of the county in which the conviction takes place *Sheriff to carry out such order.*

2241

shall cause such prisoner to be removed with all convenient despatch to the gaol of the county of Queen's County, pursuant to such order or direction. 17 V. (P.E.I.), c. 13, s. 1, *part*.

To what authority such prisoners shall be subject.

77. Upon such removal, such prisoner shall be subject to the same authority and jurisdiction as if he had been convicted in the county of Queen's County. 17 V. (P.E.I.), c. 13, s. 1, *part*.

OTTAWA : Printed by Brown Chamberlin, Law Printer to the Queen's Most Excellent Majesty.

50-51 VICTORIA.

CHAP. 52.

An Act to amend the Penitentiary Act.

[*Assented to 23rd June*, 1887.]

H ER Majesty, by and with the advice and consent of Preamble. the Senate and House of Commons of Canada, enacts as follows :—

1. In this Act, unless the context otherwise requires,— Interpretation.

(*a.*) The expression " officer " means and includes any "Officer." officer or employee of any of the classes mentioned in the schedule to this Act ;

(*b.*) The expression " trade instructors " includes bakers, "Trade instructors." blacksmiths, carpenters, masons, millers, shoemakers, stonecutters, tailors and persons employed to direct and instruct convicts in any branch of labor.

2. The twenty-seventh section of " *The Penitentiary Act* " R.S.O., c. 182, s. 27 amended. is hereby amended—

(*a.*) By substituting for the words " shall reside in the penitentiary," the words " and he shall reside at the penitentiary ; " and—

(*b.*) By striking out the words " and shall receive such allowance of fuel and light as the Governor in Council sees fit to make."

SALARIES.

3. The thirty-third section of " *The Penitentiary Act* " is Section 33 amended. hereby repealed, and the following section substituted therefor :—

" **33.** The Governor in Council may, within the limits Salaries. prescribed by the schedule to this Act, fix the salaries to be

Increases. " 2. No officer shall be entitled as of right to any yearly increase of salary, but the same may be given to him if the Minister of Justice is satisfied that he is competent and faithful in the performance of his duties :

When payable. " 3. No such yearly increase of salary shall be paid until the expiry of a year at least from the date of the officer's appointment, or of the last increase given to him :

When to take effect. " 4. Such yearly increase shall take effect and be reckoned from the first day of July only :

Certain rights saved. " 5. Nothing herein shall affect the salary of any officer whose salary, as provided in the estimates of the session held in the fiftieth year of Her Majesty's reign, exceeds the maximum salary prescribed for his class by the schedule to this Act, but the salary of such officer shall not be further increased :

No increase if maximum has been reached. " 6. No officer whose salary, as provided in the estimates of the session held in the fiftieth year of Her Majesty's reign, is equal to or less than the maximum salary prescribed for his class in such schedule, and no officer hereafter appointed shall be paid a salary in excess of that so prescribed by such schedule."

GRATUITIES.

Gratuities may be granted in certain cases. 4. To any officer—

(*a.*) Whose conduct has been good, and who has been faithful in the discharge of his duties ;

(*b.*) Who is compelled to retire from the service on account of some mental or physical infirmity which unfits him for the performance of his duty ; and—

(*c.*) Who is not entitled to a superannuation allowance under the rules in that behalf in force,—

Amount. A gratuity, or retiring allowance may be given, calculated at the rate of a half month's salary for each year of his service, up to five years, and a month's salary for each year of service in excess of five years, based on the salary that such officer was in receipt of at the time of his retirement.

Increase if infirmity results from injury. 5. Such retiring allowance may be increased by one-half the amount thereof if the infirmity which compels such officer to retire from the service is occasioned by any injury received by him in the performance of his duty, without fault or negligence on his part, at the hands of any convict, or in preventing an escape or rescue, or in suppressing a

6. If any officer dies in the service leaving a widow or Allowance to widow, &c. any person who in his lifetime was dependent on him, a gratuity may be paid to such widow, if any, and if not, to any person or persons in the lifetime of such officer dependent on him, or to any person or corporation in trust for any such person or persons so dependent on him :

2. No such gratuity shall exceed the amount of the salary Amount of gratuity. of such officer—

(*a.*) For the two months next preceding his death, if he was appointed by the Governor in Council ;

(*b.*) For the three months next preceding his death, if he was appointed by the Minister or the warden.

7. Such gratuity may be increased by one-half the Increase in case specified. amount thereof if the death of such officer is occasioned by any injury received by him, in the performance of his duty, without fault or negligence on his part, at the hands of any convict, or in preventing an escape or rescue, or in suppressing a revolt.

PERQUISITES.

8. No officer shall be allowed any perquisite except as Perquisites. follows :—

(*a.*) Any officer may, during the will of the Minister of House and grounds. Justice, occupy free of rent any house or quarters, with any grounds attached, which forms part of the penitentiary property ;

(*b.*) The grounds or gardens attached to the residence or Convict labor. quarters of a warden or deputy warden may be kept in order and cultivated by convict labor, but otherwise no convict labor shall be employed in keeping in order or cultivating any grounds occupied by any officer ;

(*c.*) Any officer who wears uniform may be allowed such Uniform. uniform as the Governor in Council prescribes.

REGULATIONS.

9. The Governor in Council may, subject to the provi- Regulations may be made as to :— sions of " *The Penitentiary Act* " and of this Act, from time to time, make regulations respecting—

(*a.*) Officers' salaries ; Salaries ;

(*b.*) Gratuities and retiring allowances ; Gratuities ;

(*c.*) The occupation by officers of houses, quarters or Houses and grounds ; grounds which form part of the penitentiary property ;

(*d.*) Officers' uniforms : Uniforms ;

(e.) The sale to officers of articles manufactured in the penitentiary shops or grown upon the penitentiary property;

(f.) Any matter relating to the establishment, maintenance and management of penitentiaries.

10. The schedule to " *The Penitentiary Act* " is hereby repealed and the following schedule substituted therefor :—

"SCHEDULE.

KINGSTON PENITENTIARY.

	From date of appointment,	By yearly increases of Fifty Dollars, to	From date of appointment,	By yearly increases of Thirty Dollars, to
	$	$	$	$
Warden	2,600	3,000		
Deputy Warden	1,200	1,500		
Chaplains	1,000	1,200		
Surgeon	1,400	1,800		
Accountant	800	1,200		
Warden's Clerk			500	800
Storekeeper			600	900
Steward			600	900
Chief keeper			700	900
Hospital Overseer			500	800
Schoolmaster			500	700
Engineer			800	1,000
Trade Instructors			600	700
Keepers			500	600
Guards			400	500
Messenger			400	500
Stoker			400	500
Teamsters			300	400
Matron			400	600
Deputy Matron			200	400

ST. VINCENT DE PAUL PENITENTIARY.

	From date of appointment,	By yearly increases of Fifty Dollars, to	From date of appointment,	By yearly increases of Thirty Dollars, to
Warden	2,400	2,800		
Deputy Warden	1,200	1,500		
Chaplains	1,000	1,200		
Surgeon	1,000	1,400		
Accountant	800	1,100		
Warden's Clerk			500	750
Storekeeper			600	900
Steward			600	800
Chief keeper			700	900
Hospital Overseer			500	750
Schoolmaster			500	700
Engineer			750	900
Trade Instructors			600	700
Keepers			500	600
Guards			400	500
Messenger			400	500
Teamsters			300	400

—	From date of app·int-ment.	By yearly increases of Fifty Dollars, to	From date of appoint-ment.	By yearly increases of Thirty Dollars, to
	$	$	$	$
Warden	2,000	2,400		
Deputy Warden	1,100	1,400		
Deputy Warden and Chief keeper, when offices held by one person	1,200	1,500		
Chaplains	500	600		
Surgeon	1,000	1,200		
Accountant	800	1,000		
Storekeeper			600	800
Steward			600	800
Storekeeper and Steward, when offices held by one person			800	1,000
Chief keeper			700	800
Hospital Overseer			500	700
Schoolmaster			500	600
Engineer			750	970
Assistant Engineer			600	750
Trade Instructors			600	700
Keepers			500	600
Guards			400	500
Messenger			400	500
Teamster			300	400

MANITOBA PENITENTIARY.

Warden	2,000	2,400		
Deputy Warden and Chief keeper	900	1,200		
Chaplains	500	600		
Surgeon	1,000	1,200		
Accountant and Storekeeper	800	1,100		
Steward			600	800
Hospital Overseer and Schoolmaster			700	900
Engineer			750	1,000
Trade Instructors			600	700
Guards			500	600
Messenger			500	600

BRITISH COLUMBIA PENITENTIARY.

Warden	2,000	2,400		
Deputy Warden and Chief keeper	900	1,200		
Chaplains	500	600		
Surgeon	600			
Accountant, Storekeeper and Schoolmaster	800	1,000		
Steward			600	800
Trade Instructors			600	700
Keepers and Guards			500	600
Messenger			500	600
Teamster			500	600"

OTTAWA: Printed by BROWN CHAMBERLIN, Law Printer to the Queen's Most Excellent Majesty.

51 VICTORIA.

CHAP. 47.

An Act to amend the Revised Statutes of Canada, Chapter one hundred and eighty-one, respecting Punishments, Pardons and the Commutation of Sentences.

[Assented to 4th May, 1888.]

HER Majesty, by and with the advice and consent of the Senate and House of Commons of Canada, enacts as follows :— Preamble.

1. Sub-section five of section twenty-eight of the "*Act respecting Punishments, Pardons and the Commutation of Sentences*," is hereby repealed and the following substituted therefor :— Section 28 of R.S.C., c. 181 amended.

"5. Imprisonment in a common gaol or a public prison other than those last mentioned,— Imprisonment.

(*a.*) May be with or without hard labor in the discretion of the court or person passing sentence if the offender is convicted on indictment or under "*The Speedy Trials Act*," or before a Judge of the Supreme Court of the North-West Territories ; Hard labor in certain cases.

(*b.*) May in other cases be with hard labor if hard labor is part of the punishment for the offence of which such offender is convicted ; And in other cases.

And if such imprisonment is to be with hard labor the sentence shall so direct. Sentence to direct.

2. Section thirty-two of the said Act is hereby repealed and the following substituted therefor :— Section 32 repealed ; new section.

"**32.** Whenever any person who has been required to enter into a recognizance with sureties to keep the peace and be of good behavior has, on account of his default therein, remained imprisoned for two weeks, the sheriff, jailer or warden shall give notice, in writing, to a judge of a superior court, or to a judge of the county court of the county or district in which such jail or prison is situate, and in the cities of Montreal and Quebec to a judge of the sessions of the peace for the district, and such judge may Notice to be given to a judge.

quent time, upon notice to the complainant or otherwise, or may make such other order as he sees fit, respecting the number of sureties, the sum in which they are bound and the length of time for which such person may be bound."

OTTAWA : Printed by BROWN CHAMBERLIN, Law Printer to the Queen's Most Excellent Majesty.

5 7 - 5 8   V I C T O R I A.

CHAP. 58.

An Act respecting Arrest, Trial and Imprisonment of Youthful Offenders.

[Assented to 23rd July, 1894.]

WHEREAS it is desirable to make provision for the separa- Preamble.
tion of youthful offenders from contact with older
offenders and habitual criminals during their arrest and trial,
and to make better provision than now exists for their commitment to places where they may be reformed and trained to
useful lives, instead of their being imprisoned : Therefore
Her Majesty, by and with the advice and consent of the Senate
and House of Commons of Canada, enacts as follows :—

1. Section five hundred and fifty of *The Criminal Code*, 1892, 1892, c. 29.
550 amend
is hereby repealed and the following section substituted therefor :

"**550.** The trials of young persons apparently under the Trial of yo
persons.
age of sixteen years, shall take place without publicity and
separately and apart from the trials of other accused persons,
and at suitable times to be designated and appointed for that
purpose."

2. Young persons apparently under the age of sixteen Imprisonn
of persons
der 16.
years who are :—
  (*a.*) arrested upon any warrant ; or
  (*b.*) committed to custody at any stage of a preliminary
enquiry into a charge for an indictable offence ; or
  (*c.*) committed to custody at any stage of a trial, either for
an indictable offence or for an offence punishable on summary
conviction ; or
  (*d.*) committed to custody after such trial, but before imprisonment under sentence,—
shall be kept in custody separate from older persons charged To be sepa
ed from ol
offenders.
with criminal offences and separate from all persons undergoing
sentences of imprisonment, and shall not be confined in the
lock-ups or police stations with older persons charged with
criminal offences or with ordinary criminals.

3. If any child, appearing to the court or justice before In Ontario
how child t
der 14 may
whom the child is tried to be under the age of fourteen years,

is convicted in the province of Ontario of any offence against the law of Canada, whether indictable or punishable on summary conviction, such court or justice, instead of sentencing the child to any imprisonment provided by law in such case, may order that the child shall be committed to the charge of any home for destitute and neglected children, or to the charge of any children's aid society duly organized and approved by the Lieutenant-Governor of Ontario in Council, or to any certified industrial school.

4. Whenever in the province of Ontario, an information or complaint is laid or made against any boy under the age of twelve years, or girl under the age of thirteen years, for the commission of any offence against the law of Canada, whether indictable or punishable on summary conviction, the court or justice seized thereof shall give notice thereof in writing to the executive officer of the children's aid society, if there be one in the county, and shall allow him opportunity to investigate the charges made, and may also notify the parents of the child, or either of them, or other person apparently interested in the welfare of the child.

2. The court or justice may advise and counsel with the said officer and with the parents or such other person, and may consider any report made by the said officer upon the charges.

3. If, after such consultation and advice, and upon consideration of any report so made, and after hearing the matter of information or complaint, the court or justice is of opinion that the public interest and the welfare of the child will be best served thereby, then, instead of committing the child for

trial, or sentencing the child, as the case may be, the court or justice may, by order :—

(*a.*) authorize the said officer to take the child and, under the provisions of the law of Ontario, bind the child out to some suitable person until the child has attained the age of 21 years, or any less age; or—

(*b.*) place the child out in some approved foster-home; or,—

(*c.*) impose a fine not exceeding ten dollars; or—

(*d.*) suspend sentence for a definite period or for an indefinite period; or

(*e.*) if the child has been found guilty of the offence charged or is shown to be wilfully wayward and unmanageable, commit the child to a certified industrial school, or to the provincial reformatory for boys, or to the refuge for girls, as the case may be, and in such cases, the report of the said officer shall be attached to the warrant of commitment.

5. Whenever an order has been made under either of the two sections next preceding, the child may thereafter be dealt with under the law of the province of Ontario, in the same manner, in all respects, as if such order had been lawfully made in respect of a proceeding instituted under authority of a statute of the province of Ontario.

6. No Protestant child dealt with under this Act, shall be committed to the care of any Roman Catholic children's aid society, or be placed in any Roman Catholic family as its foster-home ; nor shall any Roman Catholic child dealt with under this Act, be committed to the care of any Protestant children's aid society, or be placed in any Protestant family as its foster-home. But this section shall not apply to the care of children in a temporary home or shelter, established under the Act of Ontario, fifty-six Victoria, chapter forty-five, intituled *An Act for the Prevention of Cruelty to, and better Protection of, Children,* in a municipality in which there is but one children's aid society.

Religion of child to be respected.

Proviso as to temporary care in certai cases.

OTTAWA : Printed by Samuel Edward Dawson, Law Printer to the Queen's most Excellent Majesty.

56 VICTORIA.

CHAP. 33.

An Act relating to the custody of juvenile offenders in the Province of New Brunswick.

[Assented to 1st April, 1893.]

HER Majesty, by and with the advice and consent of the Senate and House of Commons of Canada, enacts as follows :—

1. This Act shall apply only to the province of New Brunswick. Application.

2. As soon as a proclamation has been issued by the Lieutenant-Governor of New Brunswick, declaring that an industrial home for boys has been established in the said province and made ready for the confinement of prisoners, the provisions of this Act shall go into force and apply to the said province. Commencement of Act.

3. If any boy, who, at the time of his trial, appears to the court to be under the age of sixteen years, is convicted of any offence for which a sentence of imprisonment for a period of three months or longer may be imposed upon an adult convicted of the like offence, and the court before whom such boy is convicted is satisfied that a due regard for the material and moral welfare of the boy manifestly requires that he should be committed to the said industrial home, then such court may sentence the boy to be imprisoned in such home for such term as the court thinks fit, not being greater than the term of imprisonment which could be imposed upon an adult for the like offence ; and may further sentence such boy to be kept in such industrial home for an indefinite time after the expiration of such fixed term : Provided, that the whole period of confinement in such industrial home shall not exceed five years from the commencement of his imprisonment. What boys may be sentenced to industrial hom Term of confinement limited.

judge of the supreme court or of a county court, in any case occurring within the county or counties for which he is such judge, may examine and inquire into the circumstances of such case and conviction, and when he considers that the material and moral welfare of the boy requires such sentence, he may, as an additional sentence for such offence, sentence such boy to be sent, either forthwith, or at the expiration of his imprisonment in such jail, to such industrial home, to be there detained for the purpose of his industrial and moral education for an indefinite period, not exceeding in the whole five years from the commencement of his imprisonment in the common jail.

Detention for purposes of reform.

5. Every boy so sentenced shall be detained in such industrial home until the expiration of the fixed term, if any, of his sentence, unless sooner discharged by lawful authority, and thereafter shall, subject to the provisions hereof and to any regulations made as hereinafter provided, be detained in such industrial home for a period not to exceed five years from the commencement of his imprisonment, for the purpose of his industrial and moral education.

Visiting clergymen.

2. The clergymen of all religious denominations shall at all convenient hours and subject to the rules or regulations governing such industrial home be admitted therein for the purpose of giving spiritual advice and instruction to the inmates therein of their respective denominations.

Commitment of boy to jail until conveyed to industrial home.

6. A copy of the sentence of the court, duly certified by the proper officer, or the warrant or order of the judge or magistrate by whom any boy is sentenced to confinement in such industrial home, shall be a sufficient authority to the sheriff, constable or other officer who is directed verbally or otherwise so to do, to convey such boy to the common jail of the county where such sentence is pronounced, and for the jailer of such jail to receive such boy and to detain him until there is presented to such jailer a warrant from the chairman of the governing board of the said industrial home, (which warrant such chairman is hereby authorized to issue under his official seal,) requiring the sheriff or a constable, or other officer, to deliver such boy to the superintendent of the said industrial home.

Conveyance of boy to indus-

7. The sheriff, constable or other officer, on the receipt by

venting his escape, or in recapturing him in case of an escape, as the sheriff of the county in which he was convicted would himself have in conveying him from one part of that county to another.

8. If any boy sentenced to confinement in such industrial home is in such a weak state of health that he cannot safely or conveniently be removed to the said industrial home, he may be detained in the common jail or other place of confinement in which he is, until he is sufficiently recovered to be safely and conveniently removed to the industrial home. If boy is in bad health.

9. No boy shall be discharged from such industrial home at the termination of his term of confinement, if then labouring under any contagious or infectious illness; but he shall be permitted to remain in such industrial home until he recovers from such disease or illness; provided that any boy remaining in such industrial home for any such cause shall be under the same discipline and control as if his term was still unexpired. Sick boy no to be dischai ed.
Proviso.

10. Whenever the time of any offender's sentence in such industrial home, under any law within the legislative authority of the Parliament of Canada, expires on a Sunday, such offender shall be discharged on the previous Saturday, unless such offender desires to remain until the Monday following. If term ex- pires on Sui day.

11. If any respectable or trustworthy person is willing to undertake the charge of any boy committed to the said industrial home, when such boy is over the age of twelve years, as an apprentice to the trade or calling of such person, and such boy is confined to the said industrial home by virtue of a sentence or order pronounced under the authority of any Act of the Parliament of Canada, the superintendent of the said industrial home may, with the consent of the parent or guardian of the boy, and in the name of the governing board of the said industrial home, bind the said boy to such person for any term not to extend, without his consent, beyond a term of five years from the commencement of his imprisonment; and the said governing board shall thereupon order that such boy shall be discharged from the said industrial home on probation, to remain so discharged, provided his conduct during the residue of the term of five years, from the commencement of his imprisonment, continues good, and such boy shall be discharged accordingly: Provided, that any wages reserved in any indenture of apprenticeship made under this section shall be payable to such boy, or to some other person for his benefit. Apprentice- ship of boy.

Discharge o probation in such case.

As to wages

Regulations
as to dis-
charge.

13. The Governor in Council may make such regulations as he considers advisable for the discharge, after the expiration of the fixed time of sentence, of prisoners confined in such industrial home under any Act of the Parliament of Canada, and such discharge may be either absolute or upon probation, subject to such conditions as are imposed under the authority of the said regulations.

Recommit-
ment for viola-
tion of condi-
tions of dis-
charge.

14. The judge of any county court or police magistrate may, upon satisfactory proof that any boy who was sentenced under the provisions of any Act of the Parliament of Canada, and who has been discharged on probation, has violated the conditions of his discharge, order such boy to be recommitted to such industrial home, and thereupon such boy shall be detained therein under his original sentence as if he had never been discharged.

Interpreta-
tion.

15. The word "warden" in section forty-nine of chapter one hundred and eighty-two of the Revised Statutes as therein applied to the reformatory prisons shall include the superintendent of the said industrial home.

OTTAWA : Printed by Sᴀᴍᴜᴇʟ Eᴅᴡᴀʀᴅ Dᴀᴡꜱᴏɴ, Law Printer to the Queen's most Excellent Majesty.

57-58 VICTORIA.

CHAP. 59

An Act to amend an Act relating to the custody of juvenile offenders in the province of New Brunswick.

[Assented to 23rd July, 1894.]

HER Majesty, by and with the advice and consent of the Senate and House of Commons of Canada, enacts as follows :—

1. Chapter thirty-three of the Statutes of 1893, intituled *An Act relating to the custody of juvenile offenders in the province of New Brunswick*, is hereby amended by adding to it the following section :— 1893, c. 33 amended.

"**16.** The Governor General by warrant under his hand may at any time in his discretion, on the application of the Attorney General of the province of New Brunswick, cause any boy who is imprisoned in the Dorchester Penitentiary, or in any jail in that province, for an offence within the law of Canada, and who is certified by any judge of the Supreme Court or of any County Court to have been, in the opinion of such judge, at the time of his trial under the age of fifteen years, to be transferred to the Boys' Industrial Home in the province, for the remainder of his term of imprisonment and for such further term in addition thereto as the Governor General, on the report and recommendation of such judge, deems expedient ; provided that the whole term of imprisonment shall not exceed five years from the commencement of the imprisonment in such penitentiary or jail." Governor General m cause trar of boys frc penitentia or jail to i dustrial home. Proviso : a term of im prisonmen

OTTAWA : Printed by SAMUEL EDWARD DAWSON, Law Printer to the Queen's most Excellent Majesty.

www.ingramcontent.com/pod-product-compliance
Lightning Source LLC
Chambersburg PA
CBHW060606030726
47498CB00005B/1561